THE MAP AND THE SCISSORS

Praise for the Book

With verve and wit, Amit Majmudar weaves the story of Mohan and Jin as they come together and grow apart, Mahatma and Qaid, Great Soul and Great Leader jousting for freedom, and rupturing, irrevocably, a land and its people.

—**Manreet Sodhi Someshwar**, author of *The Radiance of a Thousand Suns* and The Partition Trilogy

THE MAP AND THE SCISSORS

A NOVEL

AMIT MAJMUDAR

HarperCollins *Publishers* India

First published in India by HarperCollins *Publishers* 2022
4th Floor, Tower A, Building No. 10, Phase II, DLF Cyber City,
Gurugram, Haryana –122002
www.harpercollins.co.in

2 4 6 8 10 9 7 5 3 1

P-ISBN: 978-93-5489-464-0
E-ISBN: 978-93-5489-465-7

Typeset in 11/15 Sabon LT Std at
Manipal Technologies Limited, Manipal

Printed and bound at
Thomson Press (India) Ltd

FSC
MIX
Paper
FSC® C010615

This book is produced from independently certified FSC® paper
to ensure responsible forest management.

Contents

As geographers ... crowd into the edges of their maps parts of the world which they do not know about, adding notes in the margin to the effect that beyond this lies nothing but the sandy deserts full of wild beasts, unapproachable bogs, Scythian ice or a frozen sea, so in this work of mine, in which I have compared the lives of the greatest men with one another, after passing through those periods which probable reasoning can reach to and real history find a footing in, I might very well say of those that are farther off: 'Beyond this there is nothing but prodigies and fictions, the only inhabitants are the poets and inventors of fables.'

—Plutarch, *Parallel Lives*

Prologue

Imagine yourself on an island. The sea is wheat or jute, and the wind makes waves in it. You and your family and everyone else on your island makes a living off that sea, paddling out with scythes. The island is your village. Your netted catch is the sheaf you bundle and carry in your arms.

A few times a year, you get some visitors from over the sea. The occasional pedlar, maybe. A tax-collector's visit marks the end of harvest season. You pay tribute to a queen or king you have only heard of, some barbaric and hungry but appeaseable ruler who will leave you alone if you pay up. You pray that enough be left over to eat, or at least not to starve, and you pay up. For the rest of the year, it's your island, and your patch of sea.

Maybe there's a radio in the headman's hut. One day, that radio says you're living in Pakistan, or in India, and that you are free. Regardless of where you are, and who you are, this is good news because you've heard that freedom from the foreign king means no more paying up, ever.

The old men of the village say there's never no more paying up. All that changes is who's collecting.

Of course, after the first celebrations, the island is still the island, and the sea is still the sea. You paddle out with your scythes, as usual. As usual, you wade back in with sheaves. Voices inside a small black box can't change the cyclicity of hunger, or the timeless sea.

A few days and nights pass. Timelessly, as usual.

And then the raiding ships show up on the horizon.

You are a sea of wheat, or jute, or bodies. The raiders paddle into your family with scythes. They wade back out with girls in their arms.

There is no one to call before the raid, or during, or after. No sirens come rushing to help you. No policemen fire warning shots in the air. If anything, the policemen might come to watch from a distance. They're almost serving as a perimeter guard. Because they're in on it: you are what you are, and they are what they are, Sikh or Hindu or Muslim, Muslim or Hindu or Sikh.

So, no—justice is not on its way. This is an island, after all, surrounded by a sea. Justice just started playing favourites, and it isn't holding scales. It's holding a torch. Justice just pulled off the blindfold and pulled down your pants and is checking for a foreskin to see if you're one of them or not. To see what kind of justice you deserve.

And say you hide behind some piled sheaves, or jump into the swaying jute sea and start swimming for your life, or snug down under a corpse. Afterwards, you get up and plash gingerly through the blood to shake your father, your mother, your naked splayed sisters by their shoulders. No one moves.

So you start moving. Eventually you come to a continent where surviving islanders like you have washed ashore. Call it India or call it Pakistan, depending on where and who you are. Call it whatever you like, really, since it was all the same place last week.

Everyone is sharing stories. Their stories are a lot like yours. You realize that these were your people all along, and those others weren't. You start to feel like you're being exterminated, like you're ethnic detritus. And in a sense, you *have* been exterminated, seeing as you're the last of your line.

So maybe a few people who look and pray like you get together and lay out some scythes and knives on the ground and stare at them a while. One man says his cousin knows where to steal some grenades from. Another man turns to you and asks, 'Are you with us?'

What happens next is not inhuman, much less animal. It is not barbaric, and it is not irrational. It is natural.

Because violence has a life cycle, too. When you suffer it, you are the larva. When you fester over it, you are the pupa. When you contemplate inflicting it, you are the nymph. When you inflict it, you have spread your wings. Adulthood.

'Yes,' you whisper. 'I am with you.'

You are part of a band of raiders now. You set out in search of an island to raid.

All this raiding, this vengeance and counter-vengeance, can be traced back. It always starts somewhere.

It started with some cruel boys standing around a slightly older man in a police uniform with a city map in front of him.

'Don't worry,' said the older man. 'Just stick to these neighbourhoods—here, here and here—and we won't stop you. This country is ours.'

And before that, the man in the police uniform was sitting before a still older man in a kameez, chewing tobacco.

'You know what to do,' said this still older man. 'Or rather, what *not* to do. They are doing it to us anyway. And if they haven't, they will. If anyone asks questions, I'll protect you, so don't worry about that. No one will be left to ask questions, anyway, God willing. This country is ours.'

And this man in the kameez was sitting, like so many hundreds of other men his age, next to a radio. Out of that radio came the voice of a very, very old man in a three-piece suit and monocle, a man so old he looked like he would break if the rain fell on him. This appearance was deceptive, of course. He *was* old, and so thin he was a scaffold of bones and little more—but he wasn't frail.

In fact, he was unbreakable. That was the problem.

This country is ours, said that old, unbreakable skeleton of a man. *Pakistan zindabad.*

PART ONE

Opening Statements

As both are great examples of the vicissitudes of fortune, let us first consider in what way they attained their power and glory.

—Plutarch, *Parallel Lives*

1

1893. Regress Mohammed Ali Jinnah, father of Pakistan, back to a law student in London. Subtract three thousand cigarettes from his body, and his beauty grows delicate. So what if he is a common merchant's son from Karachi, picked out for his quick tongue? His look is princely.

Young Jinnah has a copy of Blackstone's *Commentaries on the Laws of England* open on his lap. Inside it nestles a copy of *Othello*: the blackamoor, the Mussalmaan, the odd man out is moving his lips with the lines.

Something about him takes naturally to acting. London is full of the sons of wealthier Indians, studying business or medicine or law. Some pass all their tests but fail their auditions as Englishmen, their tongues never quite writhing out of their accents. Even worse are the out-of-place Indian hand gestures that accompany their Indian English, the figure-eights their heads make when they say yes, their inability to eat pork sausages with the white students as if pig were no different than mutton or beef.

Not so Jinnah. He inhabits his character. One of the first professors he sees in the lecture-hall uses a monocle to review his notes. The same evening, the young student goes out and buys one for himself, shells the monocle lens off the frame, and reads his textbook before the mirror, practising his *w*'s and *v*'s, making sure he keeps them straight. Eventually, he gets his first bespoke three-piece suit and models that with the monocle.

Those first textbooks were economics. His businessman father sent him 'across the black water' to study business, like a properly money-minded Gujarati son. But Jinnah switched, without permission, to study law at Lincoln's Inn.

He likes law because he feels like he's playacting. The costume he dons during the day happens to be a barrister's black gown. In the evenings, he has done with half measures and rolls his knee-high black socks over his trouser legs: Elizabethan breeches. A turned-up collar serves for a ruff.

He leaves the library early this afternoon, murmuring, *Then must you speak / Of one that loved not wisely but too well; / Of one not easily jealous but, being wrought / Perplexed in the extreme; of one whose hand / Like the base Indian, threw a pearl away / Richer than all his tribe.* The dry cold has fissured his lower lip. When he licks it, he tastes blood.

Back at his lodgings, a slight English girl blocks him on the way to his room. Her red lips startle him; she has painted them an inch thick.

'Miss Page-Drake,' he says respectfully, warily.

He has been only three years in London, but already his accent is just as English as hers. It's as though the Gujarati he spoke in his parents' home had been a mere placeholder, and his tongue had been shaped to these words all along. In fact, his landlord's daughter speaks an English coarser than his. Jinnah would never put an *r* sound at the end of 'India'.

'Do they have mistletoe back in Indier?' She is pointing up, mischief in her eyes, and adoration.

The handsome young foreigner looks up and sees a small weed of some sort pinned to the ceiling.

'Mistletoe,' says Miss Page-Drake, meaningfully.

'Lovely.'

'Christmas tradition and all.' She waits, her cheeks colouring. 'Past two years I let you off easy, but now you're a proper Englishman, Mr Jinnah.'

'I fear I have an important engagement,' he says in a rush, raising his *Othello* as a shield. The young girl steps towards him, leading with her lips, and he slips his thin frame past her, nudging a picture on the wall askew and hastily righting it as he passes.

His 'important engagement' is at a West End theatre. For the first time in his life, he steps on to a stage. It is bare and half-lit, and six people make up his first audience: the theatre owners, James and Tamyra Quentin; the Scottish student who recommended he audition; a few of the company actors (all socialists, outraged about their own Empire); a poet; and the fellow sweeping the aisles.

Jinnah gives them Othello. He even answers himself, his own Iago. The Quentins ask for more, and he gives them *Now is the winter of our discontent*, his spine curving. He snarls and whinges and thunders. This play on the emotions, this wordplay, this inhabitation of a perspective—arguing law simply could not match it. This is freedom.

When he steps down from that high, Jinnah only vaguely registers handshakes and slaps on the back. The spell has not completely broken.

'We'll sign you,' says Mr Quentin.

His wife, enthusiastically clutching her husband's arm, beams at this dark charismatic youth, his features beautiful and sinister, boyish and wolfish.

Jinnah notices her, his eyes still distracted, almost drugged. 'Othello?'

'Romeo,' she whispers.

From ancient grudge break to new mutiny, he says giddily, *Where civil blood makes civil hands unclean.*

The fountain pen with which he signs the contract that evening ruptures all over his fingers. He rushes to the washroom—but in his exhilaration at catching a future Romeo's face in the mirror, he laughs aloud and licks off his fingers this sweet black juice.

That night he writes home to his father. This is the first of his negotiating techniques: present the fait accompli. Last time, when he informed his father he had switched from business to law, he added that he'd paid his dues to Lincoln's Inn up front. He knew that a proper businessman like his father would not sign off on the loss.

The letter sails home to Karachi, where it lands on his father's bare desk in the young man's childhood home. Weeds have broken stone, and moisture blotches the walls like tears and kohl running down a cheek. Young Mohammed Ali, the eldest son, was sent to England at great expense to become a maker of money, not a mouther of lines. The patriarch dips his pen in the bitter black juice of reproach, the poison Romeo will have to drink.

The letter races to London, black with news from home. It arrives with a murder of crows outside Jinnah's window. Well before he finishes reading it, his head in his hand, forehead sweating against his palm, he begins to nod in resignation to his role. Parentage is destiny.

He does not sleep that night. Before dawn in the still dark room, he puts on his barrister's black robe; adjusts his cufflinks; sets his monocle in place; and combs a sharp parting in his hair.

The sun has risen. He draws aside the curtains and squints into the spotlight of his future.

That future takes him to a law practice in Bombay. He knows very few people in that city when he gets there, but every few days, he can be seen in restaurants and theatres with a tall, slender young woman. No one thinks they are a couple: their identical cheekbones, eyes, complexion, laughter declare them unmistakably brother and sister. The only question is whether they are fraternal twins.

In time, she will study in Bombay to become a dental surgeon. The surgical mask will be the closest thing to a veil that proud Miss Fatima Jinnah will countenance. In most ways, though, she is pious and observant—much more so than her older brother, who has just ordered the whisky he developed a taste for back in London.

'Jin,' she says, with an eyebrow raised, 'you've come back with the stomach of an Englishman. What if the imam sees you here?'

'I shall offer him a drink. And apologize for my sister's quite shamelessly bare arms and face.'

'When in Bombay,' she shrugs.

'I say, Fati, I wonder if I might be on the city council one day.'

'Why, Jin, *this* is a new lark.'

'I have been thinking about politics for some time. Those speakers in Hyde Park! How they used to stand on crates and declaim! It was all quite theatrical. Like delivering a monologue.'

'Aren't you busy enough with your new practice?'

'Busy, but bored. I feel I could dabble in politics.'

Fati laughs. 'You are constitutionally incapable of *dabbling* in anything. If you enter politics at all, you will end up dictating terms to the Viceroy.'

'You think much too highly of my abilities, Fati.'

'I know you, brother, exactly as you are.'

And she does. Fatima Jinnah is the first to imagine the man her brother will become. Gradually, almost imperceptibly, like a shiver transmitted between a struck tuning-fork and a still one brought close, her premonition, her ambition, her will awakens a resonance in him. The future she cannot see for herself, she sees for him.

These happy jaunts with her brother around Bombay are the closest she comes to dating in the English manner. If she ever does submit to a husband, she decides, he must be a Muslim every bit as handsome, quick-tongued, open-minded and kind as Jin. Educated in London, too, like Jin; some provincial tyrant, forever expecting a calf massage when he got home, and mutton chops after, simply would not do. And as tall as Jin, since she was tall and would look ridiculous next to a short man. She would only submit to a man as excellent, in every way, as Jin, and in turn allow Jin to submit only to a wife who was his equal in every way. Not that she plans to start looking; certainly not for herself. And not for him, either…

Crack.

The cue ball shatters a pyramid of blood red balls. Jinnah, leaning over the table, his crisp seersucker sleeve against the green felt, is playing snooker. It is a game invented by British Indian Army officers and since adopted by the suited, native gentlemen of the Raj. Impact shivers through all the balls like a rumour, one impulse instantly everywhere, and they scatter in every direction, ricocheting off the cushions and into one another, complexity and chaos, no mapping in advance where they settle.

Jinnah slides the long cue back and stands with it at his side now, erect, a faint smile on his face.

1910. In only a few years, Jinnah has made connections among the richest and most influential people in Bombay. This snooker game takes place in the mansion of a Parsi magnate, Sir Dinshaw Petit.

Sir Dinshaw's ten-year-old daughter, in a Western-style frock, claps her hands with glee. She strolls around the table and touches a corner pocket.

'Now pot one in *this* hole,' she commands imperiously.

'Ruttie,' says her father, 'let our guest decide his own shot.'

Jinnah, without changing his expression, makes his calculations as he strolls towards her. The cue ball has just come to a stop when he stretches his long frame over the table and knocks that ball into another, finessing the red into the side pocket, as requested. She laughs and claps her hands again.

'Ruttie,' says Sir Dinshaw with a smile that undoes his sternness. 'You must not distract the men.'

'But you said I could watch, Papa.'

'Watch, not interfere, and only while you did the work your maths tutor assigned you.'

'But I *despise* division. Now *this* hole, Mr Jinnah!'

Jinnah obliges her again. Sir Dinshaw shakes his head with admiration. 'I tell you, Jinnah, you are good. *Damned* good.'

'Cause and effect.' Jinnah turns and says his first words to the little girl. 'Shall I clear the table, Miss Petit?'

At a nod from her, that is exactly what he does. Sir Dinshaw groans theatrically and covers his eyes. 'Now I know what these poor chaps feel when they argue their cases against you.'

'Point,' shrugs Jinnah, 'and counterpoint. Cigars?'

They step on to the balcony. Little Ruttie stays by the snooker table, digging two balls from the corner pocket and setting them up for herself, gripping the cue still warm with his touch in her little hands. It is too long for her. A few years, and she will grow into it.

Outside, in the sea breeze, Jinnah and Sir Dinshaw talk what they always talk: politics. They are both members of the Indian National Congress—a Parsi industrialist and a young Muslim lawyer.

'There is a way, there has to be,' says Sir Dinshaw. 'First trust, then unity, then independence. You are just the man to foster trust.'

'I doubt the Muslim League trusts me simply because I have a Muslim name. And even if they do, what does it matter, if they do not trust the Congress?'

'You attend our meetings. You know our leadership, and where our heart is. A free India! Tell them, Jinnah, how we are.'

'The League feels far more secure with the British in charge. A democratic India will mean majority rule. Tens of millions of Muslims can't outvote hundreds of millions of Hindus.'

'We won't be one or the other, politically. Just as I won't be a Parsi when I go to the ballot box. We will all be Indians.'

Jinnah exhales smoke at the moon, sighing, 'And free men. Finally.'

'There has to be a way.'

'I wonder if I might join the League myself.'

'And be a member of both?'

'There is no rule against it. I am not sure yet, but it is an idea. I could persuade each side to see the other's view—and I could do it from within.'

Sir Dinshaw smiles and claps his friend on the shoulder. 'That is exactly what we need. *You* are exactly what we need. Damned good, Jinnah. You are just—*damned* good.'

And he is. The cigar smoke from his mouth becomes the steam from a train as he rides the railways east to Dacca and Calcutta, north to Delhi, and south again home to Bombay. These are the train tracks the British Empire laid down: networks of neurons along which men like Jinnah flash like thoughts.

He is finicky about the cleanliness of his hands, but he shakes hands relentlessly in mansions and meeting halls, at receptions and garden parties, at clubs and restaurants where rich Hindus and rich Muslims and rich Britishers speak of Dominion status, constitutional safeguards, and 'the people'. They rarely speak to each other.

But with Jinnah?

Jinnah is their man, no matter which elite it is. Among wealthy Muslims, he is a Muslim. Among wealthy Hindus, he is 'one of the good ones'. Among wealthy Britishers, he is better dressed, better spoken, better versed in British law than any Etonian. In their diaries, they call him 'clever', the term they reserve for natives who intimidate them.

His secret is being estranged just enough from all three groups; his secret is matching, in manner and monocle, everyone's notion of a ruling aristocrat. So what if he was born the son of a grain merchant? He is the highest-paid probate lawyer in Bombay right now, the friend of sultans and nawabs and rajahs. He reads out last wills to sobbing rooms, four freshly widowed begums, each hoping for the Rolls-Royce.

Effortlessly he floats on to raised platforms: one at the annual Congress meeting, another at the annual meeting of the Muslim League. In late 1913, when His Majesty's Government asks for four Indians to negotiate with the Secretary of State for India—in London—it's merely a question of which side will get to send him as its nominee.

Soon Jinnah is smoking again, this time in the sea breeze, on a steamer headed west. He is thinking about how he is going to get his demands out of the British in London. How he is going to collapse the Indian National Congress and the All-India Muslim League into one nation of all Indians. How he is going to be that nation's first Prime Minister, with statues in roundabouts and pictures in history books and streets and maybe a university named after him.

He is thinking about glory, but he is about to be humiliated for the first time in his life.

He is about to meet Mohandas Karamchand Gandhi.

2

The boy groom and girl bride stand beside one another while grey-haired parents and sagging relatives have conversations in rustic, worldly Gujarati. The boy and the girl share the mute, bewildered look of newly branded cattle. The boy stands under a turban as big as his head. Garish garlands muffle much of his face. The girl is invisible behind a veil, like a string curtain made of braided flowers. The saree silk, too, has been pulled forward, over her face, modesty covering modesty.

The groom at this wedding could be either boy, the young Gandhi or the young Jinnah. If there's a Brahmin in saffron nearby, then the boy is thirteen-year-old Gandhi, and the girl is Kasturba. If there's an imam in a beard nearby, then the boy is sixteen-year-old Jinnah, and the girl is Emibai.

Mohandas and Mohammed were married off before they left to study in London. Whose wedding is this? The guests differ—more beards among Jinnah's Muslim relatives, who dine on mutton at the wedding feast. But little else varies between the Hindu and Muslim ceremonies. Even the Hindu God Vishnu finds a mention at Jinnah's ceremony—the Jinnahs are Khoja Shias, only two generations since their conversion out, and Khoja texts are full of references to the ten avatars of

Vishnu. Gandhi's bride Kasturba, meanwhile, veils herself in the Muslim fashion.

Because nothing is purely Hindu or purely Muslim in India. Nothing is pure anywhere, least of all Gujarati, with its Sanskrit and Farsi and Arabic and English loan words—its own words—all tumbling into meaning. Gujarati is a merchant's linguistic coin collection from around the world, a farmer's language hardy with lexical weeds.

A breeze parts the flowers now and reveals what is under the veil of one of the girls. This is Jinnah's first wife, Emibai. Quickly, look under that veil: no face. At least not one that he can remember. In his memory, she has no eyes, no nostrils, no mouth. Just blank smooth skin from forehead to chin.

Her husband will leave this wedding for the port. His mother wants to make sure her handsome boy does not 'get into trouble over there'. So one of the first words of the teenaged Jinnah to his wife will be 'avjo'. It is the Gujarati word for goodbye. The word itself means, literally, 'do come', but she is never going to come with him to London or Bombay or Karachi or Ziarat. Emibai will die while he is still a student in London. When he gets the letter, he will feel like he ought to grieve. He will try to feel grief, and to stir some up, he will try and think of her face. All he will remember of her is the smooth blank under the veil, the face on a dressmaker's dummy, a face never seen in direct sunlight and never kissed. And he will turn back to his textbook.

The teenaged widower will get his first kiss eventually, though it will take him a quarter of a century to get it. Ruttie Petit will be worth the wait.

Best to begin Gandhi's story, though, in a bedroom, in the dark. He is only sixteen years old right now, so he is not really 'Gandhi' yet, much less the Mahatma. Call him Mohan.

His ears are outsized, almost perpendicular to his skull. No spectacles yet, but his eyes are closed, the eyebrows pinched together, as if he is concentrating. He wears a long shirt of simple white cotton. Yellowish-saffron oil from that night's dinner stains the lapel. A small gold chain hangs forward and swings rhythmically. His back is arched, and the shirt covers his tiny buttocks, stirring under there like restless twin pups. Beyond it, his brown legs lie bent and braced on the bamboo bars of the cot.

He has to arch his back because of the dome of his wife's pregnancy. Kasturba has only a month to go. A black line of pigment divides her belly down the middle. That dome is tipped by the beige grape of her everted navel. She had been asleep on her side; now she is awake, and thinking about her haemorrhoids.

Three quick knocks. Mohan's concentration breaks, but his lower half is reluctant to uncouple. He pauses and turns to the door, his spine erect as a mongoose. Three more knocks. Kasturba takes advantage of this lull to pick a tiny fleck of crust from the corner of her eye.

'What is the matter?'

A servant's voice. 'Your father is not well.'

Mohan bites his lip.

'Not well?'

A pause. 'He is no more.'

Now he uncouples. Horrified, he leaps back from Kasturba, as if she had clamped him there against his will, or had transformed under him into an unclean woman. Mohan grabs the heap of his dhoti and begins wrapping himself hectically, staunching the wound of his lust with this enormous bandage.

A minute later, he is in his father's room. Mohan's foot jerks back from the threshold; he has stepped on a tulsi bead, the pressure sharp in the ball of his foot. These beads are from his father's necklace, which he clutched and snapped in despair at the end. An uncle sits at the foot of the bed.

'I was massaging his legs when it happened,' Mohan's uncle gloats sorrowfully. 'Not two minutes after you left. Not two minutes!'

Mohan thinks back to how impatiently he had squeezed his father's calves, waiting to have this chore taken over, his father too busy dying to make conversation. He thinks back to how he passed the time thinking about Kasturba; how, if she were awake, he would stand her up and turn her around to avoid the obstacle of her belly, but if she were asleep, he would let her stay on the cot. When his father's brother, chewing betel-nut slivers, had arrived to relieve him, Mohan had gotten to his feet right away and trotted off, like a dog in heat, to rut.

Weeks later, when Kasturba's bluish newborn dies, Mohan will nod at the incontrovertible evidence. The night of his father's death is not the last time he has sex. It is simply the first night he hates sex, truly hates it, like the traitor inside the city of nine gates, letting in the barbarians, come night. It will take twenty more years before he tells Kasturba, her body exhausted with five pregnancies, that he is never going to touch her again. But the seed has been planted. He will never think about sex again without thinking about death. He will think about it even at his father's funeral, during the Brahmin's chants, when, clad in mourning white cotton, a good son, he shoulders the flower-strewn bier, its brown bamboo rod gripped with both hands.

The break comes only years later—years after his time as a student in London, years into their life in South Africa.

For someone with so many qualms about sex, he certainly has a lot of it. Kasturba and Mohan conceive a son every three or four years since Harilal, their eldest, in 1888. She lives in these transitions of motherhood: waiting for the next son to be born, or, at a prod of her shoulder a little past midnight, conceived; for the second-to-youngest son to leave off taking her breast, replaced with his newborn brother; for a son's mouth to open so she can slip the next bite in.

By 1906, another son is well overdue. Five sons would be a respectable tally. They have never waited for so long an interval—but her husband has never been so busy. He is always travelling to Durban or Johannesburg or Pretoria; always writing articles for *Indian Opinion*; always finding new chores for himself, and for her, at the Phoenix Settlement.

Motherhood is Kasturba's only link to normalcy, to the life she would have lived as a wife in Gujarat. Her life in South Africa is anything but typical. She realized, very early in the marriage, that she had been married off to a strange, brilliant, exasperating man. A child in his stubbornness, a full-blooded male in his desire, a serene old ascetic in his piety and rules. Almost all Gujarati Banias are worldly-wise and money-minded—and she ended up with the one holy aspirant in the lot.

He gets only more religious in South Africa, even as he gets more political. She never catches him staring at her any more, not in the old way. He seems more interested in discussing dietary issues and rights for Indians with his associates. (Or disciples, more like, considering how they revere him.) Motherhood is the only stay she has against loneliness. Soaping four heads of hair in the morning helps her forget that she and her husband slept with their backs to each other all night.

So, she is surprised, and unexpectedly delighted, when late one August night her husband, up on one elbow, prods her shoulder. It is the old signal; she rolls on to her back.

'I have taken a vow today before God,' he says. 'I will not go back on it.'

'You cannot cut anything more out of your diet. You are already a fruitarian.'

'A vow of chastity. The *brahmacharya* vow.'

She turns on to her side again. 'I knew this was next.'

'Then you are happy for me. For us.'

She had known this was next, but she didn't know how it would make her throat hurt and her eyes blink back tears. 'I was waiting for this.'

'I must be stronger than my urges.'

She shrugs. 'We will see how long this lasts.'

'The vow will last until I die.'

She says nothing. Is she as easy to give up as cow's milk? Before his eyes, her figure under the sheet resolves into swell of hips, subsidence of waist, swell of shoulders, the wave form of his own desire. In the poor light, time loses its place, and she is twenty years younger, his new bride. He shakes his head of the illusion.

'You know this is my strongest urge. My only urge, now.'

'It is not your only urge. You still have the urge to be pure.'

He frowns, irritated; he does not like it when she tries to change the story he tells himself about himself. 'I meant my only bodily urge. Bodily urges are the ones I am overcoming. Purity is a *spiritual* urge, like truth-telling.'

'I wish you the best.'

'You support my vow, then.'

She says nothing. Desire was always something hidden, anyway. Now she must forget the place between her thighs where she hid it—desire like the key to a wall safe, tucked away long ago. In time, neither of them will be able to find it. What was in that wall safe? A fire, soon to go out for want of air.

Some kinds of life end for Gandhi in South Africa, but only because he must make room for a new life to begin and expand: his political one.

That begins as early as 1893. At the same time that the law student M.A. Jinnah in London steps on to his first (and last) Shakespearean stage in London, the new lawyer M.K. Gandhi, in South Africa, is falling—from an open train door, to the dusty ground.

First, that moment of being physically gripped and raised. The hands of the train conductor infantilize him. The words from the man's mouth sound nothing like civilized English—just syllables, demonically odd. *Off, wog!* Gandhi feels himself released into pure air, no support, no scaffolding, no family, no caste, no religion, nothing: an individual body, in freefall. He starts out in that forbidden first-class carriage as a caste Hindu, reflexively looking down on untouchables and on blacks—and on beef-eating, cigarette-smoking whites as well. *Off, wog! Whites only in the first-class compartment!*

Thrown from the train, he falls more than just the five or so feet to the ground. He falls through everything he thinks he is, down, down to the dust he is made of. He stands up, covered in dust, as the train leaves for Durban. He walks to a bench, shedding a faint brown dust the whole way. When he sits on the bench, he is still shedding it. He touches his white sleeve, and his sleeve smears brown. He sees darkness under his white fingernails. His palms have darkened to the colour of earth as well. He has never been so brown before.

The station sign says PIETERMARITZBERG, and he realizes it must be named for the Peter and Mary he knows from the Bible. Peter who holds the keys to heaven, where some are allowed in and some are not. Mary, who is said to intercede for those who are kept out. He thinks, *I must be Mary*, and for a moment that sounds perfectly logical to him.

That is the last benevolent thought he has for the next twelve hours. Because he sits there through nightfall. First comes the shame, making his face grow hot as the night grows cooler. Then the rage. And then the resolve.

By 1910, the politician in him has reached maturity. He doesn't look like a fighter: just a solitary stick figure standing on a curved road, in white jodhpurs and a white shirt that sticks with sweat to his bony back. To either side, a yellow–brown plain; before him, some low hills, bald, save for scrub and brittle grass everywhere. It is hard land, but arable.

Gandhi walks the road to a gate and through the gate to a small house. He passes a few children sitting in rows, their diligent fingers working away at some task with wicker and string. Another group is busy with chalkboards. They look up at him in awe. He wears a moustache, and carries a fob watch, and on his head is a sahib's field hat instead of a turban. He has not yet taken on his signature dress, but for everyone in this commune, he is already Gandhi.

He seeks out, in the bedroom, a blond muscular man, who stands at an architect's slanting desk. Sleek instruments lie at either elbow, and his arm, though enormous, sends a pencil with balletic grace across a T-square. This is Hermann Kallenbach. The two men's moustaches are groomed the same. Kallenbach still has his trouser legs rolled up, his gold-brick calves mud-flecked from some recent outdoor work.

'I am drafting the sign,' he says. 'The children want to paint it.'

Gandhi, his gaze drawn to a pile of books on Kallenbach's bed, says, 'You have been rereading him?'

'Yes. *The Kingdom of God Is within You.*'

'We have the same saying, you know. Isha vasya idam sarvam–God resides in each and all. It is the same.' Gandhi picks up the largest book and looks at some pages, puzzled.

Kallenbach shakes his head and waves his hand to assure his friend he need not bother with it. 'That is one of his novels. From his early life.'

Gandhi nods and sets down the book. When he first picked up this big book, he thought with some excitement that it was a compendium of articles and essays about the topics on the spine, *War* and *Peace*. Weren't these the subject of the Gita, too? He knows of the novels only by hearsay. To Gandhi, Tolstoy is a great thinker who, in a past life, had been a storyteller.

Gandhi is a devotee of the great Russian, but only the polemicist is of any use to him. Just a few months ago, he translated, into Gujarati, Tolstoy's *A Letter to a Hindu*.

> A commercial company enslaved a nation comprising two hundred millions. Tell this to a man free from superstition and he will fail to grasp what these words mean. What does it mean that thirty thousand men, not athletes, but rather weak and ordinary people, have subdued two hundred millions of vigorous, clever, capable, freedom-loving people? Do not the figures make it clear that it is not the English who have enslaved the Indians, but the Indians who have enslaved themselves?

In Gandhi's own past life, he has been a failed lawyer. In this new life, to which he was reborn without dying first, he is a fighter. His body, hard as an ant's, bears bruises that do not show up against his dark skin.

Against Kallenbach's glowing skin, though, the satyagraha stigmata show up purple and grey. He, too, is a fighter, literally: boxing is only one of his many sports, but he has given it up at his friend's advice. No violence, not even in play. Now he takes the blows of South African policemen and never strikes back, though he could lay any one of them flat. A good brisk beating feels like stepping out, after a long day indoors, into cooling rain.

Every man on the farm carries his bruises and cuts. Lumps on the head, too, from bamboo-stick thrashings, cherished little blood-fruit under the skin. Satyagraha has been gathering force, and press. Gandhi has been chased through a town by jeering whites; nasty articles about the Indians are crowding Johannesburg newspapers.

He had not come to South Africa with this intention. He had come as a London lawyer to take cases, even though he disliked the work and botched the briefs. All that arguing, those contradictory perspectives on the same matter, those games with words. How much better to have the truth and draw one's force from the truth! How much better to build this colony, with Hermann, here on one-and-a-half square miles of earth!

Gandhi sits down and begins to peel the orange he has brought with him. Kallenbach holds up the sign with its pencilled letters: TOLSTOY FARM.

'He was a writer of novels,' murmurs Gandhi, 'in his early years. But such trifles cannot be indulged in for a whole life.'

'One must grow up,' agrees Kallenbach. 'Become a man.'

The orange, stripped of its peel, splits naturally under his thumb in two. Gandhi offers his friend a half. They eat together, side by side on the bed.

'We call it sannyasa,' says Gandhi. 'When a man reaches a certain age, he renounces the things of the world.'

'You put away childish things,' Kallenbach nods.

'Do you know if something happened to make Tolstoy do so? To make him see through the world?'

'I think he wrote an account of it. *A Confession*. But I have not read it.'

'There must have been some such moment. There always is.'

'What was it for you?'

Pietermaritzberg station. 'I do not believe myself a great soul, Hermann. Not like Tolstoy.'

'He will be a good presiding spirit for the farm. Like Phoenix Farm, which rose from the ashes, yes? Always reborn.'

'We call it dvija,' says Gandhi. 'To be born twice. One birth physical, the second one, spiritual.'

'"Unless a man be born again, he cannot see the Kingdom of God." Tolstoy would approve, no doubt.'

'I want to write him another letter,' sighs Gandhi. 'But first I want to do something worthy to report.'

Rebirth: to be the same self in different bodies; to be a different self, in the same body. Simply being reborn, Gandhi knows, is not enough. Falling silent, he drifts out of the room without another word. Kallenbach knows better than to take offence at this.

Even as Gandhi goes back in his memory to the bench at Pietermaritzberg train station, Count Leo Tolstoy is dying on a cot at a train station in Russia. He has a prophet's beard and a peasant's smock and an aristocrat's everything else. Buzzards from newspapers in eight languages circle the small room, hopping sometimes to look in the window, every one occasionally stabbing a notepad with the beak of a pen. Tolstoy has forgotten those word games of forty years ago, his novels. His monstrous nostrils flare and breathe engine oil and steam and his own earthy pong. He has spent his whole life imagining he would go among the common people, dwell with them, become one of them. The farthest he will get is Astapovo.

His Indian admirer will go much, much farther. But he, too, will never quite arrive where he dreams of going.

For Gandhi, Tolstoy Farm is just a way station. Follow him now as he rises from the cot and grabs a bucket and broom to sweep out an open latrine. And now, as he washes his own clothes for the first time. Kasturba is grabbing his arms and protesting, afraid someone will see this and judge her. He says some sharp words and almost strikes her. He lets her join him as he hangs the clothes out to dry.

Follow him now as he rises and takes a train, with Kallenbach beside him, close as a bodyguard, 150 miles into the Transvaal, to the mines at Ballengeich. He enters the shaft and draws out the dark men trapped in the earth behind him. They are shouting *Vande Mataram*. Pickaxes and shovels somersault joyfully into the brush. They are more numerous than he imagined, a whole subterranean race, which he feeds now with loaves of bread. He cuts each loaf in three and digs a hole with his thumb, which he fills with sugar. They file past him, receiving their gift from his hands. Bread and sugar. It is barely a snack, but it will sustain them for the 150 miles back to Tolstoy Farm. He marches at the head of that army in the sun and heat.

From the perspective of the white South Africans, this is a stampede of beasts. In towns and telegraph offices for dozens of miles around, white men with badges and sunburnt faces feel the seismic tremor and grab their tools: handcuffs, canes, whips of hippopotamus hide. They converge along a dozen side roads, on foot, on horses, to block the dark-skinned singers in the free sunlight.

Gandhi stops and raises a bony arm.

Kallenbach hurries along the column, saying the little Tamil, the little Hindustani he knows, 'Remember, satyagraha; remember, do not resist.'

Gandhi lowers his arm.

No one steps forward for a moment. A few policemen snap their whips on the road.

As one now, the policemen advance. The officers on horses bring their rifles to the ready, just in case.

The singers have stopped singing. One miner loses his nerve and scurries barefoot into the brush, biting his lip. The others know what is coming, but they still have the taste of bread and sugar on their tongues, and they look forward to stay anchored. They do not look at the burly athlete, Kallenbach. Even now, as the blows start falling, they keep their eyes on the slight man with the large ears. They have never felt so powerful.

It is not the first time or the last that he will go to jail. At first, Kasturba was scared for him, but his letters came back curiously untroubled. The prison wasn't pleasant, but the South African whites, no matter how much they hated him, feared their subjugated dark races too much to torture or kill him. They did not dare find out what tens of thousands of non-violent Indians would do if the one man who preached non-violence died by violence.

Years have gone by since he took his vow and stuck to it. Somehow, against her expectations, they have grown closer. It's as if sexual union had been keeping them apart the whole marriage. His stubbornness and strictness don't outrage her any more.

One evening, while he is still in a Johannesburg jail, Kasturba stops suddenly in the kitchen, hurries to the sink, and vomits blood all over the dirty dishes. Word is sent to him that she is dying, but he writes her a letter that explains why he won't come see her. *If I just plead guilty, pay the fine, and come home*, he writes, *it will reduce the struggle to a farce. If you are destined to die, I think it is preferable you go before me.*

Ten years ago, that would have horrified and offended her. But Kasturba finds herself nodding over the letter, thinking to herself, *Yes, this is the truth. How right he is.*

What else is love but a madness for two?

She recovers, eventually, after a surgery. When the doctors insist on beef tea to help her recovery, she refuses, and her husband beams with pride. There is something pleasurable, she realizes, in hurting yourself on principle. Something uncommonly sweet in doing something counter to common sense.

Lying there in her own sweat, ashen, her incision aching for days like someone has taken a bamboo cane to her stomach, she feels she is the wife of Mohandas Gandhi for the first time in years.

If this is how he wants to be loved, she can love him like this.

By their last years in South Africa, thirteen-year-old Devdas's voice is cracking as he parrots the words *home rule*, while twenty-five-year-old Harilal has already gotten himself arrested. And Kasturba has finally attracted her husband again by prodding and stoking the only kind of fire he allows himself any more: the political kind.

Having marched at his side from the mines, she gets marched into jail for three months in 1913. The tiny mother of four, sentenced to hard labour, waits out her sentence. She finds the wait pleasant, even in the sun in her white saree—white, the colour widows wear, her own way of helping him keep his vow. The guards in this quarry, near Pietermaritzberg, have issued her the pickaxe, but they do not make her swing it. Kasturba is happy because she knows she is going back to India, and because she knows her husband is going to disrupt comfortable injustice on two continents, and because she has, at long last, reunited with him.

The proof: her Mohan meets her outside the jail on the day of her release. He does not care that several of his followers from Tolstoy Farm stand to either side of him, watching; he throws his arms around her and embraces her—without desire, but without reservation.

It feels like the first time. It feels better than the first time. Because she is, for the first time, his.

3

Early August, 1914. A steamer has been stopped in the English Channel. Dozens of passengers are milling about behind Gandhi, chattering excitedly, but he stands apart. The sea breeze that stirs his moustache has carried the news to the crew and passengers.

The passengers are asking each other questions like, 'How long do you think they will fight?' and 'Do you suppose it will be over by Christmas?' *They* and *it*: *they* are Germany Serbia Austria England France Russia, and *it* is war. Or rather War with a capital W, an abstraction like Life or Truth, at best a personification, like God.

Kallenbach is at Gandhi's side, but he may as well be on shore. He knows better than to disturb his friend at moments like these. Gandhi thinks one solipsistic thought: *what should I do*? And one compassionate thought: *pity them, help them, save them*.

In his mind, though, *they* are not the nations. *They* means the soldiers who will do the dying and the killing. He has seen them dying and killing in the modern way once already, while he was in South Africa during the Boer War. His fingers twitch a little at his sides, closing around the imaginary handles of stretchers. He recalls lines from the Bhagavad Gita where thousands of divine mouths crunch millions of soldiers, and Arjuna sees bits of skulls and limbs stuck between the teeth—that unbearable detail, the Universal Form barbarically feasting ... Gandhi recalls a nineteen-year-old soldier, twice his size, but with shredded thighs; delirious with pain; sobbing Cockney curses at the two 'grimy bastards' carrying his stretcher.

The steamer's foghorn startles him out of his reverie. A cable, leading down to a small tow boat, goes taut. Kallenbach points. The steamer begins to move at last—it has been stopped in the water for hours—zigzagging at odd angles behind the tow boat, which shifts course with no seeming logic.

'Has it lost its way?' he asks Kallenbach. 'Why is it turning to and fro like this?'

'Submarine mines,' he says, pointing at the waves. 'They have made an obstacle course of the Channel.'

The Boer War is still on Gandhi's mind, and he remembers himself at the front end of the stretcher, arms straight down with the weight, zigzagging among the writhing uniformed bodies on the ground as he made his way to the rear—each body a container of explosive suffering, mine after mine after mine.

In time, he gets to Southampton; in time, to London. On his way to a reception in his honour at Hotel Cecil, he passes a regiment of bookbinders. Whole neighbourhoods and guilds are signing up together. The Government wants every British citizen to play soldier. It wants the same of its far-flung Indian subjects.

The ballroom is already full of Indians, holding drinks, in bespoke suits and blue and gold silk sarees. The future enters, hands joined, in the simple white shirt and trousers of Tolstoy Farm.

All conversation stops. Some guests let out frank shouts of delight. This is the celebrity, this is Gandhi, the man who led the marches in South Africa! The guests turn and converge like sand grains towards the waist of the hourglass.

Only one guest lingers at the far end of the room, bewildered at how quickly the woman he was speaking with, the poet Sarojini Naidu, stopped paying attention and bustled past him. This lone guest is Mohammed Ali Jinnah. He approaches the ruckus reluctantly. A genteel company has become hectic rabble, and Hotel Cecil has taken on the sweaty atmosphere of a shrine on relic-viewing day.

The two men have been in London at the same time before, incidentally. In the same year M.A. Jinnah stepped off a steamer in London, M.K. Gandhi, a recent (and lacklustre) graduate from Middle Temple, stepped aboard a steamer headed for South Africa. The two men almost bumped shoulders on the quay.

Jinnah eyes the backs of Gandhi's throng a while. He, too, is an admirer—he has read and heard admirable things about Gandhi's work for indentured Indian labourers—but he cannot quite bring himself to *fawn* on the fellow. Not like this, at least. Jinnah sits down in the nearest chair, legs crossed, and takes a sip of his drink.

Presently a space is cleared, and Gandhi is introduced formally, with effusive praise. Jinnah tunes out much of it and gazes over the audience, which sits rapt. Those rapt looks turn to rapture and applause when Gandhi rises to deliver his speech. Jinnah himself has enjoyed an audience's admiration before, but this is something more than admiration. This is reverence. He turns to the object of it, and is rather disappointed in Gandhi's oratory. His English is technically passable, but slow and halting. Rather hard to imagine him holding his own in a court of law;

certainly, a native English barrister would clean bowl him from the opening statement. And the message! Indians, says Gandhi, should put their demands on hold until the war is over. Gandhi himself would organize an ambulance corps, just like the one he organized in South Africa.

He gets a standing ovation for this, to Jinnah's astonishment. Jinnah has been speaking with these same people since the day war was declared, and not one of them thought it right for a single Indian to die in Britain's name, in Belgian mud, for an Austrian archduke shot by a Serb.

Jinnah is important enough to have a seat at Gandhi's table. The table may be round, but Gandhi, without even sitting up straight, makes where he sits the head of it. The two men are introduced, but Jinnah has to wait his turn to address the great man.

So, meanwhile, he carves his roast chicken and potatoes. Gandhi has already whispered his off-menu request; Jinnah, chewing, looks up to see the waiter raise a silver cloche off two oranges and ten cashews.

Well, thinks Jinnah, *some eccentricity was to be expected.* A lull—here is his chance. 'About your ambulance corps, Mr Gandhi. And your position on India supporting the war effort.'

Ah yes, thinks Gandhi, *this is that well-dressed Mussalmaan.* 'It is only appropriate, Mr Jinni—'

'Jinnah.'

'Now is their hour of need. Surely the Indian students here in London can enlist, if the English ones do?'

As if you would have done so, or I, when we were students here. As if you or I would have been any use with a gun. 'Of course, the English are enlisting. It is their war. Britain's hour of need is our hour of opportunity. Let us cooperate, but conditionally. Not while we are slaves.'

How base it would be to press our advantage. 'Are we really their slaves, Mr Jinnah?'

Not chained and whipped, no, but slaves nonetheless. 'Perhaps not slaves—but they are still our masters. That is bad enough. We sailed here from Bombay some months ago to present India's demands, but as soon as this war broke out, they simply ushered us to the door. They take India for granted.'

This poor fellow has become frustrated. 'Let us show them solidarity, Mr Jinnah. It will be much easier, later, to negotiate as trusted friends.'

Indian tea, cotton, pepper—and now, Indian cannon-fodder? 'Slave and master can never be friends. Or servant and master, as you would have it.'

We must convert them with love. 'We must convert them with love.'

Jinnah thinks nothing at all for a moment; he is taken aback by this absurd 'holy' sentence dropped into what he thought was a political discussion. He says nothing.

Gandhi, remembering his platter, sets a cashew on his tongue, daintily. Someone takes advantage of this new lull to ask Gandhi how to sign up for the hypothetical ambulance corps. Gandhi's attention shifts from Jinnah, and with it, the table's.

Jinnah leaves without anyone noticing and smokes a lonely Craven A in the hotel foyer. 'We must convert them with love,' he mutters aloud. He takes another drag and laughs out a single pulse of incredulous smoke. 'Love!'

On the steamer home to India, Kasturba, not Kallenbach, massages Gandhi's calves. Kallenbach is not with him any longer; the carpenter-swimmer-mystic is not allowed out of London because of his German passport. Sciatica pours chilled acid down the backs of Gandhi's legs, but it gets better when he walks around the deck of the *Arabia*, which is taking him from London to Bombay. Eventually he circles back to Kasturba with a new trouble furrowing his brow.

'What will I wear?'

'What is wrong with the clothes you are wearing?'

'There will be receptions. There are always receptions for me, now.'

'The men will be wearing suits, mostly. Just as they were in London.'

Gandhi stares over the waves, recalling the image of Jinnah in London: three-piece suit and diamond cufflinks, fob watch chain dangling in a precise symmetric U, two peaks in the breast pocket's blue silk handkerchief. 'I will wear,' says Gandhi, 'a turban. And a dhoti. From now on, a dhoti.'

Kasturba shakes her head. 'But you may meet British officials. They will see you.'

'Let them see me for who I am.'

They do. Bombay receives him in the usual suits, and every pair of eyes flashes down to his dhoti and knobby brown ankles, his dusty feet in sandals, his native costume.

His fellow Gujaratis organize a separate reception for him. The first of the group to shake his hands at the garden gate has a familiar face, a familiar extreme formality to his attire. Mohammed Ali Jinnah chairs the Gujarati Association, just as he chairs every other organization he is a part of—except the Indian National Congress.

'I am so pleased to see you ...' says Gandhi, and Jinnah nods and is just letting go of the handshake as Gandhi continues, '... in this position. Not only is a Mussalmaan like you a member of our group; he is chairing it.'

Jinnah stands where Gandhi leaves him. He runs a hand over the nape of his neck to tamp the bristling there. What did that *mean*? That the ones *naturally* in charge were to be commended for letting the Muslim guest come up? That Jinnah led, not thanks to his own virtue, but to *their* magnanimity? The magnanimity of Hindus?

A small slight, Jinnah tells himself, *scarcely a slight at all, and if a slight, then surely unintentional. Mr Gandhi is an eccentric fellow, clearly. Just look at what he is wearing! He looks like some illiterate villager.*

Jinnah checks the written remarks in his pocket and follows the guest of honour to his seat. The speech he gives is generous and eloquent, praising even the ambulance corps. The speech is in the King's English, as a proper speech should be.

Now it is Gandhi's turn to speak. He rises and scratches his nose.

'Forgive me,' he begins, 'if after such a fancy speech, I talk to you, brothers, in plain Gujarati, dressed like a peasant…'

The suited Hindus are already on their feet, applauding. Jinnah stays seated, his legs crossed. This, he realizes, is an image even the best educated of them cannot resist. The Hindu holy man in rags, in deliberate poverty. It is in their blood.

The corner of his mouth twitches, once; then his hand rises, quickly, to rub the back of his neck again. *If after such a fancy speech…*

That wasn't a compliment, was it? A small slight, he tells himself, *scarcely a slight at all. But not unintentional.*

4

Total unity, total understanding, total love from a woman, without the complications of sex and romance: Jinnah has from Fatima the same pure love that Gandhi has from Kasturba. But Jinnah, unlike Gandhi, is single.

Bombay's wealthiest women, single and married alike, know it. Like this one, sitting next to him during a garden party. He is telling her a story about his early days, when he used to challenge Englishmen at billiards to pay the rent. They simply could not turn down the wager from an arrogant brown man, lest they lose face. They lost face anyway once he cleared the table.

She throws her head back and laughs, then takes another sip of her punch. When she turns back to the handsome lawyer, she starts visibly, and her smile vanishes. Dashing Mr Jinnah has been replaced in the chair. Where has this woman come from? The two faces are utterly identical—regally high cheekbones, thin upper lip, sharp nose—a cross between a pharaoh and a wolf. How can this be? Even this woman's dress is the same black with blue trim as Mr Jinnah's blazer and tie.

'Fatima Jinnah,' says the Sultana's new conversation partner, extending a hand that must have been holding an iced drink until now. The Sultana sits paralyzed by her stare. 'I see you met my brother?'

'Yes,' she chokes out. She almost wants to say she is sorry. 'Such a brilliant man. Lawyer. Such a brilliant lawyer.'

'A busy lawyer. He has so little time for frivolous chit-chat. We Jinnahs like to stay busy.'

'And what keeps you busy, Miss Jinnah?'

'My brother, for one. I am also a dental surgeon. I rip out teeth for a living. With pliers. What do *you* do?'

'I ... I am the Sultana of Daulatabad.'

'I did not ask you what you are, but what you do.'

'I do ... I travel a great deal.'

'Smile for me, Sultana.'

The Sultana, uneasy, obeys the command.

'My clinic is in Boriwali. I can only do so much for your dentition, but I do hope I shall see you there?' She smiles and rises. 'I promise to use the drill sparingly.'

The Sultana stays pale long after Miss Jinnah deserts her. Jinnah's sister finds him smoking beside the piano.

'Jin.' She calls him *Djinn*, spirit of smokeless fire.

'Fati.' He calls her *Fati*, which he knows from his Lincoln's Inn Latin is *fate*. 'I saw you terrifying the poor Sultana.'

'What number Sultana is she?'

'Number three.'

'The Sultan must name them by how many chins they have.'

'He values her a great deal.'

'Is she getting the Rolls-Royce in his will?'

'And the villa on Mount Abu.'

'Well, she won't have *you*.'

'Not every woman, Fati, is out to entrap me. Besides, I have no interest in women right now.'

'But they have an interest in you.'

'You flatter me.'

'No. *They* flatter you. As I overheard. "You are so charming, Mr Jinnah, your stories are so wonderful, do tell me another."'

'Politeness.'

'Scheming. I shall introduce you to someone, Jin, when I find your equal. None of these frivolous spoilt princesses.'

'And then shall I have your permission to make conversation?'

'Not for too long. And not so it distracts you from what is important.'

'India.'

'The Lucknow meeting. You can broker the deal. You can unite the Congress and the Muslim League at last. Now over there is Mr Das. Go pluck his sleeve. Go to work on him.'

'You are a sterner taskmaster than the British. I shall be relieved to go work next month, at my own pace, in the hills.'

'I have not heard of this new plan. Where are you going?'

'Darjeeling.'

'And whom do you know in Darjeeling?'

'A friend of mine owns a summer home there.' Jinnah drops his cigarette and crushes it with two precise grinds counter-clockwise, clockwise—of an alligator-skin loafer. 'I believe you have met him. Sir Dinshaw Petit?'

Fati does not accompany her brother to Darjeeling, so she isn't around to enforce a blockade around him.

Papers cover two side tables, one at either elbow. An ashtray heaped with cigarette butts smokes down like a ruined village. The Himalayas beyond his balcony might as well not be there. Concentrating hard on his speechwriting for Lucknow, he is vulnerable. Anyone might creep up behind him here. Anyone might slide her small pale hands over his eyes and laugh to see the elegant gentleman start in his chair.

'Do you remember me, Mr Jinnah?'

He rubs his eyes. 'Of course. Miss Petit.'

'Ruttie, to my friends. Did you know our name was, originally, Pet-*eet*? Some French merchants encountered my great-great-grandfather in a customs house, and he was so small he could swing his feet off the ledge of his chair. Like so.' The lithe young girl has pulled a chair next to him on to the balcony, and she scoots back to dangle her naked feet with their red nail polish. 'The name stuck. Pet-*eet*.'

'There are Germans named Klein,' says Jinnah, 'and Englishmen named Small and Short.'

'All of them gigantic oafs, I am sure. We stayed small, even though our name took on its own Indian pronunciation. *Pet*-it.' A small white cat has appeared in her lap. 'And this is my pussy-cat. Would you like to pet it? Pet *her*, I should say.'

He strokes the fur, and the kitten starts to purr.

'She loves you,' says Ruttie.

The loose-leaf pages of his speech, his legal briefs, the pages of his two reference books on English constitutional law: all rise on a mountain wind, dance with the silk curtains, and fly off the balcony and over a curving mountain path below.

On that path, Ruttie and Jinnah ('J', as she has chosen to call him) are strolling side by side. They round a corner and cannot be seen from the terrace of her father's house. To her right is a steep drop and dark green trees, to her left is Jinnah. She leaps delicately on to a low stone wall and walks, her arms out a few degrees, fingers splayed, balancing.

'That is dangerous, Ruttie.'

'I could jump into that abyss, and I would glide, from side to side, down on the breeze, like a leaf. There are advantages to being a Petit.'

A breeze does pick up, and she sways wildly, flinging out her arms. Perhaps a little dramatically; perhaps for effect.

It works. He cries out her name.

'Hold my hand, then.'

He does. And within moments of his doing so, she skips casually off the stone ledge. But she doesn't let go of his hand.

This stroll becomes a daily ritual, but he does not take hold of her hand until she leaps on to the stones. He is always drawing her away from the same abyss.

The only time he lets go of her hand is one week in, when he gets a craving for a Craven A. She points to the package.

'You won't share?'

'What will your father say?'

'Nothing, unless I tell him. And I will only tell him you gave me a cigarette if you don't give me a cigarette.'

She places one in her mouth and lowers her face to his lighter, gazing up into his eyes, as she has seen a femme fatale in a film do—then promptly doubles over coughing. He pats her back. He rubs her back. She grins and takes another drag on the cigarette and blows the smoke into the sky.

The cigarette smoke becomes Himalayan mist. Ruttie and Jinnah are riding through it on two Arabian horses—hers a mare with a white-spotted sabino coat and high white leg markings; his horse's coat rubican, the white hairs intermixed with dark.

Ruttie is pouting. 'Already?'

'We have ridden for an hour and forty-five minutes, Ruttie.'

'Darjeeling all around you, J, and you only have eyes for your fob watch?'

'I must get back to work.'

'Your Lucknow meeting is all the way in December.'

'It is the most important of my career to date.'

Ruttie, as casually as ever, remarks, 'I suppose Congress will concede one-third Muslim representation in the central government. They want Hindu–Muslim unity in the short term, while Britain is still at war. They will see your plan as a way to negotiate from a position of strength. Your case is already made. I daresay your success is assured.'

Jinnah's reins slip from his hands. His jaw drops, and the most eloquent lawyer in India can find nothing to say.

'Far less certain is whether you will succeed in teaching *me* to handle a cue stick.'

Mohammed Ali Jinnah is in love.

He is also in luck. Lucky in Lucknow—if luck deserves credit for a pact so dependent on political skill. Dozens of politicians from both parties give speeches, but everyone knows that Lucknow's architect and builder is one man.

'Jinnah has squared the circle, hasn't he?' 'Unflappable Jinnah, that tie of his is never a degree askew.' 'Where does he get his suits tailored?' 'Silver-tongued Jinnah has made peace between the two houses.' 'I say, are they wearing pinstripes in London these days?'

A line from *Julius Caesar* keeps running through Jinnah's head as he takes in the praise. *He doth bestride the narrow world / Like a Colossus*. One foot among the Hindus of the Congress, the other among the Muslims of the League—all of them *petty men* now, who *walk under his huge legs and peep about*.

Fittingly, it is a poet who draws him to the centre of the meeting room and urges him on to a chair, calling everyone to listen. Fitting, too, that it should be the very same woman who looked past him at Hotel Cecil and rushed to meet the newly arrived Gandhi—Sarojini Naidu. There is another chair close by, and with the line about colossal Caesar still in his head, Jinnah widens his stance to bridge them.

Meanwhile, Sarojini is delivering her panegyric. She is still an admirer of Gandhi, but today, it's Jinnah who moves her to perform. She weaves about him, beams up at him, gestures at him and bids the room applaud. The only thing that distinguishes him from a statue a pedestal is the blush to his cheeks. His whole body gets the fine warm feeling of freshly cast bronze.

'Here he is,' declaims Sarojini, 'behold the man! No politician in India's history has done what he has done. And still so young! Where are his grey strands? I present to you the genius who has brokered this Lucknow Pact between two groups so long believed irreconcilable. I present to you Mr Jinnah, *our* Jinnah—the ambassador of Hindu–Muslim unity!'

He is not going to rise higher. Not yet, at least. But he doesn't know that. He feels unstoppable, and he scans his audience. There: he breezes off the chairs with the grace of a dancer and extends his hand.

'Sir Dinshaw,' he says.

'The man of the future!' Sir Dinshaw covers Jinnah's hand—the same that held Ruttie's—with both of his own. 'I'll say one day that Mr Jinnah planned it all out under my roof.'

'I have no shortage of plans, Sir Dinshaw. But not just for unity between Hindus and Muslims. Why not the Jains and Christians?'

'Absolutely! Why not the Parsis?'

'There are ways. The communities must eat together, for example. We should hold joint dinners.'

'And concerts in the park. Everyone invited!'

'The communities must build houses side by side, too. None of these Muslim neighbourhoods and Hindu localities.'

'Right, Jinnah! The more we become neighbours, the more we will feel like citizens.'

'Citizens of one India. And they ought to intermarry, too. What better way to unite our various communities? Muslims, Parsis—'

Sir Dinshaw claps Jinnah's shoulder. 'Brilliant idea! Brilliant!'

Someone has brought cigars: Romeo y Julietas. They each take one. Jinnah is quick to strike and proffer a match, the long fingers of one hand sliding open the matchbox and picking out the match. Sir Dinshaw leans forward and puffs three times. Jinnah lights his own now and tilts it at the ceiling, savouring a mouthful of smoke.

'I say, Jinnah, you must publish these ideas in an article, if not a book.'

'I have a better idea for cultivating communal harmony.'

'Do tell.'

'I wish to marry your daughter.'

First the smile falls, then the cigar. 'What?'

Jinnah stares at the cigar smoking on the tiles. It is too late to backtrack now. 'Ruttie. I love her.'

'What about *you* makes you worthy of my daughter's hand?'

Jinnah dry swallows and looks around at the assembly hall, where some people, in the middle of conversations, are still glancing his way. He gestures vaguely around himself. 'You yourself said I was the—' He stops himself.

'The man of the future? Not of *her* future. You? How could you ever fancy yourself … For God's sake, you are a forty-year-old *Muslim*.'

Jinnah starts to tremble. Whether out of hurt or rage, he himself does not know.

'This is the last conversation you will ever have with me or anyone from my family. Stay away from my sweet little girl and don't you ever imagine I'll let you wrap her up and put her behind a curtain. Not while I live, Jinnah. Stay away from her.'

Little Sir Dinshaw turns on his heel and quicksteps out. 'Colossus' Jinnah crumbles, thunderstruck, into one of the chairs that, only moments ago, he stood astride.

At home, crestfallen personally after his greatest political triumph, he goes over the postcards he has received from Ruttie over the past months, shuffling through them like photographs of a lost loved one.

11 September 1916

Dear Mr Jinnah—

You do not remember me perhaps—but I remember you—and if nothing else, this little postcard from Darjeeling will remind you of the frivolous chatterbox who bothered you this summer when you were busy with your serious work. Do you remember her name? If not, let me remind you, it is

Ruttie Petit (Sir Dinshaw's daughter)

As if he could have forgotten those walks during which he held her hand. As if that memory hadn't been more alluring than any future he might find in Lucknow. One of the gifts she's given him is a chain of paper figures holding hands. 'A good luck charm,' she told him. Two at the centre have smiles and eyes penned on to them; over one chest, 'Me,' on the other, 'You.' He had tried to replicate it with his own scissors, at his desk, but no matter how he folded and cut, the figures came out separate.

3 December 1917

Dearest J—

Papa read your latest article and is all abuzz with your genius! I rolled my eyes and asked if you were that summer houseguest with the perfectly folded handkerchief. I do not want to read your articles; I would much prefer a letter from you. Would the Political Genius of the Age take the time to write a few words to a silly lonely girl? If so, please address it to

Ruttie Petit

He hadn't known how to write what he felt to her. She was a child—*is* a child—Sir Dinshaw was not wrong when he called her that. If he had written his love to her, things might have gone utterly wrong. And imagine the risk of that letter being intercepted! Even to bribe the postman or a sweeping-girl to deliver such a letter would open him up to blackmail. Ruttie, though, had been willing to take the risk. Here it is, trembling in his hands, that first, long, wildly scrawled letter. Love came into the open between them, all at once. Twenty days after its date, he would be asking her father for her hand in marriage.

11 December 1916

My dearest J,

I shall not send you any more postcards—only letters properly enclosed and sealed from the eyes of the world. I want to say too many things to you in any case.

This last Tuesday, when you called at our house, I cannot explain to you what elation I felt. And when you smiled my way and gave me that wink, I think I know now what firecrackers feel like when the fire touches them for the first time. These words I am writing you are beyond my control. They are the sparks flying out of the firecracker heart you lit.

I do not think you can imagine how high I esteem you. You are not so vain as to think about yourself the things I think about you. I want you to teach me everything you know. I feel that one hour with you is a shortcut to all that is wise and beautiful in the world, which I would have to live ten years to experience.

You may think I have nothing to offer you, but you are wrong. I can offer you love. That is why I am writing this letter with shaking hands and a dry mouth. Loving me, you will be free to pursue your future. I will not weigh you down at all. My very name means 'small'. I will help you along. If you wish, I can be your personal secretary. My teachers say I have excellent handwriting. My hand is not always this shaky!!

This confession may strike you as a girlish infatuation, but I assure you I have always been ahead of my age. I only pretend to be frivolous and teasing. Inside I am thinking the most serious and troubled thoughts. There can be 'old souls', as you know, and mine is an 'old soul', so you can think of my love for you as being a thousand years old, preserved in my heart as in an urn. It is new but familiar. It is ancient but I believe it is—I want it to be—my future.

Yours, whether you will have me or not,

R

Rereading this letter, something breaks in him. Is he sacrificing his happiness because he fears the wrath of a five-foot Parsi gentleman? Jinnah pulls the inkwell close and starts to write to Ruttie with all the fury of a poet.

His letters fold themselves into paper boats and navigate the roadside braids of monsoon rain. Hers become origami cranes and perch on her windowsill, pecking kisses off her cupped palm before they fly off to his desk. It is a very old story: a young damsel trapped in the tower, and the knight-at-arms promising to free her from the wicked old sorcerer.

Every tragic pair of star-crossed lovers implies at least one tragic pair of star-crossed parents. Sir Dinshaw doesn't quite fit the fairy tale. Elfin and grey-haired, he sobs into his hands, terrified by his princess' tantrums. Ruttie's mother throws her arms around him. She, too, does not recognize their daughter any more. What kind of spell has this Muslim cast on her?

'I brought that viper into my own house,' he says, after he blows his button nose. 'That snake, that seducer, that Jinnah...'

Upstairs, meanwhile, the headstrong princess writes another secret letter to her Saracen.

> ...On my birthday I will walk out of my father's house and down the street to yours. I am in such ill repute here that I do not think Papa is allowing a party for me anyway. I was born a little after 7 in the evening, you know, but I shall not wait till dusk. In fact, I will try my hardest not to slip out at the stroke of midnight!! It is very convenient, isn't it, that the love of my life lives so close by? I will bring a toothbrush and a valise of clothes, but you know I am not very strong, so I shall pack lightly—will you have a nice dress ready for me? With a veil perhaps??? And also, do think of my new name. I am always—and for now—your love, your admirer, your
>
> Ruttie

Her birthday is already here. She places a cherry-red beret on her head, smiles into the mirror, and slides the valise out from under her bed.

Her father is still snoring, but her mother is awake and rushes out of bed when she hears Ruttie's door down the hall. She grabs at her daughter's dress, but the dress is grey-blue, like cigarette smoke in the dawn light, and escapes her fingers. She cries Ruttie's name and grabs again, but Ruttie herself turns to smoke.

Jinnah, waiting for her in his study, takes the nervous cigarette from his mouth and breathes out. Smoke. His lips still in an O, he breathes in—and draws Ruttie, materialized out of that grey-blue smoke, on to his lap, into his mouth, kissing.

She slips his handkerchief from his pocket and holds it over her nose and mouth. 'Shall I be an Aisha? Shall I be a Rukhsana?'

She is playing at being a Muslim bride.

Jinnah lifts it and kisses her again. 'What's in a name?'

'Maybe I am a Zulaykha. That is romantic-sounding, isn't it? Like the girl saved from the harem in a Lord Byron poem. Or—Layla?'

'That would make me Majnun.'

'Gone mad for love! Perfect. Unless you would like me better as a Mumtaz or a Tabassum?'

'I will call you whatever you wish, Ruttie.'

Her face falls. Suddenly, she is no longer trying on names like dresses for a ball; suddenly she is just a Parsi girl pressured to convert on the eve of marrying out.

'I don't think I want to go by the new name, J. It will be too strange.'

'A formality. No different than notarizing the marriage license.'

'Will Fatima call me by my new name?'

'I cannot speak for her.'

'I will choose Fatima, then. She will never call me by it, and neither will you.'

Jinnah's smile fades, and he shakes his head. 'I am afraid Fati will not like that.'

'You have a sister named Maryam, don't you? Would she mind?'

'Less.'

'Maryam it is, then.' She nods, her eyebrows lowering slightly, deciding. 'My name is Maryam Jinnah.'

5

Prayer meeting, winter, 1918.

And when it is said to them, Do not make mischief in the land, they say: 'We are but peace-makers.'

Gandhi sits with a shawl around himself, all his limbs collapsed, like an umbrella with all the spokes snapped. He is murmuring almost to himself. Multitudes stare up at him.

'I think it is beautiful, my brothers and sisters, that this verse comes from a chapter of the Qur'an called "The Cow". Who can tell me that the cow is not holy to my Muslim brethren, too? When there is a whole chapter in the Qur'an with this title? The wisdom is universal. And very necessary, in fact, now that the so-called Great War has ended in Europe. I myself think no war is great. How will these victorious powers make peace? With violence and rancour, or with love?'

Sometimes he speaks in Gujarati, sometimes in Hindustani. Religions, too, are languages; he speaks them all as a native.

'"Therefore, Arjuna, fight." Our fight is only now beginning. We must remember that God comes "not to send peace, but a sword", as Jesus said. Our holy war must involve the use of force. Truth-force.'

Satyagraha. The crowds surge a little closer to the platform, excited. Some are clean-shaven, some are bearded. The bearded men are Muslims, drawn by Gandhi's promise to support the khalif of all Islam—the Ottoman Sultan, one of the losers in the Great War.

No one in that crowd, beard on his cheeks or red tilak on his brow, cares about what went on in Lucknow late last year. Why would they care about deft deals agreed upon by billionaires and big-city barristers who speak English to one another?

All they care about is here, in Gandhi's vernacular. Faith and freedom.

Satyagraha.

At the far edge of the field, two figures stand side by side, both thin and well-dressed. A man and a woman, arms folded, a Packard nearby with a chauffeur leaning against it. The chauffeur, his interest growing, leaves his place to go closer to Gandhi's prayer meeting. He takes off his hat as he floats past them, spellbound.

'So, this is what draws a crowd,' says Jinnah.

Fati gives a little shiver. 'A *mob*, you mean.'

'Odd how talk of non-violence can arouse the rabble.'

'"Satyagraha". Is that even a word?'

'His own coinage.'

'Political currency. But counterfeit.'

'Like this mad talk of keeping on the Ottoman Sultan as khalif. As the leader of the whole world's Muslims. And they believe he means it? Hindu that he is?'

'Even if he does believe it, does he mean to dictate terms to the Allies? To send a telegram to Downing Street?'

'Look, more absurdity. He is praying again.'

'Come along, Jin. We have seen it for ourselves now. This is not politics.'

'But it is. Lucknow will be worth nothing if he whips up the mob like this. The British won't negotiate. They will crack down.'

'Only if he makes mischief. Gandhi keeps exhorting his followers to sit down and take blows like donkeys.'

'Marches, demonstrations, strikes. He is mixing mass politics and mass prayer.'

'Oil and water, Jin.'

Jinnah shakes his head. 'Sulphur and saltpetre.'

The call for satyagraha doesn't lead to a single explosion. Instead, it sets off hundreds of small brushfires across the British Raj. India sent Indians to die at Ypres, but now that the Great War has been won, the sahibs don't just leave the sweaty coolies standing with their hands out. They keep in place the wartime restrictions on voices and pens. It's wartime all the time, as far as criticizing the Empire goes. Perfidious Albion.

Britain's money machine judders and spews smoke. Saboteurs are on the factory floor, and they are wearing homespun cotton: Congress firebrands, inspired by Gandhi. They don't lob bombs at the Viceroy, or stand there waiting, Gavrilo Princip–like, with a pistol when the coach-and-four takes a wrong turn down Baird Road. They simply refuse to cooperate with the running and maintenance of things. The knob-knees of the Empire click and give out.

Non-cooperation gives way to sabotage. The Punjab has always had Britain's admiration—they know it for a good field to harvest soldiers—but what made the British admire it before, makes them fear it now. Amritsar's burly Punjabis go particularly wild. Telegraph lines go down, cut with a knife. The Town Hall's neoclassical pillars turn to smoke. Soon the streets are chock-full of bobbing Sikh turbans. Mounted lancers slash at protesters while bricks arc overhead. Saltpetre and sulphur, at the touch of hammer to percussion cap, sends the crowd screaming and cursing.

Some men round the corner, covered in sweat, looking over their shoulders. They almost jog right by the white Englishwoman on a bicycle. She is quite unaware of what has been going on three streets over; she is on her way to teach schoolchildren. The sight of her stymies them at first. She is past them, still oblivious, when almost out of curiosity, one of the men kicks the rear wheel with his foot. Once she tumbles and hits the ground, and oranges go rolling from her bicycle's front basket, the spell of Englishness is totally broken. They strip her naked and beat her, darkening her skin perforce until her breasts and back are brutalized purple-grey. The Indian parents of her Indian pupils pull her to safety—four middle-class and decent fathers, who wave their sandals at the mob, as they might at stray dogs.

And yet, for all the smoke and violence in the air, people find a time and a place to celebrate in Amritsar. Gandhi isn't there, but his words and his ideas are.

They gather in a garden around a well, deep and bottomless and full of cool, clean water. The garden is enclosed, its walls ten feet high, with five narrow-gated passages. Spare scrub and wildflowers roughen the earth, but no hillock or ridge rises high enough to conceal a body, not even a crouched child's.

Two or three of the people are giving speeches in praise of ahimsa, non-violence. Every so often, singing breaks out. But there are no guns, no bombs, not even a torch, and why would there be? This bright afternoon in early April, 1919, is the religious festival of Baisakhi. Punjabis—Sikhs, Hindus, Muslims—have gathered to celebrate it together.

How many? A small plane has just circled overhead. Its pilot reports the crowd at 20,000 at least.

Clap your hands. Sing along, while there is still time.

Welcome to Jallianwala Bagh.

After the shameful daylight humiliation of an English schoolteacher, an order came down from the British authorities: every Indian male must crawl on all fours down that street.

'Just as they do before their idols. So they know a white woman is as sacred as their gods.'

The British officer who gave that order, and that justification for it, is riding in an armoured car. He heads a convoy of eighty soldiers in troop trucks and several artillery pieces. He knows the size of the crowd in Jallianwala Bagh. The pilot of that small plane has reported back to him.

Look at Brigadier-General Reginald Dyer's profile, his posture. The delicately trimmed grey moustache, the inexpressive blue eyes, the lordly uprightness—all convey self-discipline, detachment, nobility. It is hard to imagine terror inside that wax model of British sangfroid. But it's there.

That terror distorts and confuses everything as in a funhouse mirror. The gathering at Jallianwala Bagh has become an army; chants from the Guru Granth Sahib, the holy book of the Sikhs, garble into revolutionary slogans. Indian self-rule is Bolshevism, spreading down from Russia, and this 'Ghandy' returned from South Africa is another Lenin returned from another Switzerland.

Maybe it is easier to imagine hatred in him. That is there, too: hatred for the Red threat and brown skin and commonplace wogs like 'Ghandy' who go get their schooling and airs in England and make trouble back here. *What did they imagine? That we would clear out of India after the War? We won the War—but we lost good British boys by the millions—so we'll keep our prizes, thanks all the same. And we'll keep those wartime restrictions on sedition in place, while we're at it. That's what you get for making trouble. You get the Rowlatt Act and three slaps of a bamboo cane across the arse and sixty-five of my Gurkhas marching into your Jollywhatever Bagh.*

The soldiers he leads look very little like the people they are about to shoot. The Gurkhas have short muscular bodies, enormous smiles and almond eyes. They have come from Nepal in the northeast to Punjab in the northwest. They are known to giggle a lot. The British, privately, think of them as children. Exceptionally loyal, exceptionally lethal children.

The remaining twenty-five soldiers are Baluchis from the far western frontier of British India. They are devout Muslims and keep to themselves. The festival of Baisakhi means as little to them as Diwali or Christmas. It isn't Eid, and it isn't Ramadan. So, it isn't sacred.

General Dyer, at Sandhurst, learnt the old philosophy of *divide and rule*.

The Indians have done all the dividing already, on their own. All the British have to do is rule.

The contingent arrives now at Jallianwala Bagh. The Gurkhas have been bobbing their knees and tumble joyfully from the backs of their transport trucks. These eager boy-men, at a word from their commanding officer, go tense and orderly, like iron shavings that have sensed the magnet. The Baluchis, rifles checked, eyes sullen, join the formation. General Dyer gives an order to lock all the gates. He has his men leave the artillery pieces, though not out of mercy—the pieces are too big to fit through the passageway into the garden. His men shoulder their rifles and follow him.

What happens next will be the last thing on which Jinnah and Gandhi ever share an opinion.

Saltpetre and sulphur and charcoal, two fuels and an oxidizer, combine to make gunpowder. Add a spark, and you get an explosion. Place that explosion behind a thumb-sized piece of metal, and funnel that explosion through a metal tube, eighty times over, twelve times a minute, into a crowd of 20,000 unarmed civilians, and you get Jallianwala Bagh.

General Dyer, guiding the rifle fire, points his sabre now left, now right. In response, the crowd surges now right, now left. He sculpts an ocean with a magic wand. The gun smoke forms a halo around him and around all his soldiers. Inside it, they are invulnerable.

Before them, all around the enclosure, grown men are clambering up the walls. Children get pushed up from below by their parents. Dyer points his sabre at them. The rifles tilt, responsive. His sabre is the finger of fate, choosing you, and you, and you.

When bodies crouch under the bullets, he lowers his sabre. *Bagh* means *garden,* and he is watering these human flowers, bullets like so many drops from a watering-can. Bullets like so much rainfall from this cloud of rifle smoke.

Jove hides inside that cloud, deciding who dies. Imperial, impervious.

The bullets pass through a body and still have momentum enough to pass through two more. The people are packed that tight and shot from that close.

Some of them, grazed, or with only a leg or an arm shattered, crawl to the well, the only landmark, the only cover. Others have already jumped. The ones who know how to tread water do so, while the rest claw the smooth cement wall for purchase. This lasts only a few seconds. They are safe from bullets but not from more bodies thudding on to their upturned faces, driving them under. They splash and wrestle and cry out, but these little tussles last only a few seconds as more bodies knock them apart. The well has swallowed so many bodies that the breath bubbles, released, make the water look like it's boiling. The last person to jump into the well finds himself standing on a solid cylinder of one hundred and twenty dead bodies, his torso still above the rim, exposed to the bullets.

The firing subsides. To be precise, the ammunition runs out. General Dyer restores his sabre to its scabbard and shouts a command. His troops shoulder their rifles, spin on their heels and march, their task complete. Shrieks and sobs wrinkle the new silence. The cloud of gun smoke stretches apart and clears. Not one man glances over his shoulder.

PART TWO

Calling the Witnesses

And even if, in our comparison, we analyse each life, as we would a poem or a picture, we shall find that the rise to political power and repute in consequence of innate excellence and strength, rather than of inherited advantages, is common to both.

—Plutarch, *Parallel Lives*

6

London, 1919. The Old Vic theatre.

A gentleman is reading the newspaper in one of the balconies, his long dark fingers stained with newsprint and nicotine.

The door behind him opens. A sylph floats into the box behind him. She carries all thirty-five weeks in front; from behind, it is impossible to tell she is with child at all.

The newspaper stays up. Ruttie Jinnah leans forward and watches the audience filing into the seats below, but this fails to distract her for long.

'Catching up, J?'

Jinnah turns a page. 'A few minutes yet before the curtain rises.'

'Is there any more news from India?'

'Only two days since Jallianwala Bagh,' he says bitterly, 'and it is no longer a crime or a tragedy here. It's just another quarrel between Tories and Labour.'

'Will they bring him to justice? This killer—this Dyer?'

'Knowing the British? I half expect the *Morning Post* to take up a collection for him.'

Her husband does not look up from the newspaper. Ruttie stares at his profile, at her fingernails, at the ornate ceiling.

'I feel kicking,' she says, laying a hand on her belly. 'Baby is very restless.'

'Excited for the show, no doubt.'

'Baby would have been *much* more excited to see the latest Noel Coward play.'

Jinnah either doesn't hear this, or ignores it. The lights go down, and a man in an Elizabethan doublet and hose enters.

'Two households,' he declaims, 'both alike in dignity, In fair Verona, where we lay our scene…'

Jinnah moves his lips along with the lines. He is imagining his other life, in which he stayed with the theatre company back in 1893 and played Romeo. *Who set this ancient quarrel new abroach?* He would have been a poorer man, with a wife less young and less beautiful than the Flower of Bombay, already wilting off to sleep at his elbow. But oh, if he had done it! He would have out-Romeo'd this Romeo. *Tut, I have lost myself; I am not here…*

'J?'

She is tugging at his sleeve. He shrugs her off, rapt. But now she grabs his shoulder and rises from her chair, listing, one hand under her belly. The silk of her evening dress clings darkly to her legs. Her water has broken. A contraction makes her wince. Only a few theatregoers glance up at the commotion in the balcony, which is soon empty.

Their daughter is born at midnight, on the fifteenth of August.

Ruttie has already picked out the name. Sir Dinshaw's granddaughter will be Dina.

Ruttie never finds out whether the gesture moves him, though. Even if it does, it doesn't move him enough to speak with his daughter again. For the next week, congratulatory telegrams confetti over new mother and newborn daughter, but none from Sir Dinshaw.

Not that Aunt Fati's telegram is particularly effusive. Even when the young couple makes it back to Bombay, she holds the baby for half a minute, awkwardly, and not just for want of experience. Ruttie is, after all, the very temptress who slipped through sisterly surveillance. If only Fati had accompanied Jin to Darjeeling! Fati had known Sir Dinshaw Petit had a daughter, but she'd thought that daughter was a child. Which Ruttie *had* been, after all.

And still is, even now that she is a wife and a mother. Ruttie had the audacity to ask Fati to stay with the baby one night while she and Jinnah went to a circus in town. *Selfish child*, Fati had thought, *unready to be a mother, fancying she can still have her frivolous giggling girlhood*. Luckily for the new mother, three-month-old Dina had not made a sound, but Fati warned her brother with a look against allowing Ruttie to ask ever again.

Worse, Ruttie's body is even lovelier now, fuller in all the places a man would desire it to be. Fati wishes Ruttie's body had gone lumpy and soft after the delivery, to break the pixie's spell. Is she so beautiful, anyway? From some angles, not from all. And her forehead! Her forehead is much too small for the rest of her face. It gives her, in Fati's eyes, a vaguely simian look.

Prompting all these little dislikes and irritations is Fati's deep, unbearable hurt: that Jin picked someone who is nothing like her. The only remedy is to turn her back to mother and baby, and talk politics with Jin like old times.

This afternoon, Jinnah has joined her on the balcony. She has him to herself again, if only briefly.

'The Government should cart them all off to prison,' she says. 'Every last one of Gandhi's satyagrahis.'

'That is what the Congress members want. A stay in prison is a mark of authenticity for them. It means a promotion in the ranks.'

'Prestige.'

'You see they are all play-actors. Each invited beating is a piece of street theatre.'

'What does it accomplish? What but the breaking of windows and bones? Nothing.'

'Of substance. Yet.'

'Yet? Do you have hope, Jin?'

'Either his methods will prove effective, or they will prove disastrous. I hope the debate will be settled, and soon.'

'Gentlemen will go back to negotiating with gentlemen.'

'And I will be free again to achieve something. The way I would have been after Lucknow, if *he* had never interfered.'

'You aren't praying for satyagraha to explode in his hands, are you, Jin?'

'Every "experiment with truth" risks starting a fire in the laboratory.'

'Sulphur and saltpetre,' she smiles.

He shrugs. 'Even a modest fire will do.'

Nagpur, the very next year: another packed enclosed space, full of bodies. The Indian National Congress is holding its annual meeting.

On the other side of the hall—on the floor, having declined to sit in an actual chair—Gandhi waits for Congress to pass his resolution. It is a resolution for non-cooperation: for satyagraha to become the official policy of the nationalist movement. The people ready to carry it out are thronging outside the meeting hall; they had to be persuaded not to carry Gandhi on their shoulders from the railway station.

The well-bred lawyers and businessmen of the Congress have never seen such crowds as Gandhi brings in tow. India is his entourage.

Everyone is for the new resolution, and not just in the Congress. Even the Muslim League has decided to get behind non-cooperation.

Only Jinnah refuses to cooperate with non-cooperation. He smokes yet another cigarette to get his nerve up for his speech. The speech must sink Gandhi's tactics once and for all, must stop the mobs and make politics a game for constitutional lawyers again.

His lips move softly, practising the memorized sentences as he stares at the ceiling. It looks like prayer. He does not have to glance at the papers on his lap.

Jinnah and Gandhi really do agree about Jallianwala Bagh: they both agree that it was an atrocity. But they don't agree on what it means, going forward. For Gandhi, it's a reason to call for more strikes; for Jinnah, it's a reason to call them off.

So now Jinnah rises before the same politicians who, just four years ago, considered him their dawning star. He strides onstage, adjusts his cuffs, and begins politely.

'Mister Gandhi—'

His voice disappears. The uproar startles him, pushes him physically backward.

'Mahatma!' 'Mahatma!' 'Call him Mahatma!' 'Mahatma!'

Gandhi stares at the floor. Jinnah glances at him, but it is impossible to know if the man is smiling. Jinnah raises a hand and tries to start again.

'Mister Gandhi has presented a platform whose merits and demerits we must carefully—'

Has he even said the words? Or did he just move his lips? Jinnah cannot hear himself over the explosions of *Mahatma, Mahatma!* like so many insults spat in his face, so many pipe bombs flung at his feet. Thanks to the charismatic Great Soul, Jinnah's old club of politicians has devolved into a mob, too, shouting this absurd pacifist war cry, 'Mahatma!'

Jinnah, trapped onstage, waits for the barrage to stop. He touches his throat, feeling for his voice. It isn't there.

7

Gandhi wins Congress. Gandhi wins the Muslim League and the British press and admirers around the world. All the while, he is losing his son.

By 1921, he does not dare pay Harilal a visit. His most trusted—and most hard-knuckled—follower decides to handle the problem himself. Vallabhbhai Patel—not yet 'Sardar'—first met Gandhi four years before, during a famine in Gujarat. Gandhi had organized the first satyagraha campaign in India: the destitute farmers refused to pay their taxes to the British Government. The British sent agents to carry out confiscations and beatings, but the farmers of Kheda, inspired by Gandhi, never gave in. After the Viceroy signed the exemption, Patel had become a believer in Gandhi's methods. Well before that, though, he became a believer in Gandhi himself. Patel calls Gandhi 'Bapu', *father*.

'Is he a father?' Harilal Gandhi is shouting. 'Has he *ever* been a father to me?'

Sardar Patel wonders if this is what Bapu looked like as a young man, struggling in South Africa. The ears are tell-tale. Also the long, slender neck and thin wrists. Among the four sons, Harilal Gandhi looks the most like his father. The resemblance is so strong that it is hard to speak sternly with Harilal. But then Patel glances down at the empty bottles by the bed, and it becomes quite easy.

'Understand something, Harilal. I am not here to reconcile you and your father. He doesn't even know I have sought you out. I am here on behalf of India.'

'I should have been a barrister. He studied in England. *You* studied in England. But me? He had me cleaning latrines as a boy. Milking cows. Was that my destiny? To be humiliated like that?'

Patel, who comes from a long line of farmers, raises an eyebrow. 'What's wrong with milking cows?'

'Do you know how intelligent I am? But what good are brains in this world without proper schooling? That's what he took from me. What kind of fanatic does that to his own children? He took my destiny.'

Patel gestures at the bottles on the floor. '*This* wasn't the destiny your father had in mind for you.'

Harilal grins. 'No? The man who swore off milk didn't mean for his son to become a drunk?' He pulls a flask from under his pillow and unscrews the cap. He takes great pleasure in tilting it towards Patel and watching the stern farmer's lip curl in disgust and disdain. 'I have a message for him,' says Harilal, and takes a sip.

'You can deliver it yourself, if you ever muster the courage to stand before that great man again. And before your saintly mother. I am here to give *you* a message. Stop talking to reporters. Stop talking to his enemies. *Stop talking*.'

'Because his big satyagraha campaign is underway! Isn't that so? 1921 has been a big year for you! Don't think I haven't been following everything, lush though I am. Tens of thousands rioting when the Prince of Wales arrived in India. You're filling up the prisons with Congress-wallahs. My father is always in the newspapers.'

'His enemies are looking for ways to smear him. You're helping the British every time you badmouth him.'

Harilal, with another smirk, raises his flask a second time. With a graceful, efficient movement you wouldn't expect from so heavy-set a man, Patel knocks the flask out of his hand. Harilal is astonished to see it clatter and spill. His mouth stays open.

'I'm not your father, Harilal. When children misbehave around *me*, I punish them with my hand.'

'I thought you believed in non-violence.'

'I do. Within limits.'

'Tell my parents how much I'm drinking.'

'I'm not telling your parents anything about you.'

'Tell them I salute the Union Jack wherever I see it.'

Patel glares around the squalid room and strides out. Harilal's daughters cower in one corner of the room, but they are not looking at this eloquently thuggish stranger; they are looking towards the sound of bottles being smashed in their father's room. Patel wonders which one of these children, once he leaves, the drunk will come out and browbeat.

Harilal's wife, in the traditional Indian custom, holds a tray with a small glass of rose sherbet on it. The tray is trembling. Patel cannot refuse without offence, so he pauses and takes a sip.

Inside the room, Harilal is pounding his bed and shouting.

'Tell him I'm going to turn Muslim! Tell the Mahatma his son eats beef and loves it. Rule Britannia. Do you hear me, Bapu? Rule Britannia!'

Streets, meanwhile, are filling with heads that shine with sweat and coconut oil. The cotton khadi they wear is Hindu-funeral white. Harilal is right, 1921 has been a big year. 1922 is even bigger for Gandhi's new satyagraha campaign. By February, it has spread to big cities like Ahmedabad, Calcutta, Delhi.

Little villages, too. Like Chauri Chaura.

There are no British officials in Chauri Chaura. Only twenty-three rotund and moustachioed policemen, standing in front of a crowd of people shouting *Gandhiji ki jai!*

These marchers are not bespectacled students in self-consciously plain, traditional Indian clothing. Their Indian clothing is traditional rags and traditional dirt. They are not the sort to go to a prayer meeting in a major city and learn the jargon of 'ahimsa' and 'satyagraha'. Even if someone gave them the bus fare, they would use it to buy flour for their children. Muslims and untouchables: most have never seen Gandhi or heard Gandhi speak in their lives. To them his name means, basically, *Take power, for once.* And they are shouting it at the twenty-three men who have made the mistake of wearing uniforms in this riot.

One policeman cringes at a flying brick, another bristles, but they are both reacting the same way, bringing their rifles to bear. Hoping, perhaps, that they will stare down the mob this way. Like dogs making eye contact, the many pupils of this collective beast meet the blacker pupils of five levelled gun barrels.

The people have worked themselves up. The name *Gandhiji* is a drug. They are already beyond any sense of their own vulnerability. When the rifles pop a few times, the reports are barely audible against so many voices. No one falls. They really *are* invulnerable. The name really *is* a talisman, protecting them against all threats, justifying all actions, cleansing all guilt.

The hectic, heckling crowd begins to think as one. A man takes off his shirt as a second man rushes over with a large stick. He knots it at the top as a third man arrives, offering an ablution of kerosene, and a fourth shields with his hand a lit match. They have a torch. A fifth man drops it at the police station's door, skipping back from the flash and flare.

Flame clambers up and around the building with dozens of wild monkey hands slapping in every direction at once. It isn't long before the door bursts to let through smoke and sparks, and policemen come running, some clutching their throats, others pinching their earlobes in the schoolboy gesture of penitence. Hatchets split fat and muscle, bellies and ribcages. The few who barrel through—sightless and mindless with skull wounds, brain-dead, but their legs still going—encounter a prodded hive. They buckle on their own and get knifed and stomped. The police station is burning close enough for a heave-ho on to the mass pyre, but they do this only for two bodies. They prefer to go on stabbing the rest. Boys of seven or eight and a few girls dodge in to participate too, ritually, every knife sanctified with the blood.

Three days later. Gandhi lies on his back, arm flung over his eyes. He could be sleeping under there. He could be crying.

'It is not your fault.'

Kasturba has been squeezing the nerve pain out of his legs. His nausea matters little; on day three of his penitential fast, he doesn't even have bile to spit up. His fever may or may not be real. The doctor himself is unsure. In any case, Gandhi isn't taking any pills or tinctures. Or nourishment. Even the enema he gives himself is behind schedule. Nothing in, nothing out.

'I did not do the action. The action happened because of me.'

'How can you control every action of a hundred million people?'

'Take that orange away. This would not be difficult if I did not have its scent.'

'You are ill.'

'I am sick at heart. My body is mimicking my heart.'

She knows better than to spend too much time quarrelling with him when his mind is in a mood to hurt his body. His mind cleaves from his body and punishes it, though it's his mind that had the idea, made the decision, shaped the words.

She is walking out of the room with the bowl containing the orange when she encounters a man with brilliantined hair, who wears a three-piece suit. He is flanked by two of her husband's close associates. Her first sight of him fills her with fear, and she steps back as though she has encountered a garden snake.

'Mr Jinnah,' someone explains, distantly. 'Here to see Bapu.'

She nods and hurries on, pulling her saree fold over her head. The orange in the bowl is split cleanly down the middle, in a small puddle of its own juice. She cannot remember slicing it.

Inside the room, Jinnah pulls up a chair beside Gandhi's cot.

'Sorry about this fiasco, old boy. Every experiment runs the risk of failing.'

Gandhi lies under his sheets, having pulled them up to his chin as Jinnah entered. Bapu seems to cower under there like a spooked hare. Yet his spectacles, still visible, catch the sunlight and flash when Jinnah lights a cigarette.

'I have called off satyagraha.'

'Well done. Good of you to swallow your pride.'

'For now. The people are not ready.'

'When do you think these illiterate villagers will be *ready* for high moral musings? Either they run amok and butcher people, or they don't. You'd do well to leave them be.'

'They will be ready once I have readied them. And I cannot ready them until I ready myself.'

'It all comes down to you, does it?'

'The authorities mean to try me for sedition. I intend to ask the judge for the maximum sentence.'

Jinnah hisses smoke in a bright jet of frustration. 'Oh, come off it. Non-cooperation? It's done. It's failed. You mean to gain prestige by going to prison. For you to exploit this tragedy by whipping up a frenzy a second time—'

'I do not go to prison for prestige, Mr Jinnah.'

'Well, you certainly aren't going there for the food. Do what's right, friend. Give it up. Britain will listen and negotiate once India cools off. Running riot has gotten us nowhere.'

Gandhi has quite forgotten his ailments and hunger. His round bald head emerges from the sheets, and he speaks even more quietly than before. 'Satyagraha does not involve running riot, Jinnah. It means standing very, very still. Sometimes even in lying still.'

'In a prison.'

'And listening.'

'To the shrieks of men hacked and burnt to death. To the sobs of their widows.'

Gandhi puts his finger to his lips and closes his eyes. 'To my inner voice.'

There is no arguing with this poppycock. Jinnah strides out of the room, and behind him, the windows thicken into prison bars. Gandhi's cot and homespun cotton remain the same. He is in his gaol; he is at his goal.

Outside Yeravda Prison, paperboys as far away as London can be heard shouting the headline: *Ghandy sentenced to six years!* In India, intellectuals and villagers echo and re-echo in English and Hindustani, *Free the Mahatma! Mahatma ko chhudao!*

Jinnah strides out into the usual circuit of garden parties, clubs and political meetings of Congress and the Muslim League. 1923, 1924 … A space clears around him wherever he goes. *There's Jinnah, he's one of them.* Them: that is, whoever he isn't among at the moment. Muslims and Hindus are drifting apart again into mutual distrust. Within a few years, Gandhi himself will fast to guilt them into unity. *Can't trust Jinnah—he's their man on the inside.* Jinnah's success at Lucknow works against him in this new political climate. To have negotiated so smoothly with the League makes him suspect to the Congress, and vice versa. *There's Jinnah, that turncoat. That wolf in sheep's clothing.* The more orthodox Muslims have always thought this Khoja Shia too dapper to be devout. *There's Jinnah, that Englishman in Englishman's clothing.* The more orthodox Hindus can't get past his name.

Mohammed Ali Jinnah. He can get a seat in this or that legislative council, or argue his case regarding this or that matter of representation or tariffs, but his name just won't catch fire. His name is in the process of being forgotten. Whispered behind his back, it is a decibel away from silence—and he is a decibel away from becoming Mohammed Ali no one.

No one? No, wait. Someone…

At all the garden parties, clubs, political meetings, an opposing set of whispers is gaining volume.

'He is so young, so handsome, so *well-dressed*.'

'He is going to unite everyone. They say he'll be Prime Minister some day, if ever we are free.'

'If ever *he* frees us…'

Jinnah's ears prick up. *Wasn't this what they said about me*, he thinks, *not too long ago?* It's like the radio of elite opinion is picking up static from 1916.

'Educated in England—a lawyer of brilliance—'

All this is word for word. Are they rediscovering him?

He listens closely—and then he hears the discordant note.

'You know he keeps a bust of Gandhi in his study. He has been a fierce devotee of the Mahatma ever since he was a boy...'

Jinnah stands stock-still while the crowd rushes to the door again, this time to adore not Gandhi but a disciple of Gandhi: the man with the whitest teeth, the most handsome face, the most ingratiating manner, the most eloquent English in all Indian politics. The whispers keep growing, inexorably, unstoppably, into acclamation.

'The future of India!' say the Calcutta industrialists. 'The man of the future!' the Delhi intellectuals agree. This rising young star, according to reporters and radio announcers, will unite the people and throw off the colonial oppressor.

They aren't talking about Jinnah. Not any more. Never again.

They are talking about Jawaharlal Nehru.

8

Maryam Jinnah, by 1926, is smaller than she was at sixteen. In a mansion emptier for its high ceilings, she is wasting away.

You could call her Mrs Jinnah, but Mr Jinnah is not at home right now. The man who sits across from her has the same wheat-coloured complexion, the same small wrists. He looks like her brother, but he isn't. His name is Kanji Dwarkadas, and he's a Parsi, like Ruttie. To see them sitting across from each other at a table like this, with seven-year-old Dina playing nearby with her dolls, you could be forgiven for thinking them all one family, and a happy family at that.

'Is he speaking to you again?' asks Kanji.

'He is so very busy, Kanji. You see, he is scarcely ever here. I don't think he stays away out of anger.'

'I meant Sir Dinshaw.'

'Oh—no, I haven't spoken to him, either.'

'How is he doing?'

'You mean J?'

'Yes.'

'He has been ill. Cough and fever. But he shrugs it off and keeps working. Politics, the law practice.'

'Maybe he should head north to take a cure. It might be a good way for you to spend time together. Kashmir, maybe.'

'You're right, Kanji. We are being poisoned here. His lungs, my stomach ... May we ask Socrates for advice? He was so wise last time.'

The lights dim, except for a candle. Kanji takes hold of her hands across the table. The séance calls up the ghost of Socrates, who agrees about Kashmir; of Isaac Newton, who says she should leave her husband; of Cleopatra, who dislikes the humid air of Bombay, too.

Among the spectral figures who return from the beyond is Jinnah. Silhouetted in the doorway, he witnesses Ruttie and Kanji at the table in the dim light, holding hands, murmuring questions to the dead. He watches them a moment and floats upstairs, less interested in chit-chat than the séance's latest, surprisingly voluble visitor, Genghis Khan. The only sign Jinnah is really there in the flesh is the way cats scatter where he steps. Ruttie keeps a dozen in the house; they are good for conversation when Kanji is not around.

Upstairs now, Jinnah is staring in the mirror. *We are being poisoned here.* His cheekbones have gone from kingly to skeletal, a sinkhole on either side of his face, and his hair has gone white just to the right of his widow's peak. Is it a sign? Is he midway through his life? His hand's first impulse is to cover the spot. Should he smother it in shoeblack? Slowly he lets his hand slip, and he studies this demarcation line a while. Though it makes him look older, his lips twitch into a smile, vaguely pleased. Something in him likes this sharp stark division. This natural partition in his hair.

It is best they don't talk much. After all, when they do speak, it turns all too often into a quarrel.

'And why *not* a Theosophical school for Dina?' Spirituality, spiritualism—'Maryam' takes an interest in every holy book but the Qur'an. 'Theosophy does not teach anything that goes against Islam,' she says very confidently.

'And who told you that?'

'Mrs Annie Besant herself. She says her school is perfect for Dina.'

'A mullah would say the same thing about his madrasa,' mutters Jinnah. 'Shall we split the difference and send her to a proper school? One that teaches mathematics and science and reading? Instead of just—*magnetism*?'

At this, he points to the brooch of a doe she wears superstitiously over her heart, one that Kanji has 'magnetized' for luck. She touches it defensively.

'But what about the spirit, J? What about her inner selfhood?'

'Theosophy is just Hinduism without the extra arms and conch shells. Dina will go to a proper girls' school.'

With that he waves her away like a secretary from his desk. To think—only five years ago, she used to drift kitten-like into his legal chambers, unannounced, in a scrap of chiffon as airy as her perfume, and while he and his client discussed bequests, her naked foot would set his gilded globe a-spin—good God, so much love and death in one room! And now her presence irritates him like this scratch in his throat.

Ruttie rushes back from the door when she hears him cough violently into his hand.

'We are being poisoned, J!' She drops to her knees at his feet. 'Your lungs—my stomach and my head. The headaches I get—I don't know what I would do without the pills.'

'*You* may be ill,' he says coldly. '*I* am well.'

His door is open, and a few of Ruttie's cats wander in, as if to remind them both who the real invalids are. Blubbery and diabetic, they urinate on the rugs, a sweet yellow juice that draws the ants.

'We are being poisoned, J. Politics—all your frustrations—your energy is darkening. People do not listen to you, and you are growing dark and bitter.'

'My energy is the same,' he says proudly. 'I can do more work now than I could ten years ago. This is an important time. Don't you see the black flags on all the houses, protesting this latest Commission the British have sent to assess their "Indian problem"? All white men, not a single Indian on it. I am close to rallying all the parties together again. This is my second wind, Ruttie, and you want a *vacation*? Just last year we took that trip to America. Before that we were in London.'

'I want you to succeed. I want glory for you.'

'You hardly care for politics any more. It shows in your conversation, I might add.'

'I have been ill, J...'

'You have been communing with the dead.'

'They show me more warmth than the living.'

'Get *up*, you—you child.' He takes her by the wrist, pulls her upright and pushes her away. 'You were more interesting at seventeen than you are at twenty-seven. And you presume to say *my* mind is weakening with age?'

'Not weakening. Darkening.'

He clears his throat of bitter phlegm. 'I go from strength to strength,' he rasps.

'Have I ever held you back? Have I ever stopped you?'

'Have you *encouraged* me? What I might have done with a strong woman at my side!' He pauses, imagining, maybe, a steely woman like his own sister Fatima. 'Not a sheltered little *princess* like you. All you want is more and more of my time.'

Ruttie leaves, brushing a tear off her cheek, leaving Jinnah alone at his desk, cheek on his fist. That night, she climbs beside him for the first time in months. He lies on his back, arms straight down, palms flat against the sides of his thighs. He is so rigid, it is almost rigor mortis.

Ruttie begins to stroke his hair, desperately; this ninety-eight-pound sylph with hooded eyes and no birthmarks, the only blemishes on her body the stretchmarks on her flanks from the one pregnancy seven years ago, parallel claw marks where time lost purchase.

Jinnah doesn't enjoy this. Neither does she. She closes her eyelids on tears. He is an icicle. She wants desperately to interest him, but his interest is detached, almost disdainful. Desire stirs inside him momentarily—but it's just steam off dry ice.

Looking away from her, Jinnah wonders why religion, of all things, nags him right now. When he cares nothing for religion. Or does he only *think* he cares nothing for it? And even if he did, isn't she a Muslim now? Her legal name is Maryam, after all.

He lies on the vast snowy steppe of their four-post bed. The pillows lie in snowdrifts to either side. Ruttie begins to shiver beside her husband. It is a kind of mock ecstasy. She is not shivering from cold. Her foot is swollen and red. A tiny needle pierced it weeks before, and it required a surgical cut along the pregnant dome of the abscess. The whole foot is still inflamed.

'Are you unwell?' he asks. There is no compassion in his voice.

She shakes her head and imagines herself on a horse at a split sign that points to two mythical cities in opposite directions, both built of ice.

He does not encourage her to stay. The icicle of his desire melts away to nothing. He has uncoupled from within. Jinnah closes his eyes. She senses him retreat without seeming to move, like a glacier.

Even after she leaves, Jinnah lies on his back, motionless, exactly as she left him. As the clock ticks in his ear, his eyes sink deeper into his skull, his cheeks sink, his cheekbones rise.

He stares at a lizard on the ceiling. *Cut its tail off, the lizard grows another*.

This is the last night he will touch her. At some level, he knows this. He should never have allowed her to try this tactic after arguing. But she had insisted, imagining, perhaps, a proxy reconciliation of their bodies.

'But to the girdle do the gods inherit,' he whispers into the darkness. 'Beneath is all the fiend's.'

Downstairs, Ruttie is limping through the Malabar Hill mansion in a blue silk nightgown, her throat dry. Blue veins branch and divide on the Italian marble of the pillars, just as they do on her bare arms. It is July in Bombay, but the marble is cold to the touch. The water, ladled from a clay pot, proves so cold, her teeth smart. She can see her breath when she sobs.

At the All Parties Conference, India's scattered political parties, including the two major ones Jinnah united briefly over a decade ago, are all present. Gandhi isn't, but he doesn't have to be. Several Congress delegates are khadi-clad Gandhians.

Jinnah has argued for separate Muslim electorates as a precondition of unity—parallel, Muslim-only ballot-boxes in every province. This is something Gandhi abhors. Jinnah's Congress opponents call him a spoilt child, whining after the same candy these past twenty years.

'Will the honourable Mr Jinnah please grow up?'

Titters.

'And if not, will he please sit *down*?'

Outright laughter.

Soon, Jinnah, fist on cheek, sits outside on a bench. Apart, alone. The hall has almost cleared out, but he is still staring at his heavily marked-up and revised failure of a speech. This is when an elderly man in a handlebar moustache takes the spot next to him.

'Jinnah,' he whispers.

'Iqbal.'

'We have not seen each other for some time. You don't come out to Lahore much. Where have you been?'

'Here and there.'

'You might as well have been nowhere, for all you are accomplishing.'

Jinnah does not answer him. Only Muhammad Iqbal, the greatest Urdu poet of his generation, can speak to Jinnah this way and not get a tongue-lashing.

'You are the sharpest legal mind in India,' Iqbal says, 'and barring the poets, of course, her most eloquent man to boot.'

Jinnah takes in this praise, waiting for the sting in its tail.

'Have you ever wondered why, with all your talent, you are such a political failure?'

The answer is *yes*, but Jinnah cannot bring himself to give it.

'You have no people, Jinnah. But it does not have to be this way. Come visit me when you want to find out who your people are. How to win them, and how to win.'

Jinnah, not concealing his scepticism, says through clenched teeth: 'I am open to any advice you care to give me, Allama Iqbal.'

Allama means teacher. He doesn't really mean the word, not yet, and Iqbal knows it. 'Soon enough, my friend,' says Iqbal, patting Jinnah's shoulder. 'You need to break a little more. You still have too much hope in …' Iqbal flicks his hand dismissively, disdainfully at the assembly hall, '… in all *this*.'

Jinnah doesn't plan to take him up on the cryptic offer. He is too busy brooding.

And coughing. On the way back to Bombay, he runs a fever in the sleeper compartment. Iqbal's hint has gone somewhere deep, though, because Jinnah dreams a fever dream during those tortured hours in the rocking, clacking car.

He is paddling a small boat upstream on a great river. He can hear a waterfall all around him, but he cannot see it. The sound of it surrounds him. There's no telling if it's downstream or upstream.

He is wearing a suit, but his shoes and cuffs are not wet. It's the same suit he wore at Nagpur.

He's paddling diligently against the current when an enormous raft sweeps past him. A dozen oarsmen in Congress white are rowing it, and at the back, seated cross-legged and oarless, is Gandhi.

Jinnah paddles harder and keeps up for some time. Gandhi turns to him and says, his voice mysteriously audible over the waterfall, 'The race is not to the swift.'

Then he points ahead, and his Congress-wallahs row harder. *But races are* always *to the swift*, thinks Jinnah. *One paddles as hard as possible for precisely this reason—and* your *oarsmen, aren't* they *redoubling their strokes, even as you drop your nugget of fool's wisdom?*

So Jinnah paddles harder, even though his cough, either in the dream or in the train car, begins to bother him. He notices the heads and limbs of men drowning in the river. Here and there, an unravelled turban snakes by.

Jinnah draws up to Gandhi's raft again. Gandhi commands even more oarsmen. Jinnah points at the struggling men in the river all about them. Gandhi gestures at his own raft and says, 'Come aboard with your oar. I have a place for you.'

Jinnah shakes his head and points at the drowning men—and realizes that the waterfall, if anything, is louder, closer.

At last, he lifts his oar out of the water, and his little boat seems to spring free. Astonishingly swift, it heads the other way, the natural way, downstream. Several coils of rope lie at the bottom of his boat, and Jinnah throws these out into the water. Arms, so many he never imagined the river held so many, emerge from the rushing water and grab hold. Their faces emerge gasping, and all of their faces, under their beards, match Jinnah's own. Now he rows furiously with the current, and there is no boat swifter than his. He speeds downstream, trailing long lines of rescued men who cheer his vigorous strokes. He coughs no more; he takes joyful, deep breaths. The sound of the waterfall has vanished, and he imagines the other raft having forced its way upstream only to find an insuperable wall of plummeting water. Meanwhile he, Jinnah, tows not a dozen men but millions, all approaching the river's delta, and beyond it the trove of the sea.

While Jinnah turns in his fever dream, Ruttie is clearing her belongings out of the Bombay mansion. When he gets home, he doesn't notice her absence at first, or Dina's. The servants say nothing. What he notices, eventually, is the absence of cats on the couches and of cat piss on the rugs.

The first person he calls is Kanji Dwarkadas.

'Where is she?'

'Room 554 at the Taj Hotel.'

'For how long?'

'Until you love her again. Until you bring her back.'

9

'My name is Madeleine Slade.'

The sweating white woman keeps a broad-brimmed hat in her lap, but she refuses to fan herself. She sits across from a thick-wristed, short-necked Indian man in a dhoti. His build and no-nonsense expression is a farmer's, accustomed to bad harvests. This Ahmedabad heat means less to him than a fly on a cow's flank. Madeleine did not imagine the first Gandhian she would meet would possess so pragmatic an air. He keeps one leg tucked under himself, every inch the traditional village headman; yet his English is as perfect as any Middle Temple lawyer's.

'Of course, Miss Slade. I am aware of that,' says Sardar Patel.

She digs in her valise and brings out a tattered envelope. 'You see, I have a letter from the Mahatma. He told me I could come and see him.'

'I know. And you have come from so far away that I would never deny you an audience.'

'Is he well? I know he was only recently released from prison, after an operation.'

'He is well enough, under the circumstances.'

'After two years!'

'They had sentenced him to six.'

'How may I help him?'

Patel raises his hand to cool her eagerness. 'About that, Miss Slade. I need to make sure you understand your own request. That might make your meeting more … meaningful.'

She nods and says, somewhat formally, 'I request to join the Sabarmati Ashram.'

'You understand the weather in Ahmedabad doesn't get any cooler than this?'

'Yes.'

'Miss Slade, I am one of the few people here who speak English. You would have to learn Gujarati. And Hindustani as well, if you really wish to help Gandhiji in his work.'

'I understand the two are similar.'

'To each other. Not to English.'

'Of course.'

'And then there is the matter of food.'

'I shall become a vegetarian.'

'And work.'

'I grew up on a farm.'

Patel raises an eyebrow. 'On a farm, or *working* on a farm?'

The privileged daughter's eyes fall to the floor. 'The farm had five Jersey cows.'

'We do *work* here. Hard work. It is more than just sitting at the spinning wheel. Spinning wheels are simply what reporters like to photograph.'

'We had a pigsty on the farm, and chicken coops.' She takes the letter from the envelope and holds it out to him. 'The Mahatma warned me of everything when we corresponded.'

'Sometimes he sends his disciples out to clean latrines.' He clears his throat. 'Even his own wife.'

'Perhaps you think me an idealist who will fall away after a few weeks. I assure you, if that is the case, you misread me. I have made a decision. I have left everything behind for this.' She raises her eyes and stares into Patel's. 'For him.'

Patel raises a finger to tell her to wait, and he disappears into an adjoining room. Madeleine lovingly folds the letter and replaces it. The door opens, and she is led by the elbow, like a bride, into the room to which all the other rooms in her life have been antechambers.

The concentration of sunlight is higher inside it than outdoors. The sandalwood incense, which she smells for the first time, smells familiar. The only other time she felt this way was the first time she heard the music of Beethoven, her other love. That divinity had been disembodied. This one rises off the cot to meet her. He is at least a foot shorter than she is, and so small and thin, she fears she would break him with the embrace she wants to give. She lowers herself to the floor instead. On her knees does not feel low enough. She is on her way to a temple prostration when his hand takes hers and guides her back, weightless, to her feet. 'Young woman,' he whispers, 'do get up,' and she recalls, vaguely, a chapter in Mark where the dead child was raised from her bed. No wonder so many thousands of people are seeking him out from around the world.

Gandhi kisses her forehead, and she realizes she is his daughter. Not just that she *is*, but that she *was*, long ago, and is only now recalling this relationship. She has no mother or father back in England any more.

'Tell me about your farm, Madeleine.'

She tells him about the meadows for the cows and the stable-yard. She goes on to tell him about Sonata 17, Opus 31, Number 2, and how it transfigured Dorking Valley and the Leith Hill Range into the high waves of a tempest. How Beethoven led her to Romain Rolland, the French writer, and how Monsieur Rolland had directed her to him.

'He called you another Christ,' she says. 'Now I see why.'

Gandhi shakes his head. 'I am afraid Romain is given to hyperbole. I would prefer criticism to such excessive praise.'

'The world proclaims it. Why else do we call you the Mahatma?'

'That is not a name I deserve, or even like. Those who know me here call me "Bapu". I want you to call me that.'

'What does that mean?'

'"Father". You will be my daughter.'

'If you are my father, you should name me.'

He nods and closes his eyes to think. Some time passes before he speaks. 'You had such a lovely home in England. Your family, your music. But you gave it up to come live with me. There was once a woman who did something similar. Her husband ruled a place called Mewar, but she left it to devote herself to Krishna. She became a musician.'

He gives her the new name. It is a lot like her old one; the sounds are so close that the names, repeated over and over, shift and switch. Come nightfall, the first name dissolves entirely into the second. 'Madeleine' is, forever after, 'Mirabehn'.

Transformation.

Gandhi squats to wash his own clothes. Skeleton arms wring the garment. Patel is watching him; Nehru is watching him. See the sinkholes behind his collarbones, see his knees like tree trunks, swollen where the parasite nests. The parasite is hunger.

The parasite is lust. Impossibly, his desire still arrives at dawn when he awakens, no differently than before. What did you dream of, traitor? The 'beastly' part hungers hard. No matter how skinny the rest of him gets, this one part is thick and fat as ever. Hale fellow, well met. It is the staff of Moses, the divining rod. He urinates to drain desire of its power, and he goes to his morning prayers.

There, to his shame and torment, his followers see a holy man. They see the haggard Jesus, his body all ridges and jutting hip bones. Mirabehn, in a saree, sees the sacred cow, ribbed in famine time.

The things people say and write about him strike him as absurd. Do they know what he thinks? How much he loves his desire? Even when he tells them he is 'beastly', that he has 'beastly impulses', that his faith is 'impure', they don't believe him. They think he is being hard on himself. They have never seen him sit up in bed and try to stare down his desire. It's like staring down a flared cobra. It retreats beneath its hood.

The crowds he draws bring whole cities to a stop. London comes out to see him in his white dhoti and shawl, cheering him louder than its own Prime Minister. It feels good. He keeps his head down, willing himself not to be proud, and it only makes people praise how humble he is.

He indulges in fasts. A fast for atonement, a fast for penitence, a fast for the striking of this or that clause from a law. His mind weaponizes his body, and his body cooperates. His first release from Yeravda Prison, after the Chauri Chaura conviction, comes after an appendicitis, but his next comes when his feet swell and his throat rattles and his jailors realize he may actually die on their hands.

No one realizes how happy he is that his member stays shrivelled, sensationless, a mere conduit for pungent yellow fluid.

But he is free again. Crowds cheer as he sips his first guava juice. Sweetness restores the power grid of his nerves. What has he dreamt of? The very next morning, he is risen: risen hard, fallen hard, from Mahatma to Gandhi to Mohan.

Gandhi is standing in a river. It is the old Brahmin way of praying in the morning. His legs are so crane-thin, it seems he might tuck one under himself and stand that way a while.

No food today. He balances, perfectly, on the border between hunger and starvation. He is located in neither. The proof is in his gaze, which doesn't have the wildness of hunger or the dullness of starvation. This gaze has a sharpshooter's aggressive serenity.

He wears little cloth himself, but he sits down for hours at his spinning wheel. It marks the quartz movement of his mind, like Kant's walks or Chinese worry balls or prayer beads through a monk's fingers.

Everyone visits him. Here is Patel, the village strongman, sitting at Bapu's feet, reporting on a tax strike he has managed in Bardoli.

'The British trucked in a hundred Pathans to knock us about,' Patel snarls. 'Burly Muslims from the Northwest Provinces. Spoke not a word of Gujarati. Showed up just to kick old men in the stomach and lead off our cows. It must have been no different during the old Muslim invasions. They could have been the troops of Mahmud of Ghazni.'

Gandhi raises a hand. 'This is what the British do. What they have always done. They know how to play with our divisions.'

'Tell the Pathans this! They *enjoyed* themselves, Bapu.'

'Don't think of those soldiers as Muslims or Pathans. They are paid British soldiers who are Indian. They know not what they do.'

The Biblical reference is lost on Patel, who frowns. 'They knew all right. And they were laughing the whole time.'

'Think of them as slaves, like ourselves.'

'Well, our farmers still didn't pay the damned tax.'

'Or fight back?'

'Not a penny in taxes, not a punch in anger. Those farmers have the bruises to prove it.'

'I hear they have given you a name out there, in Bardoli.'

Patel nods. 'Sardar.'

Chief. But there are other leaders coming up under Gandhi's guidance, too. Like this young man, the son of one of Gandhi's closest allies.

'Jawaharlal!' Gandhi greets him with visible delight, the spinning wheel quickening a little. Young Nehru's excitability is infectious. 'You look troubled, Jawaharlal.'

'Our struggle is going backwards, Bapu. I mean—just look at the Nehru Report.'

'Your father's work has been excellent. You should be proud of him.'

'I'm ashamed that it bears my last name. Its terms ensure us more sluggishness from the British. They'll never leave, at this rate. And even worse, it wants Dominion status for India. Do we realize "Dominion" comes from the word for "Lordship"? Why should the British be our lords for even a *second* after we gain independence? Is that our goal?'

Gandhi nods. 'Young men are naturally rebellious.'

'Bapu,' laughs Nehru, showing his increasingly famous movie-star teeth, 'you are the greatest rebel of us all!'

Gandhi looks up mischievously. 'I am also the youngest.'

'So, you are on my side. Kick out the British entirely, and the Indian people get dominion over India. Total self-rule!'

'*Purna swaraj*,' whispers Gandhi, half to himself, using the Hindustani word for it.

'You will support me, then?'

'Motilal will not be pleased with me. You will be going against your father.'

Nehru leans forward, his hands clasped joyfully, eagerly. 'But not against my Bapu.'

'I can tell you have grown impatient,' murmurs Gandhi, 'with working for reform. It is very early in your career to be so disillusioned.'

'Only with reform *within* the British system. Outside it, anything is possible. We have hundreds of millions on our side. What can't we do?'

Gandhi is thinking how wonderful it would be to collapse Sardar Patel and young Jawaharlal into a single leader: totally idealistic, totally pragmatic; refined at cocktail parties, but a villager among villagers.

'You must be thinking the same thing yourself, Bapu. Some fresh satyagraha that upends all these talks and delays. Some new experiment.'

Gandhi's spinning wheel quickens. 'I have some ideas,' he murmurs. 'Very small ideas, as yet no bigger than mustard seeds. No bigger than grains of salt...'

10

She used to be called the Flower of Bombay. She used to be a pampered daughter, riding her own horse by six. Even her nightgowns came from Paris; she had five different ones by the time she was ten. She used to lounge on a couch, reading P.G. Wodehouse. An emptied glass of lassi, held in the air, would make some wallflower servant named Rambabu hurry over with a tray.

She went from childhood to womanhood on her eighteenth birthday, but things got even better. She used to be the wife of the richest lawyer in Bombay. She used to wear such nothings in public that her husband's orthodox Muslim aunties—and, once, an overly conservative Vicereine of India—hurried a shawl over her shoulders. She used to dance the jitterbug in London, she used to smoke cigarettes through a seven-inch golden holder in the most expensive hotel in Delhi, she used to shoo her toddler daughter off with the nanny and sit down for a séance with a good friend and schnapps and Catherine the Great.

...And now she is lying on a bed in the Taj Hotel, immersed in a miasma of cat piss.

McVitie's biscuit crumbs on the bedsheets.

Three bottles of pills on the nightstand.

Motherhood might have given her days a little structure and companionship, but little Dina is at boarding school. Not even Bertie Wooster can make her smile any more.

Ruttie can't go back to her parents' house because her father still won't speak to her.

'Can't we come live with you?'

Kanji Dwarkadas shakes his head at his best friend's plea. 'It would be a scandal, Ruttie. You want him to remember how much he loves you. It's the reason you left. So that he will come and get you.'

Neither she nor Kanji quite know their man. Mohammed Ali Jinnah is not one to grant concessions.

'I would be so happy,' she sighs, nuzzling a tabby, 'if he grew jealous. Mad and irrational and jealous! It would prove he still loves me.'

'He trusts you. He trusts me. And why shouldn't he? He has your love.'

'Magnetize some charms for me, Kanji. I need to heal. Once I am healthy again, I will charm him. I will seduce him.'

'I can bring you something even better.'

That evening, he brings Ruttie's mother to the hotel. Mrs Petit eyes this little pocket of squalor in a deluxe hotel and declares, 'Ruttie baby, we are going to Paris.'

Soon they are in a stateroom on a liner. Paris, it is true, used to cheer her up. But the liner is simply the same hotel room with a round window instead of a rectangular one. Her Paris hotel room becomes the same as the one at the Taj, going miraculously slovenly overnight, only minus the cats. Which means she is lonelier.

Meanwhile her mother, every few days, suggests divorce.

'I don't know why he hasn't done it already,' she reflects aloud. 'You know these Muslim men, when they want to be rid of their wives—the Qur'an says that all they have to do is say "Talaaq" three times. Three times, and it is done.'

The fairy goes pink with anger. 'J is not a Muslim in that way,' she insists. 'He is scarcely a Muslim at all.'

'Under the surface,' says her mother with an air of superior wisdom, though she has rarely spent more than five minutes at a time in his company, '*deep* down...'

Admittedly, Jinnah doesn't pray. And admittedly, he is drinking alcohol when he gets word she is in a Paris hospital. He happens to be across the Channel, a ferry ride and train ride north of her sickbed. He ascribes this not to Allah, but to chance; ascribes her condition, too, not to Allah, but to a weak constitution and the idiocy of French doctors. He does not imagine Ruttie herself might be responsible for it.

Her mother picks out still another cause.

'You! This is all because of you!'

Maudlin, maddened, she accosts him outside the hospital room. Jinnah observes her from his superior height, his gaze a statue's, until she remembers herself and glances sheepishly at the shocked French nurses. She slinks aside to let him into the room.

Ruttie, addled with drugs, stirs awake and sees his silhouette in a sunlit window. Her mother eyes him from a chair in the corner of the room, judging his reaction, expression, next word.

Jinnah has very little French, and the nurses and doctors eye him as a curiosity, a dark fellow in a white suit, the monocle still lodged over his eye as he studies the gibberish on her chart.

He is a comical figure in their eyes until he claps his hands and starts giving orders. He supervises the changing of Ruttie's sheets, lifting her moist body, as light as when she was a girl.

Ruttie's eyelids stir again, like moths in a troubled slumber. When she sees Jinnah setting her back down, she whispers, 'Carry me off.'

'Carry off' had been the phrase her father had always used in his rages—how dare this Mussalmaan carry off my daughter, how dare you allow him to carry you off…

Carry me off.

The words shiver through her lips again, and Jinnah cannot tell if she speaks to him or speaks to death when she murmurs, *Do please carry me off forever…*

Next morning, Ruttie is upright on two pillows, sipping beef tea. Later she takes a bowl of chicken broth and scoops the white from a hard baguette.

Mrs Petit and Ruttie are whispering when Jinnah visits next. He is expecting gratitude. He gets requests.

Will he take fewer cases now that they are reconciled? And be done with all his travels, at least until next year? And will he please send a brief telegram to Bombay? For Kanji has received no word of her recovery yet, and if he can magnetize a small steel cup for her, she will drink only from that and stay healthy during their sea voyage home together…

Mrs Petit, too, grows relaxed and voluble. She strokes her daughter's hair. 'The mind and the body are related intimately in a fragile girl like you, Ruttie. The body grows ill when the heart grows sad. The body is only a weathervane. A wife deserves love, needs love. And to deny your family *time*,' Mrs Petit says with a sidelong glance at Jinnah, 'is the same as denying it *love*…'

Jinnah sits through this show, eyeing his mother-in-law with increasing irritation. Now he crosses his legs and folds his arms. 'Are you not the wife of Sir Dinshaw Petit?'

Mother and daughter turn to him in shock, as if he has profaned the sacred name.

'The same Sir Dinshaw Petit who has not granted his own daughter a *minute* of his time in the past ten years?'

'Mr Jinnah!' cries Ruttie's mother, shielding her daughter's ears. Jinnah, with scrupulous nobility, has not said a single word against Sir Dinshaw Petit since that day in Lucknow, in 1916, when the cigar dropped from the man's mouth in horror at Jinnah's suggestion of marriage to Ruttie.

Ruttie is shaking her head. 'Your energy is dark now, J. I warned you. Politics has done this to you. Your energy has turned dark.'

'I came here out of love and duty, not out of guilt,' says Jinnah, rising. 'Clearly, this little crisis is over. Ladies, enjoy your stay in the city of light. I shall take my darkness elsewhere.'

And he does just that. He takes his 'dark energy' back to Bombay, to months of squabbles about the Simon Commission and the Nehru Report and separate electorates and Legislative Councils, and the possibility of holding a Round Table Conference in London.

He is in the midst of all this when Ruttie reminds him of herself again.

This time, by dying.

Sir Dinshaw Petit phones his son-in-law within moments of getting the news himself, but not to weep and reconcile. No, Sir Dinshaw (increasingly orthodox, as if to make up for his daughter's conversion) wants Ruttie's body disposed of in the Parsi way, laid out atop the Tower of Silence for the vultures to pick at, like an orphan hit by a lorry.

Kanji seeks him out, too. 'Ruttie wanted to be cremated,' he insists. 'She envisioned her pyre on a mountaintop.'

Fati has been waiting in the wings this past decade while the Parsi minx held her brother spellbound. Now there is no one between her and her beloved Jin. She is the only one he can ask what to do about Ruttie.

'The name on the death certificate is Maryam,' she says. 'Maryam Jinnah is your wife to bury. According to *your* customs.'

Fatima and three other Muslim women wash Maryam's wasted body before a Muslim funeral. Her hands travel up and down the limbs, over the stomach, over the breasts.

So, this is the body that sank my brother, Fati thinks. *This is the famous beauty, the Parsi princess, the Flower of Bombay. Now how cold and rubbery. How unbeautifully, permanently, finally dead.*

Jinnah, at Aram Bagh Cemetery, greets the male guests with stiff hug after stiff requisite hug. He wears a plain white kurta, the same white as her shroud. Mr and Mrs Jinnah have never dressed so plainly as on this day.

They bury the hummingbird girl lying on her right side, with her head towards Mecca. Jinnah and Fati listen to the Imam's recitations—the Imam who would have shut Ruttie's blithe bare shoulders out of his mosque.

Distracted, Jinnah recalls the pre-dawn hour he rushed to her room at the Taj Hotel. A few pills had tumbled on to the night table, and he picked them up one by one and vanished them into his pocket along with the empty bottle. The chit of paper in her hand he read once and stuffed away into an inner pocket, the waiting match instead setting alight his first widower's cigarette there at her bedside. The first lungful gusted through his clenched teeth in short sobs. The second rose passively, steadily, from his thrown-back, open-mouthed and moaning skull.

That memory is not what makes him break down weeping, though. What triggers his tears is the sight of the tombstone, its eyewitness reproach, its evidence against him: the unnatural symmetry of her birth date and death date.

20 February 1900, 20 February 1929: telltale.

The mourners have all seen, and guessed, and stayed quiet about the unlikelihood of anyone dying of *natural* causes exactly on her twenty-ninth birthday. Jinnah weeps at how his humiliation has been engraved in permanent stone.

Ruttie had spent that vulnerable birthday alone, save for her cats. When Jinnah first saw her corpse, the tabby was perched on her breast like an animal guardian. Every last one of them was purring. Ruttie did to her body, in that hotel room, what mercy would do to any suffering homeless pet.

The recitations are over. The body is lowered.

Jinnah kneels. He is still weeping. He lets the dirt fall from his hand. The mourners throw flowers on the mound. Jinnah starts experiencing strange spasms within his ribcage, and he realizes this is what it is to cry.

The mourners all crowd close to see staid cold Jinnah do it out loud in public. He cannot stop. They get their show.

Making tears is how Jinnah makes salt. In Ahmedabad, in 1930, they are wearing white, too. And they, too, make salt.

Satyagraha is on the march again, seventy, seven hundred, seventy thousand strong, south from the Sabarmati Ashram to the beach at Dandi.

Jinnah sees it happen on a Pathé newsreel. He has taken eleven-year-old Dina to a Marx Brothers movie in the hope it will cheer her up. He has already decided to move, with Fati and Dina, to London. Gandhi is the last man he wants to see, but there Gandhi is, on screen.

He is walking. Rural roads, barefoot, ten miles a day.

In each village, he lowers his head and accepts a sprinkle of water, a red mark thumbed on to his forehead, a palmful of almonds. Women come forward with a sliced mango or split papaya, inviting his butterfly appetite to alight.

If he encounters a stream, he bathes, letting the cotton dry on his body as he walks. Jinnah sees Sarojini Naidu at his side. She alone does not wear white, partly to stand out for the cameras, partly to avoid the look of widowhood.

Once upon a time, she thought Jinnah a great figure of history. Now all her panegyrics are for Gandhi. Jinnah is nowhere in her mind.

He is nowhere in Gandhi's mind, either. He might as well not exist. At best, he is a faceless spectator in a darkened theatre, watching, silent.

Cameras swarm from all over and batten on the event, mosquito-like, on tripods. Here is a *march*, with all its connotation of warfare and aggression, only without weapons, hence moral, sublime, castrated of violence. Paradoxically unstoppable.

To oppose this procession with the police, or, God forbid, with a real army, would complete the image, perfect the contrast between Gandhi's spiritual brutality and brutality of a more conventional sort. The marchers want nothing more than to strike such a pose.

Gandhi himself is the most irresistible image of all. This swami in a loincloth. This stock figure from the old Hindu myths.

See him ankle deep in a river, twisting out a cloth.

See him bend to the beach at Dandi and take up his handful of salt.

He announced, a month in advance, that he would target the salt tax. A trivial diversion—or so most people, including Jinnah, thought at the time.

The newsreel plays out the script of a master dramatist, a master director. All speechifying feels powerless and pallid compared to this Salt March. Jinnah, watching, feels unmagical in his very being. What is magic but illusion? He wonders how Gandhi coaxed the camera just there, to get that exact shot. How has Gandhi managed to star as the lead in his own picture?

Dina leans over and asks her father: 'Have you really met him, Papa?' As if Gandhi were Douglas Fairbanks.

'Yes,' whispers Jinnah. 'And I will again.'

PART THREE

Cross-examinations (I)

There is something singular in the present parallel which has not occurred in any other of the lives; that the one should be the imitator of the other, and the other his best evidence.

—Plutarch, *Parallel Lives*

11

Mohammed Ali Jinnah is playing snooker again. He breaks more efficiently now; three balls have sunk like predestination. He has had a lot of time to play snooker here in London. It helps him think. It helps him brood.

The sharp crack of the break elicits the echo of three knocks on the door. Jinnah opens the door to three well-dressed young Indian men. Law students, fresh from class at college, by the look of their ragged satchels. Decades ago, Jinnah looked much the same, allowing for changes in fashion. None of them have been here long, clearly. It is early October, and two of them are already wearing woollen mufflers against the cold.

'Mr Jinnah!' says one of them. 'Sir, we are honoured to meet you.'

'What is your business here?'

'We wish to know what you thought of the pamphlet.'

'I receive a half-dozen such things every week.'

The students look equally shocked and crestfallen. 'The one about Pakistan! By Mr Choudhry Rahmat Ali!'

Jinnah raises an eyebrow. 'About *what*?'

'Pakistan.'

A made-up word, *Pakistan*—only fitting, for a made-up place. In English, the fairy-tale nature of the idea would come through better: *Pureland*, where all the boys are true believers, and all the girls are virgins until marriage. *Pureland*, where stones are never painted and garlanded, and boys and girls never, ever engage in nine nights of dance around a tiger-straddling Goddess. Only Purelanders live in Pureland, where the water is pure, and the daughters are pure, and the demographics are pure. Religion: Islam. Nationality: Pakistan.

'I am not familiar with this,' says Jinnah icily.

'A homeland for the Muslims!' shouts one of the students. 'Hindustan for Hindus, Pakistan for Muslims. Anything less, and we will be overrun.'

Another student, crushing forward: 'P for Punjab, A for Afghan, K for Kashmir, S for Sind!'

'Baluchistan would be in there, too,' adds the third student. 'We'll work a B into the name later.'

The students are pushing each other forward, crowding through the door—to the point that one of them brushes Jinnah's seersucker suit coat. He looks down at the invisible stain and then back up at his visitors. They sense immediately that they have transgressed, and they shuffle back to stand at attention on his porch.

'How long have you boys been involved in Indian politics?'

The students glance at each other. One speaks up, but sheepishly, with none of the fanatical glee of a moment before. 'Since we got here, Mr Jinnah.'

'How about in India, growing up?'

'We were busy with our studies, sir.'

'I assume from our conversation that it was an English medium school.'

'Yes, it was, sir. St. Xavier's, sir.'

'Did you have Hindu boys in your class? Parsis? Christians?'

They nod.

'And you all sat side by side and did your work?'

'Yes, sir.'

'When it comes to school, then, it does not bother you that men of different classes and faiths sit peacefully and do their work. But when it comes to a society, to a *nation*, you need Muslims in front, in back, and at both elbows to feel at home?'

The students say nothing. Jinnah seems to have grown several feet in stature, dwarfing them.

'The *only* good thing that has come out of the British Raj is the fact that no Indian can stand the British. And that unity of disgust is the only thing that will allow us to kick them out. Once they are out, we will be one of the largest nations on earth.'

A student digs in his satchel. 'If you would only read the pamphlet—'

'When you were in India, you never looked up from your textbooks, and now that you're here, you don't look up from your pamphlets. It may be pleasant to conjure up these fantastical wonderlands on a green lawn in London, but your elders at these Round Table talks are concerned with India as it is. Go study your books. Leave politics to us.'

The students are standing with their hands at their sides, their hats askew on their coconut-oiled heads. The weather gets colder where he gazes, and he is gazing right at them. Jinnah slams the door just as Fatima comes down the stairs.

'Salesmen again?'

'Of a kind.'

'What were they selling?'

'What all salesmen sell,' he mutters. 'A fantasy of ownership.'

Fati shakes her head. The year is 1931, and they are still new to Hampstead Heath. 'I think I will answer the door from now on.'

'And you will be sweet, Fati?'

'Not at all. But at least I will help you spare your words for opponents that matter.'

Jinnah gathers the snooker balls into the triangle, but Fati does not bother to play against him: no matter who breaks, the game will end with Jinnah clearing the table by himself. Alone again: that is what he does. *Beware a diaspora*, Jinnah thinks to himself. Take a step back from a painting, and you can grasp the composition: put time between yourself and your great love, and you can see it for the infatuation it always was. Remove yourself from a place, though, and the opposite happens: it becomes a mere shape on a map, a word in a pamphlet, an idea in the heads of hotblooded young men. What a foolish idea, this Pakistan! As if water and ink could be corralled, by fiat, in two halves of the same glass! What of the granularity of villages, customs, tongues, sects, trades? Who was this Choudhry fellow, anyway? Had he done the hard, unrewarding work of politics, as Jinnah had? It was easy to scribble fever dreams in another country. Herzl had projected Zion from his study in Austria-Hungary. Ensconced in a London library, learning everything from newspapers, pamphlets and hearsay, could such immature young students even see their birthplace any more? That India of many minglings made; that quarrelsome India ... 'Pakistan' was an abstraction, not a place where people lived. Divide it once, what was to keep it from dividing over and over? Ninety-nine squabbling Balkans—while the British tsk-tsked how much better off we were under the Raj ... Jinnah shakes his head, thinking, *No, not possible*, but partly out of pity, too. *Political deadlock has got to the point that people are turning to hopeless, unrealistic ideas like this one*. Click. The white ball shivers back towards him, tracing a crescent on the green felt.

Observe that house on Hampstead Heath. The light in the dining room blinks off, and two separate lights upstairs blink on; in time, the one on the right blinks off, but the last one stays on late into the night.

What is Jinnah reading in that room? *Coriolanus*; legal briefs; newspapers from two continents. The occasional book, too. Never a novel, but on one occasion, a memoir: *My Experiments with Truth* by M.K. Gandhi.

One year, two, three: the house ages far more quickly than it should. Jinnah's black Doberman barks half-heartedly at the postman; his white Highland terrier grows less frisky. Fati's hair goes white in streaks. As for her brother, the bleach stain at his widow's peak stretches and spreads, always on one side.

Dina Jinnah, in her school uniform, flashes in and out of hallways and rooms, laughing. Sometimes she pulls her father by the sleeve to the latest Noel Coward. She sits in his lap, plays with his envelope-slitter, vanishes to school again. Somehow she seems more than a year older after every term. In his pained, adoring eyes, Dina at fourteen is already the ghost of her mother.

1933. A Rolls-Royce pulls up to the house. Inside it sits a man in early middle age, round face, round paunch, round spectacles, already balding: Liaquat Ali Khan.

His fat wristwatch and diamond cufflinks announce a different kind of wealth than Jinnah's, aristocratic and unabashedly self-proclaiming. The woman next to Liaquat is much younger than he is, and beautiful, with a smooth wheat-coloured complexion long sheltered from the Indian sun. Their titles are Nawabzade and Begum, and their look is, unmistakably, old money.

Liaquat, though, shows little of the aristocrat's self-confidence before this meeting.

'First we will meet Miss Fatima Jinnah,' he says a little breathlessly, straightening his tie. 'She will interrogate us. Nothing to fear, Sheila. Nothing to worry about.'

His young Begum's pride has been visibly pricked. 'What has she studied?'

'She was a dental surgeon back in Bombay.'

'*I* have a degree in Economics from Cambridge. Who is she to interrogate me?'

'This will not go well if you get into a contest with her. Miss Jinnah is … Miss Jinnah is her brother's sister.'

'And what does that mean?'

'You will see.'

Sheila Pant had been a Christian until her marriage. Now she is the Begum Ra'ana, with all the sense of ascendancy and aristocracy that the title entails. She gives a little sniff and hardens her gaze at the door. It is opened by a tall, brittle woman with impossibly long fingers and impossibly high cheekbones. Liaquat's spectacles fog a little when he clasps her hand. Fati gestures them inside and sits across from them.

'So,' she begins, steepling her fingers. 'Very kind of you to make a stop here. On your honeymoon, no less. We are honoured.'

Liaquat sweeps a handkerchief over his forehead. She may be frigid, but he feels uncomfortably hot all over. 'It is a pilgrimage, Miss Jinnah. I simply had to visit my dear friend.'

'He will be down in a moment. In the meantime, tell me. What prompts this … side trip?'

'I wanted to talk to him.'

'About?'

'Politics. Why he should return.'

'My brother made his attempt at the Round Table talks, here in London. He did not attend the third and last one.'

'He was not invited to it.'

It is the Begum who has dared point out this fact. Fati brings her gaze to bear, but says nothing. The Begum drops her eyes.

Liaquat hurries to fill the pause. 'Why would he attend it? Those talks were already a failure by then. Gandhi did not attend the last one, either.'

Clearly, he has said something grievously wrong; Fati's eyes fix on him now. 'Those talks were a jamboree. A mix and muddle of every last faction, a failure before they began. Gandhi's presence only made it worse. My brother was very disappointed in the whole affair.'

'And so he stayed on here, in England. But India's Muslims need him.'

'To do what, exactly?'

Liaquat has no answer. In despair, he pulls an envelope from his inner pocket. 'I have brought a letter.'

Fati leans forward with new interest. 'From whom?'

'From the poet Iqbal.'

The letter leaps vertically out of Liaquat's hand. Jinnah himself is already opening it. 'Liaquat, Begum,' he says breezily. 'Congratulations on your wedding.'

Liaquat and his wife rise as they would at the entry of a judge. Even Sheila, for all her pride, marvels. Not at Jinnah's handsomeness; he is not handsome any more. Not even at how well-dressed he is. What impresses her is his utterly imperial air. It is the same air of total command that attaches to a fur-cloaked Viceroy atop a ceremonial elephant, only Jinnah possesses it casually, by natural right. He settles down on a couch and sets his ankle on his knee.

'Allama Iqbal could not simply drop this in the post?' he asks.

'He wanted me to hand deliver it. He wanted me to persuade you in person.'

Jinnah has perused the letter's two sheets already. They vanish into his suit coat with one hand while the other produces a cigarette miraculously already lit. 'Persuade me to return to India, I presume?'

'To save us. Those were his words.'

'Flattering. But I do not fancy myself a saviour. I scarcely have a name any longer. What do the other Indian politicians say about me? Mr Gandhi, for example?'

'He is always fasting these days. Sometimes to "purify" himself, sometimes for the Untouchables. He wants everyone to start calling them Harijans, "People of God". Their word for God is Hari.'

'We shall see whether that catches on among the dour old Brahmins. Speaking of Brahmins, what about that Kashmiri Pandit? The one who follows Gandhi about.'

'Jawaharlal Nehru?'

'The firebrand. The rising star.'

'Still in prison, I believe, over the Salt March.'

Jinnah glances at Fati. 'Nehru will wear that feather for the rest of his career.'

'Fasts and prison time,' scoffs Fati. 'But only if the reporters are watching. That is the Gandhian way.'

Resurrection.

Gandhi is on his back, starving to death. Gandhi is walking. Gandhi is on his back, starving to death again. Gandhi is walking again. He almost-dies the way others nap.

His death has already become a kind of brush he dips in black paint. He raises it dripping from the can; no one wants to be smeared with it. Certainly not B.R. Ambedkar, the leader of the Untouchable caste. In 1932, after 3,000 years of not existing, millions of Untouchables won a separate electorate, thanks to Ambedkar, who was soon obliged to rush to Yeravda Prison.

'We are not separate,' murmured Gandhi, on his back again, starving to death. 'You are a part of us.'

The Untouchables are the hand that does the dirtiest work: the hand the body holds off to one side, the hand with shit under the fingernails, the hand the body will not eat with.

Ambedkar's Columbia-educated hand took up a pen and signed away his victory.

The Viceroy in full fig doesn't want the black paint on his jacket, either. A fever spikes, a pulse gets thready, and he lets Gandhi out of prison.

Gandhi is walking again, out of politics, into the villages. He isn't at the third Round Table Conference in London. Instead, he eats bare-fingered in the hut of an Untouchable. He kneels before their water pump, the heel of his hand at his lips, the water streaming along his fingers, some into his mouth, some down his chin and chest, a ritual bath.

He gives Untouchable children chalkboards and lice checks. He gives their parents a discourse on the importance of not shitting on the roadside.

He prefers these little pockets of people to London and Bombay, with their paved roads and newspapers. The great cities have opened up like giant drains. Villagers will swirl into them, and with them, India. Some call the darkness they drain towards, 'the future'. Gandhi knows it isn't the future, it's just the West. The West thinks its own present is everyone else's best possible future. But that way lies darkness, nameless and Godless. That way lies enslavement, not always to Westerners, but in all cases to the Westernized. The villages Gandhi walks among are one immense coral reef, built up over centuries, hut by hut, shrine by shrine, mosque by mosque. He cannot bear to see it bleached white.

May 1935. He gets a visitor. Fresh white cotton khadi, freshly creased white cap, freshly brushed white teeth, a small black satchel under his arm.

'Jawaharlal!' he says. 'You have been released at last.'

'Bapu.' Nehru lunges to touch the master's feet and sits beside him, on the earthen floor—after spreading the small white square of a handkerchief, embroidered with his initials. 'The British Government showed me excellent hospitality,' he smiles, 'but they seem to have tired of my company, for now.'

Villagers crowd around the hut. Small brown faces show up at the windows. Maybe it is the Packard automobile parked out front; maybe it is the novelty of Gandhi's visitor, or simply his physical beauty. Both men are naturals when it comes to ignoring crowds and photographers, such as the Englishman from the *Times* who has accompanied Nehru here, and who crouches now to get a candid shot of the two politicians in private conversation. If they look into the camera, or glance out at the gathering crowd, it will destroy the illusion. Everyone must observe this private moment.

'…August may be the month,' Nehru is saying. 'If Parliament passes this Government of India Act, we shall have direct elections.'

'Your party will do well,' Gandhi nods. 'I do not doubt that.'

'*Our* party. Congress is your party, too, Bapu.'

Gandhi rolls his head, a gentle figure-eight that could be assent or denial. 'I feel myself to be outside parties. Even Congress. This is where I belong—here, in the villages.'

'You will not campaign with us?'

'There will never be a place, on any ballot, to tick my name. Why would I campaign if I do not run?'

'Your support, then?'

'You always have my support. But my work is here. Come with me, Jawaharlal.'

Nehru follows Gandhi out of the hut, down to the river. Villagers stare at him from terraces and the forks of trees as he helps Bapu wash clothes. On the way back, his sleeves wet to the elbow, Nehru diverts into the back seat of his Packard.

This Packard drives back into Bombay, and the man who emerges is wearing a crisply ironed 'Nehru suit'. Flashbulbs go off in paroxysms.

Nehru gives a speech in flawless English. Then back into the Packard, back into the countryside. He is in simple cotton again. This time, after a speech in flawless Hindustani, the road back into the big city has filled up with admirers. Nehru has gained momentum. His chauffeured Packard can scarcely move. Palms press white against his tinted windows, and ecstatic faces peer at his profile, studiously looking ahead. The Man of the Future.

Jinnah's house on Hampstead Heath has been quiet these past two years.

Everything is the same, preserved as in a museum, even the Jinnahs. Their visitors—Liaquat Ali Khan and his Begum—are the same, too. They are on their second mission from Iqbal to secure Jinnah's return.

Fatima Jinnah sits in the same chair, steepling her long fingers. Her brother sits with the same leg crossed over the other, the same polished shoes, immaculate. And he has sighed, again, at this request that he return to India.

'I am hardly the saviour Iqbal makes me out to be.'

This time, when Jinnah asks, again, what they are talking about in India, he doesn't ask about Gandhi first.

'What about Gandhi's protégé? This matinee idol, Nehru?' He gestures disdainfully at the newspapers stacked on the end table. 'He's quite the darling of the columnists.'

'Well, I did encounter him a few months ago, at a dinner,' says Liaquat. 'He said—we spoke of quite a few things.'

'Did he say anything of note?'

Liaquat and his young wife exchange a brief, uneasy glance. *Of note*, they both know, means *about me*. Liaquat swallows. The Begum, fearless, intervenes. She has got a sense of Jinnah's hidden wound from the word he had just attributed to Iqbal: for all his flattery, Iqbal never called him a *saviour*. But a saviour is what Jinnah dearly wants to be. For all his detached superiority, he wants to be resurrected.

'Jawaharlal said you were finished.'

Jinnah raises a single eyebrow from the dead. The Begum knows she has cut deep.

'Those were Mr Nehru's exact words, weren't they, Liaquat? *Jinnah is finished*.'

12

Gandhi is humming a tune. His bent knee rises and falls, and the spinning wheel blurs in front of him. As it picks up speed, it seems to shirr in reverse, into the past. The reflection of the wheel ghosts itself on to the round lenses of his spectacles.

His lips are moving now. '*Sare jahan se achchha Hindostan hamara…*' *Better than all the world, this Hindustan of ours…*

What a lovely tune, thinks Gandhi. *Some day they will ask me what our national anthem should be, and I may well choose this song. When was it written? 1904? Just a year before the British tried to divide us all by dividing Bengal, that failed colonial experiment: riots in the streets, everyone at each other's throats … Many will expect Tagore to compose something, or Sarojini, but they would do it in Bangla. This song is in Hindustani, and almost everyone in India understands a little Hindustani.*

Best of all, Gandhi reflects, *it will be a fine gesture of unity towards the Muslims. The composer of these lyrics being who he is and all…*

Mohammed Iqbal is dying in Lahore in the year 1935, his tight bronchi whistling with effort as he wills himself to walk, in his garden, with the newly returned Jinnah.

The poet's moustache is still stylish, groomed with very tiny silver scissors, handlebars twisted to a point and upturned. He is a theatrical speaker, even in an intimate setting among frangipani flowers. His spotted, shaky hands have spread wide. He holds an idea in either one.

'Capitalism. The Hindus are money-men, industrialists, natural capitalists. Capitalism tends naturally towards hierarchy. Rich to poor. And on the other side? Caste. Another top-to-bottom hierarchy. If the Hindus take over India?' At this, Iqbal brings together his hands, pinching an imaginary throat.

'Nehru is a socialist,' says Jinnah coolly. 'And Gandhi, I hear, has been campaigning against caste.'

'Ask Ambedkar about Gandhi and caste,' Iqbal growls. 'The Untouchables will tell you otherwise. They will be our natural allies. We are both subhuman in the caste Hindu's world. And as for Nehru's socialism, don't think he can undo thousands of years of Hindu money-changing. The Hindus are the Jews of Asia. There were just too many of them to scatter.'

Iqbal is the frail one, the dying one, but it's Jinnah who starts coughing roughly, almost doubling over.

'Do you need water?' Iqbal asks.

Jinnah shakes his head. 'I think some scent or another must have tickled my throat.' Then why does he taste blood?

'Come inside. Come into the library.'

Iqbal's library has a little of everything. Among so many books, the old man's mind veers away from politics. He holds up some papers. 'Proofs of my last epic,' he whispers. 'I call it *Azazil*. It's the temptation in the garden, told from the perspective of Lucifer. Like *Paradise Lost*. Only, I followed the Sufi mystics. Mansur al-Hallaj's version. Azazil loves Allah too much to bow to Adam. He does his evil out of too much love.'

Jinnah can hear Iqbal wheezing much more loudly here. He can hear his own heartbeat, too, still startled after that coughing fit. He looks down and notices blood has sprayed on his hand and wrist. Though he uses a handkerchief to dab it away, he cannot get the flecks out of his shirt cuff.

'Who is your favourite poet, Jinnah?'

'Shakespeare.'

'I would imagine. Shakespeare was a man of the world. So are you. Men of the world like Shakespeare and Lord Byron.' Iqbal raises his nose, a little peeved. '*Englishmen* of the world, I should say.'

'I fear I do not read Urdu.'

'Or speak it. I know. That will have to change.'

'Which poet do mystics like?'

'Among the English you can find only one real mystic. William Blake. He wrote a poem about a tiger which transcends anything written about tigers by an Indian. Yet, I am uncertain if he ever saw one.'

'An Indian?'

'Or a tiger.'

'Then it cannot be a true poem, can it?'

'It is all the truer for his never having seen either. *Tyger, Tyger, burning bright, In the forests of the night. What immortal hand or eye Could frame thy fearful symmetry*?'

'Your Blake does not mention teeth or stripes.'

Iqbal shrugs. 'Or Bengal.'

'What he describes is not really a tiger. It could be anything.'

'Which is why his tiger embodies a superior terror! It is like faith. A true prophet, Jinnah, makes you believe in something you have never seen. *Belief* in its reality is where its reality comes from.'

'It's the mind that gives birth.'

'To the tiger. Or to the country.'

A servant brings in a small folding table, then tea. Iqbal's fingers are black with ink, like a mechanic's with motor oil.

'History,' murmurs Iqbal as he pours, 'writes itself in books. It makes up the best stories, better than any poet could invent on his own. I knew you would reappear just when all seemed lost.'

'What now, Iqbal?'

'Tea.' Iqbal drops sugar cubes into their teacups. 'I do not care for tea made the English way,' he says. 'I like clove. I took some with me on my last trip to England. They ship cloves west from India, you know. Tiny black torches of spice. Five rupees a kilo, over here, but sold there with a nine thousand per cent markup.'

'The benefits of Empire. They will not enjoy them for long.'

'Inshallah. Tell me. How is Dina?'

'A delight. Are you working on any new poems?'

'One. An idea for a poem, really.'

'What is it about?'

'I don't know the details. I only know one word of it, the first word. But from the first word, in time, everything else will come.'

'And that word is?'

'Pakistan.'

Monocle dangling by a chain from his vest pocket, Jinnah strides on to the stage at the latest meeting of the All-India Muslim League. He receives a standing ovation from the esteemed membership: a biscuit-factory magnate, anaemic second sons of far-flung sultans and nawabs, assorted barristers with knighthoods, a newspaper editor, the police commissioner of Lahore, and two genteel and lily-necked octogenarian patrons of the arts.

The only man of substance is Liaquat Ali Khan in the front row, his eyes full of awe and hope. *What Iqbal has envisioned*, he thinks, *Jinnah can bring about*.

Jinnah is made president of the League before he even opens his mouth about the importance of the forthcoming elections. They are only too happy to have him. There is no one else, though there are plenty of Muslim politicians. It's just that they all have their own, local parties in this or that province. They have built coalitions with Hindu and Sikh industrialists and lawyers; they have splintered off into militant marches, up in the mountains; they have allied with, or outright *joined*, Nehru's Congress.

The All-India Muslim League that Jinnah finds himself leading is a rump league. 'All-India', if India were all noblemen and old money. 'Muslim', if fear of Hindus at ballot-boxes were a sixth pillar of Islam. 'League', if men of the same class, education and religious background can be said to have 'leagued' with anyone but themselves.

'What now, Jinnah?'

It is 1936: one year away from the India-wide elections. Liaquat always sits on the edge of his chair when Jinnah is around; Jinnah, by contrast, leans back and crosses his legs, not even registering his new lieutenant's eagerness to please.

'There are four pieces on the chessboard, Liaquat. The British; the various independent princes and nawabs, who are really just clients of the British; the Hindus; and us. The British are trying to give India a Constitution on their *own* terms. Quite imperiously they grant these Communal Awards, giving this or that community a certain number of seats or a separate electorate. But none of the communities are happy with it. What we need to do is present a united front to the British. The Congress is the country's biggest party, I grant that. Gandhi made it that way. But its membership is mostly Hindu.'

'So, you are saying we approach them?' Liaquat does not want to contradict the master; but he is, at heart, sceptical. 'In the spirit of 1916?'

'Not a Congress–League settlement. Not again. This time, there has to be a Hindu–Muslim settlement. They ought to approach *us*, but I am not above writing Nehru a letter. Even if I am his elder.'

'And if no settlement is reached?' Liaquat murmurs. 'What then, Jinnah?'

Jinnah has already sent off his letter to Nehru. It is one letter among hundreds that the celebrity is receiving every month, one small voice out of the roaring crowd that follows Nehru wherever he goes now. Is it any wonder young Nehru cannot hear him? Is it any wonder he glances at the letter, writes a polite response, and moves on to the next rally?

Because those crowds are shuffling down dusty country roads, straight from the rally grounds to the voting-booths. Because it is already 1937, and the results are being counted, and the roar in Nehru's ears is getting louder and louder.

Naturally that roar drowns out the old has-been Jinnah, brooding in his newly built bungalow on Malabar Hill. Mohammed Iqbal is dead, and so is the Muslim League, more or less.

They have received a drubbing. The Congress has gained more seats in every province than Nehru himself had hoped for. As for the Muslims of India, they have voted for a variety of small, provincial parties, not the rich men's League.

They have also voted for Congress. In one Muslim-majority region—the Northwest Province—Congress has won an outright majority. That is thanks to a seven-foot Pathan named Abdul Ghaffar Khan. Or, as his admirers call him, in honour of his closest ally: 'Frontier Gandhi'.

In Jinnah's new Malabar Hill mansion, carpenters are finishing up the cabinetry. The last of the Italian marble has been installed and ground down to a perfect fit, and a fine white dust coats the floors, the windows, even Jinnah himself. It adds to the pallor of his humiliation.

Some saviour. Some resurrection.

Liaquat and Fatima sit beside him. 'What now, Jinnah?' asks Liaquat.

Fatima puts a finger to her lips and shuts the door against the futile hammering of the carpenters. 'Let him think,' she whispers. 'Let him think...'

And so, Jinnah lights his first cigarette.

That first cigarette murmurs, 'The problem is borders. It's all a matter of cartography, isn't it? In the old days, the Sultan, the Mughal, the Nizam ruled as far as his tax collectors could collect without getting pitchforked in the throat. Everything beyond that needed the army and qualified as a campaign. Maps were for generals. Peasants had no maps—only this ditch, and that hill. They were cows, grazing. The tax collector came by and milked them. The Hindus got milked a little more because of the *jizya*, the infidel tax. Set down the bucket, tug the udders, squirt–squirt, move on. Be apprised, you are all subjects of so and so! Now go back to grazing.'

'So, who drew the maps?' asks the second cigarette. 'Is there a single map, carved in sandstone, of the Gupta Empire? Of the Maurya Empire? It's all some British scholar's work, off in London, painting the subcontinent Gupta blue or Maurya yellow, seeking precedent for painting it Victorian red. None of these minutely jigged coasts and borders back then. That's why old maps look like a child's drawings, even European ones.

Cathay one blob, Aethiopia another blob, and in between, a little spouting whale to mark the salt sea. Perhaps an Atlantis somewhere in there, like a premonition of Australia.'

'If only we could go back,' sighs his third cigarette, 'and unteach these natives their sense of being a nation among nations, corralled and defined by lines on a map. Keep them as cows, that is, villagers in ahistorical ignorance. An ignorance, admit it, Gandhian: maybe the old man is on to something there. Maybe that's been his game all along…'

'Oh, but you *can't* go back,' declares his fourth cigarette. No more than Adam and Eve. The British made the maps, with help from diligent Hindu Pandits pacing the outer reaches, counting their footsteps. Jawaharlal's forebears, perhaps, obsequious eloquent Kashmiris, talented at sensing power and latching on: the Raj then, Gandhi now. No forgetting the reality of Western-style borders, once you know what they are and what they look like. The transition is irrevocable, like introducing a society to money or seated toilets.'

'Or cigarettes.' Jinnah's fifth one says. 'These people, the people, your people—whatever you care to call them—will be new to democracy, too. Self-rule. Or the illusion of self-rule, probably. As if hundreds of thousands of unlettered Bihari squatters and Balochi goat-shearers and Bengali tea-pickers can be expected to analyse 'issues' and vote. They will be susceptible to the basest, simplest appeals. Just like the English. You have seen elections in England—some ha'penny Hyde Park demagogue on an upturned orange-crate, fist in the air. There, the rhetoric pitted miners versus the mine owners; before the war, England feared strikes, feared its own underclass, worse than it did the Kaiser. And here, in a hypothetical India? Whom would a demagogue have to demonize if he wished to come to power?'

'You know damned well who,' says his sixth cigarette. 'And democracies are quite good at keeping an underclass under. Majority rule. And where there isn't a majority, just redraw the district.'

'Because the Hindus will be the new elites,' mutters his seventh cigarette. 'Count on that. Tory, Liberal, Republican, Democrat—governments change, but the money-men stay in power, as they always do in England and America. Money wins, no matter who gets more votes. Elections are for show. Even fascists hold elections...'

'...And come to power *through* elections,' cautions the eighth cigarette. 'With Hindu money and Hindu votes and sly Hindu promises (Congress commands all three), the Hindus will win both the show election and the real power. And it won't be long after that. Maybe five years, maybe fifty, but eventually some demagogue on an upturned orange-crate will discover how to get out the vote. The fist in the air will become a pointing finger.'

'And this is how it will all have started,' warns his ninth cigarette. 'With a slick Hindu whispering in the ear of a slick Englishman, with Nehru posing for an American photographer. It has always been this way, this love affair between the English and the Hindus. The "babu" has excellent penmanship. Gandhi deadpans another headline-ready quip, and a dozen pens glide across a dozen pads.'

'No, you will never enchant the journalists,' Jinnah's tenth cigarette sighs. 'Or the Viceroy, or the Viceroy's wife. Like Ruttie said once, long ago—"There's no romance in you, even on horseback." But you can get what you want, that is, what your people require.'

'Because there are ways to *make* them your people,' whispers his eleventh cigarette all too knowingly. 'You know how to do it. You know what you have to say. Preaching unity has netted you nothing. Try the opposite for once and see. You can get it all without charming the crown off the Queen, without dramatic marches to the sea, or jail time, or a homespun dhoti. All you need is the willingness to slum a little: intellectually, rhetorically. All you need is grit and ruthlessness and words.'

And another ashtray.

Liaquat has been waiting. He can't help himself. 'What now, Jinnah?'

Jinnah stubs out the eleventh cigarette. 'We fight.'

13

Sardar Patel is chewing on a pencil. It hangs from his mouth like a sceptical segment of straw. His face is turned to Gandhi at his spinning wheel, but his eyes flick to Nehru, passionately pacing back and forth.

'It really is an extraordinary letter!' Nehru almost shouts. 'So soon after his desultory showing in the elections? He has the *cheek* to dictate terms to us?'

'Jinnah has presented his requests,' says Gandhi quietly. 'We may as well consider them.'

'His *demands*. You heard his tone, Bapu.'

'I heard your tone, Jawaharlal, when you read this latest letter to me.'

'To demand a fixed Muslim share of state services! To insist we write *that* into a constitution! Is he mad?'

Sardar mutters, 'He is a Mussalmaan.'

Nehru ignores him, pacing more quickly. 'Do that, and next we shall be fixing shares for Sikhs and Christians and Jains and—and every silly sect you can think of. Communal politics! Even the Muslims are tired of it. Haven't they seen what the Congress has done to Hindu-only parties? We won our seats by sweeping away their communal thinking with a *national* movement. That's what we *are*.'

'The Muslims think they are a separate nation,' says Patel.

'Their intellectuals say that! The likes of Iqbal and Jinnah. Not their peasants!'

Patel raises an eyebrow. 'You know their peasants, do you, Jawaharlal?'

'That's my next step, of course. To travel through the countryside and make—make—'

'Converts?' Sardar asks. 'Good luck.'

Gandhi shakes his head. 'Hindus and Muslims are not two nations. One cannot tell the difference by looking at them. Look at their faces. They are the same people.'

'Iqbal's ancestors were Kashmiri Pandits,' declares Nehru, as if this proves something. 'No doubt Jinnah's grandfather was a Hindu, too.'

'When they turn,' says Patel, 'they turn completely.'

'And his thirteenth point! That the League must—note that *must*—be the *sole spokesman* for all of India's Muslims! What does that mean? We have Muslims in our own ranks. Congress welcomes everyone as Indians, Muslims included. Who is Jinnah to say we don't represent them? The presumption! Sole spokesman! As if Jinnah doesn't drink Scotch and brandy. As if the mullahs can stand the sight of his monocle and spats. This makes no sense.'

No sense to anyone, yet, except Sardar Patel. 'When they turn,' he says, 'they turn *forever*.'

While this meeting is going on, a new visitor arrives at Gandhi's ashram. The stranger looks like any of the dozen European travellers who find their way there each year. Backpack, pink skin, blondish beard. This man is barrel-chested, the torso slightly large for the legs, the look of a wrestler or longshoreman in late middle age. Just now he asked for directions at a sweets stall, in Hindustani. Now he passes white sarees and children in khadi cotton, nodding, murmuring something to himself.

One of the women, bolder and taller than the others, steps up to him. To his surprise, a white woman's face smiles out from under the saree.

'Sir?'

'I am here to see Moh … I am here to see Mr Gandhi.'

'Bapu,' she nods. 'Is he expecting you?'

'Tell him it is Kallenbach.'

Mirabehn gestures for him to rest under the shade of a pipal tree. A young man brings the traveller a cup of water. Kallenbach's old friend emerges from a small house without a stick; he is walking, but so swiftly the people around him have to jog to keep up. His arms open when he is still forty feet away. The two men embrace and clap each other's backs. Soon they are sitting in a room, alone.

Gandhi does not run his spinning wheel as he does during other meetings.

'You have found me at last!' he beams. 'Not even a letter to warn me, to prepare my heart. How long can you stay with me? Are you here to join us?'

Kallenbach shakes his head with an air of great exhaustion. He has lost the golden glow of his South African days. 'I am headed … elsewhere. I had to come see you before I left.'

'You look ill, Kallenbach. India's water has not treated you well.'

'It is not India.'

'Then what is it?'

'Germany.'

Kallenbach, as Gandhi knows, is a circumcised Jew. 'You mean Mr Hitler.'

'Germany. They are the same thing now.'

Gandhi nods. 'Perhaps that is your destiny: to start a satyagraha campaign there. I will help you in any way I can.'

Kallenbach presses the heels of his hands to his closed eyes, restraining the urge to shout. 'Satyagraha, my friend? After Kristallnacht?'

Gandhi raises a didactic finger. 'You were born in Germany. You should insist you are German, in the very thick of Hitler's crowds, and take whatever punishment they decide. *Voluntarily*, you see. The suffering must be voluntary. That is how it gains force.'

'They would shoot me.'

'At first. But over time, if all the Jews behave this way, the Nazis will be awestruck. They will admire you.'

'There will be none of us left.'

'I will help. I will write the Jews of Europe an open letter if you wish. What are the words in German for truth and force?'

'There is no force but force.' His voice trembles. 'That is what I have come to tell you, Mohan. Understand it now before it is too late. Violence works.'

'They say there will be a war in Europe.'

'Hopefully not too late to save us.'

'If there could *be* a justifiable war, it would be against Mr Hitler,' nods Gandhi. 'But I do not believe in any war. You should insist Germany is your home.'

'I have a new home. Zion.'

'The Germans commit violence against you, and you would pass it on to the Arabs? This will never end unless you end it and offer yourself up.'

'We are going to fight.'

'But you are a Tolstoyan like me.'

'I am a Jew. That is all I am now.'

'Offer yourself to be shot, or thrown in the Dead Sea, without raising a finger, and see what happens. Arab hearts will melt.'

Kallenbach tugs nervously at his beard. 'You are lucky to be fighting the British.'

'The British can be ruthless.'

'Ruthless and decent. They are not wholly one or the other.'

'They are sometimes one, sometimes the other.'

The two men been sitting on the ground, cross-legged and face to face, as they used to back in South Africa. Kallenbach gets to his feet, swings his rucksack on to his back, and joins his hands.

'I came only to share with you what I have learnt,' Kallenbach whispers, in tears. 'I pray you never encounter an enemy like ours. Because if you ever do, Mohan, you are going to lose *everything*.'

Mohammed Ali Jinnah, in downtown Bombay, turns in a tailor's triptych of a mirror. He is wearing a kameez for the first time since the wedding ceremony with Emibai.

'It is the right green,' says Fati.

'Close enough to the League flag.'

'Now for the top button.'

Jinnah raises his chin. Fatima eyes the unexpectedly loose skin over her brother's unexpectedly pronounced Adam's apple.

'How do you feel?' she asks, with a sudden tremor in her voice.

'I forgot how much of a straitjacket these are. But this one is comfortable enough.'

He steps into the mirror and turns again, eyeing the cut, the absurdly loose pantaloons. Fati strolls over to the tailor's notebook, which lies open to Jinnah's measurements. Her unpainted fingernail follows down the list. Neck, shoulders, waist...

'Jin,' she says, 'isn't your waist measurement...?'

'It was.'

'When?'

'Last year.'

'You have lost an inch off your waist. All of these measurements are off.'

Jinnah tugs at the kameez's unfamiliar collar. 'The measurements are not off. They are simply more recent.'

'I see you every day,' she murmurs. 'It has been too gradual to notice.'

Jinnah coughs and clears his throat.

'I must make sure you eat, Jin.'

'As you wish. We can begin with lunch at the Taj.' Jinnah brushes a thread off his pious, traditional lapel. 'Come. This costume has put me in the mood for a drink.'

After Kallenbach leaves, Patel circles back to speak with Gandhi alone.

'You look worried,' says Gandhi. 'I rarely see you worried, Sardar.'

'I wonder if Jawaharlal is going to say something reckless.'

'To Jinnah?'

'To anyone he comes across. He is ... *excitable*.'

'It's what makes him so adored.'

'It's what makes him dangerous.'

How dangerous? Look at Nehru now, striding into a gaggle of reporters.

'What of Mr Jinnah's claim that Congress does not represent the Mussalmaans of India? Can you reply to that, sir?'

Nehru talks, they write.

'Oh, Jinnah may say he represents India's Muslims, but I suspect I have more of a connection with them than Mr Savile

Row of the All-India Moneyed League. Does he speak their language? Does he go among them where they live, in their huts and farms, as I am doing?'

'And his claim to be the *sole* spokesman, Mr Nehru?'

'Don't we have Muslim members, too? Let each Muslim decide for himself which group best represents him.'

'Mr Jinnah has issued a statement that Congress should leave Muslims alone—'

'Who are the Muslims, in his opinion? Only those who follow Mr Jinnah?' Nehru is getting visibly excited. The reporters love this; the flashbulbs are going off rapid-fire. 'He and his League are hardly the types—monocled and cufflinked, a *Sir* before the names of half of them—hardly the types to fight for the common, hardworking Muslim at the village pump!'

The pens dance.

'But now that Mr Jinnah has come back, Mr Nehru—' 'Now that Mr Jinnah has taken charge of the All-India Muslim League—'

Nehru waves away this stale moth of a name, this wisp of smoke that curls into a J. He even rolls his eyes.

'There are only two parties in India,' declares Nehru. 'Congress and the British.'

1938. The Muslim League has assembled on a vast field in Delhi. Just a year since its loss in the elections, but already its membership is enough to fill fields like this in cities across the Raj.

Jinnah has a long enough memory to recall how Congress, under Gandhi, first got the mobs out and marching under the banner. So, he dropped the League's membership dues to four annas. Even the fellow selling chai at the train station can afford to be a member of the League now.

They are true believers. They believe that Hindus can't be trusted. They believe Gandhi, for all his Qur'an-quoting, is just a Hindu playing a clever game. They believe they see through him.

They believe in the man in the green kameez and the karakul wool cap who steps onstage and begins to speak in English, a language they don't understand. Not Great Soul, not Mahatma. Instead, Great Leader: Qaid-i-Azam.

His English (he is still some years away from trying to speak in Urdu) has all the power and mystery of Qur'anic recitation in Arabic. They don't understand that, either, but it's theirs, and that is enough. The Qaid is theirs, and that is enough.

'Pandit Nehru claims that there are only two parties in India,' Jinnah shouts. 'Congress and the British.'

These words—*Pandit, Nehru, Congress, British*—are enough to set them shouting. He clusters them like incantatory syllables to stir up the spirits. He raises his hand, and they go silent.

'Count again, Pandit! There is a third party: *us!*'

14

The Viceroy of India does not get to wear a cape of ermine. No one kisses his ring, which is a modest wedding band—white gold. An umbrella is the closest thing to a sceptre he gets, and he holds it himself against the pummelling monsoon rain when he hurries, shoulders stooped, from his office to his limousine.

Once upon a time, centuries ago, it was pleasant to be the most powerful man on the subcontinent. Sultans and Mughals and maharajahs had it much better, and the Viceroy knows it: you could lean out of your carriage and point at a slum girl, and she would be brought to you washed and combed, laid out open before you like a book for your perusing. Lord Linlithgow, the Viceroy of India, is stuck being British. Long ago, he married a statue made of talcum powder and toothpaste named Doreen Maud Milner, who dutifully bore him twin sons and three daughters, and has not opened her thighs since Stanley Baldwin became Prime Minister. For the record, that was 1923.

And this is 1939. See him trapped in his Viceregal office in New Delhi, sweating without the benefit of a slave-boy with a fly whisk. See him touch his gurgling belly—but distractedly, not taking his attention from the papers in front of him. He assumes a certain degree of indigestion as a baseline. Three towers of file-folders sit on his desk, overshadowing him. This is what it means to hold power.

It's a wonder why everyone still wants it. But they do, don't they? These 'Congress-wallahs' in their showy white cotton and their trademark caps, marching about, shouting slogans. Who taught them what 'liberty' was, in the first place? The clever ones went to study in London and came home with a whole new vocabulary. Constitution, minority rights, self-determination—*everything these fellows demand*, thinks Lord Linlithgow, *they don't have words for in their native tongues*.

That was another thing about being British. You instructed your subjects in autonomy and self-respect and hence in rebellion. You could imprison dozens when they started marching. You could imprison hundreds. But even a sly subversive like Gandhi got deluxe accommodations at the Aga Khan's palace, pen and paper, visitors, books. In earlier days, under a *native* imperium, firebrands could be thrown in a pit and left to rot. Even in England, Good Queen Bess used to hang, draw and quarter a rebel, then festoon the Tower of London with his head. But all that was 'barbaric' now. One simply *jailed* a Gandhi in plain sight and wrung one's hands over his health. *Eat, damn you*.

About the wringing of hands: an aide rushes into the Viceroy's office. He doesn't knock. The telegram in his hand seems to justify it. He waves it behind his trouser leg, like a flame he wants simultaneously to put out and hide. His voice, when he sets down the telegram, is perfectly composed.

'He's done it.'

'Poland?'

'Yes, my Lord.'

Lord Linlithgow reads the telegram and glances over at the tear-away calendar on his desk. *Friday 1 Sept.* 'Well.'

'This is it, then.'

'It is.'

The Viceroy moves to his window to look out at the people. Or rather at a vast and empty green lawn with a neoclassical fountain nymph in it; beyond that, a high wall obscured by higher trees; and beyond that, the idea of people. This much, at least, has not changed between the old empires and the present one. You still don't have to smell your subjects very much.

'Hitler doing this—what does it mean for us, my Lord? For India?'

'Same as last time, I imagine.' The Viceroy turns from the window. 'India shall come along for the ride.'

The 'last time' was 1915, when a boy accompanied Gandhi from village to village, beating a drum. The people filed out to witness the great man. They gathered close to hear his holy words—which exhorted them to join the British Indian Army. In the gentlest Gujarati, he told them they should learn how to use rifles and go to Europe to fight in the great sahib-war so that England would win. The villagers, all farmers who shared a last name (and a personality) with no-nonsense Sardar Patel, interrupted his discourse with a few forthright questions. Why should they go die for the British? What did *they* care who won in a war between white men in Europe? And how did any of this fit in with ahimsa? Gandhi ... choked. When he worked as a lawyer, he was always terrible at cross-examining. It turned out he was even worse at the receiving end. Within a week, he was bedbound with a nervous breakdown, marking an abrupt end to his 'recruitment tour'.

Now, a quarter of a century later, Gandhi is on his back on a cot at Sevagram Ashram—restless, insomniac. His memory replays that embarrassment in the village and his subsequent breakdown. Hadn't he got what he deserved for compromising on his principle, for telling his fellow Indians to come along for the ride? Ahimsa was not a political tactic to be taken up or dropped depending on expediency. Unjust or just, aggressive or defensive: it didn't matter if you were fighting a Hottentot or a Hitler. No violence meant no violence, and no war meant no war.

Lord Linlithgow has made the usual appeal: Britain and British India are one. The colony must stick by the Home Islands. Either give us your sons or suffer total tyranny worldwide forever ... and so, two days after Germany invaded Poland, the Viceroy declared India at war with Germany. He did it imperially, asking permission of no one. Not Congress and not the Muslim League.

Congress was immediately up in arms, but not for King and country. Gandhi knew the Congress protest wasn't out of love of philosophy. After the Viceroy's declaration, Congress made a specific set of demands about independence after the war. Britain gave them nothing.

Which is what brings Nehru to his ashram. Daybreak early in October. Nehru is only partly here to get counsel from the old sage. He really wants to share his latest inspiration.

'Imagine if we did it! Simply resigned all our elected seats. Gave up the leadership of eight provinces, just like that!' Nehru snaps his fingers. 'What do you think, Bapu? How is *that* for non-cooperation?'

'You want Congress to ... resign?'

'Relinquish! Isn't that the word they use in your Gita?' (*Your* Gita: for all his discipleship, Nehru's atheistic socialism always comes through in the accidental pronoun.) 'We are big enough at this point. When we walk away, it will be all India walking away! Britain will find herself standing alone!'

Gandhi takes off his spectacles. This brash new idea of Nehru's has caught him off guard. To leave Britain 'standing alone' in a time of great vulnerability will hardly foster goodwill after the war. But there is so little goodwill left already that a different point troubles Gandhi more. 'Are you sure *all* of India will walk away, Jawaharlal?'

'Of course. If Britain wants to win the war, she will have to lose the Raj.'

Gandhi shakes his head. 'I fear this will be a gift.'

'A gift, Bapu? To whom?'

December, 1939. Jinnah is meeting with the Viceroy of India.

'To be honest, Lord Linlithgow, I consider it a Day of Deliverance.'

The two men are having a drink together, not across a desk but in side-by-side armchairs. Poland has surrendered, the Nazi armoured ship *Graf Spee* has sunk its ninth British cruiser, the Soviets have invaded Finland … and Nehru, to add one more crisis to Britain's list, has just led Congress in a dramatic walkout from all its provincial governments.

'This is the nature of non-cooperation,' continues Jinnah. 'The Gandhian way. "Either let me win, or I shall take the ball and walk off the field."'

'I think of all our various parties as a family, eh, Mr Jinnah? We can quarrel to no end inside four walls, but when a stranger bursts in with fire and mayhem, we lock elbows and defend the house.'

'If it is a family, you may think of the Muslim League as the good son. I assure you that India's Muslims even now are heading to their mosques to give thanks that Congress is out.'

'And for a swift end to Mr Hitler's war, I would assume?'

'Naturally. But Poland, you understand, is no closer than neverland for peasants in an Indian village. They are more relieved to be free of their Hindu oppressors.'

'No doubt,' he murmurs. 'Oppressors…'

'No jobs. No justice. Our boys and girls had to stand up and sing that idolatrous anthem of theirs—the "Bande Mataram". Invoking a pagan Mother Goddess every morning! Imagine imposing that on British schoolboys.'

'I don't imagine such a thing would go over well at Rugby.'

'They even outlawed the killing of cows.' An ironic smile plays briefly over Jinnah's lips. '*Cows*, for God's sake.'

'Have you been in contact with Mr Nehru?'

Jinnah nods. 'And Gandhi. He claims he isn't a member of Congress, but he's their true leader, the unofficial king of the Hindus. He wrote me a letter the very day I announced we Muslims would celebrate Congress abdicating its seats.'

'To demand a promise of independence is most unreasonable. To go to war with Hitler, and lose India, all in three months' space?'

'What a blow to British morale it would be! Too much to expect, I dare say. And at *such* a critical juncture. Lord Linlithgow, you had every right to refuse them. Fortunately, we are not all madmen and daydreamers here.' He smiles. 'I assure you, *I* have no illusions at all.'

And yet the scene in Lahore, three months later, arises and shimmers like the hallucination of a demagogue.

Years later, the park will be renamed Iqbal Park, and a tower will shoot skyward on the spot where Jinnah will stand and speak. For now, though, it's still called Minto Park after one of Lord Linlithgow's predecessors. And the spot in question is an overwatered green lawn nostalgic for Old England.

Enormous tents hoist aloft on long steel legs and unfurl their wings. Automobiles, bicycles, rickshaws clot the approaches to the park. As the sun rises higher in the sky, more and more men swarm the grounds. They plant flags. They carry European-style brass instruments and traditional dholaks. Some wear uniforms and carry ceremonial-looking scimitars at their waists; others look like college students in spectacles and button-down shirts. The stalls outside the entrance sell sweets and lemonade and pictures of a gaunt old man in a cap of karakul wool: the Qaid-i-Azam. The Great Leader.

This time, his kameez is black. An eruption of trumpets announces his arrival. At his side is the slender sterile beauty with the white hair. The Arctic she-wolf. Every man thinks Fatima Jinnah is beautiful, but no man has the courage to desire her. Not even the nawabs with their military medals, who have imported and ridden big-boned Slavic blondes; not the sultans in sashes, not the moustachioed industrialists. Definitely not the crowd of poor men that stretches into the distance. They do not let their daughters learn to read; some do not let their wives show anything more than their eyes in public. But Fatima Jinnah walks with a dancer's posture, her face uncovered, and her imperious disregard puts her outside their hierarchies and village proprieties. She is their virgin queen.

No wonder there is a dual throne set up on the main platform. The Muslim League Guards—a private military with its own uniform, complete with helmets and scimitars—march around them clockwise, swords held high, led by a child holding a green flag aloft.

Fatima leans over and whispers, 'Are you still in pain? Jin?'

He keeps facing forward, and he shakes his head. The introductions have begun, and the man introduced is the Great Leader. Mohammed Ali Jinnah might be capable of suffering pain, tuberculosis, cancer, death. Not the Qaid-i-Azam.

And it is the Qaid-i-Azam who rises now, the Qaid-i-Azam who speaks.

'You are not two communities inside one nation,' he says to these assembled Muslims, *his* Muslims. 'You never were. Your history is the negative image of theirs: your conquering hero their violent oppressor, your Golden Age their Kali Yuga, your beginning here in India their end. You break idols. They sculpt them. You have one God, they have more Gods than they can count. Your music, diet, language; truth, soul, life is different, different, different—but they still tell you we are all one. I believed that. I tried, for years, to bring harmony about. But I am here to tell you that is never going to happen. Because we aren't two communities. We are two *nations*.'

This speech, like the others, is in English. The pressmen in the front rows are busy taking notes. The crowd cannot follow it, but something about Jinnah's tone, scowl, and defiant confidence transmits. He raises his hand, index and middle finger raised. It already means V for Victory, and will come, in time, to mean Peace. But here, now, it means war.

'Two nations!' he shouts.

What transmits is nonverbal, irrational. The crowd gets choppy, like a black sea under a pulsing moon. At the periphery, people begin to ululate. The League Guards, reawakened, draw their scimitars, which leap into the air.

'One nation will be theirs: Hindustan. But in the north and west and east of this land, we are in the majority. We outnumber them. We will have our nation too.'

Cloud-cuckoo-land. The land of milk and honey and blood and bombings. Paradise.

'Pakistan!'

15

'And this letter is?'

Kasturba sits cross-legged in front of six Untouchable children, a chalkboard in her lap, pointing at a Gujarati letter that looks a little like the number 4.

The children, all together, say, 'Puh.'

She chalks a vertical mark next to it. 'And if I add this line here? What sound does it make now?'

'Pah!'

She covers the diacritical line with her hand, and the letter becomes 'Puh' again. She uncovers it; 'Pah!' There was a time in her life when she would have thought this a polluting thing to do, though more pleasant than the latrine-scrubbing. Her husband has long since numbed her sensitivities.

Now, in 1942, she thinks of that young woman of half a century ago as a princess in the castle of caste—thinking it her home when it was really her prison. Her husband has denied her the conventional enjoyments of being a lawyer's wife. But in exchange for mere being and enjoying, he has forced her to live and suffer. Or rather, to live *among* and suffer *with*. So what if she has not heard from her son Harilal in years? So what if she is always nursing her husband back from the dead?

Her memory of her husband calls him into being, there, walking across the ashram yard. The children are shouting 'Puh–Pah!' with the rise and fall of her hand, and it sounds like they are calling him *Papa* as he walks by with his stick.

Gandhi is troubled, not even nodding at Kasturba as he vanishes into his spinning-room. She can sense his crises the way some animals can sense earthquakes. She dismisses the children early and seeks him out. He isn't spinning. He is reading a book, which he holds almost flush with his nose. His lips are moving softly with a Sanskrit verse.

'What has happened? Is there news?'

'I cannot hear my inner voice. I am trying to fill the silence.'

She sits down next to him and waits for him to lower the Gita. He does so, his recital trailing off.

She completes the verse in a whisper. 'Therefore, Arjuna, fight.'

'Everything has gone out of my control.'

'Was it ever in your control?'

'If I ever thought it was in my control, that was vain of me. That was my illusion.'

'Is it Jinnah?'

He shakes his head, listlessly, unconvincingly. Still, Jinnah is not all. Nehru's Congress Party is still out of office. The Japanese have started bombing Burma. While the house next door is on fire, this house is full of shouting and sulking. Worst of all, Britain's new Prime Minister is no friend. India has no hope of concessions with an Empire-loving bully like Churchill in power. His photograph headlines the newspaper on the writing-desk to Gandhi's right—mocking grin, baby-bald head with baby-soft jowls, two fingers raised in a V for Victory.

'I must make a decision,' Kasturba's husband murmurs. 'I must wager all our work on one call to act. All our work, all of it, from South Africa to now...'

'A new campaign.'

'A *movement*. Non-cooperation, all over India. Not just individuals. Not just a march in this or that city.'

'You want to bring India to a halt.'

'I do not want to break the machine.' Gandhi looks out into the sunlight and closes his book. Already he can hear the crowds assembling, the microphone set before his chin, the reverb so shrill, it will awaken, with its radical lark-song, the Tories asleep in London. 'I will simply lodge a brick among the gears and wait.'

'Until?' asks Kasturba.

He sighs, and his small ribcage shudders on the way back down.

'Until ... until they...'

'"Leave India to God,"' a young English reporter reads, his eyebrows high, '"or to anarchy."'

The reporter smiles up at the cigar-smoking gentleman who stands, resplendently obese and slightly hunched in his black coat and bowler hat, on the steps of 10 Downing Street.

'Does the Government have any response to Mr Gandhi's demand, sir?'

Sir Winston Spencer Churchill has been frowning until this moment, for the subject has been Gandhi's new 'Quit India' movement. Suddenly his face lights up, and he smiles around his cigar.

'Leave India,' he says, 'to *me*.'

Police lorries are leaving district stations. Picketers, rioters, demonstrators, radicals are leaving their houses. The horses are leaving the police stables, freshly brushed the night before, saddles burnished in preparation. The women are leaving their radios and walking into traffic, the baffled omnibus stopping short and honking in distress. The pistols are leaving the holsters. Gandhi is leaving the stage where he has just demanded that the British leave India: 'God has vouchsafed to me a priceless gift in the weapon of ahimsa.' To counter the weapon that is no weapon, the handcuffs are leaving the belt.

The arrests take place swiftly this August morning. It hasn't been twenty-four hours since Gandhi gave his speech. The newspapers reporting it are still being delivered. The mousy old man has entered the iron mousetrap. The jail door snaps shut by spring action.

Gandhi is not the only one arrested and jailed. A vortex has opened up. In goes Nehru, in goes Patel, in goes every member of the Congress High Command, and then some.

The sum is over one hundred people. By nightfall, they carpet their jail cells, lying in rows, head to head, feet to feet, like slaves in the hold of an Atlantic slave ship. 'They are getting restless,' mutters officer to officer, under his moustache. Cotton-clad dark-skinned Congress-wallahs, slight and bookish and indestructible, shuffle into prison.

One hundred prisoners become one thousand. The British wanted to prevent demonstrations, and they did so successfully. Only now, every sit-down demonstration they thwart becomes a riot that runs screaming *Do or die* through the haywire streets. Satyagraha and shutdown give way to open revolt. One hundred thousand in jail, and more people in the streets now than when they first locked Gandhi up.

And so, the bullets leave the pistols. They also leave the exit wounds, along with the blood. The breath leaves the chest, for the last time. But the clerks keep leaving their desks, and the slogans keep leaving their hoarse and tear-gassed throats. The British won't quit India, and the Indians just won't quit.

In jail, Gandhi gets word of deaths and arrests, arrests, arrests. What he doesn't get word of is his release date because he doesn't have one. How could he? There was never a trial.

His appetite leaves him, and he begins a new fast. He begins, too, to worry that he has made a catastrophic mistake.

Because the Muslim League, on the very day of Gandhi's arrest, declared its opposition to the Quit India Movement. Even as Churchill cracks down on Congress, he is scouring the desolation for an ally. And he is going to find one in the League. Will it stay loyal to Britain merely out of self-interest? Yes, but what of that? It will be loyal to Britain, and that is what Churchill wants from his Indians.

Gandhi's shaky hands curl around the bars of his prison window. The knuckles whiten. The tendons cord at his wrists and fan taut along the backs of his hands. This sinking feeling in his stomach has nothing to do with the fast. It has to do with a realization.

He hasn't left India to God. He's left it to Jinnah.

PART FOUR

Cross-examinations (II)

And then as to their errors, in the one they were due to ambition, in the other to a spirit of contention.

—Plutarch, *Parallel Lives*

16

Gandhi: forty years younger, forty pounds fatter, in a green kameez and round white skullcap. Not Mohandas, but his son Harilal.

His handlers had him grow out a beard, but the look was all wrong for their purposes. More recognizably Muslim, but less recognizably Gandhian. Also, the eyes were too bloodshot and hooded. They had him shave his beard and set round-rimmed, plain-glass spectacles on his nose: Perfect.

This Islamized Gandhi is pouring Scotch into a stainless-steel cup. He has been doing this so often that he really ought to just swig from the bottle. But he's used to that cup; he keeps it with him and gargles out of it every morning. Harilal drinks backstage, hidden from view, hunched forward in a chair. Behind him, a bearded mullah is delivering a harangue into a microphone. The words are noise to those big drunk Gandhi ears. Another two fingers of Scotch have gone into the cup when Harilal hears, and ignores, his name.

'And now we present to you the testimony of someone very close indeed. We present to you *Abdullah Gandhi*!'

Abdullah, alias Harilal once upon a time.

Bottoms up.

His exasperated handlers—the applause is dying down, perplexed—lift Harilal by his armpits and snatch the bottle and cup from him. He protests dully, as though awoken from a deep sleep.

'Get out there!' snaps a handler. Another, more gently: 'Don't worry, brother, we'll have it waiting for you when you're done.'

Harilal knows the booze isn't his until it's in his belly. He glances resentfully at the repossessed bottle, fixes his kameez cuffs, and walks across the lurching ship of the stage. There is no applause, only a curious collective stare, a collective astonishment: yes, that really is his son…

Harilal, unsteady on the tilting stage, holds on to the microphone and lets the words tumble. Politics always came first for Bapu. He never wanted to father a son. What he wanted to father was a country. Harilal, in his new name, in his new religion and new dress, knows his father will notice him for once. What he snarls about his parents on that stage—he doesn't remember it afterwards, but it feels, at the time, like exhaling after decades of holding his breath—is a way of killing that rival who stole his father's love. Or at least of slashing that rival across the face, mutilated forever, so that Bapu looks at it with horror, the same horror he feels when he looks at 'Abdullah' Gandhi.

The Muslim League members in the audience stare at this speaker with fascination and disgust. The show is well worth four annas. They don't pay attention to the slurred words of the rant, either. What's delicious are the ears and nose and round spectacles, the grotesque of Gandhi that is Gandhi's botched son. The world-famous Mahatma has a dirty secret in his house! This rambling lush is proof that Gandhi's personal virtue is a sham, and so, logically, are his political ones. Even sweeter is seeing the Mahatma's son advocates the Qaid's vision. When he does it, Harilal's League handlers agree, he is worth the bill at the liquor store. *Pakistan zindabad!*

How sharper than a serpent's tooth it is to have a thankless child.

Jinnah is pacing back and forth on the marble floor of South Court as he mutters this. Ruttie Jinnah, her arms folded across her chest, sits on a mahogany couch swing. Or no, wait, not Ruttie—these cheekbones, a little higher, are telltale. These lips are thinner.

Dina Jinnah is twenty-three years old. Her voice is more cutting than her mother's, and she has her father's quick tongue.

As her father is finding out.

'Are you quoting *Lear*? Come now, Papa Bear, has it really come to that?'

'Thankless,' he mutters. 'Insolent.'

'At least *meet* him. He admires you no end.'

'I do not care for flattery.'

Dina raises a sceptical eyebrow.

'The problem is that you never faced hardship, Dina. You are a spoilt child.'

'If I am spoilt, who is to blame?'

Jinnah glances at her with irritation. 'You have settled on a half-Parsi, half-Christian. What a bloody *muddle* of a man he must be.'

'I am something of a muddle myself! Half everything. Did you ever think of that?'

'I am the head of a Muslim political party. I am struggling to be acknowledged as the sole spokesman of India's Muslims. And my daughter, meanwhile, is trying to marry this—this—'

'His name is Neville. And do please tell Mr Jinnah, head of the Muslim League, that I had hoped to discuss this matter with my *father*. Not with a politician.'

'There are millions of Muslim boys in India. You could have had any one you chose.'

'There are millions of Muslim girls in India—but *you* picked a Parsi, too.'

Her father stops pacing. 'Your mother wasn't a Parsi on the day I married her. She became a Muslim.'

'Do you recall which sura enjoins the faithful to a biweekly séance? To table-tapping? I am old enough to remember her. I never once saw her pray.'

'You are a Jinnah.'

'In fact, you never called her Maryam. You called her Ruttie, just as Kanji uncle did. Just as *everyone* did. What's in a name, Papa?'

'If you marry this fellow, you do so against my will. You defy your father.'

She stands and shrugs. 'Call me Juliet, then.'

The Lincoln's Inn lawyer looks hard into Dina's eyes. This is the same inflexible stare that has faced down Viceroy and Mahatma, and seen out every political rival in Muslim India. Faced with a reanimated Ruttie, though, her long sylph's neck, her blue-and-yellow sun dress, her loose braid, Mohammed Ali Jinnah drops his gaze.

'Let your Aunt Fatima have a word with you,' he pleads. 'Woman to woman.'

This is the first time in Dina's life that he has referred to her as a woman. Dina does not dwell gratefully on a concession that was only her right to begin with. She comes, instinctively, from the Jinnah school of negotiation: she receives concessions and, in return, concedes nothing. 'Aunt Fati never married. And it's quite possible she has never fallen in love. What advice could she give me? She has no experience in matters of the heart.'

'I will write to you only as Mrs Wadia.' He swallows the bitter aftertaste of that name.

'I look forward to your letters, Father.'

'If I write to you at all.'

'My daughter.'

Gandhi—the teetotal father, not the drunk son—is still in jail. His jail is a palace built by the Aga Khans, innumerable arches all in a row, like the old palaces of Jaipur and Udaipur. Its nineteen acres require a small regiment of gardeners to keep it in palatial trim. Gray-furred monkeys perch gossiping on the terraces, and a boy is on the staff to bang pans and send coconut-shells spinning skyward. The occasional unclad fountain-nymph scandalously mesmerizes the help. Gandhi walks the grounds each peacock-noisy morning with a young woman to either side, each hand hooked on a shoulder, his 'walking sticks'. He hasn't used a wooden one since the Salt March. The Aga Khans's palace is a beautiful place to starve oneself to death.

Kasturba has been dying by means of her own these past months. Today's visitor has come to nurse her. She is not his daughter, though he calls her that, but his grand-niece. The Gandhi ears lie hidden under her black hair, but the shape of her mouth, too, bespeaks the resemblance. Gandhi repeats, 'My daughter, my daughter,' and grips her upper arms and squeezes, looking her up and down, marvelling at the young woman.

Manu looks down at the ground, and this shyness, this demure dropping of the eyes, brings a tender smile to her uncle's face.

'Kasturba is waiting for you. Let me take you to her room.'

He draws Manu close and slides his hand on to her shoulder. They walk together, side by side, down the open-air hallway. A few older ladies have accompanied her uncle this far, and when they try to follow, he waves them away. Such exclusivity, already? What an honour! She feels honoured, too, by the hand that trusts her for support. It's as if a free swallow had selected her body for a perch. The hand, though small, carries unexpected force in the fingers. He is not resting it. It grips her and pulls her down.

He opens a door. Kasturba lies alone in a shuttered room, propped on cushions and pillows, wheezing rhythmically. Gandhi stares at her body, shrunken, misshapen, ashen under the threadbare cotton of her saree.

'Ba,' he says. 'She is sleeping.'

Gandhi's mind, against his will, recalls that body in her youth, when they were first married, when she was sixteen, as this grand-niece of his is … how old? Scarcely budded, under her punjabi. His eyes shut with surprise and shame at the commingling of these two women in his mind, one old and dying, the other young and growing.

'My daughter,' he whispers again. 'You are sixteen years old?'

Manu nods.

'It is only fitting that you gain something from your time here.' He points her down some steps into the courtyard, and they stroll together under golden champak trees, over a garden hose, through a busy local cloud of gnats. 'Tell me about your schooling, Manu. There is so much I can teach you…'

The night of his daughter's defiance, Jinnah sits alone in his room for an hour. The light isn't on. He isn't reading. From the look of him, he isn't even breathing. Was it really so surprising that Dina should leave him? Her whole life, he had been leaving her for meeting after political meeting, court case after court case.

The light in Fatima's room goes off on the opposite side of the mansion. A moth settles on the white of Jinnah's sleeve and tries to go to sleep there. He picks it up between his fingers and contemplates crushing it. But he lets it go, and it flees under his bed—leading him there, into the past…

The towering figure is on his knees now, his long arm thrown under the bed, feeling for a handle. He pulls out a dinted metal suitcase full of fresh mothballs and ancient chiffon. One by one he flings Ruttie Jinnah's old dresses on to his bed, her wedding dress, the dress she wore to Lord Willingdon's reception, the one she got on their first trip to London. The peach-coloured dress that drew eyes like nudity, the blue scrap that scandalized the Bombayites who thought themselves forward-thinking until they saw the Flower of Bombay in her unabashed springtime. 'Jinnah's blue flower,' Sarojini Naidu had teased her—an envious ageing poetess, faced with poetry embodied.

Jinnah becomes 'J' again, and he climbs on to the dresses and sprawls there. The mothballs can't quite quench the Chanel. Is he sobbing? No way to tell in this dark; he has turned his face down, buried it in the silks.

At the bottom of the old suitcase, the treasure chest, he finds some old letters and stationery and her box of school supplies. From the stack of letters slips the old cut-out she had made him—little human figures, all holding hands in a string. They unfold in his lap, four bodies, joined at the creases. Her scissors are so small, they barely fit in his fingers. His eyes dwell on that catastrophic last note he never brought himself to destroy.

29 Feb 1929

J—

It is my birthday today, but no one has come to see me. Even Dina is at school. So I have decided to throw a little party for myself and the kitties, and to give myself a gift. I have wanted this for two years now. Didn't you know?

I have tried so many ways to separate myself from you. Love so intermixed us, I was always teasing sugar from water. I was the water, trying to shape myself to your emptiness. You were the sugar, sweetening my life. I am pouring us out and breaking the glass.

This gift I give myself is also a gift to you. Accept it in that spirit, and remember me by it. J, love of my life, my *life*, I am giving you a divorce the only way I know how. I am no longer Ruttie, but I was never really Maryam, either. But for all that, I remain, whether you will have me or not—

Mrs Jinnah

Good God, he thinks, *she was a child when I took her from her life and a child still when she died.* His thoughts wander as he stares at the chain of figures. They were never really holding hands; their sleeves simply meet at the creases. The scissors are still sharp and have been working in his unaware hand. Four human shapes lie scattered on the bed.

Another shape, supine on a bed. Human: two arms and two legs laid out, limp. Her expression is as blank as any piece of paper, but she is not yet faceless.

Kasturba's imprisonment started the day after her husband's. She simply kept one of his speaking engagements, giving a Quit India speech in his stead. The dragnet sucked her in. She fasted once last year, in solidarity with him, but now she is fasting for want of strength to sit up and chew. She is dying in a palace ringed with barbed wire.

Gandhi's requests to the British Government have been met: he is with her at the Aga Khan palace, and so are other family members. Among them, the young grand-niece who waters Kasturba's tulsi plant for her, and massages coconut oil into her hair and braids it up again, and tenderly clips her gnarled toenails, hunting the fallen slivers in the coverlet.

Two doctors visit Kasturba. One arrives clean-shaven and bespectacled, in a white coat, and clutches a black bag. The other is bearded, with a red smudge on the forehead. In a saffron shawl, he clutches herbs. She prefers the latter doctor, and so does Gandhi. The Ayurvedic healer prescribes turmeric water for her cardiac ischaemia, gooseberry jam and sesame oil for her renal failure, spiked ginger lily for bronchopneumonia. Some more theatrical bits he has picked up from watching 'Western' doctors. His fingers press the wrist's tendons, not the artery, but husband and wife are elated and comforted. She is in the care of her own tradition. And she actually feels better.

Not for long. The British physician's stethoscope picks up a crumpling-paper sound at the base of her left lung. He frowns. She is done for, he knows, unless the son can arrange for penicillin, as he says he might. Penicillin may yet clear up the lungs. No telling what that new drug cannot do; it would be interesting to see the stuff in action ... Kasturba stares at his pale, pensive profile, and the colour drains from her cheeks to match. She feels worse.

She has had three heart attacks in the past month, and her blood-choked heart has swollen in her chest. It's so big now that she can love the whole world with it. It thumps against her ribcage. It wants to get out of her chest as badly as she wants to get out of this room. Or at least off this bed, where she's sinking deeper and ever deeper, to the hallway outside. She can hear, during this brief wakefulness, the conversation taking place about her.

'How do they give it?' That is her husband.

'In the arm.' That is her son; that is Devdas.

'An injection?'

'Yes. A quick shot every four hours.'

'It will wake her up.'

'I got this flown in from Calcutta, Bapu. It is nearly impossible to get hold of.'

'You did a good thing.'

'So, let's give it to her. Please.'

'You cannot heal her. She is in God's hands.'

'This penicillin is a gift from God. Think of it that way.'

'He is testing my faith.'

'Think of the drug as a miracle, Bapu.'

'But it is a manmade thing.'

Her eyes close a little. When she reopens them, it is night, and a moth starts bothering her eyes, as though they gave off light. She closes them again, and soon it is daytime, and someone is slipping a straw between her lips.

'Have mercy on her.'

She cannot tell who is saying these things, her husband or her son.

'I will not stand in your way.'

'If that is what you want.'

'If that is what God wants.'

She sees her husband's face eclipse her field of view, filling her sky. His look is full of compassion.

'You are in God's hands,' he whispers.

Time may be passing, or not. A face presses wetly to her hand. Someone is cupping the heels of her feet. Now the pillows are removed from under her head, and her husband slides his bent knee across the top of the bed. The bone rod of his femur, with its scant cushion, is more comfortable than the pillow. It feels good to be in his lap. She has never been here before. She has held plenty of heads in her own lap: frequently her toddling sons used to lie like this, after drinking their fill from her breast; in those frenzied first years of marriage, Mohan laid his head in her lap, too, after he had taken his pleasure. But now it's her head being cradled, and it feels like a well-earned homecoming. How perfect: all she has to do is look up, and her husband's compassionate gaze downwards is all the painkiller she needs for her chest. It cools her fever. It purifies her blood. How nice to be stroked this way…

They will smear red sindoor down the parting in her hair after she dies. They do that to women headed to their pyre; they dress them up like brides. It will be a return to her beginning, won't it? At her wedding, sindoor in her hair, circling the fire with her beloved Mohan … her new life beginning all over again…

The next day, Gandhi watches Kasturba's pyre burn down. Prayers from four different faiths have been spoken over her, but when it comes to the manner of her disposal, all faiths are not equal. No ditch in the earth will degrade her Hindu body. Only a traditional pyre, and her sons chanting *Rama, Rama is truth*. All her sons, even Harilal. He has sobered up for this, and because his mother begged him, he is no longer Abdullah.

Gandhi sits under the shade of a tamarind tree. He thinks about the way the old Hindu sages used to die, as recently as Swami Vivekananda: they simply willed their own deaths, sitting cross-legged at a shrine, during prayers. He would do it if he were powerful enough. What better shrine than this? He could follow her up and out, then down and in, joining her in a womb. They could be reborn as fraternal twins and live together chastely from the very start, a love uncomplicated by romance, brother and sister raised crying into the lamplight within minutes of each other.

Manu sits down next to him to watch the flames. Harilal, perhaps not *entirely* sober, on the other side of the pyre, sees Manu's face warp, through the heat-shimmer, into Kasturba's fifty years ago, then back into her own.

Gandhi says nothing. His mourner's vow of silence commenced after the last prayer chanted before the torch-lowering.

Manu is still a few feet away. He pats the grass beside his hip, and she moves her body closer to his. He puts his arm around his grand-niece. He draws her close.

17

In 1943, Gandhi didn't eat, and neither did Bengal. Gandhi deployed his fast strategically, to break the latest impasse between Indian leaders and the Viceroy. Bengal had no choice.

By early 1944, when Kasturba dies, Bengal still hasn't eaten. It wasn't the tidal wave alone that did it, or the fungus in the rice crops, or the storm of Japanese bullets and bombs that struck Burma next door. All those phenomena weren't enough to starve one of the most fertile regions of the subcontinent. The rich, in a panic, bought up and hoarded all the rice they could—and that included the portliest consumer of all, Sir Winston Churchill. Churchill made sure the last bags of rice to come out of Bengal ended up in the stomachs of the Royal Northumberland Fusiliers in North Africa. Australian wheat shipments asked Downing Street for directions, too. They took a left turn at Ceylon and steamed west to feed the 7th Armoured Division in Salerno instead of His Majesty's Indian subjects.

At one point, Churchill's own Foreign Minister challenged these allocations.

'British fighting men do not multiply on their own,' shrugged Sir Winston. 'Famine or no famine, Indians will breed like rabbits.'

He said this just around the time, ironically enough, that the Bengalis had taken to eating grass. On all fours. Theirs *was* 'a beastly religion', after all.

Now it is 1944, and Kasturba has died, and the fire from Kasturba's pyre leaps directly into her husband's blood. Gandhi chooses for himself the same room in which Kasturba died, and the same nurse, Manu. There he lies on fire, cremated alive with malarial fever. He shudders, he sweats, he shudders. But he never cries out or even asks Manu for water; he is keeping his vow of silence, out of mourning for Kasturba. Manu learns to anticipate his thirst.

One afternoon, he writes on a piece of paper: 'I am your mother.' It's a puzzle. Maybe he's getting better. Maybe he's entering his final delirium.

The next morning, he is half-conscious, malaria's tertian fever returning and returning with the inexorability of reincarnation, this time a notch over 104 degrees.

Meanwhile, in London, Churchill gets a telegram from Delhi about the millions perishing in Bengal. The response he dictates gives pause to the hand of his own secretary.

'They are dying off, are they? Why hasn't Gandhi died yet?'

Because skeletons are as hard to kill as they are hard to the touch. Just look at Jinnah.

He hasn't fasted a day in his life, not even for Ramadan. But here, with his shirt off, standing against an x-ray film plate, he looks just as ribbed as any Bengal rabbit.

They shoot the film. He puts his shirt back on, then his vest, then his suit coat, layer after layer, to conceal the wasted torso.

Back in the office with his Parsi doctor, Jinnah's radiograph sits on a lightbox. His skeleton glows against the black film: the primitive axe-heads of the shoulder blades, the crossbow of the collarbones and breastbone.

The doctor turns from the image, adjusts his spectacles, and gestures his patient into a chair.

'What are we looking at, Doctor?'

'The lungs are the darkness,' the doctor says uneasily. 'Those are your ribs, and that is ... tell me first, Mr Jinnah, how have you been breathing?'

'Stubbornly.' He takes out his Craven As from his jacket pocket. 'May I smoke?'

'I would advise against it. You would benefit from clean, cool air; preferably mountain air.'

'I just bought a houseboat in Kashmir. Dal Lake.'

'The air there will be perfect for you. Clean and cool.'

'It gets too cool in the evenings.' Jinnah lights his cigarette. 'Luckily I have these.'

'I must advise you to cut back on smoking. Or best, stop it entirely.'

Jinnah blows a playful smoke ring that shivers and frames his doctor's face. 'I smoke the way I breathe. Stubbornly. I will stop smoking some day, but don't hold your breath.'

'This is a serious matter, Mr Jinnah. I do not care for gallows humour.'

Jinnah turns to his film on the lightbox. 'You are not the one facing the gallows.'

The doctor switches off the lightbox, and Jinnah's image goes dark, like a city blacked out for an air raid.

'Predictions, Doctor?'

'These films—medical science—we cannot tell the future.'

Jinnah nods. 'You cannot account for a man's will.'

'You must go easy on yourself. When the fever rises, or you have trouble breathing, take time to recover. Go to Kashmir whenever you can.'

'Bombay is humid,' agrees Jinnah. 'But the air in Delhi is particularly poisonous.'

'There are signs to watch for. I would like to speak with Miss Jinnah, if I may.'

Jinnah's friendly tone vanishes. His eyes hood and sink darkly into his face, and the doctor, pinned under this strange new gaze, adjusts his tie, which is suddenly choking him.

'You may *not* speak with Miss Jinnah.'

'I think it will be a great help. To have someone close to you who—'

'You may not speak with anyone. *Anyone*.'

The doctor nods his head.

Jinnah points his lit cigarette at the unlit film. 'That skeleton is not me. My lungs are not me.'

His lungs protest this assertion by detonating a cough deep in his chest. Jinnah covers his mouth with a hastily produced handkerchief and crushes it around a gob of red phlegm, which he hides from the doctor. Taking a slow, savouring drag on his cigarette, he says, 'I am my will.'

Gandhi is still dying in May when the India Office starts to worry about how the headlines will sound.

'Gandhi Dies in British Gaol' will give the old man more power than he has right now, alive, just barely, a rabbit in a gilded cage. 'Raj Lets Gandhi Die' is how the Labour rags will phrase it, no doubt. The Americans, too, get exercised about the freedoms of colonial peoples, and Sir Winston, in extremis, needs Americans more than he hates Gandhi.

The gates of the Aga Khan Palace creak open. Chicken bones wrapped in a dishrag dhoti are tossed on to the Poona street. Crowds rush to this refuse and treasure it up, shouting for joy and singing. A few even set off fireworks; the palace sentries tense their hands on their rifles, but they know it's all in celebration. The Mahatma has been set free.

Relatives and disciples piece together his body on a fresh bed in a small house. Here are the brittle wings of his shoulder blades, the holy cross of collarbones and breastbone. They recite Sanskrit verses around him. They sing medicinal Gujarati bhajans.

His skull fills with the sounds, with the joy of the crowds in the street, and all this sound and joy is lighter than air. His skull rises, ever so slightly, off the pillow. Manu rushes a glass of juice to his lips.

India is still not free. That is why Gandhi hasn't died yet. One week out of British captivity, and he wills himself on to his feet again. 'A recovery suspiciously swift,' some mutter. '*Miraculously swift*,' say others.

By July, Gandhi has written a letter to the one politician he knows he must confront, convince, convert to his way of thinking. The invitation is accepted. And so, in Bombay, in early September of 1944, Jinnah and Gandhi meet again.

The journalists—Indian, British, American, even an out-of-place Aussie—shove for position around the entryway of South Court. Turbaned and liveried footmen, along with a few policemen, mingle in the hubbub. Policemen keep the bolder sort from taking up positions on the verandah. The mood reminds the Western journalists of a prize fight just before the weigh-in. Occasionally a photographer steps back and snaps the house itself, out of awe and aesthetic pleasure, for his own collection. Mr Jinnah must be filthy rich to live in a mansion like this.

Their cameras and gazes alternate between the doorway, where Mr Jinnah will enter, and the wrought-iron gate at the far end of the near-infinite drive, where they expect Mr Gandhi's car.

Movement, in the doorway.

'Miss Jinnah!' 'Miss Jinnah!' 'Over here, Miss Jinnah!'

They are still raising their cameras when her long flat hand flicks downwards at the wrist. They fall quiet and lower their cameras, chastened like so many rowdy schoolboys.

Fati has her eyes set on one photographer in particular. She pulls him aside just as a black car pauses at the distant gate, and the reporters turn clamorously to the arrival.

'You're from the *Dawn*?' This is the official paper of the Muslim League.

'Yes, Miss Jinnah.'

'When Mr Gandhi gets out of the car, Qaid-i-Azam will stand on the porch. Up there. Look where I am pointing, young man. The Qaid up there, Gandhi down here.'

'Yes, Miss Jinnah.'

'I want that moment photographed. The Qaid up there. Before Gandhi goes up those three steps.'

The photographer nods and gets ready. The car is already here. Fati, having vanished back into the house, cues her brother's appearance on the porch steps just as the footmen rush to Gandhi's car door.

The two men are both in white: Jinnah in a three-piece, Gandhi in his dhoti and shawl. Gandhi, navigating the aggression of inquiries and flashbulbs, heads up the steps with both hands joined. He is obliged, once he is level with Jinnah, to part his hands and give a proper English handshake. Jinnah joins his hands before no one.

After this, he seeks an embrace, and Jinnah's body stiffens against his. But only Gandhi feels it. They are both smiling right now, two old friends. They have known each other for thirty years, haven't they? Since that other August when they met at the Hotel Cecil, in 1914, when Europe had just declared war on itself.

Friends? Closer than that: Gandhi makes a point of saying, 'Let's go inside, Jinnah bhai.' *Bhai*, the Gujarati word for *brother*. Jinnah sees it as a tactic, or sees through the tactic: his adversary speaking the same language their mothers spoke at home when they were children. It's meant to lull him into trust.

His answer—cordial, with a half-bow at the threshold—insists on English.

'After you, Mr Gandhi.'

The door shuts. No one has to smile any more.

Jinnah, as he takes a seat, gestures Gandhi to the chair opposite him, but Gandhi very naturally settles on to the floor, spine curved like a drawn bow, head turned down and to the right, one thigh flat, one knee up with his elbow resting on it, the hand hanging limp.

Jinnah eyes this body absurdly buckled on his Italian marble tiles. 'My condolences,' he begins.

The limp hand rises once and drops again in acknowledgement. 'We both know the grief of widowers now.'

'To the business at hand, then.'

'We are brothers in this grief. You and I, my dear Ji—'

'Have you read the League's Lahore Resolution of 1942?'

'Not in detail.'

'But you have discussed it with Congress leaders? With Mr Nehru and Mr Patel?'

'I am not here as a representative of the Congress.'

'As a representative of the Hindus, then.'

'I am here as an individual.'

'I am here as the President of the Muslim League. Why are we having these talks? If I negotiate a bill of sale, who will deliver the goods?'

'It is worth your time to convert an individual to your opinion.'

'What individual? Are you the same man I found back in 1939, dead set on one India?'

'You are cross-examining me. But I am here as a friend.'

'I am a lawyer. Cross-examine is what I do.'

'I am a lawyer, too.'

'I meant a *practising* one. The question still stands. Are you the same man?'

'I am the same man. But you may change my views, if you can. I invite you to convert me. I will be your Saint Paul.'

'You mean my Ali.'

'Your Ali, then. You see how ready I am to concede a point.'

'Hindus and Muslims comprise two separate nations, and accordingly, they must have two separate countries.'

Gandhi shakes his head. 'Any point but that. Don't you see our problem right now? The longer we disagree, Jinnah, the longer the British have an excuse not to leave.'

'There is an easy way to remedy *that*. Simply agree with me on everything.' Jinnah smiles. 'Problem solved.'

India versus Hindustan and Pakistan. One versus two.

The people, meanwhile, are busy being, not just multiple, but messy. In Bengal, one half is mostly Hindus, the other half is mostly Muslims, but they all sing the same Tagore songs in the field. In Punjab, Sikhs are in the mix: five rivers, three faiths, but in the holy city of Amritsar, you can scarcely tell their drumming, dancing marriage processions apart. In Hyderabad, the ruler is a rich Muslim, while the outlying villages are full of poor Hindus. In Kashmir, the ruler is a rich Hindu, while the outlying villages are full of poor Muslims.

Pureland itself has an impure pair of advocates: the late Iqbal, Muslim great-great-great-grandson of Kashmiri Brahmins, who lived in the Punjab and wrote in Urdu and Persian; and Jinnah, the Gujarati Muslim who spoke Sindhi as a boy in Hindu-majority Karachi and grew up to write love letters in English to a Parsi.

Jinnah is using English now, too, even though Gandhi has tried again to coax him into benign homely Gujarati. His fingers fidget, restraining themselves from lighting a cigarette so close to Gandhi's face.

'Name any test of nationhood,' says Jinnah. 'Any test. We are a separate nation.'

Gandhi spreads his hands. 'But you are converts.'

'We converted, yes. As water does to ice. Separate, and for centuries, on *top*.'

'You and I are the same race, Jinnah. Look at us.'

'Germans and Frenchmen are both whites, aren't they?'

'Is that a future? To end up like Germans and Frenchmen, at each other's throats every thirty years?'

'Americans and Canadians, then.'

'Let us all gain independence together. After that, I have no objection to some Muslim-majority districts voting to live apart, if they wish.'

'So, there will be a government at the centre, in the beginning. And we will simply vote to leave. Self-determination, yes?'

'Exactly. Just let us be rid of the Brit—'

'Until the army, commanded by the centre, puts down our secession.'

'There will be no violence.'

'Says the *individual* who doesn't represent Congress, or the Hindus, or anyone. A few missing ballot-boxes, and Pakistan will form like a few dewdrops on the map, burnt away by noon.'

'I will stand beside you and be shot for it.'

'No, you won't.'

'Try me, Jinnah.'

'You won't, because we'll be shooting *back*.'

Fatima Jinnah is listening outside the room where they are sitting. Unlike her brother, she is enjoying a cigarette through a long ivory holder, her legs crossed. Her eavesdropping is going poorly. Gandhi speaks in a frustrating murmur, and she bends forward every time he speaks. Every so often, she writes a few notes, on graph paper, in tight English letters that never violate the lines.

The kitchen at South Court has a door that opens on to the courtyard, through which have come two visitors. She answers a small meek knock on the dining-room door. It is a sub-editor of the *Dawn* and the photographer she had instructed earlier. Hours have passed since the first encounter on the porch, and his photographs have come out of the darkroom. Without a word, the photographer spreads the photographs on the table.

'This one on the front page,' she says quietly to the editor. 'This one, inside.'

'And the headline, Miss Jinnah?'

'First Day of Talks End in Impasse.' Her tone is philosophical. 'No, wait. I have a better one. "Qaid-i-Azam Rejects Compromise, Insists on Pakistan."'

She hands her notes to the sub-editor and waves them away with royal disdain, finished with them. The two men hurry outside. They speak in a hush about the Qaid's sister.

'Now you know why she never married.'

'Why no one ever married *her*, you mean.'

'Married to the cause, as they say.'

'Beautiful, though.'

'I suppose. Like a schoolteacher.'

'Rumour is she's very pious.'

'What was in that glass?'

'Juice, of course.' Titters, muted; as though she is still within earshot, even though they are well down the long driveway. 'She gave you notes for the article?'

The sub-editor has been glancing at them every so often. The letters are as precise and uniform as typescript, and this seems to fit his sense of Miss Jinnah's personality. 'Seems Gandhi won't even acknowledge the Qaid is our sole spokesman.'

The photographer shrugs. 'My uncle in Lahore likes the Congress. Shook hands once with Maulana Azad.'

'Don't tell Miss Jinnah. And definitely don't tell the Qaid. For him, every Muslim who's not a League Muslim is a sham Muslim, a betrayer of the faith.'

'Is that so? Even my pious old hajji of an uncle, who's never in his life tasted a drop of—*juice*? Will he have to prove his faith to Mr Jinnah?'

'Politics. You know how it is. The Qaid has to insist on that point to win us any concessions at all.'

The photographer pauses to take a more panoramic shot of South Court. 'Won't it be great once we actually get to live there?' For a moment it sounds like he could be talking about Paradise, or about the mansion. Then he sighs, 'Pakistan.'

'The Hindus and British will never agree to it. The question is, what can the Qaid win for us by using it as a threat.'

'You think the demand for Pakistan is a bluff?'

'Don't sound so shocked. This is politics, after all. Bluffing and brinksmanship and bargaining. Spend a few more years on staff, and you'll see for yourself.'

'But the Qaid is more than a politician.'

'They say the same thing about the Mahatma.'

'This is about more than just politics.' The photographer shakes his head, screwing the cap on to his camera. 'You'll see.'

18

The Viceroy's office has a different Viceroy. Lord Linlithgow is out, and Lord Wavell is in. He busies himself opening the day's mail. Swift decisive slices with the letter-opener please the khaki-and-eyepatch military man in him. Envelope after envelope drops into the rubbish-bin at his elbow. These gentle stabs and saws, even more than the letters themselves, take his mind off his troubles.

Because troubles are what he has. How swift and decisive life had been just a year ago, motoring across the North African desert in a game of fox-and-terrier with Rommel! The worst one had to fear was a Luftwaffe airstrike, or the smoky scrim of surprise panzers on the horizon; and even then, the bombs merely kicked up sand to one's left or right, rattling the cook-pots. What the panzers won on Tuesday, Crusader tanks took back by the week-end. Of course, Cyrenaica had been a rather hairy business, and he had failed to retake Tobruk—ergo his current assignment—but hadn't it been a far easier command? He could lay out a map and point here and here and there, and by gum, the boys shouldered their kits and marched.

But here? In India? He has no one enemy to see eye to eye with, no Rommel fighting on the same bloody terms, commander versus commander. Instead, he has 300 million Indians who disobey him like toddlers.

As soon as he arrived, he had tossed rice sacks at the Bengalis, locked up the demonstrators, held talks with the politicians and sent troops against the traitors who'd run off to fight for Japan—and he was *still* regarded, back home, as botching the job.

How much easier it had been to contend with Rommel! That had its frustrations, too—scant petrol, bad intelligence—but at least he had the hope of winning. In India, nothing he does is right.

Wavell is still working through his mail when the opener clatters on to the desk. He has made it to the packages, and the first one is from his London publisher, Jonathan Cape. The Viceroy tears it open with his bare hands. Inside it is a book.

The old soldier's chin caves in and starts quivering. A manly tear rushes to the corner of his one good eye, but he blinks it back.

'If you can keep your head when all about you,' he whispers tremulously, 'are losing theirs and blaming it on you…'

He rubs his hands over the dust jacket, spreads the pages, lowers his nose to the binding and breathes in the scent. *Other Men's Flowers: An Anthology of Verse Compiled by A.P. Wavell.* The military man has always loved poetry, and he jotted down from memory the entire texts of poems by Robert Browning and Lord Macaulay whilst his artillery fired spondees at the dusk.

It has finally arrived, his favourite poems between the covers of a book, arranged under headings of his choosing.

Music, Mystery, and Magic.

Good Fighting.

Hymns of Hate.

Wavell rises from his chair with the book clasped against his iambic heart. His eye is blinking rapidly, but he isn't weeping because it *simply isn't done, old boy.* His has been a hard lot, has it not? From losing his left eye at Ypres to getting his right one spat in, thirty years later, here in Hindoostan. But he shall persevere! He shall make it through this Conference in Simla!

Yours is the Earth and everything that's in it, he sighs, steadying his jaw. *Yours is the Earth…*

At least for now.

Simla. From the way these grown-up toddlers are scrapping around the table, Lord Wavell doesn't quite feel like the most powerful man on the subcontinent. If anything, he feels like a schoolmaster who has lost control of his class. He wishes he had a gavel, or a ruler to slap wrists with. What if he could command Jinnah to go to the corner and face the wall? Or punish Nehru for speaking out of turn by making him write *I will not interrupt* a hundred times?

The task of this Conference is simple enough, attractive enough. Lord Wavell, with London's authorization, is offering to form an Executive Council, composed entirely of Indians nominated by Indian political parties, to run the affairs of the country (except for defence, of course). Everyone will be represented—Hindus and Muslims in equal numbers, in fact, with all the other minorities thrown in.

The old stumbling block has come up again. Jinnah wants the Congress to nominate no Muslims, to prove he's the one and only spokesman for 'his' people; Nehru insists the Congress has a right to nominate whomever it wishes, Muslim or not.

As a result, Wavell must sit and watch the old quarrel play out again. Jinnah is speaking, and Liaquat is nodding as usual.

And hapless Archie Wavell is engaging in a tactical retreat to his schoolboy days.

I fled Him down the nights and down the days … he whispers under his breath, reciting 'The Hound of Heaven' as his eyes settle on Jinnah. Strangely wolf-like face the man has, a face tapered at the bottom, particularly when he glances down at a paper. Though of course, it isn't a wolf he's most often compared to. Lord Linlithgow had warned him as he left. 'Jinnah,' the outgoing Viceroy had said, 'is a cold fish.'

The cold fish is talking about Pakistan again, and Wavell finds his mind wandering, in a moony reverie, to Keats's 'The Fall of Hyperion.' A few lines run through his head like snatches of a sad old tune.

Fanatics have their dreams, thinks Wavell, *wherewith they weave a Paradise for a sect*. That is exactly what Jinnah is, isn't he? What they all are.

'Fanatics.'

Jinnah spits the word as he sits in his bungalow that night.

Fatima has accompanied him to this toy-train town the Raj's whites built for themselves. Simla. For part of the day, she strolled that hallucinated European village, but she could not bear it for long. She kept thinking about the amoral wives and burnt-pink lieutenants playing out, in real life, their novels of adultery. The wives imagining themselves young, and the rakes imagining themselves dashing, and everyone maintaining the proprieties though their whitewashed bungalows carried the menagerie-stink of sweat and copulation all summer. Meanwhile, Indians writhed on the Deccan's burning plain like the condemned in a scene out of hell. Fati came home to wait for her brother.

'Fanatics,' he repeats. 'Nehru—he gets it from Gandhi. They think they can represent *everyone*. But what are they? Hindus and more Hindus.' He snaps his cigarette case shut, and his eyes narrow. 'Scheming Hindus to a man.'

'The only solution is Pakistan,' she says simply. 'Everything will sort itself out after that.'

'If they name even *one* Muslim to the Council, they can run to the press and claim that they, too, represent us. Suddenly, *they* are the national party, drafting a plan for a free India—and *we* are a mere communal one, stamping our feet and sticking out our hands, asking for handouts. Nehru claimed it was a small point, a minor snag.'

'You are playing about with their plans. But they will always outwit you, Jin. They are Hindus, after all. It is what they do.' She rubs her fingers and thumb together. 'Deals. Always to their own advantage.'

'If it was such a minor point—whether the League alone could nominate Muslims—why wouldn't he concede it? He had no answer.'

'He doesn't *want* these talks to succeed.'

'These days are exhausting.' Jinnah holds his cigarette in his mouth, but he has not lit it; he drifts on to a couch, his face drawn. 'I do not have the time for this. I do not have time.'

'We will get you to the houseboat this Friday. Dal Lake.'

Jinnah finally lights the cigarette, his arms leaden and reluctant. The first drag triggers a violent coughing fit. Fati rushes over to rub his back; it is all she can do, since she knows better than to tell him to stop smoking.

'He is no happier sitting there than I,' mutters Jinnah. 'We make each other miserable. He fancies himself a film star, you know. A real Romeo.'

'You know he has been palling about with Padmaja Naidu. She is head over heels.'

'Sarojini's daughter? She is half his age.'

Fati folds her arms, and her right eyebrow twitches briefly with the old disapproval. 'Ruttie's friend.'

Jinnah does not catch his sister's sharp tone when she says *Ruttie*. All he hears is the name, and he stares into the distance, and his lips part, and the smoke floats passively out of his mouth.

'Jin!' she snaps, irritated at the hold Ruttie still has on him. 'You already have an answer to every quarrel with Nehru and Gandhi. Every point, major or minor. Just make the same counterpoint. It's the only solution.'

He nods. 'You cannot force two nations to live together,' he says quietly, 'any more than you can force two people.'

Fatima smiles, feeling a slight thrill of victory. 'Divorce.'

'Pakistan.'

That winter, the Raj holds its first provincial elections since the League's 1937 debacle. The Qaid orders his followers into the villages. A grandfather and grandson, both in kameezes of Muslim League green, trek together down dusty cart paths, down little corridors in jute fields, stopping only to squat and chew chapattis from a tin. There are dozens of such pairs. They stand outside the village mosque. The boy beats a drum, the old man calls the villagers to assemble with a musical call indistinguishable from the call to prayer.

Bengal.

Sind.

Punjab.

They are magicians, Pied Pipers, circus barkers, mesmerists.

We can own all of this: *Vote League*. We can conquer all of this: *Vote League*.

Many of these villagers have never heard of Pakistan. Radio sets haven't made it into this wilderness. Newspapers are what vendors in town use to wrap your roasted peanuts. But they have heard of Hindus.

The Hindus are out to enslave you: *Vote League*. The Hindus already have all the money, don't let them have all the land: *Vote League*.

There is only one solution. Let Congress win a (narrower) majority everywhere but the biggest, richest provinces, the biggest, richest prizes.

Bengal, Sind, Punjab.

The villagers there say *Pakistan* for the first time, and already it feels like home. Columns of jute-cutters and cobblers follow the drum to the ballot-box. Each one is a little kafila. The big kafilas are still two years away, but who can imagine them now, with the piper piping, the dholak drumming? Even later, when they stream Gangetically across the plains, who will connect those shuffling kafilas to these enthusiastic freshets?

Jinnah doesn't have to smoke down eleven brooding cigarettes after this election. No, three cigars will do. Bengal, Sind, Punjab.

Win. Win. Win.

19

The first time Manu saw Bapu naked, it was an accident. She had entered a room to fetch her diary, and she heard him bucket-bathing, the small slaps of water on the tiles behind a door. A half hour later, she had gone back into the room and read a book he had assigned her—written by a man named Tolstoy, and translated years ago into Gujarati by Bapu. Hearing nothing for several minutes, she had pushed the door open to find him in the small bathroom, cross-legged on the floor. Or was that the lotus position? Naked. It looked natural to her, since usually he wore so little. His eyes were shut, as if he were meditating. The tall figure of Dr Sushila Nayyar soaped his limbs. Bapu's eyes opened once to check if it was Manu; Sushila waved a soapy hand at her, and she backed out and closed the door, confused. All this happened in a matter of seconds, but she noticed every detail of Sushila's bold body and Bapu's meek, shrivelled one. Immediately she heard the pouring again, but no words; and she left the room.

There really aren't any. Even when he speaks to her in a clove-scented whisper. 'I want you to write about this.'

Tonight, he is sitting cross-legged again, this time on his cot. Undressing, for him, goes very briskly, the way a woman's updo collapses over her shoulders at the pull of a pin. The crescent moon over his naked shoulder casts him in his unmistakable silhouette, and she focuses on that, because it is a familiar object of reverence. He is speaking the whole time, explaining clearly why he needs her to do this.

'It is a way of becoming stronger,' he says, 'to call up the desire and then force it down. I had a friend once, a burly German fellow, and he used to lift the heaviest chairs and beams he could find. I would ask him, "Kallenbach, why are you exerting yourself in this futile way, lifting that wheelbarrow over your head and setting it down, over and over?" He said there was no better way to find out how strong he was, and no better way to get stronger. That is the nature of the experiment, Manu. That is what we must do.'

For her, the undressing goes slowly. Even her dupatta snags on her mother's necklace, the one she started wearing after she passed away, out of remembrance. But her Bapu keeps talking, and in time his voice, which has taught her about ahimsa and overcoming caste and the importance of a clean diet, bridges with its beauty those beautiful ideas to this queasy one. Now if only her heart would stop beating so hard. At least it is dark. Surely, he cannot even see her? But her hands hesitate at the drawstring.

'I am worried,' she whispers.

'You can ask Sushila. And Abha. They will tell you everything about the experiment.'

'I worry about people.'

'I told you. I want you to write about this some day. I will be writing an article about the benefits of this very soon.'

'With my name?'

'No one understands until afterwards, when they say, "Forgive us, Bapu. We were foolish, we were silly children." I will lie on my back now. Look, Manu. My eyes are closed.'

He is still murmuring, as if sleep-talking, when she lowers herself on to the gentle slope he makes on the cot. His leg hairs tickle her. She lies face up next to him, hands flat against the sides of her thighs and the whole of her stiff as a corpse.

'Jinnah will not rest,' he is whispering, 'until he has divided us. But there is still hope. Now the British say they can arrange the Raj's provinces in groups, according to its majority. A Hindu group of provinces, and two Muslim groups of provinces. One government at the centre, in Delhi, to govern them in matters of trade and defence ... That will work. We will be one India. But will Jinnah accept it? He wants two countries, one all to himself. And if he does accept this plan, will Jawaharlal? Will Sardar? Jinnah will not rest.'

Manu is confused. She does not know if she is supposed to turn to him so he can feel her against him or say 'Yes' to what he is saying or just lie here until he touches her. Unless she is supposed to touch him? Is that part of the experiment?

She wants to do this right. She wants to be told what to do.

Bapu has fallen silent. He takes an abrupt breath and lets it out. Now a few deeper breaths, all in a row, until his breathing steadies and goes shallow.

'I am in control,' he says joyfully. 'You can see. Look. I am in control.'

She does not look. She cannot bring herself to look, not yet. She lies for she does know how long, wide awake, in wait. The next sound out of him is snoring.

Sushila's enmity begins the next morning when Manu walks her great-uncle to his prayer meeting. Sushila watches Manu through the Gospel reading and the Gayatri mantra, and at one point, turning away, she wipes a tear from her cheek. She knows she has crossed into her thirties now; she has put on weight, too, and the desire she calls up has become less heavy a weight for Gandhi to lift and set down, lift and set down. He needs someone younger for the experiment to work, and he has found her.

Manu has become intensely aware of the other women around Gandhi. They are all watching the new favourite; they all seem to know where she sleeps at night. She sleeps well next to him, and she wakes up smelling of him.

Yet she is terrified someone will write an anonymous letter to her father in Jamnagar. Or even that Bapu, in his childlike innocence, will *himself* tell her father in the next letter, or the next. She loves sleeping next to Bapu but wants desperately to stop. She is afraid of Dr Nayyar's wordless envious glares, but she envies the older woman right back: when will *she* be invited to bathe Bapu? Why hasn't she been asked?

She is at his side even more than before: her spine his 'walking stick' in the mornings, and in the afternoons, during nap time, her lap his pillow. She kneels to help him hoist himself from the spinning wheel, and he places one hand on her bent knee, the other on her shoulder, and they rise together, his joints cracking sharply. She is at his side when frenzied reporters crowd a porch at Sevagram Ashram.

'What are your thoughts, Gandhiji, on the latest breach between Mr Nehru and Mr Jinnah?'

'Mr Nehru and Mr Jinnah are representatives of larger parties,' he says quietly. 'These differences are not personal differences.'

'The breach between Congress and the Muslim League, then. Your thoughts?'

'I have spent these past days in prayer,' he says. Manu's expression does not change, but she has witnessed him scanning three different newspapers every morning.

'Mr Jinnah—the *League*—is incensed with Mr Nehru's comments about the structure of the Interim Government.'

'I am unaware of Mr Nehru's comment.' Again, not true; Sardar Patel had visited him the previous night, shaking his head incredulously, muttering, 'Jawaharlal's been wagging his tongue.'

The reporter begins to read. 'Quote. "The Congress is only entering the Interim Government on a provisional basis. Once we have control at the centre, we may reshuffle the Muslim-majority provinces as we see fit." End quote. Mr Jinnah has called a press conference on this matter in Bombay later today.'

'Mr Jinnah will have his opinion on this.'

'And what is your opinion of Mr Jinnah?'

'I hold him very close, and I always wish to do so. I wish to keep him in my breast pocket, against my heart.'

Gandhi turns to go. Manu and her cousin Abha guide him away from the cameras and shouts. He is visibly troubled by what he has heard, and within the hour, he asks to have his calves squeezed, one grand-niece set to work on either leg. His nerves grow hot, like wires bearing too much current, and the body's pain follows naturally from the mind's.

That night, Sushila is waiting in the unlit room. The cot is crowded. Gandhi turns on his chest and says, 'Show Manu.'

Sushila begins to roll her elbow on his back. Manu's eyes flick from Sushila's digging elbow to Bapu's eyes, which are closed in ecstasy and pain.

'The pains come and go,' he whispers. 'I have had them for years.'

Sushila, after some minutes of demonstration, invites Manu to try. The small knob of her elbow bumps over Bapu's moon-shadowed ribs.

'Jinnah does not know the villages,' he says, almost to himself. 'I have spent time there ... They live side by side by putting each other out of mind. Like small boys, playing with their backs to each other. They must not be reminded of their differences. They must not quarrel over the same toy ... To divide them is murder. They will do the murdering, but the guilt will be ours...'

Ten or so minutes later, he is asleep, and Manu is left on the same crowded cot with Sushila. Both women stare at the ceiling, not speaking to each other. Eventually Sushila falls asleep. Manu cannot.

The next morning, she tells her Bapu, tearfully, that she wants to go home to finish her studies. To her relief, to her despair, he strokes her head with a paternal hand and lets her. By that afternoon, her suitcase at her feet and her diary clasped against her chest, she rides the bus out of Sevagram, heartbroken. She has her freedom, though she knows she is not really free of him. She feels cast out of history and into a more trivial kind of existence; entirely private, futile, without prospects. This freedom will last as long as he wants it to because she does not want it to last. All it will take, all she needs, is a letter from him, beckoning her to his side again, into history, into their experiment with truth.

Her first afternoon back home, and every afternoon after that, she sits by the window, waiting for the post.

20

'I hear to my amusement that Mr Gandhi wishes to keep me close. So close that I will be, quote, "in his breast pocket". What can I say to that offer? First of all, Mr Gandhi has for thirty years now given up the wearing of shirts.'

At a snap of Jinnah's fingers, the pressmen have battened like locusts on Malabar Hill. They all give dutiful laughs at this quip.

'But secondly, my friends, what does it mean to be *in someone's pocket*? Am I his fob watch? Or does he want me there, in his *pocket*, as a paid and punched ticket to New Delhi? Does any Muslim in all of India want to be *in* Mr Gandhi's *pocket*, that he might take us out, and show the world he owns us? Are we his pet mice? We are not in his pocket. We stand here fully clothed, thank you very much, with pockets of our own. In one pocket is the Qur'an, Mr Gandhi. In the other is a pistol.'

This word *pistol* excites the gaggle, and questions get shouted helter-skelter. Jinnah knows—or has learnt, rather, from his self-dramatizing rival—that a statesman must be a showman as well. So he steps aside to reveal what looks like an artist's easel, draped in cloth. With a grand flourish, he sweeps the cloth away to reveal a solid silver map of British India, with large areas of jewelled green in the northwest and the east: the new, Muslim country.

Jinnah speaks over the gasps and flashbulbs. 'Mr Gandhi and Mr Nehru strode up to the Congress throne by stepping on our skulls. And now he wants to keep me there, underfoot. How long? Does he understand that Pakistan is not a demand for territory, but a right? In 1944, I met with him for days at a time. All I wished for him to concede were very simple points. First, that we Mussalmaans comprise a nation separate from the Hindu nation—and that Mr Gandhi represents the Hindus. Let us meet as equals, but let us call ourselves what we are. Mr Gandhi called us a mere population of converts. We must clean our hearts, said Mr Gandhi, and once my heart is clean, I will forget Pakistan. Will I clean my heart of Islam for Mr Gandhi's sake? He made wily offers but refused to concede the very basis of Pakistan: that we are *two nations*.'

More questions. Jinnah is not done with his presentation; he raises his hand to quiet them.

'I am no Gandhian, as you all know,' he says. 'What is the opposite of *passive resistance*?' He waits, savouring the moment. 'Direct Action.'

They are scribbling joyfully: *here* is a story.

'On behalf of the League, I declare the sixteenth of August Direct Action Day.'

'But what does Direct Action *entail*, Mr Jinnah?' 'Why the sixteenth of August, Mr Jinnah?' 'Mr Jinnah, have you handed out specific orders to take effect that day?'

The prospect of bare knuckles makes the press eager, rowdy, like any crowd that rushes to form a ring around a street fight.

'One,' says Jinnah, 'the Muslim League refuses to join any Interim Government led by Mr Nehru. Two, *because* of Mr

Nehru's speech, we rescind our acceptance of the Viceroy's latest scheme to group the provinces while keeping India one country. And three, if not granted a sovereign Pakistan, the League will pursue unconstitutional Direct Action.'

'Mr Jinnah, could you please define *unconstitutional*?' 'Does *unconstitutional* mean *illegal*?' 'Can you give us an example of Direct Action, Mr Jinnah?'

Jinnah's raised hand spreads silence over his orchestra.

'Until now, we in the League have negotiated in good faith, with clean hands. The Congress Hindus flex their numbers at us, while the British flex their guns and bayonets. It is time they all learnt that *we* have millions, too. We, too, have a pistol.'

That word *pistol* cracks the sky again. Half a dozen more questions rain down. Hindu pressmen, too, are at this conference, and one shouts, 'Are you threatening civil order? Are you threatening the lives of Hindus?'

'I am not here to discuss ethics.'

Press-baiting, Jinnah knows, is a delicate game of tease and tantalize. They clamour again to find out what he is planning, but he knows that suspense and uncertainty and an unplaceable perfume of violence will take up more column-space than outlining a six-city strike and railway boycott.

'Go to Congress,' says Jinnah, 'and ask them their plans. When they take you into their confidence, I will take you into mine. Did you all think I would sit around waiting for scraps? I, too, mean to cause trouble.'

And with that, Jinnah strides into his mansion and leaves the reporters shouting and waving their pads. Two servants hoist the map on its iron easel. The fantasy Pakistan, in silver and green, follows Jinnah into his study, where Fati is waiting.

Iron hooks have already been driven into the wall behind his desk. Fati watches with folded arms as they heave it on to its perch. She takes a step and makes a gesture; the servants adjust the map a fraction of an inch until it hangs level.

'Perfect,' she whispers to her brother. 'Perfect.'

The telegraph cables, the phone lines along the roads and highways, the radio antennae heat up, like nerves carrying too much energy. 'Direct Action' starts acting indirectly the moment the phrase is uttered. The violence starts like something paranormal. A window shatters in anxious Allahabad. A brick soars through the air and smashes a lorry's windshield in Delhi. A body is found with its spectacles cracked and throat slit in Dacca, and it seems like just another murder until his testicles are discovered lying soggy under his Congress cap.

August is hot everywhere, except prim Simla. Mid-August is a bad time for hotheads to be saying 'Direct Action' to one another. Given all the acid whispers and electric jolts, it's a miracle that morning on Direct Action Day sees long-winded assemblies on sports fields and public parks and squares in Bombay and Delhi and Ahmedabad. Paunchy, middle-aged men in kameezes and round caps sit in the sun and listen to speech after speech. The khaki-clad police stand warily at the crowd's edges; they drift back reflexively when the slogans get shouted by the throng a thousand or two thousand strong; but no one marches, no one charges, no one attacks.

In Calcutta, though, the assembly takes place towards nightfall. And something is off from the beginning. The entire Bengal provincial government has been granted a three-day weekend. The head of that provincial government is a man named Huseyn Suhrawardy. A League Muslim, he rules his estate like a feudal baron only nominally subordinate to King Jinnah. Suhrawardy has imported his wife from Poland, his wines from France, and his cars from America. He gives a speech by twilight under the crescent moon to a sports field where the torches are being lit early.

Calcutta is a Hindu-majority city, a city of industrialists and shopkeepers and mill owners and newspaper editors. The Muslims work the jute fields far beyond the city limits. Suhrawardy needs a crowd, a mob. So, he imports it from the Bengal countryside.

They bring the countryside with them. Scythes and machetes and the flattened bats that laundrywomen use to clobber red sarees on the riverbank. Only these bats have nails driven through them.

Or that is what is said. Who says it?

Enter Rumour, painted with a thousand tongues. Rumour has it that after his speech, Suhrawardy heads over to the police station, where he unplugs the telephones and sits swivelling in the Commissioner's chair, eating Belgian chocolates. They have melted in the humid night's heat, and he sucks his fingers while Calcutta devours itself alive. Rumour also has it that he sits at the Commissioner's desk answering three separate telephones, giving commands to keep the peace, eating nothing all night but his fingernails.

'We barricaded the bridges and alleys into the Hindu neighbourhoods so they couldn't get in.' 'They barricaded the bridges and alleys out of the Hindu neighbourhoods so we couldn't get out.'

'Because Suhrawardy's speech called on his Muslim crowds to march peacefully.' 'Because Suhrawardy's speech called on his Muslim gangs to march on the Hindus.'

'That schemer Jinnah knows all about it.' 'That dreamer Jinnah doesn't know a thing about it.'

Direct Action.

Did you hear? The Muslims are banding together to descend on the Hindu neighbourhoods. The Hindu neighbourhoods are banding together to descend on the Muslims.

There is no going back now to how things were. There is no forgetting.

There is no end.

Rumour painted with a thousand tongues climbs aboard the trains, joining the people who flee the city bearing nothing but their stories. Their tongues are its tongues, and they tell their stories.

Word spreads. Blood spreads on the pavement, ink spreads in the newspapers. Black smudges on the fingers of the reading public, red smudges on the fingers of the blooded mobs. Fear is a stain that gets bigger the more thought rubs at it, a rash that gets angrier with scratching.

Calcutta is the drop of ink, of blood in a glass of clear water. The drop writhes and diffuses. And so, violence spreads to Bihar, birthplace of the Buddha, who sat under the Bodhi tree with his hand raised to say, 'Do not fear.' It spreads, too, to the mosquito-rich mud and mazy swamps—a district in the south-eastern part of Bengal, where the Ganges, mother of rivers, bleeds into the sea.

Noakhali.

21

'Why go to Noakhali? Why not Bihar?'

Huseyn Suhrawardy is sitting on a broad swing in his Calcutta bungalow, chewing betel-nut slivers. His receding black hair is parted crisply on the right, his kameez a striking white, his cheeks freshly shaven; but the sole of his foot, when he kicks back on the swing, shows pitch black. The League's top man in Bengal is entertaining an illustrious guest, who insists on sitting on the tile floor and has just refused a gracious rose sherbet.

'Because I am called there,' says Gandhi.

'Muslims are dying in Bihar. The mobs cut up their bodies and dump them in wells so the rest die of thirst. Whole districts will be emptied of us. The few Muslims who flee to the police get accused of starting the violence. Get thrown in a room and beaten with lathis. Bihar has a *Congress* government in charge, you know. The road there is quite good. Why not go there? They are calling out for any help they can get.'

'I have said I would fast unto death if it did not stop.'

'Thirty thousand,' says Suhrawardy. 'Qaid-i-Azam says thirty thousand of ours have died in Bihar.'

'Mr Jinnah's monocle must have quite a good lens,' says Gandhi, 'if he can count the dead from all the way in Bombay.'

This dig pleases Suhrawardy a great deal, though he reveals his pleasure with little more than a twitch of his ample nostrils. The transcendence is breaking down; the holy man is getting irritated. Gandhi's hand creeps down to his own calf and massages it, as though working out a cramp. Jinnah's name has triggered an ache.

'The Qaid gets daily reports of our Muslim dead.'

'Everyone is our dead. All his dead are my dead, too.'

'Then go to Bihar, Gandhiji. I can arrange a chauffeured car for you and your ... entourage. You will be in Bihar by sundown.'

'What is happening in Noakhali? You can tell me.'

Suhrawardy frowns. 'I am telling you not to go to Noakhali for your own good. It was a wet, bug-ridden hell even before this.'

'There is a story that Christ went down into hell.'

Worldly Mr Suhrawardy, given pause by that one, swings passively to a stop. 'Did Christ get malaria?'

Well, thinks Suhrawardy, *let Mahatma Christ go down among the devils*. Suhrawardy himself overflew the killing zone last month in a plane, along with some Britishers. No way to get troops into the place. The mobs had taken precautions, felling trees and flipping boats to block the canals, smashing and igniting the bridges. Smoke flowed skyward, perpendicular to the darkened rivers, which carried a debris of planks and bodies to the sea ... *Let old Gandhi go on his little walking tour. Let him see his fill of what men can do to men, and what men can do to women. Maybe then he will concede that hacking the country in half is the best way to keep it from burning alive.*

The winter Gandhi goes to Noakhali, Jinnah goes to London. The British Government flies out Nehru and Jinnah together. They say nothing to each other for the whole plane ride. They say nothing while sullenly buttering rolls at either elbow of the King of England. They even meet with different politicians. Nehru visits Sir Stafford Cripps, the fellow socialist. Jinnah visits Sir Winston Churchill.

'Romeo y Julieta?'

Jinnah is lean, Churchill corpulent; Jinnah is dark, Churchill white—but the two smoke in a camaraderie of convenience in the library, under shelves full of Churchill's own books. Campaigns against Boers, Abyssinians, fuzzy-wuzzies—imperial skirmishes all, dwarfed by the World War he concluded. Churchill has lost most of the hair off his head, and he possesses nothing like a neck. His chins and jowls layer directly on to his shoulders.

Jinnah's meetings with the Tory leadership have gone well. They have been fighting Congress for three decades and regard Congress as the cause for upstart India's demands for independence in the first place. Fortunately, they have quite forgotten Jinnah's own Congress days.

Churchill has taken Jinnah aside for a tête-à-tête. This, Jinnah knows, is how the fates of nations are decided—in private rooms in European capitals, over a decanter. This library means more than a dozen Simla conferences.

'I would take you to Chequers and show you the garden and the main wall, if it were not so cold,' Churchill begins. 'I built the wall, you know, with the might of my arm. I injured it some time ago—in India, in fact, on the quay at Bombay. I played polo with the 4th Hussars with my arm strapped to my chest.'

Jinnah waits. Superfluities of cigar and reminiscence are formalities of friendship, as in a meeting between tribal chieftains.

'As to the matter we have spoken of in our correspondence,' says the sonorous orator, 'you should know our friendship and concern for your cause holds firm.'

This strikes Jinnah as dismayingly vague. 'We supported you in the war years and stayed firm through Gandhi's rabble-rousing. I do not claim Pakistan as our reward for that. I claim it as a human right.'

Churchill takes the cigar from his mouth. 'Of course, of course,' he mutters half-heartedly.

'If we don't get it, we will live as the Jews under Hitler. The Hindus will be two hundred million Hitlers to us.'

Churchill nods vigorously. 'I have been saying for years that the Indians are unfit for self-rule. A naturally slavish people require a noble and decent master. That is simply the best way for them to get on. If one places such a people in power, they shall be petty, vengeful, cruel.' Churchill looks at Jinnah, his eyebrows rising. 'By *Indians*, of course, I mean the Hindoos. The Muslims are another matter entirely. They are a virile race.'

'There is much in common between the old Muslim empires and the British one.'

Churchill's lips and eyes flatten into a smile. 'There is indeed a similarity. These are empires that improve their subjects. If *we* got rid of suttee and thugee, who knows what Hindoo practices the Muslim got rid of when *he* took charge a thousand years ago?' He strikes his armrest. 'Abomination upon abomination.'

The afternoon is progressing nicely, with glass after glass of sherry, but still no assurance about Pakistan.

'I shall write to you as "Mrs Gilliatt", which is my secretary's name. Any notes that treat of delicate arrangements between ourselves should be read by the light of a match, Mr Jinnah—while the paper is blackening.' Churchill stops and seems to have an idea. 'I say. Have you thought of proselytizing among their Untouchables? If you persuaded Ambedkar to convert, he would bring the Untouchables along with him, and you could increase your bloc twofold.' He holds two fingers up in his famous 'V'.

'Ambedkar is an ally against Congress and caste-Hindu rule. But matters are not as simple as that.'

The old boy frowns, displeased that Jinnah has not pounced on the plan as genius. 'Well, take care that Gandhi does not get his hands on them.'

'Gandhi has been courting them for decades, unsuccessfully. Gandhi is a political nullity in any case. He used to make salt, but now he has turned to salt.'

'And glucose! You must not forget the glucose they slip in his water whenever he declares a fast.'

'Some people, even within Congress, wish *Gandhi* would quit India. They think him a nuisance. A senile meddler.'

'We've outlasted him in the end, you and I,' Churchill says gleefully. 'I may not hold the highest office any longer, but you will see that *I* am not senile or irrelevant. Quite the contrary.' He leans mischievously towards Jinnah. 'Of course, I *do* still make myself a nuisance. And I meddle. But then I have always been doing that.'

'So, you will support Pakistan in the House of Commons?'

'In every house I visit,' Churchill says, his eyes suddenly shut with determination, his jaw thrust forward. 'And that includes His Majesty's.'

Noakhali. Barefoot.

Gandhi's associates and disciples trail behind him. Only Manu is at the front. He holds her forearm tenderly as he sets out on a dirt road. A short letter had beckoned her to his side again, one without blandishment or begging. All he had to do was sign it *Your mother*. She knew that they would revert to their former arrangement, and she wanted to regain that intimacy. This past week, reunited with her 'mother,' she has been sleeping the best she has slept in months, even in the train compartment, where they could not share each other's warmth completely. Being close to him is enough. Her feet do not ache.

A shallow expanse of dark water, and a boat by a jetty. The Ganga's thick braid unravels in this part of the country. *In one way*, he thinks, *this too is holy water*. These swamps derive their moisture from the mother river. The outboard motor starts, and the vibrations carry through his pelvic bones, without buffer of fat or much muscle, deep into his pelvis. His legs spread a few inches, and his knee rests against Manu's. He regards this stirring with detachment. It is vigour he can redirect; it comes from his spirit, and he can return it to spiritual ends by force of will. Because he is in control. He is in total control of his stomach, his lungs, his desire. All these appetites he will plough back into his soul, like dung into soil, and so his desire will improve and enrich him. This is not an evil. This is a source of strength. And he will need to be strong in Noakhali.

'Twelve families used to fish there,' says one of his guides. 'Twelve families. They were among the first.'

He is drawing Gandhi's attention to a smashed clutch of huts on the water's edge. They look as though a typhoon has blown through, except the trees are still standing. Something in Bengali Gandhi cannot read has been painted on a standing wall. The sloppy red paint has dripped to the earth.

More walking until nightfall. It is November, and when the temperature drops, Gandhi wraps a shawl around himself. They enter a forest of areca palms. He is on the outskirts of the first Noakhali village. A black snake stops him, and he plants his stick on the dirt road upright, like a diviner's staff. The snake twists off the road and leads him to a twilit gully. At the end of it is the husk of a shack. Part of it burnt weeks ago, and this gives it the look of a building cast half in shadow.

The man inside joins his hands and drifts to his knees at the sight of Gandhi. He is alone, but he wasn't always. He weeps, and when Gandhi asks if he can stay the night, he answers with more weeping. Gandhi guides him to his feet again, and the man rushes inside to offer him, in one hand, a tin with two cold chapattis sitting in it, in the other hand, inexplicably, a woman's earring.

The mosquitoes make bold all night. They have no care for stealth. He can hear them in his ears, but he never slaps them dead, not even when he sees one settle and drink by moonlight. The parts of their bodies that are not covered will get bitten. He sleeps clothed that night, but close. The next morning, he asks one of his aides to find mosquito netting.

Their pilgrimage steps out. The Gujarati hymn he sings to himself draws some children, barefoot like him, out of the shadows. They peek from up ahead in the road and scatter, skipping, when he extends a hand in their direction. Soon they have made it a game, and he stretches his arm dramatically, lunging a little, to amuse them.

At the first cluster of huts, no one comes out to see him. He sits down beside a water pump and waits. It is not a deserted village. He can sense their gazes like the heat of so many freshly banked fires. So now he reaches under the folds of his shawl and produces a blue rubber ball, no bigger than an apple. He whistles and bounces it towards a shuttered shop. By its fourth bounce, just before it dies out in a roll, a boy about eight years old springs over a low wall and grabs it with both hands. Gandhi waits, nods, holds out his hand. Another child emerges several feet behind him, and another, and then, at a rough gate, one of the parents. The laughter of children breaks the spell.

In village after village, they start showing him their wounds, telling him their stories. Sometimes Hindu families come out with small plates of kumkum and wayside flowers to make a shrine of him. Sometimes Muslim families, believing he has come to damn them, hide in their kitchens and wait for him to pass by. But they can only hold out so long against the tapping of his knuckles on the door, the appearance of his bald head at the window. A father comes out and demands what he wants, and he tells his Bengali interpreter, 'I want to sit with you.' Within an hour, the courtyard is packed with Muslim strangers in beards and caps inspecting the Mahatma for themselves. They keep waiting for rancour from him. They know he has just come from the neighbouring village where survivors have been telling him about their daughter Mausami, now Mumtaz; or the whole Pal family roped together and set alight; or the forty converts of Krishnaganj, crowbars taken to the backs of their knees, brows forced to the earth in namaaz, the crowd hooting and clapping. Did that happen at all? Where is the proof, other than words said and words heard—other than hearsay? Is Noakhali reality? Is Bihar reality? Or was it all just Rumour painted with a thousand tongues?

Gandhi does not accuse anyone of anything. Not even of hunkering down and waiting it out while strangers from another district torched that house but not this one, this body but not that one.

He tells them instead that decent people outnumber men without consciences, and that kind people outnumber cruel ones. 'Didn't your fathers and grandfathers live as neighbours? What changed when you saw those headlines in the *Star of India*?'

'It wasn't the newspaper,' says one man, unexpectedly. 'I got a telegram from my sister in Calcutta.' Another bold voice asks,

'Are all Mussalmaans the same?' And that man's uncle says, 'A few do these things, and all of us get the blame.' And a fourth man: 'This is a pious family. You will go back and tell the world about the Muslims of Noakhali, but we did nothing but fear God and lose family in the city.' A fifth: 'Those goondas were not our sons. When they came through, Gandhiji, we feared for our lives, too.' And the first man, shaking his head: 'I lost two brothers and a nephew in Calcutta, Gandhiji. I didn't need a newspaper to make me angry.'

Gandhi joins his hands and nods at his translator. 'Tell them, I know they have done nothing wrong. Tell them, please.'

'Then why is he talking to us? Let him find the thugs doing these things and preach to them. Muslim or Hindu. Let him find the culprits.'

Under their reproaches is hurt and rage and fear. Distrust, too—but is Gandhi immune to it? He can scarcely admit to himself that he glances up at the shuttered windows when he stands outside a Muslim house.

In the almonds a Hindu grandmother places gratefully in his mouth after he prays with her at a household shrine, he tastes a bitter brackish kerosene taste. No matter what is said to him, or against the others, no matter how high a voice rises, he does not flee a single house.

The partition of this area, he realizes, would be a mere formality now. It has already happened. It has already been *made* to happen, and not by him, and not by 'the British'.

By one man, he thinks. *One man*.

There are no murmured monologues at night any more. He just whimpers, naked in the foetal position under the mosquito netting, 'What should I do? What should I do?'

What he does: he spins thirty yards of cloth a day in that burnt-out washerman's house. He reads and answers letters from Sardar Patel, Nehru, and dozens of politicians around the country—always writing that no, his duty is here, he will not come back to Delhi. He has Manu read him four newspapers an afternoon, including the League's own *Star of India* and *Dawn*. He visits his seventy-second village, his seventy-third ... And still the only refrain in his head, the only refrain in Manu's ears, is 'What should I do? What should I do?' Because he knows he is accomplishing nothing, reversing nothing, healing nothing. Most of the worst violence was over by the time he arrived anyway. He knows it is time to go.

As for the perpetrators, they find him. In his last weeks in Noakhali, as night falls, shapes break through the shadows and shatter bottles on the ground before his bare feet. He waits while brooms are fetched and the shards are swept away. Bloody shirts are found hanging from the areca palms one morning outside the washerman's house. A cow's head lies across his path, one of its horns stabbing a paper that says, in English, 'Hindu go home.'

He does, in January. By then, the British Empire is just a month away from making a major announcement. Lord Wavell is to be replaced as Viceroy of India.

Enter Dickie Mountbatten.

PART FIVE

Objections

It will not be easy to discern the difference between them, lost as it is amongst such a number of circumstances in which they resemble each other. If, however, we examine them in detail, as we might some piece of poetry…

—Plutarch, *Parallel Lives*

22

'Mr Gandhi, a pleasure. Mr Jinnah, a pleasure. Mr Gandhi, it is an honour. Mr Jinnah, do sit down.'

The DC-17 is in the skies over Slovenia right now. Dickie Mountbatten has ensconced himself in the sole bathroom for the sake of its mirror, to which he is introducing himself repeatedly. Occasionally he tilts his chin down and to the side and raises an eyebrow, flattering an imaginary Gandhi/Jinnah by finding his point interesting. He likes this effect, the dip of the chin leftward as the right eyebrow rises. Also, the rise of both eyebrows and a slight pursing of the lips, which says, 'Yes, you have brought up a grave matter, and I am taking it into consideration.'

Dickie gets distracted, as Dickie often does, this time by a fleck of lettuce in his teeth from a sandwich he ate over Bremen. He picks it out with the fingernail of his little finger and lifts his lip to scan the rest of his teeth, which are lovely, symmetrical and white. Then he drops the lip, and his face returns to its default gaze, which is also lovely, symmetrical and white. It's a Profoundly Regal Gaze that he knows is not the result of breeding; there are dozens of princes who look like cretins and ogres, viz. every Hapsburg with an atrocious five-inch chin. His smile in the mirror mirrors Fortune's smile on him. This closet of a bathroom is hardly claustrophobic in such charming company.

'The question, Mr Gandhi, is whether we can ensure ...' he says. And then, distracted, turning his head the other way: 'What we must do, Mr Jinnah, is reach a settlement acceptable to all parties.'

A few moments later, the face takes on a more philosophical cast. In a rather Rodinesque manner, he rests his perfectly proportioned Battenberg chin on his fist; the bottom half of him sits on the loo, khaki field trousers around his ankles. He is thinking about which medals he ought to wear to the swearing-in ceremony. *Why not all of them? All of them, then.*

To the mirror again, while he buckles his belt: 'I say, Archie, bloody thankless lot they are.' Or no, try this one: 'Winston sends his regards.' Dickie clears his throat and tries harder. 'Winston's been singing your praises—"Wavell's done a fine job of it," he told me just the other day—but you know, it's a new order, with Labour in, and all that. If it were Winston instead of Attlee—well, you know how it is, Archie. It's fallen to me to pack us up, what?'

He puts a little more gravitas in his face.

'Is it true what they say, that these chaps can't be reconciled? It's fallen to me, it seems. It seems it's fallen to me.'

The plane is over Jerusalem by the time Lord Louis Francis Albert Victor Nicholas Mountbatten, finished with his time alone, sits back down in his seat. Across the aisle is his wife Lady Edwina, who claps her Maugham novel shut.

'*Finally*,' she mutters, rising. Dickie raises both eyebrows and purses his lips. Edwina has been sipping the in-flight champagne a little recklessly, and her knee has been bobbing since the clouds over Belgrade. If they had been in a hotel, she might have rapped on the door and told him to finish his admirations; but there are five other officials on board this plane with them, and a lady must not seem overeager to piss.

Inside the poorly ventilated closet, she is assaulted by her film-star-handsome, blue-blooded husband's stink. Rage and disgust force her hand across her nose and mouth. Back outside, she finds His Serene Highness lying back with his eyes shut, his military cap tilted forward, lovely and symmetrical, at ease in his skin. But he's not asleep; he has just the thing to help with her mood. One eye opens rather rakishly.

'I have a gift for you, Edwina. Or shall I call you Vicereine?'

He brings out a flat velvet box and, reaching over, sets it with great self-satisfaction on her reopened novel. Edwina pops it open impatiently and sees a diamond-studded tiara made by Dickie's friends at Cartier and snaps it shut again. 'What is this trash?' she mutters. She drops it at her feet, under the seat in front of her, kicks off her shoes, and rests her heels on it. Dickie knows Edwina's moods well enough to give up, so he relaxes into his seat, tilts his cap forward, and closes his eyes again.

He isn't dreaming. She isn't reading.

She is thinking about Dickie's profile; how it belongs on a coin; how his face, though lovely and symmetrical, is the most unkissable face on earth. In Shakespeare somewhere—*Romeo and Juliet*, was it?—the nurse calls some empty eligible bachelor a *man o' wax*, and that is what Dickie is, a wax figure who belongs in a wax museum. Not in a full-blooded woman's bed. She has studied the problem of his unkissability, his sexual nullity for years now. It is a sort of metaphysical conundrum for her.

The top half of his face, she thinks sometimes, does not have the same flexibility of musculature, the same animation, as that of other men. His eyes do not soften when he kisses. But the lower half of his face has its own problems. It is pleasing—*necessary*, really—for a woman to see her body wrench, twist, torture pleasure out of a man at that moment. Dickie, back when they used to make love, simply expelled himself and rolled over. Never the slightest grimace of pleasure. Her lovers proved to her she had the power to wipe the civilization off an Englishman's face. Her lovers were not men of wax. Their faces might have been less lovely than Dickie's, less symmetrical, but they were living faces of living men, not marble busts from Westminster Abbey. Faces that crushed and gasped and sometimes even sobbed with gratitude.

Why hadn't she noticed any of this when she and Dickie first met? Edwina had been distracted by his title, his height, his grace on the dance floor. His dispassionate air had seemed a virtue, back then. No distress could touch him or any woman on his arm.

India should have been a tender, nostalgic trip. Dickie had proposed to her in Delhi after countless letters and two dances at the Viceregal Lodge. And now, they were returning to India as Viceroy and Vicereine—full circle. How sweet; funny how kismet works ... Though all it meant for her was hour after hour of posing in ermine and a silly tiara, playing Vicereine and hating it, and meanwhile watching Dickie play Viceroy in full fig, covered in military stripes and medals, like a wax statue of himself—and hating how much *he* was loving it.

Just as she hates how Dickie has yachted away from her resentment across the placid sea of his sleep. Not a cloud in the mind. He awakes, look, just in time to hurry off to the bathroom again and touch himself up before touchdown at Palam Airfield. On the tarmac, several officials shake Lord and Lady Mountbatten's hands with small bows and brief kind words. She squints at them in the late morning sunlight. Hard to believe that these are the rebels and marchers, hell-bent on kicking out the schoolhouse-building, railroad-laying British Empire. From the civil way they wait shoulder to shoulder, it is just as hard to believe they are, simultaneously, at each other's throats. Dickie's staff members spent an early part of the flight reading him last-minute synopses of the gentlemen who would greet him. Dickie quickly discovered his cufflinks, so he may or may not have been listening, but Edwina had paid attention, and she greets each of them on the tarmac.

Here is Liaquat Ali Khan, Mr Jinnah's right-hand man for the Pakistan movement. She thinks: roundish and bald and bespectacled, every inch a senior bank manager.

Here is Sardar Patel, an associate of Mr Gandhi's. Old and sleepy-looking; but sleepy like an alligator. And with the most startling vise of a handshake.

And here is Mr Jawaharlal Nehru, another associate of Mr Gandhi's, who recognizes her from several months back at a reception in Burma, where they had had a gay time. He dives to kiss the back of her hand, his eyes sparkling. His wide mouth moves animatedly as he asks what book that is, under her arm. Edwina thinks to herself: *Welcome to India, indeed.*

'...And then they strolled off to the limousine,' says Liaquat, 'chattering like long-lost friends.'

Lahore, two days later. Jinnah is smoking; Fatima is pacing; Liaquat is complaining.

'Apparently, they had met one another in Burma at some point. Lord Mountbatten scarcely said two words to Lord Wavell, at least in my presence. Nehru monopolized him, and very soon the Mountbattens were paying court to Nehru instead of the other way around. They were smitten with him.

At the ceremony, and afterwards, too, I found myself standing next to Patel. Not the easiest fellow to make conversation with.'

'Nehru is a seducer, a charmer.' Fatima folds her arms across her chest. 'And from what I have heard, Lady Edwina quite enjoys being seduced.'

Jinnah shrugs. 'It could work to our advantage, Fati. Suppose Mountbatten grows jealous of our Kashmiri Romeo?'

'Far likelier his wife will bias him in Nehru's favour.' Liaquat shakes his head. 'I saw them, Qaid, the three of them together. Laughing and nudging each other.'

'You are both forgetting what these people are *like*,' Fati insists. 'The husband on his way out tips his hat to the rival on his way in, and afterwards all three meet up for cocktails and snooker. That is marriage among the British upper crust. No morals. They are not Muslims. They are not—*anything*.'

Jinnah crushes his cigarette in the tray. 'They are smoke. They are all smoke. What did you learn about him, Liaquat?'

'The British guests were remarkably quick to speak ill of him. I scarcely had to pry. They all think he has gotten where he has because of his birth, and because he is Churchill's personal favourite. The two have in common a certain love of mad schemes. Mountbatten used to hatch fantastic plans during the war. A Navy officer told me "Dickie" tried to carve an aircraft carrier out of ice. Needless to say, the real military men paid him no mind.'

'Dickie?'

'His nickname. I am told they flew him about to inspect troops during the War. He photographs well.'

'Well, if Dickie does like fantastic plans,' says Jinnah, 'I shall see what he thinks of mine.'

Three days later, Jinnah pulls in at the Viceroy's mansion in Delhi.

He sizes up his opponent's armour immediately. Dickie sallies forward in a grey pinstripe with black tie. Jinnah counters with an off-white three-piece suit, a white handkerchief in the lapel and a gold tie with crimson dots and circles.

Handshakes, a few pleasantries. As soon as the door closes, Jinnah lays out his objections to the Cabinet Mission Plan—how its 'weak centre' would become a strong centre as soon as the last Britisher had sailed for home.

Dickie, scarcely listening, leans back and puts his hands behind his head, like a man in a lounge, listening to music. He crosses one leg over the other, and presently the shoe nearest Jinnah begins to bob in the air. For a moment Dickie has the look of some bored schoolchild going into a reverie. Then, without warning, he begins to recite his own life story, or rather the parts of it that have touched on India.

'I toured here with the future King back in 1920. We even rode atop a camel. David quite enjoyed it. During the War, you know, I ran all the operations in Southeast Asia from Kandy, in Ceylon. Rather rainy! Have you been there, Mr Jinnah?'

Jinnah says nothing, confused at this sudden turn.

'The monks fetishize a tooth of the Buddha. Or at least they *say* it's his tooth. I believe the first time I ever tasted sugar-cane juice was right here in Delhi...'

Dickie is trying to set Jinnah at ease the only way he knows how, by the magnetism of his own personality and conversation. Businesslike Mr Jinnah has never encountered anything like it. He is relieved when he hears photographers clamouring on the verandah. Lady Mountbatten has appeared, a pearl choker round her overlong sun-spotted neck.

Perhaps this was what Mountbatten's admirers meant by his 'charm'? Fati had counselled her brother to play charming; the Mountbattens, never at a loss for charm, she said, could only by charm be won. *This is a play like any other*, thinks Jinnah, *with costumes and scripted lines*.

He has kept a line in reserve for this moment: the inevitable photograph of Viceroy, Vicereine and himself. The blocking plays against his timing. Lady Mountbatten slips to Jinnah's left, and as he stands between the couple (part of his mind still puzzling over the Viceroy's odd monologue), the line says itself, trippingly off his tongue.

'A rose,' says Jinnah, 'between two thorns.'

He looks to his left and realizes the gaffe immediately. Lady Mountbatten says nothing, but the Viceroy throws his head back and laughs, as though Jinnah has made a sly jest. The three of them stand and chat for the photographers.

'I say, Mr Jinnah, tell us about your time in England. I'm quite curious.'

Jinnah thinks: *So, this is what it is to be charming, in these circles. To feign familiarity, to feign interest*. He plays along. 'I dreamt of playing Romeo at the Old Vic. I even signed on with a Shakespeare troupe.'

Edwina says, listlessly, 'Oh do recite for us, won't you, Mr Jinnah? We would love to hear something.'

Jinnah clears his throat. He recites a dozen lines from *Lear*—the ones about the division of the kingdom.

Meantime we shall express our darker purpose.
Give me the map there.

23

That map is burning at the edges. The violence across the Raj has not abated. Twenty-five have just been killed in the far Northwest Province, including a Congress minister, a Muslim unforgivably opposed to the Qaid. In Bihar, twelve Hindu men pin a six-year-old Muslim boy under the surface of a pond. They use a long pole, and from a distance they look like rescuers. Machetes are even now rising and diving in the Bengali jute fields.

Here, though, Jinnah and Mountbatten are talking about the issues. They discuss these matters in perfect security.

'Pakistan,' says Mountbatten, 'is only one idea of many.'

'It is already a fact in the hearts of India's Muslims. Now we are simply pushing to get the map to reflect the fact.'

The two gentlemen face each other and do not notice when blood sprays obliquely across the window of the Viceroy's study.

'Pakistan need not be considered an inevitability, Mr Jinnah. There are other ways to arrive at a settlement.'

'Pakistan is inevitable because we will it.'

'Because you want it.'

'Because our nation wills its own nation-state.'

'There are alternatives to partitioning India. May we agree on that, at least?'

'Yes, agreed. May we also agree that all such alternatives are unacceptable?'

'That is contingent on your attitude, Mr Jinnah. That is not contingent on the facts.'

'My attitude *is* a fact.'

The two men do not flinch when a bullet webs and then a brick shatters the window. Their laps are full of unnoticed shards.

'I demand what I demand to spare India a civil war,' says Jinnah, 'which will result, I suspect, in a Pakistan anyway, only with mass death beforehand. A civil war would be a terrible legacy for *you* to leave us. The historians would never forgive you.'

Dickie looks aghast—either at the prospective slaughter of millions, or the prospective disapproval of a future Edward Gibbon. Black smoke rises in the distance. A telephone rings in a far room, and when an aide picks up, hysterical garbled shrieking comes through the receiver.

'But why should there be a civil war?' Mountbatten remarks. 'Because one community's most extreme demand is not met?'

'Because the Muslims must have Pakistan.'

'Who the devil put the Pakistan idea in their heads, Mr Jinnah?'

'Is that a rhetorical question?'

'I only say that if it were put there, it ought to be possible to take it back out.'

'We are speaking of an idea, Lord Mountbatten. Not a wine-cork.'

The nymph in the fountain out front starts vomiting blood in a graceful arc.

'But if we do this,' says Dickie, 'the problem of minorities shall not go away. We will solve one minority problem and create a new one.'

'But the *present* problem will be solved.'

'*Your* problem. You will simply flip the majority. And you have not even accounted for the Sikhs of the Punjab.'

A talwar flashes just outside the broken window.

'My Sikh problem will solve itself. Or rather *I* shall solve it, once I get Pakistan.'

'How so?'

'I will assure the Sikhs they will be treated fairly.'

'I should like to hear what the Sikhs think of that.'

'If you cannot conceive that I should treat *my* minorities fairly, what makes you think Sardar Patel will treat *his* any better?'

A train blasts through the hallway just outside the door, and steam hisses around the door frame. The sound overwhelms a simultaneous burst of gunfire. Neither gentleman registers all this. Their voices remain level.

'But there will still be a minority of Muslims in this rump Hindustan,' says Dickie. 'Only a smaller minority, weaker by ninety million. The numbers, Jinnah, look at the numbers.'

'I know the numbers. If I have a fair *number* of theirs at my mercy, they will think twice before they maltreat their Muslims. It will serve as a check, this threat of tit for tat.'

More gunfire. The walls around the Viceregal mansion have erupted in a rash of hate graffiti.

'But this is taking hostages, Mr Jinnah.'

'And *giving* hostages.'

'I should like to hear what the Sikhs say about this, too.'

'There are two nations on the subcontinent. The Sikhs are not one of them.'

'The Sikhs may think otherwise.'

'Does Spain bother about her Basques? Does she wiggle her borders about to please them? There are tiny tribes everywhere.'

'They shall not give over. They are a warlike people.'

A grenade explodes on the grounds. Stray dogs streak howling through a broken gate.

'The British divided and ruled,' says Jinnah. 'Now let them divide and run.'

'We keep coming back to this point.'

'I repeat my point and repeat my point because I have only one point to make.'

'What point is that?'

'Have I made a secret of it? This is the third day of our talks. Do I play games, or have I been direct and straightforward with you from the beginning?'

'Pakistan, you mean.'

The walls are burning now. A rafter drops a few feet away. Neither gentleman coughs on the thickening smoke.

'I see I have made the point I came to make. Are we quite finished?'

'Mr Nehru and Mr Patel will never agree to it.'

'They will both agree to it, eventually.'

'Mr Gandhi—'

'Is irrelevant.'

Another train: this one derails itself, an accordion of metal and spilled petrol, just outside, on the lawn. The conversation continues; the eye contact never breaks.

'Britain has stated its intention to leave. Mr Gandhi is hardly likely to come around on this matter of partition, and he is more influential than you credit.'

'Nehru and Patel will both agree, in spite of what Mr Gandhi tells them.'

'Either the League reaches a settlement, or the League is left out of India's first government. Either way, we shall be gone by June of next year.'

A calendar starts ripping its own pages off, just beyond Dickie's shoulder. It hangs on the wall between two flaming bookshelves, under a clock whose hour and minute hands are swivelling in opposite directions.

'Nehru and Patel will concede to partition well before then,' says Jinnah confidently.

'When?'

'When they hate me more than they love Gandhi. Which should be any day now.'

Jinnah stands up, and so does Dickie, and the smoke clears and the flames go out and the grounds tidy themselves up before either man's eyes so much as glance out the window, which has sealed back up like water. They shake hands. Both men are exhausted and want to sleep early. Both have places to be tomorrow.

Jinnah's next meeting is in Bombay, with his doctor. Mountbatten's is here in Delhi, with Gandhi.

Nehru brings Bapu gingerly out of the car, holding his elbow, a hand resting on his shoulder, like a dutiful son assisting his infirm father. Gandhi has had some leg pains and vomiting for the past two days—nothing unfamiliar, his usual 'nerves', cured with guava and prayers. The Mountbattens hurry down the steps to meet them, to the delight of the photographers.

Edwina thinks it would be the most natural thing in the world to kiss Jawaharlal on either cheek right now, in the Continental fashion; but it is a mad, improper impulse, particularly in front of so many photographers, and she checks it, astonished at herself. Instead, she turns her attention to the

Mahatma, and she watches the way Nehru looks at him, this reverent tenderness. It is not a look she has seen on other men before. She has known only aristocrats, rich men, imperious each in his own way. She has never until now seen how self-abasement can ennoble a man.

She leans close to Gandhi, wanting him to like her, and wanting Nehru to see him liking her. The last time she felt this way, uneasy, eager, desperate to charm, was when she first met Dickie's parents. Gandhi behaves far more kindly to her than those blue-blooded, erstwhile Battenbergs did to a Jewish banker's granddaughter. Gandhi smiles instantly and whispers, 'Lady Edwina, you can be my walking stick,' as he places his child-light hand on her shoulder and follows her into the mansion.

After she drops Gandhi off to have his talk with Dickie, Nehru and she take the chance to walk the grounds together. Neither makes a formal proposal to the other. Eye contact is invitation enough.

'How has he felt about his talks so far?'

'The past few days have been spent with Mr Jinnah.'

'My condolences.'

Edwina smiles. 'He is a lawyer, and the talks were a ... trial.'

'Jinnah is a mediocre lawyer. His problem was that he could never win any *sympathy* for his defendants. He spent his days preparing last wills for rich men in Bombay, and a lucrative business it was. The man is a remarkable miser, you know?'

'Really? With such impressive cufflinks?'

'Imagine how much he must mint to allow himself such finery.'

'How did he end up in politics?'

'Temperament. He is a contentious fellow. Drawing up wills could hardly satisfy that side of his nature.'

'I believe Dickie saw a little of that.'

'What was his impression of Jinnah, after three days closeted with the man?'

Edwina gives Nehru a sidelong look. 'I could not *possibly* betray my husband's confidence.'

'Don't think of it as betraying Dickie.' And then, in a stage whisper: 'Think of it as betraying Jinnah.'

Leaning closer, Edwina matches his stage whisper. 'He says Jinnah is a psychopath.'

Nehru laughs, but not at the absurdity of this, rather out of delight. 'I suppose that is the only word for him, isn't it? And what does he say about ... Jawaharlal?'

She stops and turns to him; he stops, too, and the sun is behind him, so she shades her eyes and squints to gaze at him. 'Why, nothing at all.'

'Nothing?'

'*I* do all the talking about Jawaharlal.'

She turns and continues walking, her pace quickened, her companion taking a few hurried steps to keep up.

Inside the Viceroy's study, in the same chair where his rival sat the day before, Gandhi asks, 'How was your meeting with Mr Jinnah?'

'Fruitful,' says Dickie, shifting in his seat.

'There would be hundreds of miles between Karachi in the west and Dacca in the east. The two cities speak different languages. You see how his Pakistan is unnatural.'

'I did bring up those points. With a map, no less.'

'And what did our dear friend say to that?'

'He told me the distance between London and New Delhi. Four thousand one hundred and sixty-eight miles. And he added that he expected to get Calcutta as well.'

'I want to visit Calcutta,' says Edwina, 'and all the other cities where there has been unrest. I want to arrange for relief. Medicines and gauze and such.'

'Unrest is not the word for it. I fear the word is carnage. And it may yet get worse.'

Nehru's eyes have softened, his voice has shaken a little, and she is fascinated—after a lifetime spent among stiff upper lips—by his instant and extreme emotion. Without premeditation, without a thought, she slides her arm around his elbow. 'I am not as fragile as you think.'

Her bare arm is hard and freckled against his sleeve. Her chin is stronger than her husband's; her body, or what he can feel of it, as hard as a boy's. 'I know you are strong, but I still ought to accompany you,' he says. 'For support.'

'If you wish. I shall keep smelling salts in my purse.'

'That would be wise.'

'In case you faint.'

'...Then there is the matter of the independent kingdoms,' Dickie is saying. 'Substantial kingdoms, really—Kashmir, Hyderabad ... I suppose if they refused to join either India or Pakistan, we would have another Balkan situation.'

Gandhi's hand creeps nervously over his left chest, and he rubs at the pressure he feels there. 'You are thinking of Pakistan as a possibility. Your words reveal it.'

'It is one of the options, isn't it? You yourself discussed the ramifications.'

'I discuss it as an absurd fantasy. Not as a possible reality.' Gandhi shakes his head and leans forward as though nauseated. 'Lord Mountbatten, I have an inner voice.'

'No doubt, no doubt,' Dickie says. Increasingly, he senses Gandhi might be a man who has aged into senile innocence. Maybe it's the contrast of Gandhi's meek, soft-spoken style so soon after precise and cutting Jinnah. Maybe it's sentences like *I have an inner voice*. 'The voice of conscience. Very important.'

'It is a not a metaphor, Lord Mountbatten. I listen for it. In my darkest hours, I cannot hear it. But then I listen for it, and I honour its counsel.'

Dickie smiles obligingly. 'And what is it saying now, Mr Gandhi?'

'All I hear is sobbing.'

'I would love to show you Kashmir,' says Nehru. 'Dal Lake. The flowers in bloom.'

'I hear it resembles Switzerland?'

'Switzerland is pretty. Kashmir is beautiful.'

'I suspect you are biased, Jawahar.'

'Only the eyes of a lover can see the beauty of a place in full. A place or a person. I am more clear-eyed about Kashmir than other people because my people come from there.'

'The Pandits?' she says, with a touch of hesitation. She is rewarded by his delight at her knowledge.

'Yes—we are Kashmiri Pandits. Did I mention that before?'

'I don't believe so.'

'Kashmir used to be ours, long ago.' He takes a deep breath, closing his eyes, savouring here in Delhi that healing, ancestral Himalayan air. The people of Kashmir are mostly Muslims now, though its Maharajah is a Hindu; Nehru's imagination flies him, not just far north, but far into the past. For a moment, he and Edwina stroll along the shore of Dal Lake; her yellow sun-dress and pearls turn into a red saree and yellow gold. 'Centuries ago. Before...'

She waits, and then: 'Before?'

Nehru shakes his head, and they are on the Viceroy's grounds again, four hundred miles south and two empires past his daydream Kashmir. 'Before history,' he sighs. 'Before all this.'

24

At dinner parties—like this one held by the Viceregal couple—Jinnah likes to sit apart and play a game. He counts how many people in attendance would like to see him die and burn in hell.

Six, by tonight's count. It is not so difficult to imagine himself burning in hell, what with this fever spiking. In time, eight: he may have to start counting the Mountbattens, if they keep swinging like earrings to either side of Pandit Nehru's smile.

There they are at the corner of the improvised dance floor. A small band of turbaned horn-players has been tucked away behind ferns. A few British couples are doing a listless, side-to-side sway. Nehru is professing incompetence, but Edwina has pulled him out a little, and now Dickie is arranging Nehru's hands, one on his wife's shoulder, the other cupping his wife's waist. Nehru winks and begins moving quite expertly with the Vicereine, who throws her head back and laughs at the ruse.

'Is this how, Dickie?'

Because apparently Nehru gets to call him 'Dickie' now. Dickie laughs, too, and puts his fists on his waist, mock-marvelling, 'My, what a quick study!'

'My, what *lese-majeste*,' murmurs Fati, at her brother's elbow.

'Let them dance,' says Jinnah. 'The music will stop for them soon enough.'

The two women were mirror images as they air-kissed each other's cheeks earlier that evening: Fatima the virgin, Edwina the vamp. Edwina's supposed beauty, brother and sister agreed, was much exaggerated in the press. Costume any slight white woman in elbow-length gloves and a tiara, and from the distance of the gallery, those bespectacled babus who write for the *Times* will see a fairy-tale princess. Up close, brother and sister saw her for the painted, ageing woman she was. *Compare my sister*, Jinnah thinks, *haloed with dark silver, her cheekbones sharper than those of the Englishwoman opposite. We Jinnahs all have superior cheekbones. Fati and I look more ruling-class than the Mountbattens tonight*.

As for Fatima, she cannot bear to watch much more of Edwina's flirtation. The Viceroy's library is on the same floor, but far enough away from the partygoers, so she carries her drink there. In one of the two chairs is a man behind a newspaper. She can tell from the dhoti, and the stubby thuggish fingers gripping the paper, who it is; but it is too late to back out now that Sardar Patel has glanced over his newspaper at her silhouette in the doorway. She dares not shy from him lest it come across as cowardice. She picks a book at her leisure and settles into the chair across from him.

'Miss Jinnah.'

'Mr Patel.'

'No dancing for you?'

'This is a good time to catch up on some reading.'

'Agreed.'

Silence.

Then, still not looking away from his paper: 'Good book?'

'I would prefer the newspaper. Such interesting times.'

Eyes fixed but not on her, he hands over a section of *The Hindu*, his fat index finger pointing unsubtly. 'Such an interesting headline.'

61 Hindus Slaughtered in Rawalpindi, she reads. 'A tragedy,' she says coldly.

'Direct Action.'

Her right eyebrow rises. 'I disagree.'

His mouth widens into a bitter smile. 'All right: Direct Result.'

'Like the slaughter of Muslims in Bihar?'

'Like the slaughter of Hindus everywhere else.'

'This is no way to make a conversation, Mr Patel.'

'This is no way to make a country, Miss Jinnah.'

Silence. This silence lasts much longer. And then, to Fati's delight, through the open window bleeds a muezzin's call to evening prayers. She smiles triumphantly, but Sardar Patel remains expressionless. Very calmly, prepared for this contingency, he produces two cotton balls from his pocket and stuffs them in his ears.

Jinnah, alone with his drink, burns against the night at 103.5 degrees. He is a smokeless fire until he lights another Craven A.

A woman, drawn by this distress signal of a castaway, takes the chair next to him. The woman is not Fati. He does not register her presence until, tentatively, she touches his arm; her hand recoils, as though she has touched the metal handle of a pan on the flame, full of occult heat.

'Sarojini Naidu,' he says, and his lips twitch ever so slightly.

She beams at him. 'Mohammed Ali Jinnah,' she sighs. 'Or should I say, Qaid-i-Azam.'

This is the same poet who, thirty years ago, proclaimed him the 'ambassador of Hindu–Muslim unity.' The same poet who posed beside Gandhi during his Salt March, a true disciple, a devotee. Thoughts rush through Jinnah's feverish head at the sight of her. The source of Gandhi's power over people is their *belief* in him. His power is not innate, so, like all holy men, he surrounds himself with followers, and their perception gives him sublimity, holiness. *Eyes* charge him up and make his gestures electric, *eyes* like so many batteries from which he draws power. Sarojini is one such follower. Confront Gandhi with a man who has no belief in him, and he weakens. What is Gandhi then? A stage actor, a pretender, exposed. *I was always that unbeliever*, thinks Jinnah. *I grounded his charge. My genius rebutted his, as, it is said, Mark Antony's was by Caesar. Mohandas the teetotaller and hard-drinking Mark Antony were not so unalike: what self-indulgence was for Antony, self-deprivation is for Gandhi. A form of excess, the proof of a lack of control. The Romans knew such men to be unfit for leadership. But I, I am always totally in control.*

'How is the Mahatma?' Jinnah asks.

'The Mahatma is greatly troubled. You know he cannot bear the thought of violence.'

'Tell him to bear the thought of Pakistan instead.'

'He is willing to offer you everything but that. Go speak to him, Jinnah.'

'We spoke in '44.'

'That was three years ago.'

'And nothing has changed. What can he offer me? It is late. Too late.' The words rush hotly out of him, and he can't tell if it's fever or anger lighting them on fire. 'Your Gandhi has been sidelined by his own disciples. By prancing Jawaharlal over there, and by Patel. He is an idol of the rabble at this point, nothing more. Besides, it is not *Congress* presenting *me* with a choice of Pakistan or nothing. *I* am presenting *them* with a choice. Pakistan, or civil war.'

Sarojini flinches as though he has struck her. 'Such coldness,' she murmurs, although what Jinnah hears is 'boldness'.

'All the problems will be solved if we simply agree to partition the territory,' insists Jinnah. 'We have toyed until now with half-measures and Byzantine solutions. No more.'

'All you used to speak of was unity, Jinnah. Now you speak of division, partition, communalism. Have you forgotten Lucknow?'

'Congress used to be a club for educated, enlightened men. Mr Gandhi turned it into a mass party. I *witnessed* it. The mobs loved him and called him "Mahatma", and he was happy. Well, now there is a mob that hates him.'

'The same mob that calls you Qaid-i-Azam?'

'Has he sent you here to work on me?'

'You are Lucifer. Look at you. You are weeping blood.'

'India is no one's Paradise to lose. You romanticize me. I am a pleader. I am plain Mr Jinnah.'

'You are many things, but plain you are not.'

'I am no poet either, Sarojini. Instruct me: what is heaven, in your Lucifer metaphor? The Indian National Congress? Is that the heaven I fell from?'

'A united India. You used to dream of it yourself, back in your Lucknow days.'

'Why was I not crowned king of heaven then? After Lucknow? Why not?'

'You are ill. You are wasting away. You are eaten up from within.'

'Because of my Muslim name, that's why. I still speak of unity. What is one, I call one. What are two, I call two. Hindustan and Pakistan.'

'India and India,' she whispers, staring at Jinnah's face with horror and pity, like a nurse in a burn ward.

Alone on the balcony, Dickie is sad. Even good-looking rich men with names like Dickie can be sad, on occasion. His sadness has nothing to do with the fact that, just behind him, in a brightly lit ballroom, his wife is falling in love with an Indian man a foot and a half shorter than he. No, Dickie is staring up at the stars, the stars familiar to him from Burma and Ceylon and all points of his Asian tours, and he is thinking about the pity of it all. The Burmese, the Indians—these fellows salaamed a man with heart, once upon a time. And they still had that humble, earnest love of the sahib in their earnest humble hearts. He could see it still in the footmen who held the doors open, and the sweaty but big-smiling cooks before their pots, and the squatting shiny gardeners who waved back as he strolled by, and the pigeon-chested man-child Gurkhas he passed in review. It was still there; it was undying, a simple love of benevolent masters. A love that was not boastful and was not proud. It could have gone on, perhaps not *forever*, but longer, had it not been for these British-educated Indian lawyers demanding British rights using British words. It was really only the intellectuals who were discontent, and they whipped up the masses against the happy order of things. The Indian *masses* would have played along for a century or more until the sahibs stepped back at last and said, 'There, boys, you are ready.' The masses would have taken the captain's wheel and steered the ship themselves. Jinnah, Gandhi, Nehru—the educated types were rushing the whole business. They got between the manly understanding that existed between the officer and his batman, between the sahib and his chaprasi. A pity that he should have to see it at all, much less see it through.

But since it has to happen, best to get it done quickly. These Hindus and Muslims are more and more at each other's throats, and Dickie is looking damnably weak back home.

Briefly the music grows louder. The balcony door has opened and shut. Sarojini Naidu hurries to his side. She savours having been his spy and confidante tonight. He raises his eyebrows questioningly, and she shakes her head.

'Thank you for trying, Miss Naidu.'

'I have never seen him so bitter. Or so thin. He looks ill.'

'I wonder how fierce he must be when well.'

'You never saw him as a young man,' Sarojini sighs. 'I did. He was brilliant, and so very handsome. What now, Lord Mountbatten? If he will not so much as speak to Gandhi?'

Dickie has gotten distracted from his sadness. In fact, he has hatched a little plan. 'Oh, I shall think of something,' he says gamely. 'I always do, you know.'

Two days later. Afternoon at the Viceroy's mansion.

'...And the League will not accept a moth-eaten Pakistan. None of the provinces should be divided. And between the eastern and the western wing, Lord Mountbatten, Pakistan will require a land corridor. Perhaps two or three miles wide, but stretching from end to end.'

'I say,' says Dickie, looking unusually fascinated, 'that is a capital idea, isn't it?'

'It is a visionary idea,' Jinnah corrects him, visibly pleased. 'Pakistan will lay down railroad tracks and a four-lane Karachi–Calcutta highway.'

Dickie checks his wristwatch discreetly. 'Eight lanes. Nothing less than eight will do.'

'An eight-lane highway, yes. Along the route will be trading posts, where Indians can purchase Pakistani goods. Also, a

Joint Stock Exchange. I dare say a city shall flourish along that artery. It will be a new silk road.'

'What shall you name the city?'

'I have not thought of a name yet.'

'How about "Jinnahabad"?'

Jinnah nods. 'Or else "Islamabad",' he speculates.

'You are too modest. Why not "Qaid-i-Azam City"?'

An aide appears in the doorway. Dickie, having invited Jinnah for some last-minute talks before his trip back to London, has seated him in an outer room this time. It is furnished with a long couch and two plush chairs to either side, in one of which Jinnah sits. There are two more chairs at opposite ends of the room. Some whispers pass between Dickie and his aide.

'Send him in,' says Dickie with a nod. 'We shall only be a moment.'

Jinnah has been watching. 'It seems I have overstayed.'

'Not at all. It is crucial I know the League's demands in *full* before I head back to London, eh?'

'Tell them to accede Pakistan. Once we have it, we will take care of the details.'

'Ah, but the details are where the devil is.'

Jinnah does not answer. His body stiffens, and his casually crossed legs uncross. His eyes narrow.

In the doorway, equally taken aback, stands Gandhi. He rubs a spot over his heart and crumples into one of the far chairs.

'Well!' says Dickie cheerfully. 'Just the two old friends I wanted to bring together. Of all the coincidences!'

The two old friends do not look at each other, much less speak. They rest aslant on opposite armrests on opposite sides of the room, mutually repelled, like magnets of identical polarity. Dickie leaps to his feet, cracks his knuckles, and hurries over to Gandhi.

Gandhi has pulled his shawl close and, eyes shut, seems to be taking a catnap. Dickie kneels at his side and waits a moment. Gandhi opens one eye.

'Perhaps you would like me to convey a message to Mr Jinnah?'

'Tell Mr Jinnah,' whispers Gandhi, 'that time is running out, and I would like to speak with him about India.'

Dickie dutifully shuttles to Jinnah's elbow and relays the message.

'Tell Mr Gandhi,' Jinnah whispers, 'I am here to speak about Pakistan. And time, for his information, is *up*.'

Dickie takes a deep breath and nods. At Gandhi's elbow, he gets the next message: 'Tell Mr Jinnah he alone can heal the cut he alone has made.'

Gandhi's voice has risen; he has spoken loudly enough for Jinnah to hear. Jinnah does not wait for the message from Dickie's lips, shooting back through his intermediary, 'Tell him this is a surgical amputation. The cut *is* what heals.'

Dickie is still shuttling back when Gandhi says aloud, clutching his heart as though he is suffering a coronary, 'Tell Jinnah he can be Prime Minister in Delhi. Nehru will step aside. Tell him he can name a Cabinet entirely of Muslims. Tell my dear brother he does not have to settle for Pakistan. He can have India so long as he keeps it whole.'

Jinnah, on the far side of the room, has risen to his feet. 'Tell Mr Gandhi I have no wish to be assassinated.'

Jinnah strides out of the Viceroy's mansion to his limousine. And so, the last of the Gandhi–Jinnah talks conclude.

Mid-May. Dickie is in the skies over Tehran, on his way back to London. This time, Edwina isn't with him. She told him she didn't wish to fly all the way back for two weeks. There were so many places yet to visit in India. Kashmir, for example.

He takes his time in the airplane water-closet again. His staff members are going over an early draft of his plan for the partition of British India; it is still early in the flight, and only a few knees are bobbing.

Dickie practises the lines he will present to the Foreign Office and Prime Minister Attlee. The airs he wants to convey: One, exhaustion, so they will think, *Dickie's really put a great deal of work into this*. Two, hard-won inside knowledge, such as an old India hand might possess; Dickie has been in India for three whole months, after all, attending meeting after meeting with every Jack and Jinnah you would care to name. Three, resignation, as in, 'I don't like it either, but nothing else will do.'

It is a complex look, but he furrows his brow just so, and says, 'No party will be *entirely* happy with it—but that means we've done our job, eh? British fair play.'

He shrugs his shoulders at an imaginary objection. 'They shall simply have to split the assets. Fifty-fifty, like a divorce.'

And now, with offhand confidence, 'I see no reason why they should be *enemies*. Rivals, perhaps, but Hindustan and Pakistan may well settle down and become, as Jinnah says, like Canada and the United States. The people have a great deal in common, you know, save for this one matter of religion. Oh yes, a *great* deal in common...'

25

Earthbound, back in India, Gandhi is holding a prayer meeting. The crowds, to his astonishment, have been getting larger every few weeks, at this point surpassing the ones he pulled in his heyday, in the early 1920s, when it seemed like satyagraha would reconquer all. Yet he knows that Partition is coming; that his own disciples in Congress have all but signed the papers at this point. Nehru spat in frustration—frustration with Jinnah, yes, but also, though he'll never admit it aloud, with Gandhi—that if they can't get rid of the headache, they might as well cut off the head.

Gandhi feels like a failure, but his people, now more than ever, squeeze into the enclosures, reach for his feet, reinforce his chants with their voices. It doesn't make sense to him. Why rush to his prayer meetings now that men of the world have taken over? Men to whom Gandhi sounds like some old-fashioned idealist with no grasp on current affairs? He looks out at the crowd this morning and wonders if there is still hope. Surely a Partition cannot take place if so many people still believe in him?

Unless they aren't here out of hope. Unless they are here out of fear. They may not know the details of the negotiations, but they know what is coming, and they can sense hatred and distrust everywhere. This prayer meeting is a refuge from that. Do they come here as they might to a temple? A small safe patch of the world where truth has been fenced off for its own safety? A place quite consciously not 'of this world'?

He begins with verses from the Gita. *To protect the virtuous and destroy wrongdoers, for the sake of establishing dharma, I come to be in era after era.* A mala of rudraksha beads crawls between his thumb and forefinger. Usually this means meditation, but the speed is a little too quick. Someone as close to him as Mirabehn, who has seen him cycle through his beads before, knows he is nervous, unsettled, transcending nothing right now. He clears his throat. He brings the microphone close.

'I want to tell you a story today. It is a story from the Bible. You have heard of the wise Rajah Suleiman. Once upon a time, this king was sitting on his throne when two women came before him with a small child, an infant. They had both given birth around the same time, in the same house. Each woman said the infant was hers. But really one of them had rolled on to her own infant and smothered him and switched the infants in the night, the dead one and the living one. So, Suleiman had a sword brought and declared, 'I will divide the child and give one half to each of you.' One woman cried out as though she were cut through the heart. She said the other woman could have the infant, as long as he did not come to harm. But the other stayed cold and unfeeling because her heart was not clean. She said the judgement was fair. Let the infant be divided. Let it bleed to death, so long as her rival did not win the case. Oh, my friends, Suleiman was wise. He was Akbar and Birbal in one. He knew the true mother would offer to give the infant up, while the liar would let him be cut in half. But I ask you: what if Suleiman had not been wise? What if it were the Fool sitting on Suleiman's throne, the Fool who had put off his cap and bells, and set Suleiman's crown on his own foolish head? What if the Fool were such a Fool that he did not understand a living thing will die if a sword cuts it down the middle? Because the Fool cannot see the liar approved his judgement out of spite. The Fool will hold fast to his solution and cut the newborn child. But it is not justice at all. It is a new injustice in the name of justice. It is murder.'

The meeting moves on to a recitation from the Qur'an. *And they make mischief in the holy land, and say, We are but peacemakers.* The chant, the story, the sura could all sound hostile. This brittle collapsed umbrella of an old man speaks, as softly as ever, and no one can imagine hostility in him. Resistance, yes, but under his resistance is sorrow, and under his sorrow is compassion. He does not think anyone evil. Not the British, not Jinnah. That is what he picked up from the Gita: no one is evil, just deluded. If you persuade them of the truth, they will do good, naturally.

So, even as his sense of his own failure grows, he meets more and more people. Sometimes four or five meetings crowd into a single day. He meets with Muslim preachers, Reuters correspondents, English admirers who bring their own photographer in tow, student members of the Muslim League, soldiers who fought Britain with the Indian National Army, women workers, Hindu landlords, ministers from Bihar ... He talks with everyone, trying to dispel delusion. In his mind, it is *his* fault there is still distrust and violence. He is failing India.

From his prayer meeting, Gandhi goes straight to the hospital where Manu has just had an operation for appendicitis. He raises the gown, and then the bandage, to look at the incision on her belly. He puts a finger to his lips and whispers, 'Mother is here.' Dipping that finger in a small white bottle, he smears the incision with turmeric powder, and she lets him. The area turns an Ayurvedic saffron colour, and the incision oozes dark blood. He replaces the bandage, but he doesn't see her wince as he pats it down.

From the hospital, he goes home to Delhi's Untouchable colony, where he spins and writes and eats and hosts more visitors. He wants as many visitors as possible to see him here. These forty million Untouchables, had there been no caste, would have been Hindus, part of the community. They would not have allied with the Muslim League. Their leader, Ambedkar, would not have stood beside Jinnah on the 'Day of Deliverance'. Congress would have been forty million votes stronger, and India would have stayed India from end to end.

Maybe this is karma, thinks Gandhi. *First, we divided our brothers from us by creating untouchability. A partition on the map will divide us in return, making us outcasts in Sindh, in Baluchistan ... It is only fitting.*

Only fitting, too, that he is in that Untouchable colony when he gets the news.

Sardar Patel delivers it. He passes a garbage fire to ward off mosquitoes, and a defecating child staring big-eyed up at him. Every time he comes here, he has to keep himself from covering his mouth and nose with a handkerchief. Patel is no Brahmin, finicky around dirt; he comes from plough and mattock stock. He really wants to look at these people lovingly, as 'God's People', *Harijans*, as Gandhi calls them. But it is damned hard, knowing they didn't fall in line and put up a united front. Gandhi's loving kindness towards them won the Gandhian cause exactly nothing.

He finds his mentor bent over his spinning wheel, untangling a snag. Sardar is not one for small talk; he holds up a telegram.

'Mountbatten is back from London,' he says. 'He wants to show us the plan.'

The name on the flat-bottomed houseboat's keel is *Queen Elizabeth*. Jinnah wanted to name her the *Cleopatra*—because *The barge she sat in, like a burnished throne, / Burned on the water*—but Fatima had objected to this Egyptian queen as an immoral woman. Hadn't she ruined Mark Antony by deserting him, in her ship, during a naval battle? Just as soon name it the *Lady Macbeth*: at least that woman had goaded her man to glory, ruthless but loyal. Jinnah had switched out one Shakespearean Queen for another.

When his fever spikes, the houseboat might as well be burning on the water. The Kashmiri air makes his coughing fits come more rarely, but when they do, his blood and phlegm soak whole handkerchiefs. He collects them in a knapsack beside his bed. Fatima washes them by hand, wary of handing them over to the local washerwoman lest some Congress spy (no doubt they are lurking) hear the coughs and see the handkerchiefs and send a report that Jinnah is dying on Dal Lake.

He sleeps a half hour at a time, at most. It is all he can get before his lungs awaken him, but he leaps out of bed and begins to pace.

These late May midnights, with Pakistan in some form so close, he has been thinking about history. How it will fork in two if—*when*—Britain divides and quits. Pakistan's historians will write how he kept millions of Muslims free of Hindu domination—but not, perhaps, how he reined in the mad mullahs who pled with him to unleash a holy war. Or how this tribe and that wanted its own nation-state; or how this or that fanatical sect wanted Muslim rule over all of India, and reviled him for dividing what they regarded, from the Khyber Pass clear to the mouth of the Ganges, as their meat. Or how the only attempt on his life—so far—was by a fellow Muslim: a young man punched him in the jaw as he stepped out of his study, Jinnah's tall body buckling over a desk, the butcher knife rising, Jinnah's own arm risen by reflex, catching the down-glint by sheer luck ... The blade slit Jinnah's chin just as his secretary tackled the intruder. The scar tingles to life every time Jinnah recalls that five-second scuffle.

When Hindustan writes its creation myth, he wonders, *how will they cast me?* He remembers his recent conversation with Sarojini Naidu. *They have already cast me: I am Lucifer.*

This thought brings a smile to his face. The scar stops tingling. Perhaps he too will attract a Milton some day? His fever reverie breaks when a small bell sounds at the edge of the jetty. The postman's son has bicycled over with a telegram. Fatima brings it to him.

'From Delhi,' she says. 'Dickie is calling you back. He wants to meet.'

On an afternoon in early June, they all pack into one room. A fan in the corner turns from side to side. Jinnah, statuesque in his seat. Liaquat Ali Khan, nervous as if on the verge of getting exam results, fingers restless with a pencil. Nehru and Sardar Patel have the eyes of mourners. Nehru is thinking: *Jinnah has won, but he hasn't won everything*. Patel is thinking: *Divide and quit is just another way of saying cut and run*. The Sikh representative, Baldev Singh, stares intensely at his hands, right hand a fist, left cradling it in a C: aggression, protection. The two may prove the same thing, soon. For the Hindus and Muslims, Partition is a matter of shares in an electorate. For the Sikhs—clustered along the line of contention in the Punjab, small in number but every last man a fighter—whatever's in those folders is existential.

Only Gandhi is not in this room. He doesn't represent any political party, just himself. And besides, everyone knows what he thinks already—not just that dividing India is a bad idea politically, but that it's a sin like murder, or rape, or theft, being sure to give rise to all three.

At the end of the table nearest the wall, grim-faced in a grey suit, a stack of folders before him, sits Lord Mountbatten. He is the only Englishman in the room, backed into a corner. A photographer crouches to his tripod, and the faces turn to the flash.

Dickie Mountbatten hands out his folders.

Not one man present wants to hear Dickie talk him through the folder paragraph by paragraph. Like everyone else, Jinnah is riffling through the pages. He is looking for a word, and he finds it. *Pakistan*. Over and over again. *Pakistan*. They will divide Punjab and Bengal, but what of that? Parts are better than India kept whole. Because those parts will be wholly his: *Pakistan*. He eases back in his chair, and his pencil works dreamily on a pad. While Mountbatten talks, Jinnah doodles. He makes ovals that trail squiggly flagella. The balloons flank an enormous cannon, two wheels at the base. A banner, drifting down from heaven, says:

GOVERNOR-GENERAL OF PAKISTAN

26

Edwina's arms have darkened and freckled during her time here. She joins some young coolies unloading supplies from a truck—simply enters the bewildered line, grabs a crate, and carries it towards the medical tent. Nehru finds himself mimicking her, and he marvels at those thin freckled arms corded with the strain, that noble unworried face, her tall body perfectly balanced on brisk high heels through the dirt. He would have visited this refugee camp outside Delhi anyway, but alone, it would have been little more than a compassionate stroll.

At Edwina's side—as 'Edwina's adjutant', he joked in the Packard—he is hauling supplies within a minute of stepping out into the mid-June heat. Supplies which she herself, he finds out later, arranged for, putting Dickie's Viceregal telephones to good use.

Nehru cannot help but contrast spry and devil-may-care Edwina with his late wife Kamala. Edwina's body, from his few brief social embraces of it, is hard, wiry, energetic even at rest; Kamala's had been soft, her movements graceful but languid, almost sleepy. But then she had been sick so often—all those joyless months in sanatoria—perhaps if she had stepped *out* into the world, out of the sheltered world of a rich Brahmin's daughter and into the suffering and heat of the world, like Edwina—might not her health have been better? If she had hardened her constitution a little?

Edwina could have lived an insular life if she wished. But she never wished that.

She wishes instead to go from bed to stinking bed, asking in Hindustani, as best she can, where patients are from, if they are well, what she can do for them. Nehru trails her. He watches her wash and dress machete wounds like a student watching a surgeon. When her hair falls forward over her cheek, he wants to tuck it back behind her ear. He stares at the lock until she rights it herself, unthinkingly, sometimes with her finger but sometimes, if she is gloved, with one brisk broad shake of her head. The sight gives him a brief thrill, as if his thinking it prompted her to do it.

'You are pensive today,' she says. She is taking a break, and he brings her a canteen of water. 'Is everything all right, Jawahar?'

He takes a deep breath, and the mingling of her perfume and her sweat, and the maddening earthy glimpse of the damp cloth under her arms, the highest privilege and the most selfless willingness to sweat for suffering strangers ... she makes him dizzy. He drifts down on to an upturned crate, not as close to her as he would wish. She folds her knees together and tilts them towards him. Nehru knows her reputation back in England; he knows, as everyone does, about her 'ginks', her American polo players, her Grenadian lounge singer, her colonel in the Coldstream Guards, but the way she rests her legs, sitting on this crate, having just helped two nurses set a broken bone—she strikes him as demure, fearless, wise, innocent, deep, simple—

'Jawahar?'

'I was thinking,' he says, dabbing a handkerchief on his forehead, hiding his eyes. He thinks quickly. 'Thinking about

... these poor refugees. I suppose we have avoided more of this, now that we have reached a settlement. Even if it did cost us a united India.'

'It has all worked out for the best.' Casually she holds the bottle out to him. He puts his lips where her lips were. 'A civil war would have been unthinkable. It was Dickie's greatest fear.'

Nehru shakes his head. 'How easily Jinnah changed the question!'

'How do you mean?'

'For years, we used to ask, "When will the British go? And once they do, how will we make our new democracy as fair as possible?" But somehow the question became, "Do we partition the country, or do we fight a civil war?" Changing the question was Jinnah's doing. He did it so easily. Ten years was all it took! I could not stop him.'

She wants to put her arm around Jawahar, but there are so many people about, it simply would not do. She resists reaching for his hand. 'What he played on,' she says, 'the anxieties, the distrust—they were always there. They had to have been. One man cannot conjure such feelings out of thin air.'

'I knew India as she used to be. I saw the crowds marching with Bapu. We failed him.'

'Your job is only beginning. And you shall be a rousing success at it. I have no doubt.'

Nehru puts his lips to the bottle's mouth again, dwelling a moment like that before he tilts and drinks. 'I do have a job ahead of me.'

'You really do, as a matter of fact. Another truck has just pulled in.' She rises. 'No adjutant of mine is allowed to mope while on duty, Jawahar. Roll up your sleeves and come along.'

At that moment, over at Jinnah's Delhi mansion on Aurangzeb Road, the Pandit and the ageing party girl are a topic of conversation. Fatima has placed a chocolate-box full of letters on her brother's desk. Jinnah browses their alternating scrawl.

'Real or forgeries? How did they come to us?'

'From one of our ministers,' says Fati, 'who got it from a chambermaid at the Viceregal Lodge.'

'Was she paid?'

'I assume.'

'How much?'

'Ask Liaquat.'

Jinnah already knows Nehru and the Mountbattens are close—but *this* is a different sort of intimacy.

'Publish them all,' says Fatima. 'Invite the press to inspect each one and publish.'

'I have seen Nehru's handwriting. I can vouch for this, Fati. But why would both halves of their correspondence rendezvous in the same box?'

'What does it matter, Jin? If they are up to some depravity, expose them.'

Jinnah reads on. *You forgot your handkerchief and before Dickie could spot it, I covered it up*. Something rather literary about this dropped handkerchief. Suspicion, jealousy, Desdemona and the blackamoor—yet should he dismiss the detail simply because it conformed to a convention? Adulterers have been misplacing handkerchiefs for centuries. It is a cherished ritual among the louche. (Rarely, though, do they misplace entire correspondences.) *I have fond memories of Simla—riding and your touch*. That 'riding'!

'Edwina has gone walking in the mountains with him. Let them answer for it, Jin. Let the world jeer at her.'

Jinnah tosses the letters in the box. If he publishes these letters, which would surprise no one, the cuckold would be angrier at *him* than at his wife or her beau. He needs no further leverage, after all; his people are already lifted.

'Caesar's wife should be above suspicion,' he says—and closes the box. 'Have Khurshid put these in the burn pile.'

Fati, disappointed, slides the box under her arm and leaves his office. Before delivering the letters to her brother's secretary Khurshid, she reads the letters over to herself one last time. She tells herself she pities these two, greying at the temples, for not transcending hectic giddy lust and sweat beads on the upper lip—as she herself has done since her teens. These filthy British women with their husbands, lovers, sailors, flings! Fati's eyes may be narrow with outrage, but, unaware, she chews her lip until it bleeds.

That evening, Jinnah and his sister drive down Kingsway to the Imperial Hotel. At this meeting, the Muslim League will ratify the Partition plan. The plan is not ideal—the two richest provinces will have to be split down the middle, half Muslim, half Hindu—but it is more than they ever imagined they would get five years ago.

'King of Kings' is how Liaquat introduces Jinnah: the 'Shahenshah' of Pakistan. Fati beams up at her brother, who takes the stage before 500 League delegates. Their Qaid-i-Azam raises his hand at the applause and declares in ringing regal tones, like Caesar declining the laurel crown: 'I am only a soldier of Pakistan.'

The applause has exploded all over again when, outside the hall, shrill police-whistles and deep-throated shouts make their hands pause in the air. Heads turn to the closed ballroom door.

Dark twilit figures have rushed through the hotel's palm-tree palisade with sharpened spades. Jinnah stands his ground on stage and speaks of the 'tragic necessity' of dividing the provinces.

Glass crashes downstairs; a whole chandelier seems to have fallen to the tiles.

An insurgency of shouts arises within the hall itself, at Jinnah's feet, as Bengal's old jute magnates, and a few men with property in what will likely be India's half of Punjab, wax defiant. Fatima stands up just as defiantly, glaring at the culprit delegates. Outside, so close the voices must be partway up the marble stairs, she can hear 'Get Jinnah!' and 'Kill Jinnah!' but her brother keeps his speech going.

'I never *handed over* halves of the provinces we *don't* possess,' he snarls. 'I *snatched away* the halves we *do*.'

Sporadic rifle shots. He forces his words through the din. Now his whole audience is touching their cheeks with handkerchiefs, and he, too—as he keeps speaking, defying those who defy him—feels a sting in his eyes, the tears welling up. 'It is a truncated, motheaten, shaven lion of a Pakistan,' he weeps, 'but Pakistan it is, an ark for a hundred million.'

The police have deployed tear gas on the ground floor of the hotel. Two canisters, lobbed to the top of the stairs, have rolled stepwise back down, hissing.

Jinnah's would-be assassins, forty of them, have been tackled, bludgeoned, disarmed, shot, wrestled, handcuffed, tear-gassed. The League guardsmen know exactly what to look for: they line up the bodies and yank down the trousers, checking for circumcision. The assassins are Muslims to a man, Punjabis enraged over losing half their province.

Not one has made it into the hall proper, much less to the stage—but the tear gas has risen and spread, as words and gases do.

The delegates are all weeping relentlessly as Jinnah proposes—and the League passes—a resolution ratifying Pakistan.

Dickie Mountbatten is facing a crowd of his own just then. He is usually quite at his ease facing a crowd of reporters, but this evening the barrage comes in rather hot. *You are in command,* he tells himself, fortifying his resolve with a glance down at his naval uniform.

'When will the British be leaving?'

'We look forward,' Dickie says with stately self-assurance, 'to a prompt and speedy transfer of power.'

This satisfies no one. 'What date, Lord Mountbatten?' And then, from places around the room: 'The date!' 'Give us the date!'

Mountbatten nods. A raised hand buys him a few seconds. A *date*! He should have thought of a date ... 'The fifteenth of August!' he blurts, and the date surprises and pleases him, for it's quite a lucky date; it's the very date he received the Japanese surrender on behalf of the Allies in Singapore, just two years ago. Kismet! '1947,' he adds, just in case there is any confusion. He could have said '48, but that would hardly be prompt and speedy.

The reporters take it down. Dickie smiles; no one seems to have sensed it was the first date that came to his mind. Dickie himself does not notice that the watch on his wrist has started spinning at a brisk clip, three seconds a tick. Outside, on the grounds of the Viceroy's mansion, the crickets quicken. A pale cloud crosses the moon and tears apart to nothing.

Dickie feels his own pulse speed up, giddy, lightheaded, skipped beat after skipped beat.

'Last question,' he says to the crowd, and points to the first hand that rises.

'My question concerns the border, Lord Mountbatten,' says the reporter. 'If provinces are to be divided, who shall decide the location of the border?'

In London, it is already morning. Sir Cyril Radcliffe is just lowering his lips to a saucer of steaming Earl Grey when history punches an enormous bloody hand through his roof.

Shingles clatter all around him. Photographs of his parents and grandparents are knocked askew. Dust and chips of plaster sprinkle his Airedale, who barks up in astonishment at his master being lifted, by the pyjama collar, into the sky.

'Where are you haling me?' cries the terrified Sir Cyril, gazing down at the Low Countries. 'May I at least fetch my good spectacles?'

To India, says History. *And the less clearly you see what you are doing, the better.*

'But I am no one at all,' gibbers poor Sir Cyril. 'I am a nobody born in Nowhereshire, and I know nothing at all of India or Indians!'

That's why you are just the man for the job, says History. *A true innocent.*

History drops him on the verandah of a decent enough bungalow. His job is to be an easy one: simply draw a line on the map. Sir Cyril explores the bungalow and finds biscuits in the cupboard, a sweating glass pitcher of water, two bottles of whisky, and, in the study, eight waist-high towers of maps and census reports. The maps are intricately shaded and detailed with bizarre names. *Chittagong*: what did one sound like, struck with a mallet? *Dera Ghazi Khan*: might that be one of Kubla's sons? *Kashmir*: why, he has heard of that, at least. And he remembers *Lahore* from a Kipling story.

He is not entirely lost, then. All he has to do is page through these stacks and determine who is where. Actually, before that: where *where* is. Or ideally, before *that*, who is who.

He checks the day calendar on his desk, whose top page—*8 July 1947*—is already starting to shiver and kick, as if a brisk wind is going to rip it off prematurely.

He has about a month.

Chop chop, he thinks. *Draw them their bloody line.*

Chop chop—

Everyone is moving herky-jerky and double-time. Gandhi, Patel, Jinnah, Fatima, Dickie, Nehru, Edwina: the newsreel they are trapped in is running a bit too fast. The sun edges across the sky all too perceptibly. No one can trust clocks any longer. They keep racing from midnight to midnight to midnight.

June.

No, July. Already?

Dickie sets up, in his office, a tear-away countdown calendar to the Transfer of Power. It is locally printed on thin local paper, and on twelve separate occasions, the top page falls off prematurely, and he has to tape it back.

Events crowd out events. None of them retain any memory of these weeks afterwards. They only skim the pages of the history book they are writing as they go.

The unborn twins are already competing. Independent princes with independent kingdoms—three hundred and twenty-five of them—speckle and spot the map of India. They must be courted; they must be coaxed into one country or the other. Jinnah knows that some kingdoms are buried too impossibly deep in Indian territory to invite into Pakistan—but he cajoles the largest, Hyderabad, ruled by a Muslim Nizam, to stay out of both.

Dickie, Nehru and Patel, meanwhile, work as a team. Dickie waltzes up and shakes hands and asks the Rajah about his horses, his villa on the Riviera, his dogs. When that doesn't work, Nehru tap-dances up and riffs about democratic freedom nation secular rights future signature accession India. When that doesn't work, Sardar Patel lumbers up with unsympathetic eyes and says what isn't technically a threat but sounds like one anyway. 'You can sign this whenever you like. But you're going to sign this. Ideally, now.'

Here is Dickie doing what he does best: reviewing the troops. The brigades of the Punjab Boundary Force look impressive, collected on a field. Once they're actually in the Punjab, each man will have to cover two-and-a-half square miles. But for now, what crisp uniforms.

The date is approaching. Speed up the newsreel.

Edwina, inspecting the decorations at her anniversary dinner; Jinnah, inspecting the first green flag of his personal country; Nehru, scribbling the names of his first Cabinet in a notebook, then turning the page and scribbling a letter to Edwina.

Gandhi, praying. Telling a prayer meeting that the fifteenth should be a day of contemplation. Maybe even a day of mourning.

Gandhi on a train to Calcutta, where he intends to stop the violence that he alone knows is coming, though he does not know if he can, or how.

Cooks vanish behind the steam from raised lids and families vanish into the steam around stopping locomotives and Delhi footmen arranging their fanned turbans and photographers polishing camera lenses and Sikh men counting rifles laid out on ancestral farmland that may or may not be theirs tomorrow and serving men in New Delhi arranging butter knives and bank clerks in Karachi stamping Raj rupees with the word *Pakistan* late into the evening so the country has its 'own' currency and rose sherbet and navratan korma and festive firecrackers loaded into seaside mortars in Bombay and bullets loaded into rusty Enfield rifles in Pathan mountain country and Nehru touching up his speech by candlelight and Edwina touching up her lipstick and Jinnah spitting blood into a wastepaper basket and Dickie in full fig and—*ding!*

Time's up.

Beware the ides of August.

PART SIX

Verdict

Such being the story of these two great men's lives, without doubt in the comparison very little difference will be found between them.

—Plutarch, *Parallel Lives*

27

Shortly before Independence, Jinnah arrives in Karachi by airplane. He was coughing relentlessly after take-off from Delhi, but when mid-flight the coughing subsided and his fever poured out of him as sweat, Fatima, fanning him with a folded map, whispered: 'We must have crossed the border.'

Sure enough, he gains strength at the first footfall on the tarmac at Mauripur Airport. A cheering mob awaits him there, but no one lines the streets for him. Pakistan's capital city, the city where he feels most at home, has a Hindu majority.

The Governor's House is bigger than even his Malabar Hill mansion. He stumbles on the top step, coughing again, but Fati bears him up. Her eyes are shining.

'Welcome home,' she says.

An Indian, still in the old Colonial livery, stands at the door, saluting. Jinnah sweeps his hand at a hallway. 'That is your wing, Fati,' he decrees. She rushes down the hall, opening each door to each room that will be her own for as long as she lives and after. Jinnah strides to his left, stroking a balustrade, admiring some salvers, a globe he spins and spins inside its brass crescent, hunting rifles crossed on the wall … He decides quickly on the place where he will hang his portrait. The star of dawn will spotlight him through a high window.

Upstairs, he claims his new writing-desk, complete with the Governor's stationery with its British Seal watermark. Already faint when raised to the window, the watermark fades to nothing under his gaze.

In the library, Jinnah begins to cough again. He goes through the mansion room by room, coughing harder, doubled over. Fati, innumerable rooms away, calls his name. He keeps going upstairs, towards the brightness. By the time he gets to the terrace, his handkerchief is red. But he stops coughing at the sight of the new flag, green and white, the flag of Pakistan. His moon and his star. His moon, waxing. His star in the ascendant. At the zenith.

Shortly before Independence, Gandhi arrives in Calcutta. He has come up with a plan. He will find a deserted Muslim house in a Hindu part of the city and persuade everyone to invite the Muslim family back home. Then he will move to a deserted Hindu house in a Muslim part of town, and persuade the neighbours to invite the Hindu family back home. But he is not doing this alone. Here, in this deserted Muslim house in Beliaghat, he has a companion.

Beliaghat is not somewhere Suhrawardy would have been willing to go with a military bodyguard. But the League leader is doing this with Gandhi at his side. It is not a large house. No fence, no high wall, no lawn interposes between the street and the windows.

Which is why the latest brick sails so forcefully through the window. Gandhi does not flinch, focused on peeling an orange as if it were surgery of great importance. The grand-niece and one of Gandhi's white hangers-on start sweeping; they were standing with brooms at the ready.

Suhrawardy feels a deep unease in his bowels, but graffiti has found its way into the lavatory—PAKISTAN scrawled on the wall, with an arrow pointed down the hole. The stink drives him back into the main room.

Outside, the Hindu crowd is shouting, 'Gandhi go home! Gandhi go home!' Suhrawardy wonders what strange magnetism in the old man compelled him to agree to this mad idea, this scheme of mutual protection. Gandhi is the one who's supposed to keep them both safe in the Hindu neighbourhoods. Yet here a Hindu mob is livid at Gandhi for trying to prevent them from lancing the city's minaret-sized abscesses—and for urging peace beside the very man, Suhrawardy himself, whom they believe responsible for the Calcutta killings last year. He should have foreseen this. But how could Suhrawardy imagine the Mahatma would attract, so quickly, the ire of his own people?

'What now, Gandhi?'

'We invite them in for a talk.'

Jinnah is delivering his first address to the Constituent Assembly of Pakistan. A great knot has come loose in his stomach. In his own country at last, he fears no one. No back-room cleverness afoot against him here, no enemy handshake to draw him close for the knife thrust. He is safe from Gandhi's wiles in Wardha and Nehru's pillow-talk summits with the Vicereine.

'You are free to go to your temples,' he finds himself saying, 'you are free to go to your mosques or to any other place of worship in this State of Pakistan…'

Slowly his hair begins to darken. The streak to the left of his widower's peak lingers, then goes black.

'You may belong to any religion or caste or creed. That has nothing to do with the business of the State.'

His skin goes smooth. His chest and cheeks fill out.

'In England, long ago, Protestants and Roman Catholics persecuted each other. In time, they ceased to exist, in a sense. They became equal citizens of one Nation…'

The sherwani ceases to feel like a sherwani on his limbs. It has the hang and fit of an old suit, the black pinstripe he wore in Lucknow, luckless years ago. His voice becomes conversational, softer, and there in the audience is Ruttie, beaming up at him, because it is 1917 again, and he is the ambassador of unity. He doesn't register the perplexity on the faces of his fellow Pakistanis because he has gone thirty years back in time.

'Now I think we should keep that in front of us as our ideal,' he announces brightly. 'You will find that over the course of time Hindus will cease to be Hindus and Muslims will cease to be Muslims, not in the religious sense, because that is the personal faith of each individual, but in the political sense, as citizens of the State. We will all be citizens. We will all be equal.'

No applause. Fatima bites her lip, wondering why her brother ignored the paper in his hands. Jinnah himself shakes his head. Does he wake or dream? His young man's fingers shrivel and turn to hooks, crushing the paper. The left half of his widow's peak bleaches from the roots. What did he just say? He is not that young fool any more: Ruttie is dead, and J died with her.

He is the Qaid-i-Azam. His fight is over.

His fight is beginning.

On Independence Day, Gandhi stands inside a roundabout in Karachi. The Hindus of Karachi swore violence if the bronze statue were removed, but the new owners of Karachi had to do something about the stubborn old man. That is why Gandhi is wearing a Turkish fez.

In an open-top Rolls-Royce sit Jinnah and Dickie Mountbatten. Their Rolls is part of a small motorcade.

A sparrow shows up just in time to displace the fez off Gandhi's downcast head. Another one settles atop of his bronze walking stick, two more on his shoulder. Dickie smiles at the sight and playfully salutes the bronze Mahatma. Jinnah, resting his left elbow on the door, keeps his hand dangling while his eyes stay on the statue. Just as the motorcade peels off the roundabout, the hand rises to show Gandhi he hasn't failed to see him there. But his arm chooses not to stir. Jinnah understands the notion of a salute between generals, the victorious one showing respect to the defeated one, as the sword is handed over and the surrender signed on a desolate plain. By God, though, not today. Not on his day.

They ride in silence, Governor-General and Governor-General. Dickie had indulged in fantasies of holding the office in both countries, gracing his own roundabout in either capital, but Jinnah nominated himself. That peek at Edwina's correspondence with Nehru, forged or not, had confirmed a decision he had already taken.

The two men glance at each other only when they catch a smell of sulphur and smoke. Jinnah looks to the roadside, for it seems to be on the breeze. Nothing in sight is burning. Dickie sits forward and cranes his neck. The hood of the Rolls starts spilling smoke, and the driver waves his hand before his face, as though warding off locusts.

'Push on,' Jinnah commands.

The Assembly Hall is only a block away, and he does not want to arrive on foot. They coast the last few feet with the engine dead. Cranking the hand brake, the driver leaps from his seat and starts waving his cap at the engine. Liaquat hurries down the steps. With the agility of cowardice, Dickie scoots up on to the trunk and swings his long legs over the side of the car, as far from the smoke as possible. Jinnah, stubbornly regal, waits for Liaquat to open his door. He steps on to the pavement at the moment a great flame shoots up from the engine, like the flare of wine off a pan. They hurry up the steps and observe the car settle into a steady burn. Mountbatten looks away politically and shakes the nearest hands.

Liaquat, though, looks on in a sweat. His handkerchief is out.

'It is not an omen, Liaquat.' He nods at Jinnah's whisper. 'And even if it is—that is a *British* car.'

Jinnah has ordered only one high-backed throne placed in the Assembly Hall. He hurries inside to plant himself in it first. To the lower, wooden chair at his right elbow, he graciously gestures Mountbatten, who stands perplexed a moment. A large electric fan, placed directly behind the Qaid, keeps him cool. It makes a circle like a sun behind his head. They are all arrayed before him: thrones, dominations, princes, virtues, powers. Under his breath, he repeats '*Pakistan zindabad*', once and only once, too quietly for anyone to hear. Yet a stillness overcomes the assembly, instantly. Even Mountbatten stiffens to attention and turns his crumbling marble head. Everyone is looking up at Jinnah now. He rises to speak.

These festivities take place on 14 August, a day before India's celebrations. In Calcutta that afternoon, Gandhi stands before a crowd, too, in Beliaghat. It is a prayer meeting in pandemonium. Only Sanskrit slokas calm down his fellow Hindus. They are a motley crowd—some in Congress caps, some in saffron bandanas, all of them in a sweat. He sings to them the verses Arjuna sang when faced with his relatives drawn up in formation against him: *I see omens, Krishna, inauspicious ones! And I foresee no good in killing my own people in battle. I don't want victory, Krishna, or a kingdom, or happiness! What's a kingdom to us, cowherd?* Understanding no Sanskrit, but knowing the words are theirs, they look up, pacified like children by a lullaby.

Now for the test. He gestures a boy on to the stage. The boy holds a green book. On the top of his head is a small round cap.

'Now for another recitation,' says Gandhi. 'An injunction against *himsa*. We hear it in all faiths. Let us hear it again.'

He nods at the boy. The boy is so fearful, he wouldn't have been able to say his own name if he were asked to. These words, though, he can speak. They are quarantined from his fear. *Whoever kills a soul*, he begins. His lips go on to form the words that say whoever kills a soul *kills all mankind*, but the rest is uproar, his lips moving but no words heard. The protests themselves can barely be made out—'Whose side are you on?' 'Gandhi, go home!' 'Shut your mouth, kid.' 'Grab him! Get him off the stage!'—but Gandhi also hears several voices clamouring for Suhrawardy. Part of the crowd rivers away with an ominous, ant-colony orchestration. A more unruly part surges on to the stage, howling slogans.

Clearly the prayer meeting has adjourned itself. Several of Gandhi's associates bring him away, but Gandhi points to the boy, and they smuggle him clear and into Gandhi's radius. The house at Beliaghat is already surrounded. The mob lets Gandhi through; they are spitting, but not at him. The Muslim boy, still hugging his book, tilts his shoulders and moves as though carrying an infant brother through rain.

Inside the house, Suhrawardy is sitting on the flat swing, eyes downcast, listening to his name turn into a chant. He is not so dapper a dresser as the Qaid, but he has put on a new silk shirt this afternoon, bright white, so the blood will show more vividly in the photographs afterwards. The shutters are closed but rattle occasionally when a stone strikes. All thought of his miscalculation has left his head. A brief bitterness flashes across his mind as he thinks of Calcutta gone mad last year, and how all they will write of him one day is that.

So what, Shaheed, he thinks to himself, *if they badmouth you when you are dead—you ate well in the time you had, and twisted a ballerina's golden hair round your hand, once upon a time. Hold on to that image, and laugh at them all when they break through.*

The swing has eased to a resigned stop. And here is death tugging his white sleeve, ever so gently. No, not death: Gandhi. Suhrawardy rises and follows the old man to the shutters, but when they rattle again, he falls back.

'Talk to them,' says Gandhi.

'What do I tell them?'

'Truth.'

Gandhi opens the shutters on to the mob crying more and more violently for 'Suhrawardy, Suhrawardy, bring out Suhrawardy, drag the bastard out.' They see the Muslim politician and begin to bay, but Gandhi sticks his hands out the windows, and the stones stay on the ground

A few screams break through the hushed crowd. 'The Calcutta killings!' 'Take responsibility!' 'Admit it!'

Suhrawardy looks out into all these eyes, and thinks how strange the human creature is—bloodthirst and panic look identical. 'Yes, I take responsibility,' he says, and it is easier than he ever imagined. 'I was Chief Minister then. Your safety was my responsibility, gentlemen. And I regret it.'

The crowd, baffled, stares up at him. Gandhi joins his hands. Suhrawardy does, too. Someone in the crowd, maybe someone who lost someone, lets a rock fly. It chips the wall to the left of Suhrawardy's head, but neither he nor Gandhi flinches, and a few scattered shouts of protest gather force. Soon they are beating the man who threw that rock, a wholly local stir in the crowd. They beat him perhaps a little half-heartedly, since the beating lasts only a minute in the mosquito twilight. Soon the culprit takes off running in his torn shirt, unpursued. It is the last violence that night.

28

The last violence, that is, in Calcutta. In Lahore, the temples and gurudwaras are already on fire.

No matter. Stay calm and carry on with the festivities. A little torch-flinging was only to be expected. The speech is the thing, and Nehru delivers it as written.

'Tryst': a private, romantic rendezvous between lovers. Lady and Lord Mountbatten have flown back into Delhi to be present at the stroke of midnight. 'Destiny': the events that will necessarily happen in the future. A few buildings will burn, a few effigies, a few bodies. This was only to be expected. The barbarians will have their celebrations, too. *The past is over, and it is the future that beckons to us now.*

The future. But precisely at midnight, a sharp note out of distant antiquity turns the heads of the assembly. No one knows or will be able to recall who the interloper blowing the conch shell is. Was it auspicious or inauspicious? More than one God holds a conch shell in the old paintings. In the Bhagavad Gita, though, warriors on both sides—all cousins—blow their conch shells in the first chapter. Blowing a conch shell alerted the gods to come watch the action. It meant *Enough talk, let's start this civil fucking war.*

Next night, at the Viceroy's party in the Mughal Gardens—gardens criss-crossed with mosquitoes and waiters, lit up against the night like a gurudwara in Lahore—everyone steps out of their roles, though they stay in costume. Congress radicals, British functionaries, army officers shortly to drive off to bases on opposite sides of the border, Muslim nawabs, Hindu maharajahs: all raise their glasses and offer toasts, now to the King, now to the new Prime Minister, as if the one hadn't imprisoned the other just three years ago.

Here in the Mughal Gardens, the rival teams have resolved into individual gentlemen. It was all a game of cricket after all, played between members of the same class, on the club pitch.

Well played.

It isn't true that Gandhi is the only person to have fled the Independence Day festivities. There is one other.

Sir Cyril Radcliffe is back in London, staring out of his window at the morning traffic. He's finally gotten around to that pot of Earl Grey he left to cool last month—because he snapped all his pens and rulers and left India early, declining the fee for his service, 'all thirty shekels of it'.

His Airedale rests beside his chair, where she is disturbed now by a newspaper drifting on to her head. This has slipped from Sir Cyril's hands, which have risen to cover his face, newsprint smudging his fingertips, his forehead. His stained fingers rub that newsprint into his eyes, which go kohl-dark.

The Airedale sniffs the front page and growls low and hostile. She smells blood, she smells fire in this headline.

Elbows on the table, meanwhile, Cyril is murmuring, 'My God, what have I done…'

You may think you weren't alive then. You were; just not in your present body. You are alive in another body then, and now: trapped in that time, now still, where you lived once.

You are living in a stranger's house. He is not the kind of man who washes much. His hands are on your shoulders, pushing down. The smell of him is rotten-orchid sickly sweet, his groin fat folds full of fungal blush. You have never smelt cum before, and for hours after, it is in your sinuses. Your new life. You would go back to your old one if you could, because he falls asleep on top of you after the second go. Let's say you make it back to your house and your parents and your brother. Are you supposed to look at their faces? Or let them look at yours? With you knowing, and them knowing. Your brother so beautiful, more beautiful than you: you saw him once when you were a little girl, with his turban undone and his long Sikh hair covering the cobra-flare of his back and broad shoulders, and you thought, with a shiver of forbidden anticipation, *I will be the bride of a warrior some day*. That brother you grew up with is praying right now for you to be dead so he can mourn you instead of having to think about you out there. You could run home right now but there is no home. Your new 'husband' says that if you run, he will catch you and take you and carve his name with a knife into your forehead like tree bark. By the end of the week, you are cutting okra in the kitchen with his other wife who has not spoken a word to you. And you think, *How badly I must want to live if I am cutting okra for these people. How shameful that I want to go on living.*

No. Wait. You are that barren first wife. Getting old and seeing this new bride brought in from some village and having to listen to her getting fucked. The Sultan in his harem with his slave girl. The water for tea is boiling on the fire and you walk over to where she is cutting your okra, and you tilt that pot on her head and pretty young face. No. You are the village imam who married the Sikh girl to her husband and chose her new name. She should be grateful she is being married, not rented out or used by a crowd. She would have lived her whole life and never come to peace. This one has been dragged; at least she has come to it. Her eyes may be red right now, but after she bears him a son, it will get easier. In a few years, she will not remember that life at all. The childhood she misses will forget itself like a dream. The name she thinks is hers right now will come to seem a lie.

Not everyone is so unlucky. Maybe you are one of the lucky ones. Some British or American photographer, say. No one has had such an exemption from ongoing torment since Dante toured hell. When you kneel and take your photographs of the old man with his hands cut off, your compassion is pure. Later, safe in your dark room, when you develop the film, you will assess your photographs on aesthetic characteristics, detachedly. But not entirely detachedly. You will wonder, as each photograph fades into timelessness, whether *Time* will buy this one. When *Time* does, you will be pleased, elated even. When you receive an award for your work, and the illustrious figure introducing you calls attention to the moral importance of your work, you will think yourself important and moral. What happened in Europe, you and your colleagues agree to call *inhuman* while secretly in sacred awe of the human ingenuity involved. What happened in India, you will call a *humanitarian catastrophe* while secretly contemptuous of the savages. You will have a story to tell. Maybe you will even make a memoir out of it some day, or a novel.

Maybe you are just a little unlucky. Maybe you are that little girl in the big house outside Amritsar. Maybe you will grow up to be a grandmother one day in Edison, New Jersey. Your athletic grandchildren will look up from the first homework of the new school year and ask you where you were, how it was, and you will tell them how some young men washed their swords in the courtyard one day. You watched from upstairs while the serving girls brought out buckets. One man poured while the others held out their swords, forearms, and eventually their legs, their trousers rolled up to the knees, like washing sand off after playing on the beach. They were very polite with your father. As soon as they left, he turned and ordered the servant girls to scour and sweep the stones with thick grass brooms; and pitched into the street the sandals that touched that dark puddled runoff.

Maybe all you lose is your father's house in Delhi, maybe he sends you and your over-bundled mother (she's wearing all her gold jewellery under the shawl) to live with his sister on the other side as early as March, when things look bad. Maybe he joins you by the end of May. He has cashed everything out, but he hasn't been able to sell the house. So, three years later, when you all visit as citizens of a foreign country, you find a doppelganger family, identical to yours, living in that house; and a boy who looks identical to you sleeps in your bed each night, and looks down at you suspiciously from the window where your three toy horses still guard the sill. And there is no legal recourse to undo this substitution.

Of course, it's also possible that you are one of the men rigging the train tracks, plugging your ears while your cousin pushes the plunger. Maybe you charge the wreckage with a sword. You haven't lost anyone yourself, but you have heard from the kafila, arriving in Delhi, what they are doing to yours, so you are doing this back to theirs. The violence you do is the first violence you see, but you haven't started it. They started it. And not this century, either. Your exhilaration is pure, purer than any ancient warrior's because your enemy has no weapons. You don't have to fear because there is no risk to you. Your power is pure. You are more powerful, working your way through these train compartments, than the Prime Minister of India. Can Jawaharlal Nehru do this? Stick a sword through a man so the point punctures the seat behind him? And then turn and do the same to his grandmother? You tower over them. The smell of these people comes from the meat they eat. They are prey now. Thin their numbers on the Pakistan Special. And in their villages, break and enter their girls. They are all converts, anyway. You're really only taking back these wombs. The men dead and the women put to good use incubating replacements. The oldest stain scrubbed out. The country clean like new. This is the most intense pleasure, and the only power, you will ever know. You will recall this power years from now, when you are stamping the forms of strangers behind a window, or dropping black weights on a scale against a housewife's eggplant, or kneeling to fit a man with new shoes. Some believe that a piece of the divine is within each person; but you *know* it is, because you are accessing yours right now. Unsheathe. Unzip. Do whatever you want. You are omnipotent right now. You are the luckiest of all.

Where is Dickie's Punjab Boundary Force in all this? Like God, everywhere and nowhere. A meeting in Lahore dissolves it. Or rather, splits it: Muslim soldiers to this side, Hindu and Sikh ones to that side, estranged last handshakes in the mess hall.

These soldiers go the way of everything else belonging to the Raj, divided and distributed. Where there are fourteen inkwells in an office, the bureaucrats squint and decant one into another, one into another, until they are all level down the line; then seven are slid to the right side of the desk, seven to the left. A Hindu clerk and a Muslim clerk in the Muzaffarabad Post Office, confronted with asymmetrically thick tape-rolls, tear and compare and tear again until they compare two cardboard rings. In Delhi, a typewriter is found missing an N key; the N key gets shelled from its opposite number before the crates leave for Pakistan. So it goes for the chairs and desks, for the unused manila envelopes, this last one an odd number, ripped down the middle and rubbished. So it goes for the paperclips, shaken out on the floor and counted.

So it goes, too, for the people. Lahore: Jinnah is sitting next to Fati in the back of a Packard limousine, part of a small motorcade, which cruises regally now to a stop among shivering tarpaulins and sunken tents. Jinnah gazes out through a tinted window.

'You should stay in here,' he whispers.

'Why?'

'You will never get this out of your mind.'

'I would not want to.'

'This will unsettle you. You are still a woman, Fati.'

'There are women refugees in that camp. If they can live there, I can visit.'

The chauffeur has hurried around to open her brother's door. Fati opens her own and strides ahead of her brother and his two guards. She speaks far better Urdu than her brother; she is the one who kneels and inquires. *Look here*, she thinks, *and do not look away*.

An old imam, acne-speckled with tiny burns. Five Hindu boys, all of whose parents he knew, had swaddled his head in belts of firecrackers. They did not mean to deafen or blind or burn him, though they did all three. 'They did it for sport. They were celebrating.'

A long public ravine, at the edge of camp, where some men stand and some squat. Where do the women go? There may have been a space clear of tents around the ditch once. But there is none now. Everyone just looks away.

If only there were somewhere else to breathe. Fati holds a handkerchief over her mouth and nose.

'You can go back to the car and put the windows up.'

'I am your sister, Jin. I am steel.'

A twig reaches out of the ditch muck. Jinnah catches the glimpse of a bony hand. Here is a woman with lopped-off nose and ears, the stubs crusted—but the left earlobe still attached, with a pretty earring. Another woman, fallen asleep, head to one side. Her dupatta has slipped. The skull is hairless; not even eyebrows. The bite mark on that neck is not a dog's.

Boys run past the Qaid-i-Azam and his sister, oblivious, giggling, striking a hoop with a stick. The hoop hiccoughs over a mound under brightly coloured rags. The boys run on and over the body, as if it were a feature of the ground. The hoop wobbles but keeps going.

Odour of burning tyres, not altogether unpleasant. The colonel guiding the Jinnahs through the camp studies Jinnah's face.

'You are unwell, Qaid,' he says suddenly. 'There is the medical tent. I can have them infuse my healthy blood into you.'

Odours of sawed bone and rubbing alcohol. Jinnah shakes his head and stumbles on. A doctor emerges from the tent in a butcher's apron. He is bespattered. He has one stretcher-bearer, who collects the suffering in a wheelbarrow, like a bee going flower to flower. 'We had a stretcher, but the sheet between the rods was white, and we think someone stole it for a shroud.'

Odour of people. They are trying to touch Jinnah's sleeve or slacks, their mouths moving. Fati does not have to translate for him. He knows the Urdu for *Save us*. Jinnah, disoriented, answers in natural English. They are baffled but calmed: a man in two turbans, one atop the other, one of cloth and one of bloody gauze; a man who presses his lips to Jinnah's spats. 'Qaid, Qaid.' As if now that the Qaid has advented himself, even the puddles are potable.

Somewhere a man clears his throat repeatedly, impossibly loud, like the mating-call of a monstrous auk. Jinnah looks around in a daze, searching. Fati touches his arm to bring him back. His eyes blink rapidly, but he refuses to let the tears out. A slight woman, seated atop two metal trunks, a knife across her lap, distractedly picks her nose. Behind her, twin girls lie asleep, mirroring each other, as they might have in the womb.

The same boys circle past now, still laughing and striking, only now, instead of a hoop, they're striking a crook-legged crack-voiced shuffling dog.

Fatima, to his left, is speaking to someone. 'This is the housewarming gift they send us. This.'

The spattered doctor says, 'Delhi is worse. We huddle on the lawns of consulates, and they call to us to come out. "Oh Hassan, oh Husein," they call, "come out, come out."'

Jinnah is tugged at again. Fati translates. The man says he pulled a body over his chin like a blanket. Sikhs with talwars,

Hindus with pitchforks. Then the train moved on. Slaughter had been one more station.

An old man with one empty eye socket. The other eye rolls freely, like a ball-compass, until it fixes on Jinnah. He says, rising to his feet: 'Pakistan zindabad.'

Jinnah in his white three-piece suit drifts down to the bare Pakistani earth. Fati and two guards rush to hold him up, but he has already buckled. The monocle has tumbled from his vest pocket and hangs, by its gold chain, in the dust.

'My God,' he whispers, 'what have I done?'

29

'My God,' shouts Nehru, 'what are they *doing*?'

And with that, he is out of his open-top car and running into a crowd on a Delhi street. His question is rhetorical; he knows exactly what this crowd has been doing, and they are making no secret of it, slogans in unison, tall bamboo staves, the men's kameezes translucent at chest and back with sweat drench, smeared in some places as if with Holi-red sindoor.

Edwina, in the seat beside him, dares not move as quickly because she wears a skirt, and now a soldier blocks her from following Nehru. Some others chase Nehru into the crowd, where he has grabbed one adolescent by the throat. He zeroed in on that fellow in particular out of horror at the way he was walking with his bamboo stave: a wide stride, the lathi set two paces ahead and rowed back, exactly like Bapu with his walking stick on the Salt March. The visual echo appals the disciple.

'You dog!' is all he can say. 'You dog!'

And maybe there is something, in that word, of the nobleman drubbing a jumped-up commoner. The rioter doesn't fight back. His eyes bulge, but his grimace seems like a smile. A secretary and two army colonels pull their Prime Minister off. The other rioters are strolling backwards with infuriating smiles on every face. 'You dogs!' Nehru says one more time. The rioter hurries to join up with his pack, but he turns and drops his jaw impossibly low. The lathi fits crosswise and level in his bite. He stares down Nehru a few seconds in that pose, then spits the long stave into his waiting palms and gives two mock barks. He celebrated Independence with halwa looted from a Muslim sweet shop. He has more celebrating yet to do.

Back at the idling car, Edwina has just pushed past the guardsman. It is all she can do to resist taking this shaky, stumbling Jawaharlal in her arms right there. The crowd that gathered to watch the rioters pass through has just witnessed the great Pandit Nehru showing bravery, or loss of self-control, or both. Now they are watching her, so she holds back, giving him nothing more than eye contact.

'Bapu did it in Calcutta with his presence alone,' Nehru is murmuring. 'His presence alone…'

The chauffeur has busied himself raising the top and securing it. This way, the two passengers retain some modicum of privacy—but more importantly, the PM will have a barrier between him and the dogs, should the car come across this kind of parade again.

Sardar Patel, meeting with Governor-General Mountbatten, has spread two dozen weapons on a cloth, all seized from 'Muslim troublemakers'.

Dickie turns one of the rusted blades in the light. 'I wonder,' murmurs Dickie. 'You are sure they weren't a lot of *farmers*?'

'This is what they are using. They've set up an informal network in Delhi.'

'Old rusted blades like these?'

'Crude blades for crude work,' Patel says, irritated at Dickie's scepticism. 'They can't do their killing with Maxim guns.'

Dickie opens his mouth—but pauses, thinking over that last bit. Just then, Nehru bursts into the room and drops himself dramatically into a chair.

'It is absurd!' he cries. 'If they all just sat down for ten minutes in one place, they would look around and see Delhi is the same city it was last month. And for centuries before last month! Just now—coming back from a camp with—it is beyond belief! If we had known! If we had ever imagined! What must the world think of us?'

'It's a shame, an absolute horror,' Dickie commiserates, 'but there was just no way to predict all this.'

'Bapu predicted it,' mutters Patel. 'We didn't listen. We acquiesced.'

Nehru, elbows on his knees, stares at the floor, either nauseated or pensive. 'These hooligans. These good-for-nothings. They have all gone quite mad.'

Patel shrugs. 'Is it madness?'

'What do you mean?'

'A hundred thousand refugees from West Punjab enter this city. They bring stories of what happened to them. They bring facts.'

Nehru stands. He and Sardar Patel, allies for decades, find themselves in a wholly new arrangement. Face to face, nose to nose. Dickie drifts back. The two Indians hold very still for a moment.

Nehru's stillness is kinetic: a tea kettle, moments from the whistle. Patel's is geological: his features a landscape, indifferent.

'There is no excuse for this killing.'

'I didn't excuse it. I explained it. The Muslims have pushed us and pushed us.'

'Us? We are all "us". India does not care what faith a man is.'

'Indians do.'

'Not *this* Indian. Nor any Indian in my Cabinet.'

'Every Indian should put India first. And love it wholly. Without divided sympathies.'

'These two faiths spent centuries as neighbours. It proves they can live together.'

'Did that argument work on Jinnah?' Patel snaps. 'All that this ongoing disaster proves is that they need a policeman. Not a historian, and not a speechmaker. And if our prisons get too full, there's always Pakistan.'

'We are speaking in terms of *millions*!' Nehru objects. 'What would they write in the history books? Have you thought of that?'

Patel gathers up the rusted blades with a swift upward movement of the cloth on which he has arrayed them. He waves a hand dismissively. 'This may all be for nothing in the end. In a few months, a year at most, they will beg us to undo this absurd partition of theirs. And I do mean *beg*.'

'Millions,' says Jinnah.

'Locked up in their treasury?'

'Five hundred and fifty million, to be precise.'

'You don't say!'

Karachi: Jinnah's study in the Governor-General's mansion. The man sitting across the desk is an American, Paul Alling, a 6' 6'' Connecticut innocent with a side-part and an overbite. Fati, ever more ghostly where she haunts the top of the stairs, has let no visitors through to her ailing brother in the week since his collapse—except for two. One was the Finance Minister of the world's richest Muslim, the still-independent Nizam of Hyderabad; the other is this ambassador from Washington.

'You see my absurd situation,' Jinnah appeals, his empty hands palms-up. 'To be one of the most powerful men in the world, and yet to be a beggar.'

'But that's your money, isn't it?'

'Not until India releases it.'

'What's the hold up?'

'They are waiting for Pakistan to starve to death.' Jinnah's hands come together and clench, and Alling sees how bony they are. It's as if his body were Pakistan's body, and this talk of starvation were literal. 'All I ask is a morsel. A morsel for the starving man. It is in your interests, too. Nehru is a socialist, a natural ally of Stalin.'

This is the red button Jinnah knows he must press. Alling's ungainly sunburnt head begins to nod. What, Jinnah wonders, do they *eat* over there? It is as though excessive geographic empty space allowed their bodies, physically, to expand, as in a vacuum. The same is true of Russians, whom the Americans fear, Jinnah knows, with no small frenzy. The Americans have more money, but they have seen how easy-going Stalin is when spending Russians.

'Islam is egalitarian, Mr Alling. Our Prophet presaged your Jefferson. All Muslims are brothers, all men are created equal—we are saying the same thing. You need a power on this subcontinent that will stand up to the Soviets with a pistol in each hand. Can you trust Nehru to do that? Nehru is a socialist.'

'You know, Mr *Jin*nuh,' stressing the first syllable, barely pronouncing the second. Jinnah does not correct him; the lender is always right. 'You know, we have a flag back home we used to rally behind, during our own revolution against the Brits. Had a snake on it, and the words "Don't Tread on Me". Reminds me of what went on here, with you and your independence struggle, and I want you to know, we're all just bursting at the seams with admiration and sympathy.'

'Two billion US dollars will buy us breath for a week.'

Alling takes the cigar from his mouth and nods a little less emphatically. 'I'll see what I can do for you in Washington.'

'Not for me. For democracy.'

Alling's handshake feels firmer now than it felt when he arrived. Jinnah takes it for a good sign. Even a fraction will buy him a Royal Pakistan Navy, which consists right now of four minesweepers and two trawlers; and a Royal Pakistan Air Force, which doesn't exist yet.

And a limousine. Jinnah, exhausted by the thirty-minute meeting, drops on to his bed that afternoon, but the next day, he pages through a Cadillac catalogue while riding to Lahore. The current Packard humiliates him. It's no ride for the Qaid-i-Azam, not when Nehru enjoys a small fleet.

In Lahore, at the Governor's House, he writes a letter stating his decision: a silver nine-passenger Imperial plush, black leather, custom coachwork monogrammed *MAJ*. Fati rushes into the room. She holds a telegram crushed to her chest. A blood vessel in her left eye has burst, dyeing it a livid red from tear duct to iris.

India has landed troops in Kashmir.

Who started it?

Ask Jinnah, and he will blame Nehru, the Kashmiri scheming on Kashmir. Ask Nehru, and he will point to Maharajah Hari Singh of Kashmir, currently hurtling south in a fleet of Rolls-Royces while a squadron of Indian planes hurtle north. Didn't he sign Kashmir over to India? Before the planes took off, or just after—what does it matter when?

Ask the Maharajah, and he'll blame the bearded and cross-eyed Pathan tribes, who have shaken their rifles over their heads and piled into buses and happy honking lorries—and are raping and gunning their way to his capital even now, the only hiccoughs in their progress a periodic pause to pray. All those irregulars, so easily distracted by Catholic nuns and other sweetmeats, drop their foreheads to the ground on some mysterious collective cue, all lined up, like a tumble of iron shavings arranged rigid around a magnet.

Ask those (Muslim) Pathan tribesmen, and they'll blame the Maharajah's (Hindu) Dogra soldiers, who have weeded Kashmir's sloping southwest of Muslims. *Cry 'havoc' and let slip the Dogras of war.*

Ask the Maharajah's soldiers, and they'll blame Pakistani officers in plain clothes, tiptoeing over the border. *Pakistan zindabad*, or *Death to Hindus*, whichever works: for weeks they've meant the same thing anyway. Jinnah doesn't know anything about the whisper war, but only because he interrupted his own briefing with that very assertion—*I don't know anything about this*—eyes shut, his thin hand covering the unrolled map.

Ask those officers, and they'll blame Sardar Patel, who has paved the sole dirt road to Srinagar. He has been trucking gasoline and weapons north for days now on the sly. Ask Sardar Patel, and he'll blame Jinnah.

Ask Jinnah...

'What do we do?'

Past midnight in Lahore. Jinnah—Governor-General of Pakistan, Qaid-i-Azam, rich man, poor man, beggarman, thief—wears his tie askew for the first time in forty years. The only power on earth capable of doing that used to be Ruttie Jinnah's beauty. Tonight, it is the equally exquisite Kashmir.

The room is full of eyes, all fixed on Jinnah: scattered aides, a secretary, and here, beside a telephone, the Governor of West Punjab. The Governor is a sunburnt British holdover named Sir Francis Mudie, loyal to Jinnah and to Glenlivet. The question he fires at Jinnah has a drunk's surliness to it. The odour of alcohol—Sir Francis has spilt some on the carpet—only makes this moment giddier for Jinnah.

He doesn't answer at first; he keeps pacing, wondering how he can make war on the country that still holds all his cash reserves. Every time he approaches the window, his chin jerks up, nervously birdlike, and his eyes scan the night sky. The crescent moon matches the one on his new flag. Is it waxing or waning? He never learnt how to tell. A star blinks, and Jinnah watches to see if it moves, a wing light; or falls, an omen. He doesn't *expect* a bomber squadron from across the border, but anything seems possible right now. India has bared its teeth.

Now he must bare his. He is a lawyer, not a military man. How do you do this? How do you cry 'havoc' in real life? Jinnah takes a deep breath, but his eloquence lies dead on his tongue. No inspiring Shakespearean monologue is forthcoming. The question shoots him from behind again, garrulous, surreal.

'I say, Qaid! What do we do? Shall we let Pretty Boy have it or what?'

Jinnah pivots, deciding. His eyes shut with concentration. The white-green electric afterimage of that crescent moon pulses against his eyelids, and a new headache throbs with every pulse. 'Send them in. One group into Srinagar, the other to block the road into Kashmir. Send them in.'

The aides look like they want to scatter to separate tasks, but they, too, don't know what to do. Tipsy Mudie points at one. 'You! Stevenson! You heard the Qaid!'

The aide gets on the telephone with the army. The Lieutenant-General who picks up on base is still another Britisher. Their conversation is hushed, clipped, jargon-laden, inscrutable. Finally, the aide turns to Jinnah, still holding the receiver, and shakes his head. 'They cannot deploy, sir.'

'Good God, why not? Have they been attacked?'

'Stand Down order, sir.'

'Who ordered them to stand down?'

'Says they have standing orders, sir.'

Jinnah stares incredulously at his British underling's British underling.

Drunk old Governor Mudie snatches the earpiece and waves his early-Christmas whisky-ration at the aide. Some of the whisky splashes on the aide, who pats his shoulder as though it were flame. Mudie listens a moment, scowling; then erupts: 'Orders is orders, you twit! I don't give a fig about British officers on the other side! ... The head of bloody *state*, that's who!'

The tirade blunders on; Mudie's speech gets so slurred, and his pauses last so noddingly long, Jinnah wonders if anyone else is on the line.

'They shan't budge, Qaid,' declares Mudie at last, batting the whole telephone to the floor. 'Not tonight at least. They're flying in tomorrow by noon to explain it to you.'

Jinnah shakes his head. 'There is nothing to explain.'

Mudie drops a few disjointed comments, then leaves off in favour of a chin-on-chest catnap. He has quite exhausted himself.

Turning to find his own chair, Jinnah finds Fatima immediately behind him, shaking her head.

'Those Indian planes were waiting on their airstrips,' she whispers. 'Fuelled and ready to go.'

'Our British officers say they won't fire on Nehru's British officers. I am paralysed.'

'This is all a scheme. Mountbatten, Nehru and Hari Singh. Every detail of this is crooked.'

'That was the K in Pakistan.' Jinnah finds his chair and sinks into it, cigarette held between his lips distractedly, unlit. His tone is airy and disbelieving. 'They are there right now, Fati. By morning they will be dug in. No plebiscite. Kashmir is as good as Indian territory.'

Fati crosses her arms. 'It doesn't have to be, brother. There are ways.'

30

Birla House, Delhi.

A small pile of cloth lies bunched on a cot. It looks like a bed someone has left unmade. Here, at one end, are two dusty stones: heels, with fissures so deep they look like they were gouged with a razor. At the other end are a small clutch of oak-bark twigs, knuckled where they crook inward: fingers. That's a body under there. Or the mummified remains of one, withered under its grave wrappings. Small spectacles flash in a cloth cave, where the head hides. Behind those spectacles, eyes—fallible, mischievous, cunning, wise.

Enter Nehru. He kneels at one end and makes his confession.

'Maybe I was hasty,' he whispers, 'going in. Sending the planes, the soldiers. It is my home. I am fond of it. Maybe too fond of it. I could not bear to see it sacked.'

Haste: did he have the Maharajah's accession in hand, or did it reach Delhi the morning after the troop planes took off? When did he send a telegram across the border to Jinnah? Or didn't he, until afterwards?

'I suspect it would have come to this anyway. That does not mean I know how it came to this. We are at war, Bapu!

We believed in you and your message, Patel and I. But we are at war.'

War: the infiltration began in earnest with Pakistani soldiers, spry, roguish, hungry; soldiers who, if they weren't soldiers, would have been smugglers or horse thieves. And to rattle the hive and aim the swarm, trained men, lean and bearded and kameezed within a ring of tribesmen, their only distinguishing mark the educated military crispness of their Urdu. They pointed down at a hamlet in a valley, eyed the grey crags, distributed mortars—and reported back to base with a radio set. Ghazis in disguise, half colonel, half scoundrel, but no cards or tags under their tribal garb. Sly unscrupulous slippery men, on paid leave for six months: and *given* leave, by the highest authority in Karachi. By the Qaid-i-Azam. They went out and gave those lusty looting Pathans a little discipline as they slipped across the border by the thousands, cross-eyed bearded fanatics emerging from the hintermountains. Fanatics, yes, but the Qaid's fanatics now. They hand out tins of rations and wave the trucks through by moonlight.

'It is *himsa*, Bapu. It is war outright. And now regular regiments are clashing. Our soldiers—they are fighting their own comrades. They tell me they recognize each other across the passes, through binoculars. They call and answer each other by name between exchanges of fire. But it is too late now. I cannot *not* fight this war.'

It is almost an echo of Arjuna, centuries ago. *I will not fight.* The plain of Kurukshetra, where the Gita was sung, is covered in refugee tents. Edwina Mountbatten has arranged for a hundred tons of flour, lentils, sugar, and cooking oil per day, and 3,000 miles of blanket against the coming winter night—and film projectors. The refugees, 15,000 at a time, watch Mickey and Goofy and Donald climb a giant beanstalk to the giant's castle.

Fee, fi, fo, fum. Their laughter is so loud that schoolchildren half a mile away approach the camp in curiosity and envy. The giant's name is Willie, his sidekick's name is Gruesome Gulch. They have stolen the singing harp that kept Happy Valley happy.

'I know you think all war is evil. But we did not make this war. We are only fighting it.'

At last Gandhi speaks. 'I did not know there was a difference.'

'What do you want me to do? I cannot pull out. I cannot simply give Kashmir up.'

'I want you to follow your conscience.'

'My conscience says fight.'

'Then why have you come to me, Jawaharlal?'

Another prayer meeting at Birla House. Military planes headed north to Srinagar roar overhead while he gives his sermon.

It isn't a sermon in praise of the war, but he doesn't condemn it, either. In Gandhi's home state of Gujarat, the dog-fancying Nawab of Junagadh acceded to Pakistan, giving Jinnah a dot of green along the underbelly of India, with a port to boot. Junagadh's royal family was Muslim, her people, Hindu—a perfect inversion of Kashmir. Indian tanks have encircled and seized it in the name of the people; Gandhi's own nephew led the rebel government.

Junagadh is two rail stops away from Porbandar, where Gandhi was born. So he knows what it is to want his homeland to join India; he knows what Nehru feels about Kashmir. But he also knows what it is to see people of his own religion handed over, en masse, by a petty princeling scribbling his name on a piece of paper. So he knows what Jinnah feels about Kashmir, too.

During the prayer meeting, Sardar Patel stands off to one side, next to Manu. He joins his hands during the Gayatri

Mantra, but during the Qur'anic recitation, sura 82, *al-Infitar*, Patel cracks his knuckles and thrusts his hands behind his back, left hand gripping right wrist, fingers flaring and making a fist, flaring and making a fist.

He has not asked for this audience after the prayer meeting, as he has so often before. This time, he has been summoned.

For a while, he watches his adored frustrating master fiddle with the spinning wheel.

'There is a saying in the Bible,' Gandhi begins at last. Quietly, unassumingly, as always. 'A saying of Jesus. We should render unto Caesar what is Caesar's, and unto God what is God's.'

'This is about the money, isn't it?'

'Whose is it? Five hundred million rupees, I believe. Is that money India's?'

'Five hundred and fifty. And no.'

'Then whose is it?'

'Jinnah's.'

'It belongs to Pakistan. To the Pakistani people. Not Jinnah. I want you to meditate on that saying of Jesus.'

'I don't intend to pay Caesar while Caesar is shelling my troops.'

'India must not commit a theft against her sister, Sardar.'

'Pakistan *itself* is a theft. We saw it happen. Daylight robbery.'

The spinning wheel slows. Gandhi has no answer to this.

'As soon as we settle Kashmir,' Patel pushes on, 'I will write Jinnah a cheque. The same day. But not before.'

Enter Manu. She brings her Bapu his lunch on a tea-saucer. Patel waits while Gandhi shifts and dines almond by individually pinched almond. The Mahatma is an aged, delicate, magical mammal, and Patel wants to explain that the world is young, brutal, unmagical, reptilian.

Or no, maybe not the world. Just Pakistan.

'During the war,' Patel says slowly, as though explaining to a child, 'the Americans built massive factories for bombs and planes and mortars. Then, one day, they won the war. What do you think happened to those factories, Bapu?'

Gandhi reflects. 'I imagine they were shuttered. Never to reopen, I hope.'

'They weren't. Because they were business ventures. Shrewd, unscrupulous men had invested in those assembly lines.'

'Perhaps they began making construction cranes, to rebuild what the war had destroyed.'

'They kept the assembly lines going,' Patel says through clenched teeth. 'They looked around for someone new to sell to.'

Gandhi looks Patel in the eyes. 'It is Pakistan's money.'

'To buy bombs with. To buy bombers with.'

'You must render unto Jinnah what is Jinnah's.'

'After Kashmir. That is all I beg of you. After Kashmir.'

'I am going to announce a fast tomorrow, Sardar. For Hindu–Muslim unity. A fast unto death.'

'Don't do this to me.'

'I will set certain conditions for the breaking of my fast. I will not announce this one, regarding the money. But I am setting it now. Between us.'

'Don't do this.'

'Churchill did not let me die, Sardar.'

'Don't…'

'Will you?'

31

'Mohammad Gandhi! Mohammad Gandhi!'

He grew so weak so fast, his assistants had to carry him out in a chair to show him to the crowd at Birla House. Behold the man. The crowd members said later that they felt the fever heat coming off him. Back on his cot, he read a short prayer into a recording device, his head never rising off his bent arm. One of his disciples read out a list of seven demands.

'Mohammad Gandhi!'

Today he has broken his fast, and Pakistan is 550 million rupees richer.

Sardar Patel, making the announcement to the press, his eyes never lifting from the paper he reads from, insists it has been done as 'a gesture of good will'.

Crowds of young Hindus have rushed to the streets around Birla House this morning, where Gandhi sips lemon water and takes two bites of the banana Manu holds by his mouth.

The street has found a new name for the Mahatma.

'Send him to Pakistan.' 'Traitor.' 'Jinnah's brother.'

'Down with Mohammad Gandhi.'

The bomb goes off in the middle of the first prayer meeting he is strong enough to give. The rhythm of his speech does not falter.

'Oneness is all. To love someone, you must dissolve the wall of your self. And so must the one you love. Neither can be self-seeking. Love requires equality. So do all good things that man seeks, like justice, or God, or freedom. There must be equality first.'

He does not pay attention to the half-dozen, the three dozen men rushing to the flower-lined gates of Birla House, or the uneasy shifting of his audience, or the distant frenzied shouting on the street, or, now, the police whistles.

'In politics, this also holds true. I hope the future Prime Minister of India is a girl right now, or a young woman. Not just a girl but a girl of the sweeper caste. What we won in August was mere independence. Now that we are independent, what will we do? When one day a girl from the sweeper caste becomes Prime Minister, you must turn to one another and say: we have won our freedom. India is free.'

That night in his room at Birla House, he sleeps between Manu and Abha again. They are both fast asleep and have turned to him in their sleep, Abha with her knee bent and her thigh resting on his. Abha always sleeps with her hair loose, but the tie has slipped Manu's staid braid tonight. So her face, too, is hidden behind her hair. Gandhi lies awake. The familiar faces of his grand-nieces are hidden. In the moonlight, they are just young women. They could be any young women at all. They could be apsaras, celestial dancing girls in the court of Indra, exhausted after a performance. They could be two whores from the whorehouse Mohandas visited as a young man, when he made friends with his ship's captain, and the captain showed him how sailors amuse themselves in a port city. Gandhi begins to regress between their suddenly feral bodies. His moustache grows bushy and black, and his hair returns, and the wrinkles of his face smooth out as his face swells. It isn't just his face that swells but his whole body, taking on flesh and bulk again. And then, when he has filled out to a young man again, his desire swells towards his navel. Very subtly his pelvis stirs, begins to thrust at the ceiling, at the night sky, the full moon. He gasps, and his half-awake dream breaks in horror. His body is the same as before, seventy-eight years old, bald and emaciated. The bomb blast earlier that day gave away death's hiding place out in the brush, and the old pointer dog has scented death and points his muzzle, rigid.

Gandhi rises from the cot and stands at the foot of it, overshadowing the two naked young women. He whispers, 'Rama, Rama.' His desire shrivels and backs down, cowed. The sacred name has commanded lust to heel. He whispers 'Rama' and slides between them again. He is instantly asleep.

The next morning, when Manu is writing down a dream in her diary, he puts his hand on her shoulder. Her pen stops.

'One day, you must write about our experiments.'

She nods.

'You must write everything, some day, when I am gone. I want you to do so. I order you to do so.'

'Yes, Mother.'

'You must explain what we did here.'

'And what we did not.'

'Everything.'

Ten days later. It is half past three in the morning on 30 January 1948. Gandhi's eyes flutter open, and he stares at the ceiling of his ground-floor room at Birla House. His eyes, as if they saw some intense light while they were shut, don't adjust to the darkness. For a few moments, he thinks, *I have died*. Slowly, his eyes seek out and collect the traces of light in the room. The figures of his grand-nieces come into focus, and the outlines of the room and window. He tries to awaken them by shaking their shoulders. No response. Outside the room, their bedding laid out on the floor, some of his followers and his doctor sleep as well. He tries to awaken them, too, but they don't even stir in their sleep. He cannot hear them breathe. And he wonders again whether he has died; whether this is some residual illusion of embodiment that stands, and walks about, and imagines it touches these sleepers. After all, he hasn't walked without help since his fast. Over there, in the room, is where he has died; he must go back and lie down on the cot, he thinks, so they can say that Bapu died in his sleep. And this is what he does. He lies down between his grand-nieces and closes his eyes. When he opens them again, it is half past three in the morning on 30 January 1948. He touches Manu on the shoulder. This time, she awakens. The day begins.

Everyone else is asleep at that hour. In Delhi, Dickie Mountbatten and Edwina are asleep in the same bed, in parallel, on their backs. Their hands are folded on their stomachs and their skin is bleach white in the moonlight, like the marble relief on a tomb. Nehru is asleep, too, alone in a maelstrom of bunched sheets, his limbs flung each in a different direction, one pillow on the ground. Sardar Patel is asleep, too, an arm flung over his eyes, his snores so loud they seem industrial, the crickets in the bushes startled silent.

In Karachi, Fatima sleeps on her side, her hair tucked back to expose her ear. She is a light sleeper; her bed set up with its head by the open door, she will hear any stray cry or cough her brother might give out. This has been another bad night, but Jinnah himself is asleep right now. His desk is covered in draft pages for a constitution, a face-down copy of *The Tempest,* letters from Dacca and New York and London, a personal bill he plans to challenge, books of law, and a pad on which he has doodled a fanciful coat-of-arms—a lion rampant, a crescent moon crossed with a scimitar, and a motto on a banner, *Don't Tread on Me*.

In Delhi, Gandhi chews his neem twig and spits.

In Karachi, Jinnah coughs and turns his head from side to side. Fati appears at his door with a steel cup full of water, watching him, waiting as he settles back to sleep.

Gandhi, too, has developed a cough since his most recent fast. It is particularly bad this morning. Manu brings him a steel cup full of lemon water. She usually brings him clove powder, but she has run out.

'I will make some for you later this morning,' she promises.

He shakes his head. 'Don't bother. Who knows if I will need any, by tonight?'

It sounds as if he were certain of his recovery. Or at least she interprets it that way. On the porch, in the lavender unlight before sunrise, Manu sings the Gita, as her mother the Mahatma has taught her. She begins, as usual, with the first chapter, but he stops her and asks her to recite the twelfth. The twelfth is the chapter recited at funerals.

After she finishes, he rises airily from his cross-legged seat, like a puppet teased aloft by a string.

Manu smiles in astonishment. 'This is the first time you are walking on your own since the fast.'

Walk alone, walk alone, he whispers. She does not recall, at the time, that he is quoting a poet. *Walk alone* were Tagore's last words.

Manu's morning devotions, her daily offices continue. She brings three inches of steaming water, fills the rest of the bucket with cold, and washes his body, intimate intermittent splashes on the tile, the only child she wants or will ever have. He calls himself her 'mother', but it is Manu who rubs ghee into his heels and holds the cup of goat's milk to his lips, Manu who sets him chalk and slate for his writing exercises. She holds the book open just above the slate that rests on his knees. The language he teaches himself is Bengali because he plans to go back to East Pakistan. The line says, 'Joydeep's home is in Naihati', but he copies it as 'Joydeep's home is in Noakhali', and puts down the chalk. 'I will finish all this next time.' He does not let her wipe the slate.

The rest of the morning and afternoon pass in meetings. Gandhi has allowed thirty of Patel's policemen on to the premises, some in uniform, some in plain clothes. All they do is mill about, because Gandhi has refused Patel permission to rifle through bags or pat down pockets.

Sardar Patel himself is Gandhi's final visitor, arriving late in the afternoon. Gandhi saw him just a week ago, but today, he sees Patel as if for the first time in years. He can see just how much weight Patel has lost, how the skin of his jowls and forearms hangs loose. Exhaustion and sadness hood his once-sharp eyes. They both know what Patel is here to discuss.

'You and Jawaharlal,' says Gandhi.

'It is a marriage gone bad.'

'What happened?'

'The Partition. The killings. Kashmir. Everything. We agree on nothing any more. One of us has to go.'

Gandhi shakes his head. 'You were not meant to agree. You keep one another in balance. I wanted it that way.'

Patel eyes Gandhi, but Gandhi is looking studiously at the ground, refusing to meet his eyes. 'Back when Congress was deciding who would be Prime Minister,' Patel says quietly, 'it came down to me and Jawaharlal. Before August. Everyone was shouting my name.'

'I remember.'

'And you wrote on a chit of paper and tucked it in my hand.'

'I asked you to withdraw your name.'

'We never spoke about it since. I never asked you, *why not me*.'

'I love you. You can ask me anything you wish.'

Their eyes meet. 'Why not me, Bapu?'

The throngs outside Birla House are the usual crowds. The numbers always start swelling an hour before a prayer meeting by Gandhi. There's no reason for any of Patel's policemen to note the tonga pulling up some distance down the street, or the slight man stepping out of it in a crisp new khaki jacket.

Pinched but full mouth, high cheekbones tapering to a small chin, eyes dark and sunken. When he pays the tonga-wallah, he counts the coins out with his free hand. The right hand doesn't leave that jacket pocket.

Manu Gandhi listens quietly in the neighbouring room.

'Your allegiance is to your blood,' Gandhi is saying. 'Jawahar's allegiance is to … ideas. Ideals.'

'That is not true.'

'I thought that then. Perhaps I was wrong. But I would have you no other way than how you are.'

'My allegiance is to you.'

'And when I fail you?' Gandhi coughs. 'When I disappoint you?'

'You never have.'

'And when your blood cries out that Gandhi is a fool in his old age?'

'My allegiance is to India. But that is the same thing as saying, "To you."'

'You are both indispensable to India. And to me. I have written to Mountbatten, and he agrees.'

Manu does not hear his response. Two new visitors have arrived outside, wanting an audience with the Mahatma. They are the most obsequious gentlemen from Porbandar, his home town, who have brought a crate of kesar mangoes as a gift. 'So the Mahatma might taste his childhood again.'

Before Nathuram Godse was born, a family curse carried off brother after brother. The curse targeted male children, so his parents dressed him in a girl's clothes for the first five years of his life. Nathuram's parents were so thorough with the ruse, they fooled the curse. They even pierced the baby boy's nose. A dark divot still pocks his left nostril.

Nathu-ram, *Rama with the Nose-Ring*: the ideal Hindu man, feminized by a diamond. Born a boy, raised a girl, Nathuram remembered fondly ever after the tinkle of anklets when he walked. Though maybe *Godse* had its own meaning, its own promise. God se: *From God*.

God-sent is how he feels today.

In fact, he was born a Brahmin, though he has been reduced since to the work of a tailor. He has measured the waists of men, kneeling before them even though he didn't have to; has measured the busts of women and felt nothing. A lisp, a delicate jaw, a slight frame. No wonder he joined the RSS—virility and religion in one—thighs fleshy in the khaki shorts as he did his exercises. Squat, stand. He has learnt all about Shivaji embracing Afzal Khan, the Mahratta holding the warlord close and stabbing him. Killing could be intimate, a passionate embrace between men, their mouths open, bodies locked, until at last, at the climactic penetration, came the grimace, the jerks of the spine, the crying out. The aim of his mentors was to teach their young men to love who they were. Hate came in only as an instructional tool.

Truth be told, it's not that Godse hasn't been there at different points in Gandhi's story. He's just never been seen. Go back to Gandhi's visit to Jinnah's house on Malabar Hill, to discuss whether Indians were two nations or one. A crowd of young men blocked his car until several ashram workers shoved them aside and parted that sea. Godse was one of the faces heckling the tinted windows.

Or again, when Gandhi came down with malaria shortly after Kasturba's death, and the British released him from prison. The crowds meeting his release were not all cheering with joy. And in one of those crowds, chanting the slogans, was the same young man who paces the grass now on the Birla House grounds, near the wooden platform where Gandhi will pray this afternoon.

Manu brings Gandhi's snack into the room. 'Two more visitors,' she says, 'from Porbandar.'

'Tell them I will meet them after the prayer meeting,' says Gandhi, 'if I am still alive then.'

Patel flinches at this offhand remark. He rubs his chest, just to the left of his breastbone. The hand climbs nervously to the left side of his neck and drifts away. He gets these pains in his chest sometimes. More often, in the past six months; and always when he worries about Kashmir, or the refugees, or, as now, Bapu.

'You need more security here.'

Gandhi smiles. 'No, Sardar, *you* need more security here. I am quite secure.'

'You are lucky. I am responsible for your safety, and luck isn't on my payroll.'

'It has been ten days since that bomb went off. It sounded like something boys set off at Diwali.'

'You've refused to let us search the people coming to your meetings. There are at least 300 at each one.'

'They are coming to prayer. What if they wish to take notes?'

'I'm not worried about paper and pens.'

'God has protected me until now. In Noakhali, in Calcutta…'

'That was before Kashmir.'

'If I allow this, I will be saying to everyone who comes to pray with me, "I suspect you."'

'Let me do the suspecting for you.'

'How can there be love after that? How can there be communion?'

Two accomplices have joined Godse, but they stay at a distance. The men have planned out where each will stand. Godse nearest the platform, thirty feet away from Gandhi; the others, ready to push back the crowd while what has to be done is done.

Patel has covered his face. 'I am an old man, too,' he says. 'Maybe I am a fool in my old age.'

'We cannot understand love without a little foolishness.'

'I cannot bear this strain, Bapu. I do not sleep any more. Not more than two hours at a time.'

'Try cinnamon and turmeric in honey before bed. I will prepare it for you myself.'

Patel shakes his head. 'Tell me if I should step down. Tell me.'

Gandhi answers with three words of Sanskrit, from the Gita. *Tasmad yudhyasva Bharata*. The epithet used for Arjuna—*Bharata*—is also one of the names of India itself. *Therefore, Bharata, fight*.

Manu and Abha peek into the room again. 'You are already late,' says Manu. 'It is past five.'

Gandhi and Patel look at one another again, and Patel nods.

'I must tear myself away,' whispers Gandhi. 'It is time.'

Godse keeps his hand in his jacket pocket. The other is forming and releasing a fist. A distant commotion tells him Gandhiji has been sighted. He turns his head, waiting for the crowd to part. *Now they have their own land,* he is thinking. *In a hundred years, there will be none of us left there, on that side of the border. Overrun, converted, killed, expelled. That is what they do. That is what they are. They show no mercy. But we are ordered to show mercy. Forced to, by him. And what do we get in return, here? A mixed country that won't even call itself Hindustan, where they stay and their mosques stay, and we must be meek, retiring, hospitable, accommodating. The way his admirers look at him: the way I once looked at him myself: what couldn't he have accomplished for the Hindus, if he had been on our side? If only he had stood on that wooden platform and ordered us to fight back as one. If he had said, 'Hindus, unite, you have only one place and one chance on earth, fight now and burn them all out, push them out, drive them under, hurry, fight or you will be strangers in your own home forever. Clear a space for yourselves now, just as they have cleared a space. For there is no other place for you on earth ...' But he is not our Jinnah. No, he is a traitor, shrewdly sick to set the world sobbing, blackmailing everyone with his fasts.*

There he is. That fragile figure, supported by two girls, the three of them shuffling over the grass. Closer. I could do it right now. There is a corridor of green between me and him. People will speak evil of me for doing it, even my own people, but after the hate is spent, we will look around and realize we can do anything now, untroubled, unwitnessed by that conscience shuffling over the grass. Closer, closer. And as my people slaughter them in Kashmir and Hyderabad and everywhere, they will cry for joy: 'He has set us free, Godse has set us free!'

Look at him, so close. I could just walk up to him. I could do it right now. Point-blank. Gazing in his eyes. Point-blank. I could do it. Point-blank.

They are chatting quietly in Gujarati. Nothing religious. Gandhi is poking fun at his own dietary scruples.

'The Sardar and I were speaking of such grave matters,' he teases Manu, 'and then you brought me that raw carrot.'

'But you always like your carrots raw!'

'It was hard for me to stay serious when I was crunching so loudly. He misses his farm, you know. I told him I like cattle feed.'

'Ba used to call it horse fodder,' says Manu.

'I relish what no one likes to eat,' murmurs Gandhi. He smiles. 'Or at least no beast that walks on two legs.'

They stop. A man bends low across the path, hands joined, reaching for Gandhi's feet.

The pistol between Godse's hands is a piece of colonial debris. It has wandered a long way to this point. From Mussolini's Italy, in 1934, it travelled south to Abyssinia, where Italy, the runt of the European litter, had found, at last, a territory so isolated even Italians could swagger and slaughter there. Olive-skinned preyed on black-skinned, south preyed on equatorial—but there was no escaping the old colonial pecking order of colours and latitudes. In time, a blond-haired British officer stripped that pistol off an Italian soldier in the desert, a private trophy from El Alamein.

Redeployment. The pistol travelled, with its new sahib, on the sea route through Aden to Bombay. A servant of the newly arrived sahib saw the pistol in its teak case and thought it must be worth something. The pistol fit snugly under his turban.

This was an old pistol, the pawnbroker explained, good for nothing. The Germans made good pistols; a German pistol from the war was a true find and could still fetch a price. These Italian pieces were trash, scarcely worth the risk of selling on the black market. Who knew if it would even fire? Thirty rupees and no more.

Better than nothing. And so, the pistol had changed hands again, disgraced from its high station. Sleek colonial enforcer became museum-piece trophy in a teak case became war rubbish in the back room of a pawn shop—sold, months later, to a sucker named Nathuram Godse.

The pistol has shrunk in size over the course of its travels. Who knows if it will fire? It is small enough to hide between Godse's small hands, joined prayerfully now, as he lunges to touch Gandhi's feet.

'Namaste, Gandhiji.'

Manu knows Bapu doesn't like it when people press their lips to his feet. And this fellow has bowed unnaturally low. The things she carries for Gandhi—mala, book, and spectacle-case—shift to the crook of her right arm.

'The Mahatma is already late for prayers,' she says, bending slightly to guide Godse up with her left hand. 'Brother, why are you—'

The young man's arm shoves her, heel of palm to collarbone, as he rears to his full height. Everything in the crook of her arm has dropped, but all she sees is the mala, 108 sandalwood beads with a tassel of red threads, fallen in the grass. Bapu has cycled those beads through his fingers thousands of times, saying 'Rama, Rama' under his breath. Her attention follows this sacred object that must not touch the ground.

Godse has straightened to his full height. His arm straightens, too. The small, shabby pistol barely peeks past his hand. To one half of the crowd, it looks as though he reaches out to touch Gandhi's heart. Manu has bent down, arm extending, as if to touch his feet in reverence. The mala has fallen midway between the facing men. Her fingertips have just brushed a sandalwood bead when inches above her head God says 'No' three times.

They are on the grass.

In this forest of legs, they make a clearing unto themselves. Mother and child. Virgin mother and sacrificed child.

Blood smudges her glasses. She smells gunpowder and marigolds.

She places his head against her thigh. She strokes his cheek.

Whatever state of being a man remembers when he gives up his body, that is where he goes in the end.

'Hey Rama ... hey Rama ... hey Rama...'

Three shots: because twenty-three years from this day, the country he envisioned will be three countries. Three shots because three faiths killed and died and fled in the land of five rivers. Three sounds comprise the sacred syllable, *ah, u,* and *mah*, Aum, and he alone declared that the *ah* in Brahman was the *ah* in Allah, but Jinnah said no, no, no. *Verily, I say unto thee, That this night, before the cock crow, thou shalt deny me thrice.* Brahma, Vishnu, and Shiva the destroyer. The Bapu, the Son, and the Holy Ghost. Three shots because, in the Ramayana, three exiles set out into the wilderness. Three shots because Gandhi would be reborn three times: once in Porbander, once beside the train tracks in South Africa, and the last time here, thrown to the ground again. Bleeding out through three bullet holes, three rivers, the Ganga, the Yamuna, the Saraswati, the mystical confluence that washes away lust and ambition and vanity. The Gita Gandhi heard the morning of his assassination is the Gita his assassin will carry to the gallows on the morning of his execution. *Therefore, Bharata, fight.* Gandhi dies in possession of no mansion in Bombay, no Rolls-Royce, no three-piece suit. Gandhi dies owning a pair of spectacles and a case, a beggar's bowl and plate, the sandals on his feet, a Gita, and a watch. *Now I am Time, destroyer of worlds.* It's shortly after five in the afternoon when he gets shot, shot, shot. The watch joins its hands in a farewell namaste. The watch stops at midnight.

32

Karachi. Mohammed Ali Jinnah is surviving. At 5.17 p.m., when the shots hit Gandhi, Jinnah was napping, restless, feverish. He did not remember his dream, if he had one, but he awoke a few moments after the shots in Delhi to cough up three gobs of greyish, blood-streaked phlegm. He let them drop one by one into the spittoon at his bedside, then rolled back exhausted on to the pillow, and slept until Fatima burst in to tell him the news—how Gandhi had been shot, and who did it.

With the moon at his elbow, Jinnah sits at his desk now. He is writing and correcting, praising and qualifying his praise. The phrases must be just right. Nothing too extravagant or memorable—for the first time, he does not want Western newspapers to quote him—but not at odds, either, with public sentiment in India, Britain, America.

> I am ~~saddened~~ shocked to learn of the most ~~devilish uncalled-for~~ dastardly attack on the life of ~~Mah~~ Mr Gandhi, resulting in his death. There can be no controversy in the face of death.
>
> Whatever our bitter political ~~quarrels~~ differences, he was [one of] the greatest ~~personality man~~ men produced by

> the ~~Indian people~~ Hindu community, and a leader who commanded [their] universal confidence and respect.

The fountain pen hovers, pensive.

> I wish to express my deep sorrow, and [sincerely] sympathize with the great Hindu community and his family in their bereavement at this momentous, historical and critical juncture so soon after the birth of freedom ~~from~~ [for] ~~India~~ Hindustan and Pakistan.
>
> The loss to both newborn countries the Dominion of India is irreparable, and it will be ~~impossible challenging~~ [very] difficult to fill the vacuum created by the passing away of such a [great] man at this moment.

There. It shouldn't have been so difficult. Jinnah shakes his head, staring at the tortured draft.

On a fresh piece of paper, he writes a fair copy of his announcement. Maybe he grips and presses too hard. The fountain pen ruptures in his hand, bleeding all over the paper.

His room has a smell. It gets worse when he has a stretch of bad days. He cannot smell it, but his sister can. She suspects he is too weak to bathe himself properly but too proud to ask for help. She would do it herself, if he were her senile father, but he is anything but senile, and the brother–sister relationship has its unspoken decorum. She listens but doesn't hear splashes on the tiles when he bathes. More than once she worries that he has fallen or fainted because he takes so long. In the end, the whole odour, cigarette smoke, sweat, breath, stale coffee, and under them all the unmistakable and ominous smell of old age, stops her one morning at the threshold. She pulls a chair next to his bed.

'I can arrange for a servant,' she says delicately. 'Just to rinse, Jin. You can soap.'

'I will not have a girl in the bathroom with me,' he snarls. 'Am I Gandhi?'

'A man. I should have said a man.'

'He will sell a memoir about it some day.' Jinnah looks at his clenched hands. '"I bathed the Qaid-i-Azam," he will tell some historian, "and it was like bathing a corpse."'

Fatima closes her eyes on her tears. She is heartbroken that he thinks these thoughts, and heartbroken, too, that she has stung him into doing so.

'I am strong,' he insists. 'No fevers. I am all better.' Whenever challenged by Nehru or Gandhi or Dickie, he always blazed through his sickness to prove his point. He proves his point again, this time to Fatima, by rising out of his sickbed. 'Meet me downstairs for dinner, as usual. After that, we will see a show. The courier has delivered the reel.'

'What show?'

'Gandhi's funeral.'

That evening he shows up smelling of soap, brilliantine and cologne. His three-piece suit shows a thrice-pleated handkerchief in the lapel, and he has so vigorously combed his hair back that the grooves show. By force of will, he does not cough all through the tense dinner.

'These Pathans charge the Indian lines in honking lorries,' he says bitterly and without provocation, 'but they speed off the other way as soon as they take some mortar fire. They are amateurs, after all. We can give them food and fuel, but only soldiers can fight soldiers.'

Fati knows this for the best, most reliable sign of health. Her brother is better than reconciled with her; he is *back*. 'But what about the Stand Down order?'

'Our British officers have started to see the asymmetry of it. This is becoming a proper war. They may phone each other beforehand, but they will fire the shells. Just wait for the thaw. We shall have three brigades there by May.'

In a side room, curtains drawn, they watch the Pathé newsreel in side-by-side chairs. They have received no accompanying music or commentary of any sort, only the flickering film. Sometimes Jinnah's eyes shift focus and see flecks and imperfections in the wall.

First comes some footage of mourners. A peacock feather stuck in the bed of ashes, multitudes on terraces, multitudes clogging a courtyard, a straggle-haired woman bawling in a shawl. Here is Dickie Mountbatten in naval uniform, dark blue presumably for mourning. He sits swami-like, cross-legged on the ground.

The Indians, Jinnah sees, have placed Gandhi's body on a missile carrier of some sort, and this monstrous vehicle goes like a river-barge through streets full of people. Nehru stands on the platform in front of the body, while Patel sits on high with his elbow on the bier.

Soon flowers fountain triumphally from all directions. The procession moves thickly, like lava in sandals.

Military trucks with canvas coverings. A small thicket of turbans and bayonets. *Curiously military trappings*, thinks Jinnah, *for the champion of ahimsa. This really is the country that invaded Kashmir.*

Now the first smoke of the pyre occupies the foreground, and immediately behind it, silhouetted and above it, stand two photographers on ladders, fiddling with a tripod-mounted film camera. A police-wallah on a horse keeps back the crush of mourners by laying about himself with an enormous stick.

As the pyre begins to smoke in earnest, Jinnah goes into a coughing fit. The Mahatma's pyre blazes, and the Qaid's fever spikes and sends prickles down his back. Jinnah stands up into the cone of shifting light, doubled over and illuminated, his shadow on the scene. Fati shouts to have the projector turned off. The pyre vanishes from the wall. Jinnah stops coughing. Brother and sister linger in darkness.

She is increasingly scared for him. And not just about his lungs, and not just about Kashmir. Liaquat has brought word of protests in Dacca, in the eastern half of Pakistan that lies on the far side of India. Jinnah finds himself thinking in these terms—that Karachi, in West Pakistan, is the *centre*, and Dacca, in East Pakistan, is the *other half* of his country. His Bengali-speaking citizens sense this when they discover the new currency of Pakistan has no Bengali on it—only unfamiliar Urdu lettering. Educated Bengalis, every one of whom fancies himself a connoisseur of Tagore's golden language, need a translator to fill out the most basic government forms, just as illiterate jute farmers do. It was always the risk in constructing a country like this.

'Their demand,' explains Liaquat, 'is for two languages on the currency. Urdu on top, perhaps, and Bengali right below it.'

'Silly scribbles clipped to a clothesline,' mutters Jinnah into his tea. 'I won't have two official languages. That is Babel.'

'It is not unknown, Qaid. Canada—'

'There is already too much distance between our halves. Give me one generation, and I will convert them all to Urdu. Who is protesting?'

'University students, mostly.'

'Naturally.' Jinnah, his spine hooked over his teacup, shakes his head. Muslim students were among his first and most strident supporters, joining the League hundreds at a time. And now they have turned on him? 'I will go and give them a dressing-down,' he declares.

This means yet another trip. He is constantly on the move—inaugurating an air base in Quetta, stonewalling the mullahs from his judiciary, reassuring nuns on Christmas and Karachi's Hindu businessmen on Holi when red powder stains white shirts. They kept the celebration hidden on private terraces, out of sight of Muslim refugees from India. Most of them stuck to the green dye and bright pink. It would be Karachi's last Holi; within a year the last Hindu bankers would be gone, taking their capital with them. *So many trips racking his body*, thinks Fati, *and now add Dacca*.

Which is as restless as an occupied city. And all over nothing more than *language*. Urdu versus Bengali: such a trivial quarrel. Fati watches her brother from the front row, surrounded by policemen.

Jinnah, his voice airy in spite of the microphone, lays out his case for Urdu. The crowd cannot follow his English, so he says 'Urdu' clearly for their ears each time. Urdu and again Urdu, and still they blinked like cows. When the British were in charge, they studied English. Now the Qaid is in charge, and the Qaid says, 'Learn Urdu.'

The word, repeated often enough, works as an incantation. Jinnah sees his Bengalis register the word 'Urdu'. They begin twisting their faces. Students jump up like frogs on to their seats. The heckling reminds Jinnah of how he was heckled once, as a young man in Bombay, at one of his earliest Muslim League meetings. A nasty Maulana had berated him for *not* speaking Urdu. These students—students, once his most fanatical constituency—berate him for the opposite reason.

Fati turns and shouts at the students. 'After all he has given you! After all he has done!' No one hears her. They are hooting and booing ecstatically. A few members of the crowd start smiling broadly, and Fati turns to see her brother shuffling back to his seat, the rest of his speech given up. She does not make the mistake of helping him off the stage because that would signal his weakness. But she begins fanning him as soon as they get clear of the onlookers. He is grateful for water.

A crowd blocks and follows his Packard, which inches along.

'What a pretty ending it would be,' he says, 'now that a Hindu has shot Gandhi, if a Muslim shoots me.'

Fatima's dupatta covers her face. Only her eyes show: stern; unshaken by the Bengali shouts. Now she drops it and shouts back at them through the windows, but in their frenzy, they cannot see or hear her.

'This is the Qaid-i-Azam!' she shouts. 'He saved you!'

Her brother touches her hand to calm her. Instantly she goes quiet; they do not touch often.

'These are your people,' she says, 'whether they like it or not.'

'I have backed the wrong horse, Fatima.'

Fati does not answer him, staring instead at the furious palms that blanch every time they slap the glass.

On the drive back from Karachi's airport late that night, Jinnah's burning head rests on Fati's lap. When she puts her cool hand on his forehead, he falls asleep and suffers a fever dream.

When he sits up, he finds himself riding in the same limousine, alone, at high noon.

He sees a refugee camp. He orders the car stopped and steps into the heat.

The refugees have left their tents and ditches to cluster around what looks, at first, like a fight between dogs or brothers. Within moments, hundreds of people have surged to the circumference, their hands out and reaching for something at the centre, no matter how far away they stand. The scene looks much as he imagines the Hajj must look, except that women and men are all mixed up, and no one has bathed. He cannot imagine elbowing, even for his soul's sake, into so much sweat.

A new chanting or shouting has struck up. It sounds to Jinnah like 'Ma', *mother*, or 'hath', *hand*. This last sounds like nothing so much as 'hot', perhaps because the fever or the sun has risen so high.

But that cannot be, Jinnah reflects. These coarse villagers know no English.

No one notices the Qaid because no one looks behind himself. Some old women fan themselves and chatter hysterically to each other.

'He has come back,' says one.

'His heart was so heavy, they had to move his body on a giant truck. He stepped out of the fire and stood unseen among his own mourners.'

'You know he walked all the way here on bare feet, don't you?'

Jinnah's chauffeur and bodyguards seem to hesitate, their necks craning. Jinnah orders one of his two bodyguards, Major Ahmed, to fire his pistol in the air. This hushes the multitude, and they turn to Jinnah.

Their chanting has broken off, and now, in a scattered fashion, the word 'Qaid', 'Qaid', 'Qaid' ricochets from mouth to ear to mouth. They kneel as one and shuffle on their knees to make a sea split by the stride of Moses. Jinnah's bodyguards follow him to the centre.

There he sees the familiar bald head, but without spectacles. The loincloth is unusually filthy. The garlands on his chest have withered into threads, and only a few curled brown petals here or there are still caught in the cloth folds.

Close to the old man, also kneeling, is a mullah of some sort in a small round cap. He has stuck his index finger, knuckle-deep, into one of three small holes offered up for his inspection. Jinnah approaches as the man draws out the finger bloody, saying, 'It is real.' Then more quietly, seeing Jinnah, and crawling backwards on his knees—but the finger still raised: 'It is real.'

The old revenant extends his hand, his body tilting, his hand turned slightly outward, as though bidding Jinnah take a walk with him.

Jinnah makes a gesture with his hand, and his bodyguards rush to either side of the old man. Handcuffs are produced, and at a nod from Jinnah, the old man is handcuffed in plain sight of the refugees. The guards frog-march him into the back of the limousine, his light body suspended entirely between them.

Jinnah sits knee to knee, studying the face to see if this is the man himself redivivus or an impostor. Outside the tinted windows, the crowd rises and stumbles about bewildered, like sickened bees.

The two men begin their drive into Karachi. It is an impossible, endless drive, but Jinnah does not give his prisoner permission to speak, only studies him unblinkingly and without wonder.

Now it is night, and Jinnah lights a cigarette. The ember at its tip provides the only light between them, for there is no moon.

'So, you have come back,' says Jinnah, 'where you were never wanted.'

No answer.

Jinnah says, 'We are barristers, are we not? Very well. I will make my closing statement. Then you can make yours. You see I have no petty interest in having the last word, as they say. You fancied I would take your hand? That I would go on a march with you to the border, gathering followers from camps as we went? I know what you envision. When we reach the border, you will take a handful of soil from one side, I, a handful from the other, and we will mix the two soils together, quite symbolically, for the photographers. Then all the refugees on both sides will stroll back to their original villages and homes, nodding as they pass one another, the cut will seal, and the whole Partition will be forgotten, like a dream on waking. Is that what you imagine? Is that why you offered me your hand?'

Jinnah blows smoke in the old man's face, and it emerges in wisps from the three holes in the chest.

'These were never your people. It was only your hubris that made you think so. You had more obscene hubris than any dictator. Even Hitler wanted to bend to his will only the *next* thousand years of history, and he conceded he could not do it alone. He knew he needed armies and factories and pilots. You too wanted to write the next thousand years of history—and *un*write the *past* thousand—as if preaching and prayer-meetings could un-sack Somnath seventeen times or make a Brahmin kiss the foot of a pariah. You imagined you could do all that by yourself, simply by speaking. Simply with words and grand gestures. Who did you think you were? Christ? *He* never imagined he could drive out the Roman legions *and* be a prophet to Jews and Romans alike. There has been no one as proud as you since Satan. You cleaned your share of latrines, I do not doubt it, but even Satan crawled on his belly in the dust to work his will.'

The limousine passes a cluster of cookfires in a field, and the cigarette's tip seems reflected several times in the window.

'I knew you,' says Jinnah, 'for an unnatural man from the beginning. All these fasts, and days of silence, and enemas, and those bizarre diets of fruit and water ... I suppose all that found its culmination in you lying there old and naked, unnaturally, next to your naked niece. Did you think I would not know of this? Everyone knew, and everyone thought it unnatural. Fool, the natural state of mankind is dividedness. Why else politics? People do not care to unite *for* anything. All that comes naturally to them is uniting *against*.'

The old fakir puts his chin to his chest.

'You tried to unite Hindus and Muslims in support of *India*. So did I, once. But that failed. So you united the Hindus against the British, and I united the Muslims against the Hindus, and that worked, because division is only natural between oil and water. Bloodshed, too, is only natural. Do you think my own people will come to curse me some day, simply because their grandmothers died in a refugee camp? Do you see that fantasy? Now that there *is* a Pakistan, Pakistan is who they are. It is best they bleed for this country a little. Their bleeding, too, is foreordained, a blessing in disguise. It ensures they will never rejoin Hindustan, no matter how they suffer. Blood seals the pact. I will always be theirs, and they will always be mine. To question the Qaid will be to question Pakistan, and to question Pakistan, to question the faith. For all three are one now. Faith, country, and founder, linked. I am not just their Qaid-i-Azam. I am their Pakistan. I am their Islam. I rest my case.'

Jinnah awaits the rival barrister's closing statement. But his rival takes off his neck the denuded threads of the garlands he wore on his pyre. He places them on Jinnah. To his horror, Jinnah sees the threads flower on his chest. His rival smiles and kisses him on the forehead.

In the limousine, with his sister's cool hand on his forehead, Jinnah startles awake.

33

Nanga Parbat crackles and echoes and crackles again with gunfire. The sound is hollow and distant even to the men who squint over the bucking machine guns. A flash on the summit of Amarnath, a flash at the bottom of Sonamarg Pass. Pine trees bristle upright, like hairs on the nape of a neck. The mountains loosen and trickle, but pickaxes peck at barren stone thousands of feet above the treeline. Spindly soldiers in turbans and sunglasses trudge up a near-vertical snow field, hip deep, their rifles held overhead. They grow used to the shrill wind and the guttural thutter of the tents. Pakistani bullets, Indian airplanes vanish, equally dwarfed by these mountains, blown off course. Detached tank turrets swing on winches over bottomless ravines. Mule track becomes paved road becomes convoy route, all in a matter of weeks. War has come to pass at Shangri-La. Tanks, mortars, binoculars have come to the pass at Zoji-La. A reattached tank turret swings to bear on Ladakh and coughs. A puff of smoke rises from its barrel. It coughs again.

He can't stop coughing. Elevation, his doctors tell him, will do him good. In Quetta, Jinnah takes penicillin lozenges and bedrest, but he isn't high enough off the earth. He needs drier, higher air. The crescent moon would be curative, Kashmir would be salutary, but in Kashmir the wounds and flowers compete to blossom. Baluchistan will have to do. It doesn't have a Dal Lake, but it does have a bungalow, once a sanatorium, on a low mountain: Ziarat. The juniper shoots fork-like ice crystals of living green, and the chestnut trees are always good to lean against, and breathe, and breathe.

Fatima joins him for his walks. She pretends to do it for the sake of companionship, but she stays as watchful as a nurse. Frail though he is, his praying-mantis body a collection of stilts, he never uses her for support. An imperious monocle inspects the flowers on the property with the unforgiving, unblinking gaze of a Spanish inquisitor. He does not descend to a walking stick. Gravity wouldn't dare.

On his fifth day there, struck by a thought, he turns to Fati and asks, 'This retreat. Ziarat. What does the word mean?'

'I don't know, Jin.'

Just ahead of them, one of the gardeners squats at his work. Jinnah has exchanged words with him before; he is an army private given the post after losing his left hand. Jinnah approaches him. He has picked up just enough Urdu to ask the question himself.

'What is the meaning of *Ziarat*, young man?'

The gardener holds one handle of the pruning-shears fixed in the crook of his crippled arm. He answers without hesitating, shears still nipping at the green growing tips. 'Saint's tomb.'

A new doctor, Colonel Baksh, has him spit phlegm into a cup and hurries it off like a treasure. An X-ray machine is brought up from Karachi. Jinnah stands shirtless and lets them take their film.

'Do you know how many politicians, Doctor, have dreamt of standing me against a wall and shooting?'

Jinnah recognizes his spine and ribs. That is all his torso is now, after all. The black void is lung tissue, or what is left of it. The disease has the look of frozen smoke.

'Tuberculosis,' whispers Colonel Baksh. 'And I believe that part of this may be cancer as well.'

'John Keats, the Dauphin of France and myself.'

'Miss Jinnah wishes to sit and hear the rest. About the treatment. We have a new drug, streptomycin. We are flying it in from America.'

'You have not told her, have you?'

'She stood by while the film was developed. She did not leave my side, Qaid.'

'You shouldn't have told her. She is a woman. It will be hard on her.' He waves at the door. 'Let her in.'

Fati opens the door on her own just as the doctor turns to it. 'I will be steel.'

He nods. 'Naturally. You are a Jinnah.'

No cigarettes. Legalistically, he holds the smoke in his mouth, then gives it up like the ghost. Fati lights two and sets them in the ashtray to smoke down as incense. An injection in his right arm leaves him shuddering, sore, and covered in hives for six hours. Jinnah matches his physician's injunction with another: no medicines. The only treatment he allows himself, after that, is light therapy. He lies feverish in its ultraviolet blue wash, a burning man trapped in a frozen lake.

No 'mental unrest', either: doctor's orders. Luckily, Jinnah has lost interest in newspapers on his own. Even his reading of Shakespeare retreats to the simpler verse line of the early history plays, the turgid enjambements of *Coriolanus* too turbulent now.

Yet he finds no serenity. All it takes is news from Kashmir. Sentry, secretary and nurse, Fati rushes to a shout that sounds like pain.

'They have pushed us back again!' Her brother, unsteady on his feet, crushes a telegram and throws it at his feet. 'What is that mediocrity Liaquat doing? I must manage everything myself.' Jinnah feels like a wolf with only lapdogs in his pack.

She guides him back to his chair. 'It is not our fault,' she soothes him. 'There was nothing any of us could do.'

Her words only set his jaw. 'This is Hindu fraud! This is the Mountbattens at work! They decided these borders over pillow-talk. Nehru and Edwina. Disgusting.'

'They say she goes about with her hands joined and a dot on her forehead.'

'Dickie, too. He is a pukka Hindu now. Dickie sat cross-legged on the ground at Gandhi's funeral. This disgusting arrangement. If we are all brothers, who is Abel and who is Cain? They are Cain! Cain down to the marks on their foreheads!'

Already he is fading to sleep, exhausted.

She brings him guava wedges and a box of halwa when he awakens later that afternoon.

'What is the halwa for?'

'Independence Day,' she whispers. 'Sweeten your mouth, brother. We are one year old.'

Fati intercepts her brother's visitors. They wait in the front room, with no magazines on the table or art on the walls to keep them company. Miss Jinnah hurries upstairs and hurries back downstairs, in almost all cases, to convey the Qaid's regrets.

One of the few visitors Fati lets through is Liaquat Ali Khan. Fati gestures him up the stairs, where Jinnah is waiting in the study. Fati has dressed and groomed him. Liaquat takes it all in with one glance: Jinnah made to resemble Jinnah, like a wax statue at Madame Tussaud's. He sits complete with a Craven A inserted between his contracted index and middle finger.

For a moment, Liaquat feels confident, ascendant. Then Jinnah speaks, and he realizes that a leopard mind still paces the cage bars of the body.

'Tell me, Prime Minister,' he says, 'why you have come here to Ziarat.'

'To report to you, Qaid. We are helping the Nizam airlift weapons into Hyderabad. It does look as though Patel is spoiling to attack. Fraud, then force in Kashmir; force alone in Hyderabad. The Hindus are pressing their advantage. The country of Gandhi, yes? And then of course Kashmir is being discussed at the United—'

'Nothing that couldn't be conveyed in a telegram,' Jinnah says, his body rigid, his face a mask. 'Why did you come here?'

Liaquat scoots forward on his chair, leaning towards Jinnah, as always. 'To see you, Qaid.'

Jinnah's lips stretch. 'I thought so. Well, you have seen me.'

When Liaquat leaves the study, Fati seeks out her brother.

'Do you know why he came to see me?' Jinnah asks her. 'He wanted to see how long I have.'

Without Fati's help, he walks to the window of his study, where he sees in the drive Liaquat's Packard quite put in the shade by the Governor-General's new American limousine. Liaquat makes for the Cadillac, and Jinnah's driver Nasir emerges from under an awning, putting on his hat and wiping his hands on his jacket. Jinnah watches Liaquat banter with the driver for a full minute before Nasir opens the passenger door. Liaquat sticks in his head and has a look about, his left hand on the roof and his knee on the seat. When he leaves in his own car, the bar rises for him well in advance, and the sentry at the gate gives him a salute.

Bile rises brackish at the back of Jinnah's throat. He thinks of all the mediocrities who have risen under him, beginning with Liaquat. Such mediocrities will inherit his power when he dies. Pakistan will not stand a chance. Even if it survives—God, in what state? He hasn't even managed to draft a constitution for it…

Jinnah's eyes refocus, and he sees his own reflection on the window. Unless it is Fatima's. His eyes blur with tears as he thinks of India drowning his new country in refugees. How is *Liaquat* going to feed all these people? The reflection blurs into a softer, hazier face. Ruttie. Her lips are moving. She is telling him something. His eyes crush with grief, and when he opens them, she has disappeared.

'How long have I been here?' Jinnah chokes out. 'How long have I been buried alive?'

'Six weeks,' answers Fati.

'I am caught in a trap at Ziarat,' he whispers. 'Take me back to Karachi, Fati. Take me home.'

For the first time, he places his hand on his sister's shoulder. From the window back to his chair is a single glide path downwards, Fati embracing him and weeping. She shouts for the doctor, whose boots thump up the stairs. Jinnah is still conscious and almost desperately lucid. He feels himself slipping.

'Don't mourn,' he says. 'I don't care if I live or die. You shouldn't, either.'

'Inshallah you will live, Jin. Inshallah you will live.'

Colonel Baksh, the doctor, finds Jinnah's feet swollen and his pulse weak. 'It is your heart. We must get to a lower altitude.'

Jinnah turns his head to his sister. 'Do you see? I told you. Karachi.'

'We will have to move you today.'

'I will have no one see the Qaid-i-Azam wheeled about in a chair. Or carried on a stretcher. They must see me walk from the ambulance door to the threshold. Fati?'

'They will see you walk.'

'Every detail of my dress upheld, Fati, like a parliamentary point of order. Fati?'

Fati slides the socks back on to her brother's feet and the shoes back over his socks. Baksh holds him forward off the pillows while Fati helps her brother into his suit coat. It feels good to be embraced with both arms. Today is the first time he has been embraced since Dina wed her Wadia. He should have called Dina over to come see his country. She is just across the border even now, Ruttie's living image in Ruttie's living city, unreachable…

The ambulance, though it never switches on its siren, spreads the word along the road to Ziarat. The driver tells Fati that the crowds are already lining the streets.

The nurse in the ambulance is a nun, one Sister Dunham. Jinnah lies in the ambulance with a sister at either elbow. Sister Dunham slides an armband up his arm that swells when she pumps the bulb but scarcely presses on him.

'I fear he requires the smaller cuff,' she tells Fati. 'The one for children.'

The ambulance begins its descent. Much of the road is moth-eaten earth. The stretcher jars so much that the wheel lock gives way. He has to be chocked in place with a book and Fati's sandal. The descent takes them juddering into early September swelter. Jinnah closes his eyes, and his head bobs with the terrain. Fati checks on her brother every so often, and on two occasions, Sister Dunham shines a pen light on his pupils, just to make sure. He is awake, but barely. Consciousness is slippery.

The ambulance goes still. Fatima waits. Her dupatta slips back, drenched, off her forehead. Even chilly Miss Jinnah can sweat. Sister Dunham fingers her crucifix. An unbearable odour drives Fati to push open the loading door. To her astonishment, she sees the 2,000 huts of a refugee camp. Truckers and bell-thumbing bicyclists go past, oblivious. A cow turns to her and chews the cud.

The driver stands at the front, ostriched in his engine.

'What in hell is going on?'

The driver joins his hands. 'Two minutes, Miss Jinnah.'

'Do you know what the problem is?'

'Five minutes, Miss Jinnah.'

Jinnah blinks in the heat. Briefly he is convinced that Sardar Patel has arranged for him to be cremated alive in this box. The panic passes when he sees Sister Dunham, fleshy and bland of face. He can make out the huts.

And then, from the direction of the huts and the open sewage stink, he sees the flies.

The flies walk on eyelash legs over his closed eyes. They colonize his arms and investigate his nostrils and ears. He is covered with buzzing like a beekeeper among his boxes. Only he has no benefit of a mesh headdress. They interrupt the sneeze they trigger by getting lodged in his nostrils. They tickle the palms of his hands. He has a vision of Ruttie, but flies spill out of her mouth. When he opens his eyes, Fati is waving her arms against the wing smoke. Sister Dunham, hiding in her habit, has sweat drops hanging off her cleft chin and the tip of her long pink nose. Fati cries, 'Why is there no breeze?' The flies enter her mouth, and she turns aside, disgusted and spitting. In horror she shuts the ambulance door. They are locked in with the flies now, and the heat keeps increasing. She throws the door open again in frustration, and the flies are waiting, blown in on a dusty gust from a passing truck. She shuts the door again, and the three of them sit there, trapped, licked and trekked on by the preening flies, dark-red head-bulbs tended by dexterous front arms, the rear leg drawn lovingly down each wing. Jinnah feels them investigating his scalp, the hollow at the base of his neck, the whites of his briefly opened eyes. His white shirt soaks through and sticks transparently to his skin. Any hotter, and his skin will go transparent too. Consciousness slides. Consciousness freefalls. Sister Dunham lifts his eyelid and sweeps the light across his eyeball again. A powerful searchlight, but what she looks for is lost in some other sky.

Fati leans close now, her breath cold against his burning ear as she whispers, eyes clenched shut against the flies, 'Inshallah, you are going to live. Brother, listen. You are going to live forever...'

Epilogue

A compartment on a train that idles at a railway station in Delhi. Manu Gandhi, in big glasses and a punjabi, sits with her hands folded. Across from her, elbows on his knees, sits Gandhi, forty years younger: Devdas, his youngest son.

This is after the assassination, after the funeral. Two million people in attendance, and she was the last to get up from beside the pyre. Sardar Patel had knelt beside her and guided her to her feet again. Today, all cried out, she is headed home to Jamnagar. Her train will not leave for another twenty minutes. Devdas, at a look from Patel, volunteered to accompany her to the station. He has stowed her bag and made sure she is comfortable. Now he is broaching the subject.

Manu stays serene. Devdas fidgets.

'I wanted to have a word with you, Manu. About the … experiments.'

Her voice is level, passionless. 'You can ask me anything.'

'Did he leave you any instructions about … that?'

'Yes.'

Devdas swallows. 'Which were?'

'He wanted me to write about it.'

'An article.'

'I want to write all about my time with him.'

'So you are thinking about a book.'

'I don't know. I will write about him some day. He was my mother, after all.'

'Right. Manu, I was hoping to persuade you to...'

'To disobey him?'

'For Bapu's own good. For the good of his work and his memory.'

'He was unashamed. So am I. There was nothing anyone could speak ill of.'

'I don't doubt that. But you understand that doesn't matter.'

'Talk to Dr Nayyar. Talk to Abha.'

'I intend to.'

'They will tell you the same thing. We will all testify.'

'That doesn't matter. What matters is that it ... happened at all. Do you see that? Do you see what people who hate his memory can do with something like that?'

Manu's voice has stayed steady until now. There is no quiver, no transition; she just brings her dupatta over her face and starts sobbing. Devdas, awkwardly, leans forward and tries to put his arm around her, then hesitates and pats her shoulder. He looks out the window, at the corridor of the train. A vendor balancing a teacup and saucer walks by, announcing chai. Two coolies balance enormous bags on their heads, like circus performers, while a pale woman in a saree strolls behind them. Devdas waits out Manu's tears.

'All he has done. All he has thought and struggled for and championed.'

'I know.'

'And this is all they will talk about. They will always have this against him.'

'I won't say a word.'

'Have you already written about it? In your diary, maybe?'

She nods.

'How many pages?'

'Not many.'

'The train is leaving in a few minutes. I don't have much time, Manu.'

'What do you want me to do?'

Devdas points at the diary sticking out of the small knapsack she keeps at her feet. 'Can you find the pages?'

'I cannot give you the book.'

'I don't want the book. I want the pages, Manu.' She doesn't stir. The train hisses steam, and passengers milling about on the platform toss their bidis aside, or grab the wrists of their children, and hurry aboard. Devdas grabs the diary and sets it on her lap. 'Can you find them for me?'

She doesn't move. He forces open the diary on her lap and points at her closely packed Gujarati handwriting. 'Do it to protect your mother. He took you in, didn't he? Protect your mother's memory.'

She finds the pages easily; the spine is creased there and falls open naturally, even if a marigold bookmark hadn't been pressed dry there. She tears the pages out two at a time and hands them over.

'That's all?'

She nods.

The train has started inching out of the station. Devdas leaps from his seat clutching the pages and down the corridor, wriggling past a man struggling with his outsized trunk, finally on to the platform. Manu cranes her neck to see him growing smaller, her diary pages bent and clutched between his teeth while he bobbles a matchbook, spilling matches but striking,

striking, lighting the one in his fingers, its quick flare lost in the steam.

Sardar Patel is worried. No one imagines it's possible from the unsentimental look of him, but he tosses in bed all night and feels nauseated after every meal. Five brigades in Kashmir keep his lassi sour. Reports of close contact between Karachi and Hyderabad keep his pillow full of rocks.

After the assassination, he never found any evidence of involvement by the RSS leadership. That hasn't stopped him from outlawing the whole organization. He would have liked to hang more than just Godse and his cronies. Gandhi's sons had pled for Godse in the name of ahimsa, but Patel knew that would only set the saffron-swaddled bullies cheering. Fanatics on both sides keep Sardar worried. These past-fixated young men are forever playing Mahrattas versus Mughals, or jihadis versus infidels—with no sense of good governance or building a modern nation-state out of illiterate peasants, snobbish elites and a baker's dozen of different tongues. All the while running a war in Kashmir, and housing and clothing and feeding millions of refugees, and navigating Nehru's moods.

No wonder he feels a bitter brash at the back of his throat; no wonder he has mysterious aches and sweats out of nowhere. Like this ache, over his ribs, which comes and goes. He felt it the night he and Nehru ordered planes into Srinagar. He felt it that afternoon he spoke with Gandhi at Birla House. He feels it now when he reviews the latest dispatch from India's representative to the UN. World opinion, says the report, is turning in favour of Pakistan. They are starting to think India the aggressor, Kashmir just a land grab, violating the will of the people. And here is a tally of last month's arrivals in the camps; this number's just the living bodies. And here is word of another spate of killings in this very city. He's also aware of the speculation that Pakistan will have a sympathetic fifth column, tens of millions strong, inside India. He fears that, but he fears, too, those who believe that. Unless India succeeds in ensuring India's Muslims feel Indian first. It must be possible. But if Bapu couldn't do it, how will lesser men? Bapu, whom he could have saved. If only he had accompanied him to the prayer meeting. He might have stepped between the Mahatma and the bullets. What a fine death that would have been, what glory…

The papers in Patel's hands shuffle and confuse. He cannot read the words any more, and the pain over his ribs digs deeper now, and prickles up his neck, and creeps down his arm. Sardar, right hand over his chest as though pledging allegiance, finds himself in the hallway outside his office. No one is around him. He calls his daughter's name. No one is around to see his body, which seemed so solid and immense, shrink and go frail. This afternoon, the great Sardar is just another seventy-three-year-old man having a heart attack.

Unbending, like a tree axed at the ankles, he falls in one piece. But he falls.

The date Mohammed Ali Jinnah dies is 11 September 1948. On that day, Nehru authorizes Indian forces to enter the independent princely state of Hyderabad. The disciple of the Mahatma signs off on a Strike Force, a Smash Force, and a Kill Force. He sends in the Gurkha Rifles, the Hawker Tempests, the Poona Horse.

After it is done, he sets his elbows on his desk and covers his face. On his desk is a cast of Abraham Lincoln's right hand, which signed the Emancipation Proclamation. Next to it is a photograph of Gandhi. Nehru is not religious, but he has placed a small red tilak on the photograph, and he keeps a few fresh flower petals at the base of it, like any dutiful mourning son. He covers his face because he cannot bear to look at either memento on his desk right now.

What breaks his mood's darkening spiral is a cool white hand on his shoulder and a familiar perfume. Edwina has appeared beside him, just when he needs her, and his mood is so vulnerable that he turns his head and lets her press his face against her stomach, cradling his head. They rest like this. Finally, he pulls away.

'Where is Dickie?' he asks.

'I don't know.'

'He must have told you. We are going into Hyderabad today.'

'I thought you might be troubled. I thought you might like to see a friend.'

'Stay with me a while, Edwina.'

In a corner of his office, Nehru keeps a gramophone player. A gift from the American ambassador, along with some American records, it has seen no use in the past year. Edwina puts her red lips together and blows the dust off it. She finds a record that pleases her and lays the needle tenderly in the groove. When she turns around, and Nat King Cole starts singing '*For Sentimental Reasons*', Jawaharlal is waiting for her. One hand settles on her waist. His other rises and waits for hers. Their bodies line up, their faces line up, parted by the distance of a breath. They sway.

* * *

On a hill in Karachi, two dozen workmen are bringing pickaxes down on solid stone. Sunset silhouettes their small, frenzied bodies. One man stops because his pickaxe has snapped off at the handle. He shows it to the foreman.

A rotund old man in a mourner's kameez waddles up the hill. The foreman drops the two parts of the pickaxe and hurries down to meet him.

'They are minutes away,' says Liaquat. 'Why haven't you started? Where are the drills?'

'We have been waiting, sahib.'

'How long will it take once the drills get here?'

'No telling, sahib. The ground is hard.'

'You didn't test the ground yesterday?'

The foreman shrugs. 'We came this morning. We have been working since dawn.'

'Why did it take you until noon to decide you couldn't do it? This is a disaster.'

The foreman points. A truck has just drawn up behind Liaquat's limousine. Its loading ramp slams the pavement, echoing like a rifle shot. The workers swarm an enormous spiral drill and ease it down the ramp. It rides on a wheeled wooden platform, and they cluster behind it, their bodies straining to get it up the hill.

Meanwhile, to Liaquat's horror, the massive funeral procession has emerged far down the road. He squints in the harsh sun and blinks through his sweat. Dabbing his forehead with his handkerchief, his bald head glistening and soon to peel, he hurries down the hill to meet it.

At this kafila's head is Fatima Jinnah. She holds a widow-white dupatta over her cheek. She alone does not sweat in the heat. Behind her, two nawabs and four cabinet ministers shoulder the Qaid-i-Azam's coffin in grimacing agony, their white kameezes soaked through. As Liaquat approaches her, she raises one long hand, and the procession behind her—consisting of tens of thousands of people—stops at once.

Liaquat swallows, his hand nervously working his soggy handkerchief.

'Yes?'

'The site is not ready.'

'Why not?'

'They had to order drills from Karachi.'

'How long will it be?'

Liaquat shrugs helplessly. Fatima looks to the top of the hill. The hydraulic drill lowers to the intractable stone and shudders. Stone shrapnel sets the workers hurrying down the hill, two men shouting, their hands clapped over their eyes. Pulverized stone smokes white from the drill tip. Fatima watches, her face motionless, her eyes unblinking. Behind her, the six coffin-bearers bend at the knees, lowering their burden to the ground. When it is just two feet off the ground, she says, very quietly, still looking straight ahead, 'No.'

The six men struggle back up and hold the coffin aloft. One minister in particular looks ill; Fatima sees this, too, without turning her head.

'Relieve Nishtar, please. And someone get him a drink of water.'

Her voice is controlled, and in control. Liaquat hurries over and manages the transfer. The monstrous stave digs into his shoulder. The coffin feels like it will crush his collarbone and flatten him. It must be made of iron. Unless the slight and wasted body inside it accounts for so much weight; unless the Qaid himself was made of iron.

'Up,' says Fatima.

The six sweating men straighten their spines under the coffin. Thousands of mourners keen in the sun and pound their chests. The drill on the hilltop grinds away thunderously at the solid rock of the burial site. That ground is Pakistan, in the image of its maker. It will not break. It will not break. It will not break.

Acknowledgements

A book like this does not concern Etruria or Khazad-dûm. Bygone or imaginary kingdoms these are not: the national and religious identities involved are very much alive and have gone to war in living memory. It may be an act of literary madness to make art out of charged figures like Jinnah and Gandhi. Far safer to focus on 'regular people' who get 'swept up' in historical upheaval. Here can go materials proper to a novel: a love story, the horror and the trauma, the poignancy of memory and displacement ... A writer can elide the knotty, nasty bickerings of political-religious factionalism in the interests of portraying characters in their Common Humanity.

I should know; I took that route myself, once upon a time with *Partitions* (2011). This subject stayed with me long after I wrote that novel. I felt my engagement had been incomplete. I needed to know more, needed to know the *how*, not just the *what*. And that *how* led to a different set of *who*s. To people usually the domain of non-fiction—of history, biography and autobiography.

My opinions on the Partition have changed since I began this book six years ago, and they continue to evolve. Overall, though, I do not think a phenomenon this complex deserves a value judgement. That is the main difference between the debut novelist of *Partitions* and the novelist you're reading right now. For that author, 'Partition' was purely a negative—tearful and bloody. The author in his present iteration would need more information before he *might* judge the Partition positive or negative, in that *specific* situation. What part of the subcontinent? Which religious identity? Rich or poor? Are you asking about the short term, medium term, long term? And the final agnosticism: relative to what, exactly? That same group or person's life, had Gandhi's vision won out and Partition never taken place? Or if the British never left at all? Because those are experiments we cannot run. We have no way to compare the possible with the actual. What is, *is*.

To create a work of fiction that reimagines what 'really' happened instead of presenting a timeline of events, I have stayed very close to my non-fiction sources. Any reader will be able to see the stylistic touches, speculations about psychology, imaginative flourishes, but the narratives (and, in some cases, quoted statements) come from these sources. Luckily for us all, there is a wealth of excellent writing being done on these figures and their time.

First, two excellent accounts of the Partition itself, Alex von Tunzelmann's *Indian Summer* and Nisid Hajari's *Midnight's Furies*, stayed at my elbow for the pertinent scenes. My understanding of the political quarrels benefited from various online archives, more voluminous than any human being could read in one lifetime, or three. Stanley Wolpert's *Jinnah of Pakistan*, an early biography, served as an excellent basis and as a corrective for later hagiographies that seek to invent a 'Qaid-i-Azam' rather than document the lawyer and husband, M.A. Jinnah. I read selections from the work of Ayesha Jalal and

Jinnah, Pakistan and Islamic Identity: The Search for Saladin by Akbar Ahmed. *The Man Who Divided India* by Rafia Zakaria, and *Sources of the Indian Tradition: Vol. 2*, were also on my bookshelf at the time of writing. Gandhi's *My Experiments with Truth* and his copious essays, as well as Joseph Lelyveld's *Great Soul: Mahatma Gandhi and His Struggle with India*, gave me insights into Gandhi's life and personality. Various Gandhi biographies slender and thick have passed under my gaze over the years, though I did not read them specifically for this book. Sometimes my readings exceeded the character's role: William Manchester's three-volume *The Last Lion*, as well as two shorter biographies and several Churchill-authored speeches and articles loom behind what ended up being a couple of cameo appearances. Some research did not involve reading at all. For a novelist, there is much to be gained from staring at a period photograph, or watching and re-watching a black-and-white Pathé reel.

Some might find this book skewed in favour of this or that figure or community: such were the risks in writing it at all. The effort while writing has been to keep partisanship at bay, and the books mentioned enabled me to stay even-minded, and helped correct my own biases as well. The writing, and the readings that guided the writing, have been their own reward. I recommend the above books to anyone interested in the era. This book owes those authors a life debt.

I would also like to thank my editor, Prema Govindan, and the rest of the team at HarperCollins India. I am grateful that they greenlighted this ambitious book. I am also grateful for their due diligence. They sent the manuscript to a team of lawyers to be assessed in the manner of a non-fiction book; I was challenged to produce sources in every chapter, sometimes more than once in a chapter, and the process strengthened the work's historical accuracy. It has been a bracing and beneficial process—but, given the subject matter, necessary.

As always, I want to thank the first reader of all my prose, and my own favourite children's novelist—my wife, A.B. Majmudar, author of *The Torchbearers*. Thanks to her faith in me, I strive and fail and strive again. Some people start out as one, then get divided, and grow apart. Some people start out separate and, utterly, permanently, unite.

Amit Majmudar
Westerville, Ohio
June 2022

About the Author

Amit Majmudar is the author of five critically acclaimed novels, four collections of award-winning poetry, a translation of the Bhagavad Gita with commentary, as well as a forthcoming memoir and a three-volume retelling of the Mahabharata. The former first Poet Laureate of Ohio as well as a diagnostic and nuclear radiologist, he lives in Westerville, Ohio, with his wife and three children.